SACRIFICED: HEART BEYOND THE SPIRES

BAAL'S HEART
BOOK TWO

BEY DECKARD

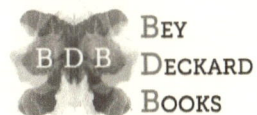
BEY
DECKARD
BOOKS

ISBN (Hardcover) 978-1-989250-14-3
ISBN (Paperback) 978-0-9937017-5-7

CONTENTS

AUTHOR'S NOTE

A heartfelt thanks to my fans and friends.
No really.
<u>Thank you.</u>
Thank you for leaving amazing reviews of my first novel. Thank you for all your suggestions, comments, re-tweeting, re-blogging, re-whathaveyous. Thank you for your wonderful support.
I couldn't have done it without you.

CONTENT WARNINGS

abuse, murder, dubcon, torture, and a lot of rough sex and general pirate shenanigans.

SOUNDTRACK

https://geni.us/SacrificedOST

PART I

JON

Every day is a journey, and the journey itself is
home.

— MATSUO BASHŌ

Six Weeks Ago

"You're going to wear a groove in the boards and make Calum throw you overboard if you don't stop your pacing, Jon," said Baltsaros, looking down at Jon.

Jon laughed, but he felt completely frantic with worry. Tom had said that he would come give them their answer early this morning, but it was now noon, and there was no sign of him.

"It's not like we have to leave immediately, Jon," said the captain. "If Tom's not ready today, maybe he'll be ready tomorrow. He can be extremely proud, like his mother. I did him wrong, Jon… and an afternoon spent playing on bedsheets won't make it all better. We can afford to wait a day or two."

Jon nodded. He hoped it was the case. He'd already made two trips back to the mainland to see if he could find Tom on his own, with no avail. They could also put off the trip for this season if Tom was unwilling to join them. Jon was sure he could convince—

"Bloody fuckin' hells, Da! What in gods have ye done to my fuckin' boat?"

Jon started and looked over his shoulder.

The ocean-eyed, burly youth swung himself up over the edge of the raised gunwale like nothing was amiss and landed on silent feet on the deck next to Jon. After dropping his bag with a thump and ruffling Jon's hair affectionately as he passed by him, Tom swaggered to the stairs of the quarterdeck and looked up, feet splayed and hands on his hips.

The captain, his relief and amusement obvious for a mere second, brought his stark brows down in a fierce scowl.

"*Your* boat?" the captain repeated loudly. "She'll be yours over my dead body." Baltsaros allowed himself a small smile, and Tom grinned wide. "Whip these boys into shape, if you remember how," said Baltsaros as he lifted his head to look over the gathering crowd.

"First mate on deck!" shouted the captain.

Some of the old-timers reached out to pat Tom's shoulder as he made his way down the deck while the newer shipmates just peered curiously at the tattooed sailor that was built like an ox. However, when Tom started bellowing, everyone jumped quickly to obey.

"All right ye lot o' bleedin' twats, move yer asses. Shore up that fuckin' clutter and tighten those lines, ye bilge rat. Aye! I'll drown ye meself if ye don't heed, boy…"

Jon grinned, listening to the first mate yell out orders in his non-stop, rolling mainland accent that was thickly peppered with cursing and laughter.

He looked out over the calm water and took a deep breath. Jon knew there would be trying times in the coming months, both from inside the ship and from without, but at this precise moment in time, he felt he could face anything.

Jon picked up the bag that Tom had dumped unceremoniously beside him and trotted to the captain's quarters to throw it inside. With a glance up at the tall, dark man above him on the quarter-deck, Jon smiled.

There was nowhere he would rather be.

PRESENT DAY

J on pulled the woollen cloak tighter around himself and shivered. His fingers ached from the cold; damp from salt-water spray, his gloves were scant protection from the frigid weather. He'd give his soul just to be back in Baltsaros's bed, warm and far from all this fucking snow and ice. Miserable, he tried once more to undo the ropes tying the crate of supplies to the mast.

"Fucking hells!" Jon yelled into the icy wind when his numb fingers refused to close around the knot. He clenched his teeth and kicked hard at the wooden crate, his shoulders tense and hunched.

"What's wrong, love?" asked a deep voice from behind him.

Jon let out an exasperated groan and rubbed his face, leaning wearily into Tom's side as the first mate put an arm around his shoulders.

"I am so tired of this weather," he said, embarrassed by how peevish he sounded. "I can't get anything done. I'm just so fucking cold. Tom, I can't even feel my hands." Jon flexed his fingers, and tried to form a fist but failed. When he looked up, he was annoyed to see that the muscular first mate was looking at him in amusement.

"It's not funny," said Jon. "I'm serious… I've seen what frostbite can do."

Tom's green-blue eyes creased at the corners as he grinned wide at Jon.

"Here, mate, let me see. It can't be that bad," he said, reaching for Jon's gloves. Peeling them off the shivering man's hands, he frowned; Jon's fingers were bone white from cold. Tom pulled him closer, lifted up the bottom edge of his thick sweater, and shoved one of Jon's hands against the warm skin of his side.

Jon let out a low moan and quickly tucked his other hand against Tom's flank; it always amazed him how incredibly warm the big man was. During the last few weeks, as the weather got progressively colder, the crew began to resemble moving piles of fur. Not so with Tom; it was only when the deck was consistently covered in ice that the first mate grudgingly put on a pair of boots. Even now, Tom went around bareheaded in the cold, the smoke from his cheroot adding to the constant halo of steam from his warm breath.

When Jon's hands touched Tom's skin, the first mate hissed through his teeth from the shock; chuckling, he put a big, gloved hand around the back of Jon's neck.

"Listen, love. Why dont'cha warm up here a spot," said Tom, his voice low and fond. "Ye won't lose yer fingers, Jon. Not on my watch, see?"

Jon nodded and leaned into the bigger man, thankful for his presence; he was glad that it was finally so effortlessly comfortable between the two of them.

Six Weeks Ago

"I'm very sorry you feel that way, Tom," said the captain with a frown. "I had assumed that we would be sharing my quarters."

Tom rubbed the side of his thumb against his stubbled jaw. With ocean-coloured eyes wide and seemingly focused on nothing, unable or unwilling to meet the captain's glare, he flared his nostrils slightly and shook his head.

"And why the fuck would ye think I'd just leap into yer fuckin' bed like a lust-wet strumpet, all big eyes and heart full of forgiveness, Da?" said Tom, his deep, gravelly voice taking on the edge of anger. "I'll be yer first mate, but I won't be sharin' yer bloody bed. Not now. Not yet."

Tom's eyes flicked to the captain's face for a moment, unmistakable pain in his gaze, before looking away again.

Jon let out a nervous sigh and ran his fingers through his dark-brown curls; his hair hung loose past his bare shoulders, and it tickled the back of his neck as he fidgeted with it. In dismay, he watched Tom bend slowly to pick up his sack of belongings, slinging it over his shoulder as he turned to leave.

Jon had assumed, like the captain, that the three of them would be sharing the large stateroom, and it was to these quarters that he had brought Tom's belongings when they had set off earlier.

The day had been incredibly busy, seeming light-hearted and hopeful to Jon. However, as the sun dipped below the horizon on this first day of their journey, when it came time to retire for the night, Tom had looked almost horrified at the prospect of sharing a bed with the captain.

As he stepped towards the door, Tom looked over his shoulder at Jon, his brow creased and eyes serious, before he let himself out into the salt-tinged night air, the door banging shut behind him.

At the creak of the bed, Jon turned to see that the captain had sat down on the edge of it, his eyes closed and fingers pinched over the bridge of his nose. Without looking up, Baltsaros held out his hand, and Jon crossed the room to press himself into the older man's embrace.

"Stubborn as a mule," muttered Baltsaros, shaking his head.

Jon looked down at the man leaning against his side and nodded; he brought his hands up to stroke the captain's shoulders and thought to himself for a moment before answering.

"I don't blame him, you know," Jon said softly. Beneath his

hands, he felt the captain stiffen slightly. "You said yourself that you didn't think Tom would forgive you right away. And you were right. So... be patient."

Baltsaros looked up at him, his brown eyes almost black in the sombre lighting. Jon could feel weariness and anger in the captain as the man shook his head.

"I'm disappointed too, if it makes you feel any better," Jon murmured. He leaned down and pressed his lips to Baltsaros's high forehead; after a heartbeat, Jon pulled back, paused, and smiled before skimming his mouth over the older man's lips, hoping to turn the captain's mind away from Tom's unexpected rejection.

The captain let out a low growl and reached up to cup the back of Jon's head, deepening the kiss. When Jon started tugging at Baltsaros's loose shirt, the captain let out a sigh.

"Yes, patience," he agreed when he pulled away from Jon. The captain's hand closed tight over Jon's forearm, his stark face going still and cold as he stared up at him.

"Don't go to him," said Baltsaros slowly. "Don't seek out Tom by yourself."

Jon straightened and blinked at the captain, disconcerted by the older man's words. They were spoken as a command, the tone unmistakable.

"I mean it, Jon," warned the captain. "As long as Tom won't come to me willingly, you're not to go see him. I... won't have it."

The soft spark of passion that had begun to take hold of Jon sputtered and expired, and he pushed away Baltsaros's hand when it came up to pull him in for another kiss.

"The hells I won't," he said angrily, taking a step back. "During the day, as captain you can order me around all you want... but this? Baltsaros, you're being absurd." He watched Baltsaros's eyes go flat, devoid of emotion.

The way that the captain could suddenly seem so completely inhuman was unsettling, and it always triggered the ghost of something primordial within Jon, buried deep in his genetic makeup: the instinct to flee from a predator.

Run.

As he shook his head to dispel the feeling of unease that had slid into his veins like ice water, Jon held up his hand.

"Listen to me. Tom is angry at *you*... not me," he said, trying to keep the resentment out of his voice. "Do you think that forbidding me to spend any time with him will make Tom any more amenable to you?"

Jon frowned when Baltsaros dropped his eyes, a slow exhale rounding the man's shoulders. When the captain looked back up, the younger man was amazed by the fury in Baltsaros's gaze.

Without a word, Baltsaros stood, tucking his shirt back into the waistband of his black pants. He moved to open the chest at the foot of the bed and pulled out a blanket before walking towards the door. Looking back at Jon, Baltsaros finally spoke.

"If I stay here, I will *hurt* you," said the older man, his words deliberate. He turned his head towards the exit. "And... I'd rather not." Jon heard Baltsaros take another deep breath. "I will be above if you need me, but I do hope you won't."

With those words Baltsaros stepped out, closing the door quietly behind him and leaving Jon alone in the dark of the stateroom.

PRESENT DAY

When his hands were finally warm, Jon gratefully accepted Tom's big gloves in exchange for his frozen ones. The first mate slipped on Jon's gloves and curled his hands into fists.

"I'll have these warmed up for ye in no time, ducky," said Tom, his pink lips curled into a crooked grin. The first mate then reached behind him to pull the long knife out of its sheath, and he quickly sliced through the knot Jon had been trying to loosen. When Jon exclaimed in surprise, Tom just lifted one shoulder up in a shrug.

"We have plenty of rope, ye daft boy," he said. "Now get to work haulin' this to Cook or he'll make ye eat last." Tom reached out and pulled him forward again to press his forehead to Jon's before taking off at a brisk pace down the frozen deck, whistling a jaunty tune as he went.

Jon looked around. Seeing the eyes of a few of the deckhands on him, he coloured slightly. It was never going to be easy being seen as the captain and first mate's cabin boy, regardless of what his actual role was on the ship.

When a gangly, tow-headed deckhand they had picked up during their stop at the *Jewel* sniggered, Jon scowled at him and picked up the crate.

He had to do something about the teasing; it was blatant and getting out of hand. However, it wouldn't do to let Baltsaros or Tom know just how much it was bothering him. Both had a penchant for violence and an overprotectiveness of Jon that almost guaranteed excessive punishment for anyone involved.

Six Weeks Ago

J on woke up when the sun's rays came through the stained glass at the back of the captain's quarters. As he opened his eyes slowly, he reached for Baltsaros and frowned when his hand encountered nothing but the cool sheet next to him. Jon lifted his head; the stateroom was empty. The previous night's drama came back to him in a rush, and he groaned. After turning over onto his back, Jon rubbed the sleep-sand from his eyes with the heels of his hands. What was he going to do?

Tom would be furious if he knew that Baltsaros had

forbidden him from spending any time alone with the first mate, and the captain would be equally livid if Jon disobeyed him. The last place he wanted to be caught was between the demanding captain and his hot-tempered first mate. It was a shitty position to be in, and Jon desired nothing more than a quick resolution.

Sure, but... then what? he thought nervously.

After slipping off the soft bed, Jon paused to look at himself in the mirror above the teak dresser. Sleep had not come easily to him, and it showed in his face. He pressed at the bags under his eyes and frowned to himself; tilting his head up to the light, he scratched his chin and realized that he was also in dire need of a shave.

Abovedeck a short while later, Jon was astounded to see Tom and Baltsaros working companionably side by side as the morning checklist was run through. Munching on Cook's good sourdough and drinking a steaming cup of black coffee as he hung back, Jon watched the two men discuss the replacement of the starboard lines running up the mizzenmast. He could almost believe that the night's arguments had never happened. However, as he stepped up to them, it was obvious that not all had been forgiven.

Baltsaros's eyes were tired and aloof when he looked down at him, and Jon noticed immediately that Tom was purposefully keeping a set distance between him and the captain. When he got closer, Jon caught the smell of stale sweat and whiskey emanating from the bigger man; evidently Tom's first night aboard had been equally restless.

Achingly uncomfortable, Jon put his cup down and chose to address the air between the men rather than make eye contact.

"Cook says that someone has been nicking more than their ration of rum," he said blandly, scratching at his jaw. "He has an idea who it is—"

"Who?" asked Baltsaros, his voice harsh.

Jon winced. It didn't bode well for the man accused; the

captain was just looking for something to sink his anger into. Before he had a chance to reply, Baltsaros held up a hand.

"Forget it. I'll go see to it myself," said the captain, turning his head towards the galley. "Tom, you stay here. Jon, go find something else to do." Jon clenched his jaw and stood his ground, ignoring the captain. Baltsaros looked back, and Jon finally met his gaze. Dark eyes wide at the expression on Jon's face, the older man stayed a moment longer before taking the steps down from the quarterdeck two at a time.

Tom chuckled.

"I never thought I'd live to see the day that ye'd stare down the cap'n, love," said the big man, his roguish face creased in a wide grin.

Jon sighed and scratched at his cheek.

"Yeah, well, obviously things change," he replied faintly. Rubbing hard at his neck, Jon shook his head. He started when Tom's hand cupped his chin and turned his head.

"Do ye have fleas, lad?" asked Tom with a laugh. "Will ye stop bloody scratchin'? Yer makin' me itch."

Wary of the captain's return, Jon's eyes darted to the stairs as he pulled his face out of Tom's callused hand.

"I just need to shave," he said, stroking his hand slowly over the hollow of his cheek. Over the course of the past year, Jon's beard had finally filled in, and he found it a constant annoyance.

"Then… shave," said Tom. His eyes had narrowed when Jon had pulled out of his grasp, and he crossed his arms across his broad chest. His gaze flicked towards the stairs and back to Jon. "What's stoppin' ye? Hm?"

"Kat used to do it for me. Since then, it's been either the captain or Cook," said Jon. He cringed when Tom suddenly let out a surprised laugh.

"Aw shit, ducky. Yer a grown bloody man," said Tom, his eyes shining with amusement. "Please tell me ye know how to shave yerself."

His face hot, Jon touched the sparse patch on his right cheek where one of his attempts had landed him a scar, and he chuckled ruefully.

"I haven't gotten the hang of it. I know, I know. Stupid, right?" he said, hoping he wasn't as red-faced as he felt.

With another glance at the staircase, Tom grabbed Jon's arm in a vice-like grip and pulled the slighter man down the steps.

Jon quickly tried to free himself, but Tom was built like an ox and just as strong; in the end, feeling like a child, he let himself be dragged belowdeck by the first mate.

Nervous as they passed the galley doors, though the captain was nowhere in sight, Jon followed Tom to a tiny storage room next to where the coal was kept.

He blinked and looked around. The room was no more than a large broom closet, but it looked like someone had been living there for some time. There was a thick mat on the floor to one side with a bright blue blanket pulled over it. Against the far wall was a rough, hand-carved shelf that held a few books. Atop a small crate sat a silver pitcher and a cup, as well as a delicate, little wooden box with an inlaid pattern on the cover. Jon frowned and looked at Tom.

"What is this?" asked Jon, confused. The room smelled faintly of the big man despite the open porthole: whiskey, tobacco smoke, and a scent that was Tom's own.

Tom shrugged, his wide frame almost comically large in the tiny room.

"Where do ye think I go when Da kicks me out of his bed, lovey?" he asked, pulling down a wooden bowl from another shelf set high above the foot of the bed. Tom eyed Jon. "Ye don't think yer the first reason I've been left in the cold, do ye?"

Jon's eyes widened. He shook his head after a beat even though truthfully it hadn't occurred to him. He felt weirdly betrayed by the information.

Tom set down the bowl next to the pitcher and poured a little of the water into it. Using the long knife at his belt, he shaved off a few flakes from the block of dark soap he held in one scarred hand and proceeded to churn the mixture together with a short-bristled, round brush. In no time the bowl was filled with thick, milky-white, sandalwood-scented suds.

"Sit," Tom said, pointing to the floor.

Jon looked down, furrowing his brow. His mind was a mess. Was this considered "seeking out Tom", he wondered; and, if so, what would he say if Baltsaros found out? Sure, he had stood up to the captain earlier, but...

"Hells, Jon... do ye want me to show ye or not?" asked Tom with a scowl.

With a startled nod, Jon sank to the hard wooden floor. A moment later, Tom sat behind Jon and pulled him back against his chest, his legs bracketing the smaller man's.

Instantly, Jon's heart started to crash against his ribs. Tom laughed low, and Jon felt the first mate's voice rumble against his back.

"Listen... I know he forbade ye from seein' me, lovey. I ain't stupid, and I've been with the captain long enough to know what he's like," said Tom softly, depositing the bowl in Jon's lap. "But I didn't come back aboard just to please Da."

Tom held up a mirror in front of Jon's face, and he could see the first mate's green-blue eyes beside his own blue-grey ones.

I came for you too.

Jon blinked and looked down. He gestured weakly to Tom's room.

"He didn't throw out your belongings. He kept your room," he said, his voice strangely hoarse. It was hard to breathe. Jon looked back up and saw that Tom was still staring at him in the mirror. The first mate nodded stiffly.

"Aye, lad. That he did," said Tom, finally looking away. "That he did."

PRESENT DAY

After hauling the crate belowdecks, Jon finally managed to wrestle it through the doors of the galley. He looked up and smiled.

Behind the thick, stained wooden countertop stood Baltsaros with a long knife in one hand. Stripped to the waist in the humid heat of the kitchen, the captain held a large fish flat against the cutting block as he looked solemnly down at it.

Jon laughed and tugged his borrowed gloves off, draping them over the set of bars Cook used to dry his towels on. After unwinding the scarf from his neck, Jon shrugged out of his thick cloak and left both in a pile in front of the hot coal stove.

"You'll never get the scales off if you hold it that way," he said, approaching the captain from behind. He passed his arms through Baltsaros's and shifted the man's hand to the left. "And you should be using a dull knife to scrape, not something so sharp... You know Cook is going to kill you for getting scales everywhere. How you've lived aboard a ship for so long without learning how to properly scale and debone fish is beyond me." Jon chuckled and shook his head. "Especially you... You who can prepare quail eggs six different ways and make vegetable stew taste like it was a gift from the gods."

Baltsaros turned his head with his stark brows high, a twist of amusement on his graceful lips. The beard he had grown over the past month was lightly streaked with grey, and Jon found it an attractive contrast to the captain's smooth, tanned skin.

"Do you want to make supper, Jon?" asked the man with the knife, his northern accent lending sibilance to his words. "Or will you let me work in peace?" At the last, Baltsaros smiled wide, his teeth sharp and white.

Jon moved his hands to the captain's chest, stroking down the thatch of curling hair to the waist of Baltsaros's black leather pants. Pressing himself up hard against the older man, Jon slipped his fingers below the wide waistband.

"What if I said neither?" he grinned and ducked his head to bite the captain's shoulder.

Six Weeks Ago

Jon was amazed when Tom started to show him how to shave in earnest. It hadn't been a ploy to get him alone to seduce him, and Jon was both relieved and disappointed. Shrugging away his misgivings and swallowing his pride, he paid close attention to Tom's hands as he slid the long blade along the curves of Jon's jaw.

It was strangely exciting to be letting a man who once plotted against him handle a sharp knife against his skin. But, if for nothing else, Tom's warmth felt good around him. While Tom had an easy physicality about him, Jon still felt a little odd sitting in another man's embrace, and he was glad that the first mate made no big deal about it. Tom was simply, and very patiently, teaching Jon how to shave. That's all it was.

And that's all that Baltsaros needs to know, he thought.

As if reading his mind, Tom wicked away the last of the shaving suds with his blade and then leaned down to bite down softly on Jon's shoulder, his tongue coming out to taste the flesh between his teeth.

With a gasp, Jon closed his eyes. His skin broke out in prickles, and he felt lightheaded, unable to move, drowning in the sudden torrent of *want* that poured over him. The reality of the situation broke through to him a second later, and he pulled away, up onto his knees, the wooden bowl tipping and suds smearing over the planks in his rush to flee. Jon scrambled to his feet and leaned into the door, his fingers clutching the brass handle.

"I... can't. I'm sorry, Tom." Jon felt his heart crashing, and the rush of white noise was loud in his ears. "Just... please. Ok? Shit, I don't even know what to say, but—" he stammered as he fumbled the door open. His breath hitched at the look of misery that flitted over Tom's face before the first mate's expression settled into one of exasperation. "Tom, we've got to do this right. Or else..." Jon frowned and shook his head. "I'm sorry." He turned his head away from the man on the floor and staggered into the hallway.

Walking blindly for a few steps, Jon crashed into the stairs and grunted as he caught himself. He glanced up and saw Cook looking at him curiously from the galley doorway. Jon gritted his teeth into the semblance of a smile and coughed out a small, embarrassed laugh before clutching the handrail to pull himself up the steep stairs.

PRESENT DAY

As Jon kissed his way across the captain's broad shoulders, fingers working at the laces of his leather pants, he heard the sound of someone clearing his throat. Startled, Jon turned his head and saw that Cook was standing next to the crate of vegetables he had just hauled in, embarrassment plain on his craggy face.

"Should I find somewhere else to be?" asked Cook, pulling his woollen sailor's tuque off and rubbing his bald head.

"Mmmmyes, I should think so," said the captain softly, pulling away from Jon and dunking his hands in the soapy water of the basin. "I will send someone for you when the galley is free."

Turning around to face Jon as Cook left and slid the door closed behind him, Baltsaros smiled his sharp-toothed smile and pulled Jon's hands back to the waistband of his leather pants.

"Continue," said the captain and leaned back against the edge of the counter. A low, pleased growl came from deep in his chest as Jon leaned in to kiss him, his fingers deftly pulling apart Baltsaros's laces.

BALTSAROS

---

*There is no way to ease the burden. The voyage
leads on from harm to harm, a land of others
and of silence.*

— DONALD JUSTICE

SIX WEEKS AGO

Baltsaros returned above deck once the man who had been
stealing rum was thrown in the brig, the captain's mood
not much improved by the task. Clenching and releasing
his fists as he walked up the narrow stairs, Baltsaros felt hot frustration like a fire burning deep in his belly.

Tom had *never* refused him; it was completely ludicrous.
And, Jon…

Baltsaros glanced up as he emerged from below and saw that
neither his first mate nor Jon were on the quarterdeck where he
had left them. Jealousy reared up, clawing hard at him, and he

clenched his jaw. He would be damned if Tom thought he could get away with touching Jon if he couldn't bring himself to submit to the captain.

As he tried to swallow down his ire, Baltsaros made for the door to his quarters instead of mounting the steps; he needed to get a hold of himself. His anger was getting out of control.

The captain pulled open the door and stepped into the relative darkness of the large stateroom. The addition of the stained-glass windows had definitely improved the disparity of light on entering, but it still took a moment for his eyes to adjust. As he made his way to the long mahogany table in the middle of the room, Baltsaros heard a noise and turned his head.

There were dark shapes moving on the bed.

Suspicion sharpened his anger, a howling tempest that churned inside him: *Tom and Jon.*

As he approached, barely able to breathe for the fury that choked him, the captain saw with relief that Jon was alone. When the young man sat up and turned to him, his eyes wide with worry, Baltsaros felt his anger shudder and go still inside him. There was a deep ridge etched between Jon's dark brows, and his face was drawn.

"Please," was all that he said.

With a deep sigh, the captain climbed onto the bed and took Jon into his arms, curling around the young man's slighter frame to bury his face in the back of Jon's neck. How could he refuse this solemn, dark-haired creature who looked at him with such love?

Shifting in Baltsaros's grasp after a few minutes, Jon's fingers tightened over the captain's hand, tugging it down to press it against the soft mound at the front of his pants.

Chuckling softly at the unexpected invitation, Baltsaros obliged and slid his hand up and then under the thin material to cup the soft warmth beneath. At his touch, Jon's cock began to stiffen, and Baltsaros pressed a smile against his nape. With a quiet, needy sound, Jon moved his hips back so that he was snug against the captain.

"I know you think I'm being absurd," Baltsaros murmured, "but I'm just frustrated."

Jon let out another soft noise, and his fingers stroked down the captain's muscular arm.

As he kissed Jon's neck slowly, Baltsaros closed his eyes and rubbed the ball of his thumb over the head of the younger man's cock, sighing in pleasure when he felt Jon tremble against him.

"You have to understand, my love," he said gently. "It never once occurred to me that this would happen."

At his words Jon pulled away slightly, twisting onto his back to look over at Baltsaros with a frown.

"What? That Tom might have spent enough time away from you to realize that he wants to be more than just your punching bag?" asked Jon. The words, though blunt, were spoken in earnest.

Baltsaros's hand, which had stopped moving, resumed stroking Jon gently, his gracefully curved cock sliding slowly within his grasp. The captain pondered for a moment and nodded, his lips pressed together in a rueful smile.

"Something like that," he answered, looking down to watch his hand moving below the sun-bleached fabric of Jon's pants. "I thought after our time at the *Jewel* things would be... normal. Though, to be fair, I don't really know what 'normal' would be. I don't yet know what's required to reach an equilibrium."

He glanced up at Jon's face and saw that he was being watched with curious eyes.

"What did you say to him?" asked Jon. His cheeks were infused with a flush, and his breathing had quickened.

Baltsaros frowned.

"When? At the *Jewel*?" he asked, and Jon nodded.

"Well... I said that I was sorry, and I called him my tomcat. Then I said that I wanted him to come *home* with me," answered Baltsaros with a smile. He remembered how his heart had begun to race when Tom had finally stepped into his arms, the big man's scarred back warm against his hands, his scent so familiar...

"And what did he reply?" asked Jon; eyes closed, he licked his bottom lip before grazing it with his teeth. He had begun to move his hips in an achingly lithe roll, matching the speed of Baltsaros's hand.

Baltsaros laughed loud, and Jon looked up at him, confused.

"He said, and I'm quoting word for word, 'If you ever whip me again, I'll cut your bloody cock off'," chuckled the captain.

"Here I thought it was something heartfelt," grinned Jon.

Baltsaros shook his head in amusement and leaned in to kiss him. With surprise, he noticed that Jon was freshly shaved and smelled of sandalwood soap; smiling, Baltsaros moved his lips slowly over the smooth skin of Jon's jaw as he changed his grip on his cock, moving faster. Jon closed his eyes again and moaned softly. Baltsaros could tell it wouldn't take long before he was panting and straining against him.

"Oh... it was heartfelt, that I know," murmured the captain. He closed his eyes, falling into the rhythm of his hand. Jon was right. Patience. Patience with Tom... and an open mind with Jon. He would work at it. But that could wait until later.

Baltsaros opened his eyes and pulled his hand away from Jon's cock.

"On your knees now, my love," he said and began to work the laces loose on his own pants.

PRESENT DAY

Jon slid his hand down the front of Baltsaros's leather pants, and the captain inhaled sharply at the icy touch. Chuckling, he pulled back from the kiss and frowned.

"Gods, your hands are frozen," he said, curling his own around Jon to pull him closer.

Jon grinned crookedly, his face impish as he stroked the captain's cock with one hand while tugging down the black leather with the other.

"You should have felt them before Tom warmed them," Jon said, leaning forward again to begin kissing down the side of Baltsaros's neck. "But my mouth is very warm, that I can promise you."

At the mention of Tom, Baltsaros felt a residual jealous twinge. His feelings about the two young men being alone together he kept buried deep, but he knew there would always be a tiny flame of resentment that flared up, no matter what. Closing his eyes as Jon slid his warm tongue over one nipple, teeth gentle yet firm on the sensitive flesh, he tried to make himself relax.

As if reading the captain's mind, Jon laughed as he sank to his knees on the galley floor.

"You're a controlling, possessive asshole, and that's never going to change, is it?" Jon said before licking a wide stripe up under Baltsaros's testicles to the base of his cock, his tongue flat and velvet-rough.

Baltsaros stroked Jon's long dark curls out of his face and solemnly shook his head. While watching the boys "play" together was something he rather enjoyed, the thought of them doing anything without his presence was still something he was learning to deal with.

FIVE WEEKS AGO

Leaning over the quarterdeck railing, the captain watched Tom reach out to touch Jon's cheek and nod with a smile. Baltsaros frowned but didn't move from his spot.

Patience. Understanding, he thought to himself.

However, when Jon's face immediately swivelled to glance up at Baltsaros with a guilty look, something *twisted* in his gut, and he turned away.

It had been a week since they had set sail, and Tom had yet to make any attempt at reconciliation. Working closely with the big man again was immensely satisfying; but, though the two fell quickly into the easy, practiced rhythm that made them the perfect team, gone was the steady underlying current of desire that had always been there before. In its place was… nothing.

Not nothing. Aloofness.

Baltsaros turned again to look below and saw that Jon had gone. Scanning the deck, the captain saw Tom standing on the port gunwale, one brawny arm curled through the ratlines. The first mate watched the captain with the coldly appraising look that the older man had come to abhor. Why did Tom think he could judge him so?

Then, as the captain was about to look away, the burly pirate dropped his eyes, raising them almost immediately with a small yet unmistakably coy grin on his face. It was gone in an instant when Tom jumped down and made his way towards the bow of the ship, but Baltsaros didn't doubt what he had seen. Watching his first mate walk away, the captain wondered what it meant.

For the rest of the day, Baltsaros kept an eye on Tom, curious to see if the muscular young man would again break from this strange, detached version of himself. The captain was finally rewarded with another brief, sly smile right before they parted for the evening meal.

Tom had always chosen to eat with the rest of the men rather than share the captain's table and, upon his return, he had resumed the custom. Afterwards, the first mate was almost always found sitting on the quarterdeck bench, eyes narrowed into the wind with a black cheroot between his lips as he manned the helm. It was this habit that the captain was counting on.

When Baltsaros and Jon finished eating that evening, the captain excused himself and left Jon reading one of the many new books they had brought aboard. As he made his way up one of the staircases leading to the quarterdeck, a mug of dark ale in each hand, Baltsaros was relieved to see that Tom was in his usual spot.

"It will start getting cooler soon," he said by way of greeting.

Tom turned his head; his brow furrowed and his blue-green eyes became suspicious slits in his sun-darkened face as he stared at Baltsaros. He worked the cheroot in the corner of his mouth for a moment before letting out a short grunt with a small dip of his head. Encouraged, the captain took another few steps and held out one of the mugs. After staring at it silently for a moment, the first mate finally accepted it with another nod.

"Thanks," Tom mumbled, gaze shifting back over the water.

Baltsaros sat down on the other end of the bench and leaned back on the painted boards. As the two men sat in silence, the sky slowly deepened to the true black of night above them.

Sipping his beer, Baltsaros studied Tom's profile. The man had a high forehead and a shapely brow that creased so often in amusement or consternation that Baltsaros could see faint lines there despite Tom's relatively young age. Though he knew Tom's nose had been broken a few times, it remained largely straight and seemed almost too aristocratic for his roguish looks. Below that were full lips that were often quirked into a smile, making Tom appear both sensual and boyish—a dangerous combination. It was a handsome face, with its scars and scratchy dark-blond stubble, and one that the captain had sorely missed.

"What else can I say?" Baltsaros murmured. "What can I do to make things better for you?" When there was no reaction from Tom, the captain thought he had not heard him, and he leaned forward with the intention of repeating himself.

Tom turned his head slowly and lifted his shoulder in a small shrug, his eyes focused on nothing.

"Tom, talk to me," said Baltsaros, reaching out to touch the first mate's shoulder briefly. When Tom didn't move away, the captain slid closer to him on the bench.

After taking a last drag from his cheroot, Tom flicked it overboard, and his eyes followed the orange spark as it arced through the darkness.

"When have ye ever cared about what I had to say, Baltsaros?" he asked, turning his gaze back to the captain.

Baltsaros frowned. Tom had been calling him "Da" for so long that it was startling to hear his name fall from the first mate's lips.

"I've always listened to you," said Baltsaros slowly, confused. It was true—whenever there were decisions to be made aboard the ship, the first mate's opinions were invaluable.

Tom huffed out a small, sardonic laugh; as he looked down at the mug clasped loosely between his knees, the first mate shook his head.

"I don't mean the bloody fucking ship, ye fucking idiot," said Tom, looking up with a wry grin. "I mean... about..." The first mate sighed, his brow deeply lined. Tom lifted the beer to his lips and drained the contents in a few swallows. After depositing the empty mug on the deck next to his feet, he wiped his lips and turned his eyes to Baltsaros again, a distraught look on his face.

Baltsaros put his own cup down on the bench beside him and stared hard at Tom.

"I thought you enjoyed our arrangement," he said, sitting back.

Tom laughed and nodded his head.

"No, no, Da. I do... It's just... Why did ye set me aside so easily?" he asked, his eyes going quickly from sad to aloof as he looked back out over the water.

"This isn't about me whipping you," said the captain; it was a statement.

Tom's lip curled in disgust, and he shook his head.

"That's just the bloody icin' on the fuckin' cake," he said, his deep voice just a low rumble in his broad chest.

With a sigh, the captain reached out and curled his hand around the back of Tom's head, the short dirty-blond hair soft against Baltsaros's palm.

At the touch, Tom closed his eyes.

"I thought I made it clear when we came for you that I'm sorry for everything that happened, Tom. Putting you aside for Jon the way I did was an unfortunate mistake, one that I would like you to forgive me for," said Baltsaros, making his voice gentle. "I was like a child with a new toy. I understand that now. It was cruel beyond cruel, and you paid dearly for my whims."

Baltsaros stroked his hand down Tom's neck, his thumb sliding along the side of the first mate's jaw. Tom kept his eyes closed, the muscles of his strong jaw moving fluidly under his deeply tanned skin. The captain watched Tom swallow, the crease between his eyebrows deepening.

Yes, he was terribly fond of this young man.

When Tom opened his eyes to look at the captain, Baltsaros leaned forward and brought his mouth hard against the first mate's. Tom went rigid with surprise but kissed back, a rough-edged embrace that awoke the desire in Baltsaros. He pulled Tom closer to deepen the kiss; there were things that Baltsaros craved that he could not inflict on Jon, and finally the drought was over.

With one hand he quickly reached down to undo the belt at Tom's waist, and when the man tried to push him away, Baltsaros pulled back and backhanded him. Tom grunted with the impact of the captain's strike and lifted his hand to his face, his eyes unreadable in the dark of the quarterdeck. Baltsaros chuckled, his lust sharpening. With a low growl the captain pulled Tom from the bench and, caught off guard, he landed hard on the wooden boards. Tom tried to sit up, but the captain hit him hard again. Baltsaros dropped to his knees between Tom's legs and continued to work loose the fastenings of his pants.

"Stop," said Tom, his voice harsh. He shoved at Baltsaros's hands again, and the older man felt a moment of doubt.

"Don't play, Tom," he said, a frown on his face. He pulled open the first mate's pants, and when he started tugging them down, the captain realized that Tom had stopped struggling. Glancing up, he saw that Tom had turned his head and closed his eyes.

"No, Da. If ye do this, ye'll be forcin' me," said the big man beneath him, turning his furious ocean eyes on the captain. "I'm sayin' no."

The captain sat back on his heels. In disbelief he watched Tom pull his pants together and sit up slowly, breathing hard.

This was no act.

Once he'd staggered to his feet, Baltsaros balled his fists but resisted the urge to lash out at his first mate. He turned and, without a backwards glance, the captain left Tom alone in the dark.

Startled, Jon looked up when Baltsaros threw the door open to his quarters. He got to his feet quickly and crossed the room, his dark brows low over his storm-grey eyes when the captain leaned hard against the edge of the table.

"What happened?" asked Jon, placing a worried hand on Baltsaros's shoulder.

With eyes closed, the captain shook his head. He was at a loss.

Jon's fingers tightened on him.

"Tom?" asked Jon, his voice low. At Baltsaros's nod, he dropped his hand.

He looked up and saw that Jon was staring at him, apprehension clear in his eyes.

"What did you do to Tom, Baltsaros?" asked Jon, softly. Accusingly.

The captain sighed and straightened. It seemed that he had no choice; fate was forcing his hand.

"Go to him," Baltsaros said gently. The words stuck in his throat like bitter bile, but he made himself calmly place a steady hand on Jon's arm. "Go to him, and see if you can't make some sense of this. Go to him, and help me *fix this*."

Worry and suspicion flashed across Jon's face. After pulling away from Baltsaros, he just stared at the captain for a moment before turning to leave.

Alone in his quarters, Baltsaros glared down at his bruised fist wondering whether he would ever know calm again.

PRESENT DAY

The captain turned his head with an annoyed growl when he heard the galley door slide open behind him, but when he saw who it was, his lips curled into a pleased smile.

"Now, now... what's goin' on in here?" asked the first mate, stamping snow from his big boots and chuckling. Tom came around the counter and looked down; he put a large, scarred hand on Jon's head and softly stroked the young man's glossy dark hair.

Jon made a small noise, and the vibrations felt good on Baltsaros's cock.

The captain let out a soft groan, turning to watch Jon take in more of his length before he drew back to work his tongue against the underside of its head again.

Tom's hand curled around Baltsaros's neck, and when he looked up, the big man brought him in for a long, slow kiss.

Too soon, Tom broke away, and Baltsaros was dismayed to see the seriousness on the first mate's face.

"I'm sorry, Da... but yer needed above deck," said Tom, eyes down to watch Baltsaros's cock, shiny with spit, emerge from Jon's open mouth.

The kneeling young man looked up, worried.

The captain frowned and rubbed his beard. Another setback?

"Snow squalls, Malik called them," continued the first mate, ruffling Jon's hair. Tom looked up at Baltsaros, his cheeks ruddy from the cold wind. "The rest of what that bloody shipwright said was bloody fuckin' gibberish, but the gist is he needs ye to look at the ship. I ain't understandin' half of what he says... so..." Tom brought up his hands in a sheepish gesture.

"Can't this wait?" asked Baltsaros, though he could feel himself getting soft. The ship always came first.

Tom shook his head and put a hand over his nose. The tip of it had been icy against the captain's cheek, and Baltsaros realized that, for once, the first mate was actually cold. The captain sighed.

"All right," he said and started tucking himself back into his pants. He closed his eyes briefly, forcing himself to say words he didn't want to say. "Why don't you and Jon go warm up? There is no reason why we all have to suffer the weather. Go on. I will join you when I can."

Tom helped Jon up as the captain pulled his shirt on over his head. Baltsaros couldn't help but wonder at how protective and gentle Tom was towards Jon; even for the short journey to the captain's quarters, the first mate carefully draped the woollen cloak around the smaller man to make sure he wasn't cold.

Frowning to himself, Baltsaros watched them leave, trying to turn his mind from bitter thoughts to the dangers of sailing a ship through icy, winter seas.

TOM

"Not I, nor anyone else can travel that road
*   for you.*
You must travel it by yourself.
It is not far. It is within reach.
Perhaps you have been on it since you were born,
*   and did not know.*
Perhaps it is everywhere on water and land."

— WALT WHITMAN, LEAVES OF GRASS

PRESENT DAY

Tom watched Jon pull the woollen scarf off his face and reached out to help when he saw that the end of it was caught underneath the edge of the thick cloak. Grinning, Jon shook his head, letting himself be unwound by Tom.

"I can undress myself, you know," the dark-haired young man

pointed out ruefully even though he obliged and raised his chin when Tom lifted the cloak up and off of him.

Tom let out a short grunt and nodded. Turning to hang their wet outer clothes on the nails he had set into the wall for that purpose, he felt a small twinge of embarrassment for how much he doted on Jon. It was more than a little ridiculous, but he couldn't help himself.

He rubbed his thumb along the edge of his stubbled jaw and glanced back at Jon; when he saw that he was smiling at him, his blue-grey eyes fond, Tom grinned wide. It always amazed him that Jon had forgiven him for everything… Tom would have killed him had their positions been reversed.

Jon cocked his head to the side, his eyes growing dark suddenly as the tip of his tongue came out to touch his top lip. His hair was mussed; a few long curls had escaped the thong at his neck, and they followed the curve of Jon's jaw as he studied Tom.

"Come here," he said, beckoning.

Instantly Tom's heart rate accelerated, and he quickly moved forward to obey. When he brought big hands up to Jon's slender waist, he felt—as always—a little shy and wondered briefly if that would ever pass; he didn't really want it to.

Jon leaned forward to brush his lips softly against Tom's, and the first mate closed his eyes with a sigh, his breathing a little ragged. Would Jon be kind or cruel to him today? Tom tightened his hold on the smaller man, savouring the anticipation and thanking whatever gods there were for gifting him with this passionate, unpredictable creature who was able to take him apart with equal measures of pleasure and pain.

FIVE WEEKS AGO

Pressing his fingers lightly to the bruises on his cheek, Tom winced. Baltsaros had a wicked backhanded strike that always made the world explode into bright colours when he hit him, and he did so often. Normally, it didn't bother him but... tonight...

He tongued the place where his teeth had sliced the inside of his lip and sighed as he leaned back against the bunched up pillows. Bumping his head lightly against the wooden boards, Tom closed his eyes.

Fucking Baltsaros. Actually... that was the point. Why *wasn't* he fucking Baltsaros?

He lifted the flask to his lips and grimaced when the rum burned the cut. After swallowing down the sweet, fiery liquid, he touched his cheek again. His mind was a worse mess than his face, that was for bloody fucking sure.

When he heard soft footfalls outside his door, he tensed, thinking it was the captain come to finish the job. However, he realized that there was a note of hesitation to the steps and, as far as Tom knew, Baltsaros had never had a moment's hesitation in his life.

Tom waited and smiled when the knock finally came, soft and timid; there was no one else on the ship it could be.

"Who the fuck is it?" he yelled, trying to mask the sudden excitement that had him smiling despite the pain in his face. When he saw the shadow under the door start to move away uncertainly, he swore under his breath.

Gods be fuckin' damned, Jon, he thought, shaking his head. *Grow a bloody pair.*

"Come in or get gone," he said loudly, flipping the corner of the blanket over to cover himself when the door opened a crack in response.

"Tom? It's me..." said the slight dark-haired man, peering around the wooden door. He was starkly outlined by the brighter corridor behind him; all Tom could see was the curve of Jon's shoulder and his head surrounded by a nimbus of curled wisps that caught the light. "Can I come in?"

Tom chuckled.

"What part of *come in* did ye not understand, lad?" he said, smiling. He saw Jon's shoulder lift slightly and knew that the serious young man would have a deep wrinkle between his brows. Tom reached up and shifted the dented cover on the lantern to make the space a little brighter as Jon stepped into the tiny room, closing the door behind him quietly.

After standing a little awkwardly next to the thin mattress where Tom was sprawled, Jon finally decided simply to sink down into a crouch. Looking worried, he licked his lips and swallowed before speaking.

"What did the captain do?" Jon asked, his eyes taking in the bruising down the right side of Tom's face. "Are you ok?"

Tom took another swig of rum and hissed in pain. He looked at the door.

"Does he know yer here, lovey?" Tom asked quietly; his heart was a quick thing knocking against his ribs, and it was making him a little lightheaded.

"He sent me," replied Jon, his storm-blue eyes wide. "Tom, what did he do? It had to have been something really shitty for him to send me to you. I automatically assumed that he beat you bloody..." He made a small noise and looked away quickly when he finally noticed that Tom was very obviously naked, covered only by the edge of the blanket.

Tom smiled; Jon was amusingly uptight. Making as if to stretch his shoulders, the first mate shifted under the coverlet a little to expose more of his inner thigh and grinned as Jon's eyes tracked the motion only to dart away again almost immediately. However, when Tom saw the way that the young man's lips parted after a slow swallow, he let out a hitched breath; he was falling prey to his own teasing. Quickly, he moved his hand over the bulge in the blanket ands rumpled the material to camouflage his sudden, unexpected arousal. The room felt very hot.

Tom lifted the flask again, and he took a deep swallow, his mouth now numb to the sting. He cleared his throat to try to cut the tension with words.

"Uh... aye, Da came up to see me above. Said some more about bein' sorry. And then... he bloody kisses me," Tom said, frowning.

Jon turned to Tom, confusion and concern on his fine-boned face.

"That wasn't what you wanted?" he asked.

"Oh, that was fine, lad. He just never does," Tom replied, realizing immediately by the way Jon blinked in surprise that the same wasn't true for him. As he swallowed against the sudden tightness in his chest, Tom went back to leaning his head against the wooden wall and stared up at the wavering shadows cast on the low ceiling. "Aye, that was fine. Nice, even. It was when he tried for more, the randy bastard." Rubbing a hand across his mouth, he scowled. "Somethin' just, don't know"—Tom gestured to his head vaguely, not able to put into words the feelings that had washed over him—"and, I said 'no'."

At a soft sound, Tom turned his head and saw that Jon had settled down more comfortably, legs crossed in front of him as he leaned forward, listening intently to Tom. The lantern threw exactly half of the young man's features into total darkness.

"And how did he react?" asked Jon, folding his fists under his chin.

Tom grinned crookedly; the right side of his face felt tight and swollen.

"The bugger actually stopped," he said, shaking his head in disbelief.

Lying on his back on the quarterdeck planks with Baltsaros kneeling between his legs, Tom had felt almost like a spectator when he heard himself tell the captain to stop. Even though his cock had been rock hard and raring to go, he had repeated his refusal, staring in amazement when the captain simply turned and left him.

"I was under the impression that you enjoyed being forced

into compromising positions," said Jon quietly, a tiny reflection of the flame in his eyes. "What changed? Why did you say no?"

Why? Tom rubbed a hand over his lips again.

Why indeed.

PRESENT DAY

Murmured against the side of Tom's jaw, Jon's words made the breath hitch in the big man's chest.

"Since you're so goddamn thick that you had to come interrupt the captain and me, I think you *owe* me something in return, don't you think?" purred Jon. "You need a lesson in manners, Tom, and I think you'll take your punishment in the form of my cock in your ass."

Tom licked his lips and nodded, wincing slightly when Jon's sharp teeth nipped his earlobe hard. He shivered as the other man's hands slid up along his ribs, Jon's touch confident as he held Tom hard against his body.

"You're going to take your clothes off and lean over the table. Spread your legs, chest down. Do it," said Jon with a sneer, pushing him away.

Tom almost grinned, but the trick to nurturing Jon's sadistic side was not to appear too eager, something that was difficult considering how much he enjoyed Jon's inventiveness.

Tom reached between his shoulders and drew the thick sweater he wore up over his head, discarding it on the floor before quickly undoing his belt and long trousers. After kicking off the big boots he hated wearing, Tom stepped out of his pants and stood naked in front of Jon for a moment, his hand covering his cock not out of modesty but in an attempt to hide his growing excitement.

Down boy, he thought.

"What are you staring at?" asked Jon, his voice low and harsh.

However, as Tom moved to obey, he caught the dark-haired man's appreciative glance and allowed himself a hidden smile as he turned his head away.

He leaned over the mahogany table, spreading his legs just as he was ordered and lowered his torso down to the cold wood. Jon hadn't specified where he wanted his hands, so Tom just clutched the sides of the table, his body taut with anticipation. The edge of the table was a hard line below his hipbones; Tom would no doubt be bruised by being driven against it... and he looked forward to it keenly.

FIVE WEEKS AGO

Tom went to take another sip from the flask and found it empty. Swallowing, regardless, just to wet his mouth, he realized he was stalling on answering Jon. The slender young man sat staring at him patiently, a soft worry in his eyes.

"I... don't fuckin' know, love. I don't fuckin' know," Tom muttered. "Be a dove and get the bottle? The little one." He pointed to the small crate holding the pitcher of water.

Jon leaned over and reached for it, fumbling at the sides of the crate until he realized that the front of it opened on leather hinges. Inside were two bottles of rum in stoppered earthenware jugs and one small bottle of good whiskey in a narrow, green bottle; Jon held the last out to Tom.

"Will ye join me... and come a wee bit closer?" asked Tom hopefully, taking the bottle from Jon.

After a moment's hesitation, Jon crawled onto the hard mattress and sat hunched beside Tom.

"That's not what I meant, ducky..." grinned Tom, pulling his knife out from under the blanket to slide the point around the wax at the top of the bottle. "Listen, love: If Da asked ye to come see me, don'tcha think he might be all right with us touchin' a tad?

Can't ye see how much I'm hurtin'?" Tom chuckled and pulled the cork out with his teeth.

Jon turned his head and smiled crookedly before easing himself back against Tom's outstretched arm. However, as soon as his shoulders touched Tom's warm skin, the timidity left Jon, and he leaned against the bigger man's side with his head on Tom's wide shoulder. Tom's heart beat double a few times before settling down into a rapid rhythm; as he took a sip of the smooth whiskey, he wondered if Jon knew how nervous he actually felt. He passed the bottle to Jon, the only thing from the *Jewel* he had brought with him.

"I think you're scared," said Jon, just holding the green glass bottle in his hand for a moment.

Tom started, a little dismayed at how transparent he was. He licked the taste of whiskey from his top lip.

"Nah, I ain't scared of much, lad," he replied, closing his eyes.

When he had finally washed ashore after being swept overboard by the storm, Tom had spent a week just lying in a spare bed at the *Jewel*, recovering from the extreme dehydration he had suffered from. He had nearly died from exposure; fighting to stay afloat, he had held onto the barrel for dear life even though his arms had trembled and his brain had gone numb from exhaustion.

Once he was able to leave the bed on his own, the first thing Tom had done was steal a large batch of sleeping powder.

The man who found Tom collapsed on the floor realized right away what had happened and managed to empty his stomach with a tube.

Afterwards, Tom had been watched more carefully.

Fresia, whom Tom had always been friendly with, had looked at him sternly and said that she couldn't understand why, after fighting to survive, he was trying to take the coward's way out.

A coward.

That's exactly how he felt.

It was agonizing to be forced to endure Jon's presence from a distance for fear of driving the captain to extremes. A bad idea. Bloody stupid. Tom never wanted to face Baltsaros's cold wrath again. Ever. He was stupid for even having Jon in his room right now, regardless of what the captain had said. He blinked—maybe it was a bloody test. Tom scrubbed his hand over the top of his head, trying to block out his worries. Jon broke through his thoughts a moment later.

"See, I thought you were angry. That's certainly how you've been playing it—wounded pride and all that—but fear is the only thing that makes sense for why you're acting this way," mused Jon, rocking his head against Tom's arm.

Tom opened his eyes and sighed.

"Ye think I'm actin' the fool, love?" he asked, taking the bottle back from Jon. "I ain't scared of him. Not the way you're thinkin'."

Jon shrugged.

"Listen, ducky. Before the captain came along, every bastard who wanted to put his cock in me, did. No choice," Tom swallowed some whiskey and shook his head. "Same with beatin' me. I kept fightin' them but just sorta got numb. When Da bought me for a few coins, I was in a real bad way. I almost fuckin' killed the bastard the first time he laid a hand on me, but he was just fixin' me up. I kept waitin' for him to make me his bed boy and it just kept on not happenin'. After the shite with Abetha, well... I just crawled into his bed and sucked his cock. He got bloody rough with me..." Chuckling, Tom smiled at the memory. "And I fuckin' loved it. He's got this *way*... Came so hard I saw stars. Ye know, he's the only soul I ever went to for it. The only one."

The edges of his mind were starting to get blurry from drink, and he was tired, so very tired of thinking and talking about the fucking captain. He felt around for the cork and pushed it back into the neck of the bottle before wedging the whiskey between mattress and wall. Looping his arm around Jon, he pulled them further down on the bed to lie face-to-face.

Jon looked at him with a rueful smile.

"What do you call *this*, then?" he asked, sliding his hand around Tom's waist.

Tom closed his eyes and let out a soft sigh.

"This... this ain't what's good for anyone, that's what it is," he said with a frown. "I'm thinkin' it was a fuckin' mistake to come back. I'm thinkin' maybe ye should leave me to my bloody proble—"

Tom's ears were filled with a rush of white noise, his pulse jumping, as Jon's warm mouth touched his. With a groan, he opened his lips and pressed hard into the kiss.

Present Day

When he finished tying Tom's ankles to the base of the table legs, Jon smacked the back of his thigh with a bare hand.

"Arms behind you," said Jon, standing.

Obediently, Tom placed his arms behind him and winced as Jon tied his wrists together tightly. The room was warm from the pot-bellied stove that Malik and Baltsaros had installed as part of the Devil's Isles modifications, but Jon's hands felt cool against his skin as they moved to trace the tattooed lines that curled and twined over his left side. Tom let out a low groan as Jon slid his fingers lower, stroking down the furrow of his ass. Breathless with anticipation, Tom closed his eyes as Jon poured something cool on him, fingers pushing into him quickly to get him ready. The penetration was perfunctory, done without any gentleness; Tom didn't expect any. That would come later.

Tom let out a grunt when Jon's cock breached him, sliding deep inside him in one motion. He opened his eyes and craned his neck, glancing back at Jon when the man remained motionless. Confused, Tom watched Jon smile and lean over to pluck one of Baltsaros's good white candles out of the heavy wrought iron holder. The motion caused him to push into Tom, and the big man exhaled slowly. He placed his head back down on the table and closed his eyes, ready for anything Jon could dish out.

"You told me once that you weren't afraid of much. How about fire?" asked Jon.

Tom heard the unmistakable sound of a match being struck against the side of the table and felt the first twinge of real fear. His heart beat fast and hard wondering what Jon intended; when it came to finding new ways to abuse him, Jon was creative. He grunted again as the hard cock in his ass pulled back, only to plunge into him once more.

"Let's see if I can make you beg..." said Jon, and Tom gasped when the first drops of burning hot wax hit his skin.

FIVE WEEKS AGO

Tom rubbed his face sleepily and took another deep swallow of rum. Bleary-eyed, he reached up and pulled the cheroot out from behind his ear to tuck it into the corner of his mouth.

"Matches, bloody matches..." he muttered, patting at the pocket sewn into his rolled trousers. When he thought he had found one, he tried pulling it out, but it snagged on the material and went flying off into the dark. Tom blinked and fumbled again in the pocket. When it was obvious that there wasn't another match, he scowled and tried to stick the slim cigar back behind his ear.

"Don't need no fuckin' match any—*Cock and bloody balls!*" he yelled as the cheroot dropped to the deck, rolling off into the dark to join the wayward match. With a string of low, muttered curses, Tom squinted and saw that his dicing partner had fallen asleep against the stack of crates; the man was snoring, mouth open and stinking.

Rubbing his eyes again, Tom fought his own desire for sleep. He had to stay away from his room for fear that Jon would come find him again. With a groan, he leaned his head against the rain barrel.

Jon. Passionate and gentle. Jon with his boundless hope that the three of them would find some kind of arrangement.

"Bloody fucking naïve fucking Jon," slurred Tom, shaking his head. The boy had been so soft in his hands, warm, willing. Tom had finally sent him on his way after regretfully breaking from the kiss. How could he explain to Jon that he was a coward? That he was terrified of being set aside again by the captain. That the reason he had been so late coming aboard that first day was because he had decided not to come at all rather than face Baltsaros and Jon.

Standing on the deck of the Sainte-Marie, Tom clutched his bag. He had spent the night tossing and turning, almost sick with unease, before boarding the small passenger schooner bound for the midlands.

The previous afternoon spent with the captain and Jon at the *Jewel* had been almost perfect; enough so that he had fooled himself briefly into thinking that everything was back to normal.

When the first twinges of doubt had struck him as he lay next to the two men, his body cooling, he wondered how it could ever be normal when Jon was involved. His desire for the dark-haired young man was like a slow-burning fire in his veins; Baltsaros would never put up with it. Jon would remain a constant threat, one that would have Tom beaten and banished again eventually.

And... he just couldn't live with being ousted from the captain's side again. There was no one else in the world that Tom respected or loved more; Baltsaros was his life. He knew that it was almost blind devotion, but he didn't care. For all that the man was a blatant sadist, no one else had shown him trust or friendship like the captain had; and, in the rare moments of gentleness between them, Tom had thought maybe even love. That fool's notion had been blown to bits the moment he saw the way that Baltsaros looked at Jon.

Jaw clenched, Tom turned his eyes away from the painfully familiar mizzenmast that could be seen just past the harbour wall. *Baal's Heart*, the only true home he had ever known.

No, he would go to the midlands and find work, maybe as an apprentice blacksmith or a personal guard for a small lord... nowhere near open water. Captain Baltsaros would never find him, and Tom would eventually forget and grow numb; his constant dreams of a dark-haired sylph with Jon's eyes and gentle hands would fade away.

He would become nothing.

Tom closed his eyes, trying to push away the ache that was growing inside him, making his chest tight.

Fuck it.

When the schooner's first mate cried out to push away from the dock, Tom let out a long sigh before jumping down from the ship. As he made his way along the floating dock, Tom whistled loud to hail one of the small boats that ferried those to the bigger ships just outside the harbour, apprehension like a heavy cloak around his broad shoulders.

"Well, well... lookee, Dan! What d'we 'ave 'ere, aye?" growled a voice nearby.

Tom pulled his eyelids apart, blinking slowly at the approaching shapes. Licking his lips, he was dismayed to see that his drunkenness had reached the level where images were overlapping. When he closed one eye, Tom saw that instead of four men swaying up the deck towards him, there were two. He scratched his jaw, trying to coax recognition out of his brain. All he could remember was that the two were part of the new batch brought aboard after the massacre on Madierus.

Tom hiccupped a laugh when the memory coalesced: *Dan.* They were both called Dan. Big Dan and Little Dan. Both were trouble.

Big Dan, who rivalled Tom in size, walked slowly up to him and kicked the sole of his bare foot. Tom grunted; he wasn't in the mood for any foolery. When he tried to haul himself to standing, the world spun on a different axis, and he found himself down on the planks, the boards smooth and worn beneath his palms. There was raucous laughter from above, and Tom wiped at the corner of his mouth before turning his head with a scowl.

"Ye know what I 'ear about this 'un, Dan?" asked the bigger of the two. The smaller man kept silent, and Tom recalled that he was a mute. It made him wonder if his name was Dan after all or if the big brute had just named him such as a lark. Tom shoved himself to sitting and shook his head hard, trying to clear it enough so he could stand.

"I 'ear that Tom 'ere is a regular cock'ound. Aye. I 'ear 'e likes to take big fat todgers in 'is little pink man-pussy," drawled Big Dan, an ugly smile on his weatherworn face. "I 'ear 'e fuckin' *loves* it. Mebbe if I fuck 'im in that sweet little ass cunt of 'is, 'e'll think twice about makin' me swab the bloody fuckin' deck again... What do ye think, Dan? Do ye think maybe 'e'll come warm our cocks at night like 'e does the captain's?"

The man's hands had gone down to his belt, and Tom could

see that he was unbuckling it. Anger crashed through him followed fast by a cold finger of fear when he realized he was probably too drunk to fight Big Dan off.

"Aye, 'elp me 'old 'im down, Dan," growled the big one, and the two men fell on Tom. He tried to shove them away, but Big Dan landed a blow to his temple, and he was overcome quickly as he lay there stunned. Tom was soon on his stomach on the boards, growling like a trapped animal, as his pants were yanked down past his ass.

Not again, thought Tom, breathing through clenched teeth, his chest crushed to the deck by the man sitting on his back.

There was a strangled gurgle, and Tom felt something hot and wet hit his shoulder.

"Tom is mine, lads," said the captain in a soft voice as the man above him slumped over and collapsed like a sack of potatoes on the decking next to the first mate's head. Tom opened his eyes and watched as Little Dan's pupils went slack, dark bubbles of blood popping and spattering along the deep cut in his neck. Confusion was immediately replaced with astounded relief, and Tom lifted himself up on his hands and knees, swaying slightly. He heard a loud thump and turned his head, hauling his pants up with one hand. There was a splash and then a gentle long-fingered hand helped him up to his feet.

Baltsaros had saved him again. Saved him and claimed him, just as he had so long ago. Tom's chest hurt, and his eyes burned.

Letting himself collapse in the captain's arms, Tom buried his face in the man's shoulder. He smelled Baltsaros's scent—the subtle musk of him, cologne, clean skin, ocean air. Tom clutched at him, gathering handfuls of the captain's loose white shirt at his back,

"Da, I'm sorry. I'm sorry... gods, I'm sorry..." he sighed over and over against the captain.

"Tom, you're completely inebriated. What are you apologizing for? Everything will be all right. Can you stand? Here... hold onto this for a moment please," said Baltsaros, leaning him against the big rain barrel. Tom swiped at his eyes and steadied himself as he watched the older man drag Little Dan across the deck. Leaving a wide, red streak behind him, the captain then lifted the dead man up and over the gunwale.

A graceful smile widened the captain's curved lips when he turned back to Tom, his hands bloody as he reached out to take the big man's arm.

"There's no need for apologies, my tomcat. You're *mine*... Which means you're mine to protect. Do you understand me? Gods you stink—how much have you had to drink? No wonder you get yourself into such trouble," muttered the captain, shaking his head. "Now, are you listening to me, you stubborn thing? Jon told me you were scared, and I think I know why. Tom, there's no justification for your fears. It's really very simple: I want you by my side... I *need* you with me. How can I get that through your thick skull, boy?" He reached out and touched Tom's face, thumb sliding along his sore cheek. "*I* am the one who's sorry."

Need. Tom looked away as his heart stumbled and his breath was torn from him. With that simple word, his doubts sank along with the dead men overboard. The captain *needed* him.

"Aye, Da. If ye'll still have me after all my foolishness," he replied with an awkward grin.

There was no mistaking the fondness in Baltsaros's dark eyes as he smiled back at his first mate. With a nod, Tom looped his arm around the captain's neck for support and let himself be led to the stateroom below the quarterdeck.

As he ducked through the doorway, Tom groaned softly. Through the haze of alcohol, he began to realize just how hard Big Dan had hit him. He felt a stickiness on his jaw and neck that wasn't drying and figured it was probably his own blood. There was a rustle in the darkened room.

"Baltsaros?" came Jon's voice, confused and hoarse from sleep.

"Jon, can you please light some candles? And get my surgical kit please," said the captain as he helped Tom to cross the room.

Tom squinted as a match was struck. Jon, standing naked next to the bed, leaned over the table to light the candles at its centre. Turning to look at Tom, his shadow-blue eyes widened.

"Tom! Oh gods, are you ok? What happened?" asked Jon, reaching out to help Baltsaros lay him down on the bed. The dark-haired young man's brows were pinched together in worry for a moment, his hand gentle on Tom's chest before he went to fetch Baltsaros's surgical tools.

"I'm ok, lad. Just got into a fight, aye?" Tom said as he glanced at Baltsaros; the captain nodded once in understanding. "Fucker beat me when I was down on my luck at dice... Me, three sheets to the bloody fuckin' wind." Tom grinned when Jon frowned and clucked his tongue once; there was no need to tell him what had nearly happened. As the captain said: everything was going to be all right.

"Ach, my bloody face," he complained when Jon leaned over him to start dabbing at the wound at his brow. Tom saw the captain smile wanly as he threaded the needle with catgut. "Why does everyone hit me in the *face*? Ain't I ugly enough?"

PRESENT DAY

While it was bitterly cold outside, the two men in the stateroom glistened with sweat. Tom, his arms bound behind him and his ankles tied to the legs of the table, grunted and hissed as another stream of hot wax landed on his bare skin. Jon groaned in response; he loved the way Tom's muscles tightened over his cock with the sudden pain. He thrust himself into Tom's body a few times, his hands sliding over the tattooed skin of the bound man's side.

The candlelight made Tom's skin pure gold, and Jon thought it was beautiful.

The door banged open behind them, and Jon turned his head.

The captain stepped in amidst a swirl of snowflakes and quickly shut the door against the wind.

His cheeks were red with the cold, and the collar of his great-coat was pulled high over his ears. He yanked his gloves off, sighing happily from the heat in the room, and nodded at Jon to continue.

Jon turned back to Tom and spilled some more burning wax on him, moving within his body. With the captain's eyes on him, Jon felt his pleasure mount quickly, and soon he was pounding into Tom, a harsh growl bursting out of his chest as he pulled his cock out to rain his seed down on the bound man's back.

Breath heaving fast in his chest, Jon began untwisting the hempen ropes that were binding Tom. He looked curiously at the captain. Baltsaros's face had darkened with lust at the display; he loved to watch the boys "play", as he put it. However, he made no move to join them as he usually did.

Tom straightened and flexed his wrists, his head cocked curiously at Baltsaros.

"What is it, Da?" he asked, still using the ridiculous title though the two were no longer related through marriage.

Baltsaros smiled wide.

"I thought you boys would like to know that we've arrived within sight of the Devil's Isles," he said.

Jon and Tom looked at each other in excitement. It had taken nearly two months to reach them; finally it was the time to see what it was they were up against.

PART II

1

THE SPIRES

Jon shivered and squinted against the snowflakes that stuck to his eyelashes and whirled around like maddened, ghostly flies over the quarterdeck. Against his side, the captain was a solid presence as he peered through his binoculars at the looming mountain range ahead. Tom let out a long, low whistle that the wind attempted to snatch away. Leaning forward against the railing, the grinning first mate turned to look over his shoulder, his sea-green eyes wide with amazement.

"Bloody hells, Da," he chuckled. "Have ye brought us to our doom?"

Jon felt, rather than heard, the captain's bark of laughter as he lowered the short, custom-made, double spyglass. Curious, Jon took the binoculars from Baltsaros's hand and held them up to his own eyes.

What he beheld was mind boggling. Monstrous. Nothing Malik and Nathaniel had described nor what was written in any of Baltsaros's books could have prepared Jon for the overwhelming reality of the Devil's Isles. Out of a frozen, pale-grey sea sprouted colossal black spires, like clawed fingers or fangs that reached up into the snow-washed sky. There were seven of them, arranged in a slight outward curve, that jutted from the impass-able mountain range that split the world in half from the northern isles to the frozen, uninhabitable wasteland to the south. Only through the relatively narrow gap between the third and fourth spires could a ship theoretically pass and *only* during the warmest weeks in this barren, snow-blasted land; at least that's what it said on the mouldering text that Nathaniel the cartographer had found. It still remained to be seen if *Baal's Heart* had made it in time and could navigate it at all. To Jon, it seemed like a frozen impasse ahead.

The Devil's Isles, the captain had explained, were formed from the same stone that the rest of the western mountain range was composed of. He theorized that there had been a softer stone between the veins of hard black granite and that, over the ages, the elements had worn it away to leave behind the hooked spires that clawed up from the frozen sea. Though Baltsaros's explana-tion made sense, it did nothing to still the nagging Jon's nagging belief that nothing natural could have created something so terrifying.

At a thump and loud creak, Jon started. His heart beat double for the moment it took to remind himself that it was only floating chunks of ice hitting the reinforced hull of the ship. They had lowered Malik's "bumpers" over the side of the prow the previous day when they began to encounter more substantial pieces of ice floating in the cold sea. Attached to the iron-and-wood struts that caged the hull, the bumpers were packets of leather-wrapped straw sewn onto a large net that swathed the entire front of the ship. The shipwright had been confident that they would be enough to deflect the ice long enough to make it through the gap. However, when the snow had started piling up at the bow earlier that day, he had started to worry that the weight would be too much and that the ship would start to be pulled nose-down into the icy water.

Jon had to smile; all it had required was that the snow be scooped overboard, something that Tom could very well have handled on his own. Instead, he had begged off, claiming igno-rance before coming to interrupt Jon and the captain in the galley. Tom caught his eye then and, as if reading Jon's thoughts, the first mate winked with a sly grin.

Jon wrinkled his brow at the first mate. Had it been latent jeal-ousy or simple desire to get out of the cold? No matter how much time Jon spent with Tom, he still had trouble reading the bigger man's honest intentions.

Tom slid away from the railing and pressed himself to the captain's other side as the three of them stood on the frozen deck, watching the approach of the looming spires.

With his hands clamped tight over his ears, Jon groaned. Even with Tom's heavy arms around him, no matter what he did, he couldn't block out the screams.

The evening after the Devil's Isles first came into view, the snow had finally stopped, and an eerie calm had fallen as *Baal's Heart* sailed towards the spires in the pitch dark. The submerged chunks of ice had increased in number and size, and Baltsaros had contemplated anchoring for the night out of safety; however, the wind had died down, and Malik had cautioned against it, pointing out that to be motionless could mean getting trapped in the ice. In the end, the captain had put himself, Tom, and Calum on short shifts overnight.

As Baltsaros was just settling into bed beside him, intending to take the second shift, a loud screech had filled the cabin, turning Jon's blood to ice. Heart lurching in his chest, Jon had sat up, wide-eyed and blind in the dark.

"What the hells was that?" Dry-mouthed, the words had come out as a mere croak, and he had flinched when Baltsaros's hand came up to touch his back. Moments later a second scream had rent the air, and Jon's heart had stuttered again, beating hard against his ribs. The sound was ghastly, inhuman. Terrified, Jon had choked when the door to the cabin was thrown open, and a big shape shambled in. When Tom's deep voice had called out, Jon's nervous laugh had been shrill from relief.

As he had lit the candles, the first mate had explained that they were encountering yet bigger pieces of ice and that these were scraping slowly along the sides of the ship; the sound, reverberating through the *Heart's* hull, was amplified. As if eager to lend credence to Tom's words, another long scream had echoed through the darkness. Even the stalwart first mate had blanched at the sound.

"Aye gods, that's a sound right outta the black hells, ain't it?" Tom had laughed, his eyes dark in the dim light.

Tom was no longer laughing.

The screeching had picked up in frequency, and soon it sounded like a chorus of men, women, and children were being continuously tortured to death outside the ship. No one would be getting any sleep that night.

Gritting his teeth, Jon tried to shake the images out of his head; he had worked a long time in the dungeons, and the sounds of the ice squealing against the sides of the ship were triggering images of torture that he had thought were long buried.

Tom pulled him against his warm chest, a big scarred hand around the back of Jon's neck.

"It's just ice, lovey," he kept murmuring against Jon's hair. Jon nodded, and squeezed his eyes shut tighter when there was a particularly jarring shriek.

"Do ye want to go back out?" asked Tom softly. Outside, the noises weren't nearly as loud. However, the air was a bone-numbing cold; even with the braziers burning hot on the quarter-deck, no one could stay outdoors for very long.

Jon pulled away and rubbed his face. His jaw was sore from clenching it.

"Yeah. Maybe for a bit. I'll be all right, I swear," he said. Both the captain and first mate were taking him very seriously, but Jon felt deeply ashamed of his reaction. It was just ice against the hull, but the noise brought back memories of the nightmares he used to have: the black water, the ship full of blood, the tortured dead crawling over its sides.

Shuddering, Jon grabbed for the thick sweater he always wore under his cloak and pulled it on over his head. Tom watched him for a moment, his eyes narrow with worry, before sliding off the bed to fetch their outer clothes.

When Jon stepped out the door, he let out a sharp gasp; the chill in the air made his breath burn like white fire in his lungs, and the inside of his nose crackled with ice. It was a terrifyingly bitter cold. After lifting his scarf over his face, he took the steps up to the quarterdeck two at a time, followed by Tom. He was exhausted and shaking with cold, but at least out here the sounds no longer sounded like screams—they'd been transformed back into icebergs scraping the ship's sides.

Standing by one of the braziers was the captain, his hands out over the crackling fire to warm them. Jon knew that Baltsaros hated having so much open flame on the ship, but they had no choice at this point; frostbite and death were the alternatives. With a glance towards the bow, Jon could see at least ten other bright spots of fire where men were huddled. They were like a floating island of light in a blackened sea.

When Jon joined the captain, he was bracketed by Tom's warmth on the other side; the first mate pulled out one of his small cigars and bent low to light it on a flaming brand.

"Still can't sleep, Jon?" asked the captain, his voice gentle. He'd started wearing a thick sailor's tuque low over his forehead, and with the big collar of his coat pulled high, his face was barely visible.

Jon shook his head and held his hands over the flames, trying to stay warm. Tom slung an arm around him and leaned into Jon's side as he passed his cheroot to the captain.

"We'll be through by mid-morning by my calculations," said the captain, taking in a lungful of the pungent smoke. "Then we can all sleep."

At dawn, the sun rose up behind *Baal's Heart*, a pale, sickly thing in the bone-white sky. Sitting swathed in blankets on the hard bench, Jon felt like every muscle in his body was screaming, and his head felt strange and numb, like he was only half-awake; the night had been so very long.

"Get up," said Baltsaros, grabbing a handful of the younger man's cloak. "Jon, get up."

Jon blinked slowly, moving his eyes from the low, flickering flames that burned in the big bronze bowl. He looked at the captain in confusion.

"Jon, you have to get up and move around. You're going to freeze just sitting there," growled the older man, stamping his feet on the deck. "Get up. Get up now."

So cold.

"I'm ok," replied Jon, his voice faint. "I'll be fine. Just let me stay by the fire." He turned back to the flames. The flames would keep him warm.

"Gods be damned, Jon," said the captain, yanking hard on his cloak. "You have to get back inside."

Jon gasped and tumbled off the bench, landing hard on one knee. He barely felt it.

"Don't make me go back inside, Baltsaros. I'm half insane from the sound... I don't think my nerves could take it. Please. I'll stay here with Tom," mumbled Jon, turning his head. The big man was nowhere to be seen. Had he fallen asleep on the bench? He couldn't remember Tom leaving his side.

"Tom is taking care of something. You have to listen to me, Jon. You have to stand up. Can you stand up for me?" The captain reached down to grasp Jon's arm, and he let himself be hauled upright. Groaning, Jon stood shakily on feet that felt like blocks of ice.

"Stamp your feet," ordered Baltsaros. "Get your blood flowing."

Jon felt like crying but obeyed. His feet began to burn and itch as he stamped the feeling back into his toes. When he heard a splash, he turned in time to see Tom pushing a body over the side of the ship; the cold was starting to claim victims.

"How many?" gasped Jon, looking up at the captain.

Baltsaros's eyes were in deep shadow as he looked over the ice-covered deck, his mouth hidden behind the high collar of his greatcoat.

"At least four," muttered the captain. "And there are sure to be more." Baltsaros's gloved hands were fists at his sides, and Jon could tell that the older man was trying to master his temper. The captain had put his men's lives in peril; he had made them victims of circumstances he couldn't control. One glance at the spires showed Jon that the captain's prediction of a mid-morning pass through them had proved ambitious. Sometime in the night, the wind had died almost completely; limp sails and a constant push against the floating ice meant that they were moving at a snail's pace. Tucking his hands under his arms, Jon tried not to panic. It could be *days* before they made it through, if at all.

Maybe Katherine had been right. Maybe this expedition had been built on madness.

"I can't believe we're really going," laughed Jon, dipping his finger in the dark foam at the top of a second mug of Maya's stout beer.

Baltsaros, stripped to the waist and, leaning back in his chair in the shaded patio of the *Grog Blossom*, curled his lips into a wide grin.

Chuckling again at the youthful excitement that infused the captain's eyes, Jon shook his head.

"You're insane, you know that, right?" he smiled and lifted his mug to his lips.

"Jon, there's nothing holding me here. Abetha's going to run things fine. I have confidence in her," replied the captain, resting his own beer against his thigh as he peered out over the water. The turquoise lagoon was alive with activity as jolly boats made their way to *Baal's Heart*, loading her up with supplies for the coming journey. "I've been making the same rounds, year after bloody year... It's time for a change."

Eyebrows raised at the captain's use of profanity, Jon studied Baltsaros's profile. There was excitement for adventure there, yes. However, Jon knew that the older man was also impatient to set off to find Tom; a dangerous journey that required the first mate's extensive skills was the perfect excuse to track him down.

Frowning, Jon tapped on the tabletop thoughtfully. The tropical blooms that surrounded the tavern were fragrant, and the sea air was a warm, salty kiss on his skin. Though he too was anxious to start the search for Tom, a dangerous journey through icy waters was so far from Jon's current reality that it seemed vaguely ludicrous. He thought of the recurring dream he'd been having:

They were on the ship, and the giant black lion stood on the deck, eyeing them. From its fangs dripped blood, and Jon saw that the boat was littered with the dead. He turned away. Beyond the horizon rose the impossibly high jagged teeth of a monster. From there came the sounds of a heartbeat, and Jon recognized it instantly as his.

When Baltsaros turned to look at Jon, his eyes were serious.

"Are you ok?" asked the captain.

Jon looked down and saw that he was rubbing at the scar on his chest; a finger's width to the left, and the knife would have claimed his heart. He dropped his hand to the table.

"I... dream about the Devil's Isles. About them and Tom," he confessed. "All the time."

The captain's eyes narrowed, and he nodded.

"I know, Jon. You sometimes yell out in your sleep," murmured Baltsaros. He leaned forward in his seat and wrapped his long, sun-darkened fingers around Jon's wrist. "When you were gravely injured, you carried on about them." The captain's thumb stroked the thin knife scar along the inside of Jon's forearm, the one that symbolized the oath between them.

Baltsaros's sudden smile was wide, and his teeth looked sharp and white in his tanned face.

"Something is telling you to go there," said the captain, leaning back again and taking a long pull from his mug of beer. "Maybe I *am* a little superstitious after all."

It was nearing twilight when at last the ship was within half a league of the looming black spires. At this distance, the Devil's Isles took up the entire sky; they seemed infinite, their tops lost in the hazy winter clouds high above. Though the temperature had risen a few degrees, the crew was in bad shape, listlessly going about dumping heavy snow and ice overboard. Strangely, the icebergs had spaced out again, and the squealing screams had become less frequent.

Jon was sprawled out on the bed, wedged against the captain's side, when he heard the first shouts. He lifted his head, groggy after finally catching almost an hour's sleep in nearly thirty-six.

When there was no further sound, Jon lay back down on the feather mattress.

Nauseous with exhaustion, he jerked awake a few moments later when there was another shout; this time he recognized Tom's voice. He turned to the captain and saw that the older man was blinking slowly in confusion in the wan light.

"What now?" muttered the captain, groaning as he pushed himself up. Baltsaros placed a hand on Jon's shoulder when he tried to sit. The captain shook his head. "Sleep, Jon. I'll go see what's amiss."

Exhausted and only too happy to oblige, Jon closed his eyes, letting the warm darkness claim him once more.

Baltsaros stood outside the door to his quarters and stared curiously at the scene before him. A thin fog had risen up over the sides of the *Heart*, and it reflected the lantern light in a misty, white cloud around the whole ship. There was a strange quality to all the natural sounds of the ship; a drip of water from the prow sounded loud and close, as if falling down a deep well next to the captain. The creak of the boards beneath his feet sounded oddly muted. Voices seemed muffled and disembodied. Peering into the fog, Baltsaros tried to make out where Tom was.

As he walked slowly forward, the captain stepped to the side when two men grappling at each other nearly collided with him. With a deep frown, Baltsaros increased his pace, dismayed to see another fight taking place along the deck through the thickening mist. Finally, he heard Tom's voice raised in a shout, and the familiar, bulky silhouette of the first mate came into sight at the starboard gunwale. The big man had one hand extended as he leaned out over the frigid, ice-strewn water.

"Tom! What is going on?" yelled Baltsaros, reaching for Tom's belt to pull him back.

With a grunt, Tom stepped down, and the captain saw that the first mate's nostrils were flared and his lips were tight with anger. Or worry? Looking into Tom's wide sea-green eyes, Baltsaros was amazed to see fear there.

"What is going on?" he repeated, quieter this time. Tom started, as if breaking out of a trance and shook his head slowly. Turning to look back over the water, he simply pointed.

"Just... look," replied Tom.

The captain peered over the side of the ship and was confused by what he saw there. Three men were standing on ice floes next to the ship, and Calum was among them. Next to Baltsaros, Tom yelled out again.

"Calum, ye bloody fool, come back to the fuckin' tub, mate! There ain't nothin' out there for ye to go to!" Tom's deep voice boomed out over the cracked ice, and Calum turned to look at him.

"Aye, lad, Marg'ry is waitin' fer me! Can't ye see her? Can't ye see my beauty?" yelled Calum. Turning back to the ice and mists, he waved an arm over his head. "I'm-a comin', my love!"

"Who in the bloody hells is Margaery, Da?" asked Tom softly, his face slack with incomprehension as he looked at Baltsaros.

The captain frowned over the water, unease settling over him like a greasy second skin.

"Margaery was the name of Calum's wife," he replied, tightening his grip on the metal cleat as he leaned further over the gunwale. Out of the corner of his eye, he saw Tom peer over the side again.

"But, Da... She's been dead for nigh forty years... Ain't she?"

2

___

THE MIST

Tom blinked slowly, staring at the captain for a moment before he frowned over the gunwale again.

"He's seein' bloody ghosts?" he asked, incredulous. Nothing in his life had ever made him hold with the notion of ghosts; it was superstitious hogwash as far as he was concerned. However, Old Calum was seeing *something* out there on the ice and, whatever it was, it was going to end up killing him.

As Tom and the captain watched, one of the other men stepped further and fell into the frigid water when the ice floe beneath him tipped under his weight. Without so much as a shout, the sailor slipped into the black water and was dragged down by the weight of his furs. The sheets of floating ice drifted, and the space between them disappeared.

Tom let out a surprised grunt. Though he didn't really give a shit about the pirate's chilling death in the frozen sea—the man was a complete bloody picaroon—Tom was rather fond of Calum. He had to do something to get the old codger back on board before he shared the same fate.

An idea struck him.

"Holy hells, Calum! Ye old dog!" he yelled out over the ice. The older man turned his head at the sound of Tom's voice, but he didn't stop inching forward on the cold, slippery surface. The first mate could see that Calum was getting dangerously close to the edge, and he clenched his fists in frustration as he continued. "Ye never told me yer woman had such gorgeous tits! Lookee here! Margaery has some fine lookin' knockers!" Tom's gravelly baritone carried easily across the distance; he took a hopeful breath when he saw the old man stop and turn again to peer up at them.

The captain furrowed his brow and nodded, urging Tom to continue.

Helplessly, Tom shrugged. He was at a loss for what else to say. He had no idea what the woman had looked like; for all he knew, she'd been as flat as a board. Leaning further out, he bellowed at Calum, hoping the old man was loopy enough to fall for his bluff.

"Aye! Calum! Ye wouldn't mind me touchin' the missus, would ye? Eh, Calum? Just want to get my fingers wet... ooh boy! She's a fine lookin' slut, and she's moanin' for my cock, mate! Lookee here!"

From where he was standing, Tom saw instantly that his words had the desired effect. The old man's face twisted into a mask of fury, and he turned back towards the ship.

"He won't be able to get back aboard," muttered the captain. "The ice is too far from the side now... We're drifting. How did he get down there to begin with?"

Face bleak, Tom pointed to the Jacob's ladder that had been lowered over the side. In the distance, the second man fell through the ice, and the first mate shook his head in disbelief. Why had everyone suddenly gone mad?

Tom glanced around him and frowned at some men grappling on the deck. It looked like two of them were trying to pin down a third so they could bugger him, and the smaller man was bleating like a sheep. A complete madhouse.

Rope. I need rope, he thought.

With a low growl, Tom jumped down from the crate and levelled a kick at one of the men. Tom's boot caught the man in the jaw, and the big northman went down like a wet rag on the snow-strewn deck. After scrambling to his feet, the other took off at a run, ricocheting off the forward mast before disappearing into the thick mist. The man on the ground stared up at him, his eyes devoid of intelligence and, with another pathetic bleat, he crawled away on all fours. Tom watched him go, a sick feeling in the pit of his stomach, as he took up a length of rope. Chewing the corner of his mouth nervously, he shook his head again; this was beyond comprehension. He turned back to the gunwale and saw that the captain was staring at his palm, his stark brow low over his dark eyes.

The fear that kept trying to break through to Tom finally slid its cold fingers into his veins as he watched the captain blink and shake his head as though groggy from drink.

Not the bloody captain.

"Da! What the fuck is goin' on? Please don't fuckin' crawl out onto the ice. So help me gods, I'll tie ye to the bloody mast if I need to," he pleaded as he coiled the rope around in his hand, one end now a slipknot.

Baltsaros just rubbed his fingers together and pursed his lips, lost in thought.

Tom clenched his jaw and looked away, hoping that he could get Calum aboard before the captain fell prey to whatever stoked the madness around them.

Leaning over the side of the ship, Tom anchored his weight by wedging his calf between the gunwale and the ratlines that ran down from the rigging. Calum was nearly at the edge of the ice closest to the ship, and Tom grunted as he threw out the rope, trying to snag it around the old man. On the second try he was successful, and he braced himself against the side of the ship; the old man's boots dipped into the icy water as he fell and was dragged forward. Tom let out a growl and hauled on the rope hard, the muscles straining in his brawny arms as he began to quickly hoist Calum into the air.

"Da! Da, wake the fuck up and grab him, will ye?" he shouted, gripping the rope tightly in his gloved hands. The sound of his voice roused the captain, and Baltsaros leaned over to pull Calum up over the edge. When the old sailor landed with a thump on the frozen boards, his eyes were roaming sightlessly; it was as if all intelligence had fled in the face of insanity.

Tom pressed his lips together—the situation was beginning to overwhelm him. He glanced at the man that he had always relied on and was utterly stricken with how dazed the captain looked.

"Da... Da, please," he groaned, fear beginning to unravel him. Clutching the captain's arm, he tried to shake Baltsaros from his stupor. The older man stroked his hand along the gunwale and squinted at his palm again, ignoring Tom completely.

"It's a spore. Not a mist. A spore. There must be some mould on the rocks... The warmer weather thawing... releasing a spore. Causing visions... Though, I wonder whether the men indoors are as affected. Hm," murmured Baltsaros, talking to himself. "I must conduct experiments."

Tom's breath stuck in his throat as he listened to the man he loved start muttering to himself in his native tongue, completely oblivious to the first mate clinging to his arm. There was a shout from the stern, and Tom turned to peer through the haze. He couldn't see anything for a moment and then...

No.

Tom's heart began a swift staccato rhythm that stole the breath from his lungs. He narrowed his eyes, hands dropping from the captain's arm as he gaped at the spectre in the mists. The balding head, the sloped shoulders... the cruel eyes and crueller hands. The man would smell of lavender but, when Tom's face was forced against his crotch, all he ever smelled was stale piss.

Tom shook his head to clear it, and the ghost was gone from sight for a moment. He looked around and saw that the captain had disappeared. He let out a low moan of terror.

No... No, gods, please no, no, no...

The man of Tom's nightmares strode again from the mists, the long whip curled in his hand as he sneered at Tom.

His master.

The man who had broken him over and over again from the time he was just a boy of seven.

Tom shook his head, tripping backwards and landing with a harsh grunt on his ass. The split end of the whip slithered across the deck like a leather snake, hungry for Tom's skin, and he cried out.

"I *killed* ye, ye bloody bastard. I fuckin' killed ye... lords in hell, go back to yer grave!" Tom choked over the words in his panic to get away as he crawled backwards on his hands.

Something. Something the captain said. Spores. The air filled with the poison of dreams.

Tom's master licked his lips and bared his yellowish fangs before taking another step towards him. Closing his eyes, Tom forced himself to think. The man was dead; Tom had slit his throat as the cocksucker lay sleeping in his bed, hot blood spraying into Tom's face and puddling in the sheets as the man's body twitched and then finally stilled. There were no ghosts. It was something wrong with the air. The men were sucking in madness with every breath; he had to make himself believe it.

When Tom opened his eyes, the ghost stood before him, his whip at the ready and thirsty for his blood. Against all the instincts that screamed at him to flee, Tom reached out a shaking hand to touch the man... and his fingers passed through nothing. He let out a short laugh, his body trembling in relief.

"Nothin' but air and mists that cause visions," he muttered to himself. "Nothin' to piss meself over. C'mon, Tommy boy..."

Tom pushed himself to his feet and, fighting the urge to run, he forced himself to walk right through the man with the whip.

J on blinked sleepily up at the shadow that stood by the bed and smiled.

"Is everything ok?" he asked, holding up his hand. The captain's fingers closed around Jon's wrist, and he sighed when Baltsaros nodded. "Oh good. I was worried that yet another thing had gone wrong. Come back to bed?"

The older man stood still, his grasp tightening around Jon's arm as he murmured something; Jon felt a tingle of fear at the incomprehensible words.

"Baltsaros?"

Gasping as he was wrenched from the bed, Jon pushed against the captain, confused. Baltsaros's grip was like an iron shackle as he forced Jon face down on the long table. There were more foreign words, muttered as if spoken only to himself, before the captain addressed Jon with a chilling voice devoid of emotion.

"I must conduct an experiment. I will infect you with these spores; you must tell me exactly what you feel," said Baltsaros. "Then, I will look inside you."

Jon panted as he struggled, panic rising in him. He was still sluggish from sleep and unable to turn himself around, but when he felt the hemp rope loop around his arm, Jon started to buck against the captain in earnest.

However, the older man just reached down and almost leisurely pressed his thumb hard into the nerve cluster behind Jon's ear. With a low, pained gasp, Jon stopped moving and let himself be tied. There had to be some explanation for the captain's erratic behaviour.

"Please... Baltsaros... What are you doing? What's happening —" Jon grunted as his head hit the table.

"Quiet now. I need to concentrate," muttered the captain, releasing his hold on Jon's hair.

With growing horror, Jon watched as Baltsaros pulled out his surgical kit and held a sharp blade up to the light of the candle.

After he'd hefted Calum over his shoulder with a grunt, Tom walked towards the trap door leading belowdecks. As he leaned down to pull it open, he paused and frowned, remembering the way the captain's hand had come away from the railing covered in a pale powder.

Spores.

Tom had no bloody clue what the hells "spores" were, but when he looked down at his arms, he saw that he too was covered in a dusting of powder. He patted hard at his sweater, sending the dust flying, and did the same with the insensate Calum before he descended the narrow stairs.

Thankfully, because the shrieking of the icebergs had ceased, most of the crew had retreated to their bunks early to catch some much-needed shut-eye. They blinked groggily at Tom when he burst through the door carrying Old Calum. The first mate's eyes skimmed over the room, quickly counting the humped shapes in the long row of bunks. Nodding, he let out a satisfied grunt; there couldn't be more than eight souls left above, and it didn't seem like any of the men in their bunks were suffering from the effects of the mist. He dumped Calum onto his bed and turned to the rest of them, raising his hand to point at them.

"Yer to bloody well *stay put* if ye know what's good for ye. Any dog who touches that goddamn door, I'll measure for his chains, savvy?" he growled, jabbing his finger in the direction of the exit. Without another word, he turned and left the bunkroom. As an afterthought, he put his back against the stack of heavy crates outside the galley and pushed them in front of the bunkroom door.

Gritting his teeth, Tom pulled the neck of his sweater up over his nose and mouth and debated climbing the stairs to the upper deck once more. His decision was made for him when, a moment later, he heard a scream laced with pain and fear split the air.

Jon.

Baltsaros muttered distractedly to himself in his northern tongue. His big hand was wrapped around the back of Jon's neck, holding him down as he planned his cuts systematically. Coughing against the pressure in his throat, Jon's head throbbed and he licked his lips, grimacing at the grainy bitterness of the powder Baltsaros had smeared on his face. Fear squeezed his heart hard as the man above him took up the sharp blade, and he whimpered, no longer sure that it was the captain holding him down... He felt the hot breath of a devil against his skin and saw the barbed shadow of crooked horns cast upon the wall.

Jon filled his lungs to let out a terrified scream as Baltsaros's knife slid stinging along his flesh; the captain was going to tear him into pieces and eat his heart.

Tom growled and pulled Baltsaros away just as he was adjusting the knife in his hand to deepen the cut. After flinging the captain to the floor, the first mate let out a strangled sob and kicked him hard in the ribs, hoping the older man would stay down. In despair, he watched the captain sit up slowly; Baltsaros's dark eyes were wide and staring, his teeth bared in a fierce grimace. It was the face of utter madness.

"Please, Da, please stay down," begged Tom, pulling his glove off and balling his fist hard. His lungs burned from the harsh breaths that heaved past his clenched teeth.

Baltsaros let out a low chuckle and sprang at Tom, his hands reaching for the bigger man's neck. Tom let out another breathless whimper, and he smashed his fist hard into the captain's face, his knuckles registering the crack of cartilage against them. Tears coursed down Tom's cheeks as he pulled his hand back to punch

Baltsaros again and once more, blood pouring from the older man's face as he went limp on the thick, handwoven rug.

With an agonized cry, Tom fell to his knees next to the man who had tamed and freed him, who had claimed Tom as his own, and he pressed his forehead to Baltsaros's shoulder.

After a few shaky breaths, he heard Jon's keening moan as he lay tied to the table, and Tom shook himself, realizing that he had to work fast before the captain came to. He stood in a daze, fumbling for the rest of the hemp rope as Jon's terrified blue eyes watched him.

"It's ok, Jon... Hush, hush, pet, I'm comin'," he murmured as he bound the captain's wrists together. In misery, he made the loops tight, not sparing Baltsaros any gentleness in case the man woke up a maddened animal once more. Brow deeply furrowed, Tom's chest ached as he stroked the side of Baltsaros's face.

"Oh, Da... forgive me," he whispered. "Gods, let this be over."

When he staggered to his feet again, Tom quickly undid the ropes binding Jon to the long table. He saw that the cut was superficial, but before he had a chance to find something to staunch the trickle of blood, Jon backed away from him with a low moan. The dark-haired, naked young man stared openly at Tom, eyes round and scared and without a trace of recognition. When the first mate reached for him, Jon cringed from Tom's touch.

Tom let out a long sigh; the adrenaline that had kept him going was starting to ebb, leaving him exhausted and brittle. The ship was adrift, and part of the crew had gone mad; he could only hope that they were being carried away from danger. He felt there was nothing else he could do until the captain awoke and was clearheaded again. Tom was at a complete loss as he pulled Jon to his chest, wrapping his thick arms around him when he began to struggle.

"Hush, lovey. Hush, it'll be ok, Jon. Stop your fightin', it's just me. Old Tom's goin' to make things better..." he murmured into the other man's hair as Jon began to sag against him. "That's it, pet. Hush now."

He wondered what waking nightmares were burning in the clever young man's brain as he drew Jon onto the bed with him, holding him tight and burying his face against his sweat-damp neck.

Tom's rough, scarred hands stroked Jon's smooth skin until the trembling stopped, and he closed his eyes, humming a soft nursery song that he barely remembered from a life stolen from him so long ago.

3

PAST THE SHORES OF LUNACY

Baltsaros woke slowly, the left side of his face a throbbing web of pain, nose burning and so swollen he could barely breathe out of it. For a moment he couldn't tell where he was and why he couldn't move his arms. After he'd flexed his fingers a few times, he came to the conclusion that his hands were tied behind him, and the rough, crusty surface beneath his cheek was the rug in his quarters. Blinking slowly, Baltsaros took a few deep breaths, grimacing at the dull ache in his ribs, and tried to make sense of his situation.

Calum on the ice. Tom yelling. A strange scent in the air... The captain closed his eyes and saw again the pale yellow powder clinging to the fingers of his glove. He remembered his desire to check whether the spores had affected Jon, asleep behind closed doors.

A knife?

Suddenly an image of Jon, tied down on the table and bleeding, flooded his mind. His own hand held a knife. Baltsaros's eyes flew open.

Jon.

He let out a grunt as he tried to lift his head from the blood-soaked rug, his heart beating a swift rhythm as his mind tried to put the memory back together.

Where is Jon? It was a small, mewling, panicky thought. With dread he let his mind touch the possibility that he had ended Jon's life while under the hallucinogenic influence of the spores. A hoarse moan escaped his lips at the sudden sharp twist in his gut, far more agonizing than the pain he felt in his face.

From across the room he heard a rustle and felt the thump of something landing on the floor reverberate through his cheek. He thought he smelled tobacco; the captain closed his eyes with a sigh.

"Da! Shit… Tell me yer back to yerself." Tom's warm hand closed over the captain's shoulder.

Baltsaros frowned and nodded.

"Yes, Tom. I'm all right," he said, his voice strangely nasal. "Where's Jon? Please tell me I didn't kill him." He grunted in pain as the ropes binding his wrists were quickly cut; blood rushed back into his hands, and he rolled over onto his back, his face coming away from the rug with a sticky pull.

"He's fine, Da. Ye put a knife to him, but I stopped ye," said Tom, on his knees next to the captain. The first mate's hand closed gently on his wrist; moving up to squeeze at Baltsaros's palm, Tom's touch helped relieve the itching and tingling.

With the numb fingertips of his other hand pressed to his nose, Baltsaros winced.

"I think you broke my nose," Baltsaros said, gingerly prodding at the swollen bridge; he couldn't immediately tell if it needed to be rebroken to set straight or if he actually even cared.

With brows deeply furrowed, Tom pressed his lips together and nodded. His face was an almost comical mask of worry as his gorgeous eyes took in the damage his fists had wrought.

"I'm sorry, Da," the big man whispered, shamefaced, and Baltsaros let out a hoarse laugh, groaning again at the pain in his ribs. "I… might'a kicked ye in the side too," Tom added quietly, though this time the corner of his mouth quirked into a rueful grin.

Baltsaros squeezed Tom's hand and chuckled, curling his arm around the first mate's side.

"Help me up, you savage brute," he grinned, but when the muscular first mate hauled him quickly to his feet, the captain let out a sharp gasp. Baltsaros rested against Tom for a moment, dizzy from loss of blood and from being tied up for so long.

The ship... The spires. The only thing immediately important to him right now was making sure that Jon was all right; his questions could wait.

The captain pulled away from Tom and took the few steps to the bed, leaning across it with a frown. Jon slept, sprawled on his stomach with a crude bandage covering the left side of his back. Baltsaros saw immediately that there was no blood seeping through and let out a relieved sigh. The damage seemed minimal.

Jon's eyes were sunken, and his skin was pale, but he was breathing easily. As he stroked his fingers gently along the curve of the young man's face, Baltsaros glanced at Tom. When he saw the affection in his first mate's eyes as he looked down at Jon, Baltsaros had to accept a somewhat bitter truth: Tom would always protect Jon, no matter what, even from the captain himself. Gritting his teeth, Baltsaros pushed away the resentment and let that fact sink in. There was nowhere safer in the world for Jon than in the protection of his fierce tomcat, and he should be happy about that. After all, the first mate had just saved Jon from becoming a simple puzzle of flesh and bone at the captain's hands.

"I never thanked you for saving Jon's life the first time," he said, thinking of the storm that had nearly robbed him of so much.

Tom looked both pleased and embarrassed; dropping his blue-green eyes to his hands, the big man's shoulder came up in a tiny shrug.

"Just doin' what's right, Da," Tom muttered.

Baltsaros turned back to the dark-haired young man on the bed and smiled softly.

Just over a year ago, Baltsaros would have laughed to hear

Tom say he was doing something simply because it was right—even now, he had expected his first mate to claim it had simply been his job to protect the captain's interests.

"Jon is special," murmured Baltsaros, watching the younger man's back rise and fall in the easy rhythm of sleep.

Tom grunted in gruff agreement and walked to the little cast-iron stove. When Tom opened the grate and poked at the fire within, Baltsaros thought they had reached the limit of the stoic man's comfort with such talk. He blinked in surprise when he heard Tom's deep voice break the silence a moment later.

"He sees the good in me, Da, plain as day. That's somethin' worth fightin' for. Maybe even dyin' for." His words sounded strangely choked.

When the captain turned to his first mate with curiosity, he was amazed to see that Tom's brow was low over eyes that shone with moisture, his jaw clenched and shoulders hunched as he stared into the fire. The night had taken its toll on Tom, and Baltsaros suddenly realized that the first mate was barely keeping it together.

"Tom, come here," he murmured.

Tom's lips worked together as he swallowed; he sniffed hard and passed a brawny arm across his face before lurching to his feet. When Tom leaned into the captain's arms with a sigh, Baltsaros felt a shudder run through him.

"You did good, Tom. You did very good. It's all right," he said, smiling against the younger man's hair. "Tell me everything, from the beginning. We'll figure things out from there."

The demon wielded the sharp knife, intent on taking Jon's heart from him. Jon couldn't move, couldn't see the monster's eyes. He could only feel its hot breath on his neck. Fear made him cry out... and a huge, tawny cat with crackling green-blue eyes let out a deep growl, pouncing on the devil's back. Confused, Jon saw that the devil was

actually the black lion that often walked beside him in dreams. He screamed out at the cat as its claws made bright red streaks in the giant lion's fur. It didn't matter, he wanted to say. His heart was his own to give...

Jon tasted the residue of sleeping powder and rubbed his face against the soft, dark sheets of the bed. His back was a dull ache, and he thought he could smell the captain's healing salve. Groggy and confused, he lifted his head and saw that the room was empty. Something pulled at his back as he sat up slowly, and seeing the bandage when he glanced over his shoulder, Jon realized that he was wounded. Try as he might, he couldn't remember what had happened.

There was a thump from above, and he heard the first mate's booming laugh. For a moment, Jon had a strange memory of Tom's voice gentle in his ear, soothing away a terrible fear... and then it was gone, caught up in the eddies that swept away pieces of a dream laced with terror and darkness. Running his hand through his tangled hair, Jon realized that, for the first time in weeks, he couldn't see the fire burning in the pot-bellied stove across the room. Yet the room was warm.

He slid off the bed and walked to the closest porthole. In amazement, he saw that the sky was a bright blue and no ice could be seen in the water.

How long have I been asleep? he thought with alarm.

He looked around for a shirt to wear and put on the first one he found. Quickly pulling on his pants and boots, Jon then reached for his woollen cloak and threw it over his head before he opened the door. When the bracing, cold wind he was expecting did not immediately assail him, Jon's heart began to beat faster in excitement. While there was still a brisk chill in the air, it was far from the bone-numbing cold of the past few weeks. He could hear voices above on the quarterdeck as he stepped out the door, and when he looked up, he saw that the sails were bulging and straining with a strong wind.

Jon climbed the wooden steps, smiling as the captain and his first mate turned to look at him. Both men were holding metal cups in their hands, and Jon could smell coffee. Tom sat at the bench, one booted foot on the felloe of the ship's wheel, and Baltsaros stood to his side, long strands of his hair whipping loose around his head as he smiled at Jon. As Jon squinted into the crisp wind, tears were whisked from the corners of his eyes by strong gusts. The Devil's Isles, the colossal spires that had taken up nearly the entire sky the previous day, were now just pale grey fingers rising up in the fog-shrouded distance.

In a daze, Jon looked at the captain.

"Have I been asleep for days?" he asked.

"No, my love. Only one night's sleep… " Baltsaros laughed and shook his head.

Jon frowned; though largely hidden by the captain's beard, the mottled hues of new bruises showed along one side of his face. Under his eyes were dark, yellowish shadows, and his nose was red and swollen. The captain looked like he had been in a fight.

Before Jon could ask what had happened, the captain started describing the night's terror and mayhem that, in his exhaustion, Jon had missed entirely. He stood breathing quickly, aghast at the stories of spectres and shocked by the deaths that had taken the crew whilst in the throes of some potent reaction to a mould in the air. Thankfully, most of the sailors had been spared; owing to Tom's quick thinking, those out of the mist had remained unaffected, and Calum had recovered swiftly once he'd been locked in the bunkroom with the others.

Nine men had been lost that night; it was a hard blow to a crew already diminished in number by the brutal cold but not an insurmountable obstacle to their survival.

However, none of what Baltsaros told him answered the two questions at the forefront of his mind.

"Wait, how did we get this far with no one manning the helm?"

asked Jon, accepting Baltsaros's cup to take a sip of black coffee. "Why didn't we run aground?"

Tom's stubbled cheeks dimpled in a wide grin, his teeth slightly crooked but white in his handsome face.

"Malik," said the first mate, laughing. "The bloody fool thought he was in a navy battle. It's a bloody boon the squiffy bastard managed not to bilge us on the rocks! Sailed us straight past the devil's pointy cocks, and then the wind picked up... Blew us straight an' true all night. Malik's sleepin' off a night's holy terror, but I'm plannin' on pourin' my share o' rum down his bloody throat tonight." Tom's blue-green eyes twinkled in merriment, but Jon could see how deeply relieved the first mate was. He had to smile when he imagined the surly shipwright wresting the ship away from the imminent threat of a sea battle with phantoms.

Turning his eyes to the captain, Jon felt his heart thrum quickly for a moment in his chest, and he frowned. Though he didn't know why, his second question was suddenly hard to voice. When he moved his shoulder under his cloak, he felt the pull of the bandage and the ache of the wound again. Jon cleared his throat and made himself speak.

"Why am I wounded?" he asked quietly and felt an odd pain in his chest at the way the captain's eyes lost focus at his words.

"Ye fell on some ice, lad," replied Tom. "Sliced yourself up bad, but I fixed ye up smartly."

Jon tensed and looked at the first mate. On the big man's face was the same bland openness Jon had seen when Tom had lied to him about being in a drunken fight while playing dice—a fight that in no way explained the fact that Tom's belt had been undone, nor why there had been a long rip along the side seam of his pants. Jon's eyes flicked back to the captain's, and he pressed his lips together when he saw that Baltsaros was staring at Tom with a strange expression.

A lie to protect the captain.

A shiver took Jon and he swallowed, turning to look at the horizon.

Float above it, don't think...

When he looked back again, Baltsaros was gazing at him with solemn fondness.

It didn't matter, he thought reluctantly; if Tom was lying for the captain, then it must be important.

Forcing himself to smile, he gestured to his face.

"Don't tell me you fell on the ice too?" he asked the captain playfully.

With eyes narrowed at the setting sun, Baltsaros took a swallow of rum and passed the flask to the young man leaning against his side. It was amazing how much warmer it was on this side of the spires. Something about the mountain range must be altering the climate on this side, causing the weather to be milder. Nature was ingenious in its many forms.

He could see a few stars already sparkling where the sky was a deepening indigo, and he thought about how curious it was that, even though they had come so far, the same twinkling lights looked down on them. The firmament that held them in place must be further away than what was assumed, he mused to himself. Or maybe, like the sun and the moon, they were free agents, gliding through the sky in some intricate pattern.

"You're mumbling to yourself," said Jon, looking up at him with amused grey eyes, "which wouldn't be so bad except I can't understand a word of what you're saying."

Baltsaros laughed and nodded, accepting the flask again.

"I'm sorry, I think in my native tongue; it seems a natural progression that I'd think out loud in the same fashion."

He frowned as something occurred to him.

"Jon, do you want to learn to speak it?" he asked quietly, turning his eyes to the brazier that burned nearby. Maybe if Jon had been able to communicate with him while in his trance, the young man wouldn't have faced vivisection at the captain's hands. Baltsaros felt the corner of his mouth twitch as he shunted aside a scenario where Tom hadn't been there to use his fists.

"I'd like that, yes," said Jon, and he lifted his hand to twine his fingers in the captain's hair. The touch was confident and possessive and when Baltsaros turned to look at Jon, the breath caught in his throat at the fierce desire obvious in his eyes.

Smiling slowly, Baltsaros leaned forward to capture Jon's lips in a light kiss and let out a low growl of pleasure when the younger man moved his hand to the captain's neck to pull him closer.

Baltsaros nudged Jon's lips open, breathing him in as their tongues shared space, and he moved his hand beneath the blanket to place his palm against the firm warmth of Jon's cock through his pants.

Pulling his head back, he furrowed his brow at Jon.

"What did I do?" he asked, amused and charmed by how Jon's pupils became deep pools at Baltsaros's touch.

Jon's tongue touched his bottom lip before he answered. Moving against Baltsaros's hand, he sighed.

"Whatever it is that you and Tom are keeping from me... it has to do with how much I mean to you," he said, shifting so that Baltsaros's hand had space to slip between fabric and flesh. He let out an exhale that ended on a chuckle when the captain's chilled fingers closed over the head of his cock. "Fuck, that's cold. I can't wait for warmer weather," laughed Jon. Leaning back against the captain's arm, he let out a small groan as Baltsaros started to move his hand.

The captain watched Jon closely, intrigued that the boy knew there was more to the story yet seemed content not to pursue the matter. What Jon had spoken was the truth—the omission was fundamentally tied to how very much the young man meant to him. Baltsaros would have been thrown into torment if he had achieved the savagery of relieving Jon of his viscera, and he felt like an utter failure when he thought of the promise he had made.

Jon knew there was something monstrous about Baltsaros, but it was Tom who was intimately acquainted with the captain's particular predilection; the first mate had jumped in to protect him as always, and for that, Baltsaros was glad. As much as Jon wanted to know everything, there were things about the captain's compulsions that were best left concealed. The best course of action was not letting Jon know just how *easily* he would have killed him. Yes, Tom had been right to step in with his lies. There was no need to alienate Jon with the truth.

His thumb slipped smoothly over the head of Jon's cock, wet with the young man's arousal, and Baltsaros let out a slow breath. Turning his mind to the gorgeous brute asleep below them in their quarters, he realized that it had been a while since he'd been entirely alone with Jon. Shifting on the bench, he pulled on the laces holding the front of his leather pants together and dug his thumb beneath them to free the hard cock that had hugged the curve of his thigh. As he stroked himself with the same rhythm that he used on Jon, he smiled.

"I know it's cold, my love, but could I entreat you to remove these?" he said lightly and plucked at the fabric of Jon's long pants. He watched Jon turn to him with cheeks flushed by lust. "There's nothing in the world I want more right now than to have you splayed over my lap, full of my cock," he explained with a grin. When his words were met with a breathy moan, the captain leaned to help Jon remove the offending clothing.

4

AN EDUCATION

The roots of education are bitter, but the fruit is sweet.

— ARISTOTLE

Jon groaned as Tom pulled away, Jon's spit-wet cock bucking up once in protest before settling down on his flat belly. The first mate then moved forward to press soft lips to his chest again, kissing along slowly and pausing to tease his velvet-rough tongue over Jon's sensitive nipples.

Shaking his head, Jon clenched his jaw in frustration.

"I was almost right," he complained in a hoarse voice as his heart thundered against his ribs.

Tom stopped his kissing and raised his eyes, quirking an eyebrow up at the man behind Jon.

"No, Jon. Almost right does not cut it, I'm afraid. Start again. What is the word for 'ship'? Tom… continue," said Baltsaros, his voice rife with amusement.

They had been at this for nearly an hour. Jon groaned and put his head back, leaning against the side of the captain's neck as

Tom resumed teasing him with his tongue. Eyes closed, he took a deep breath and searched his exhausted brain for the right word.

Agreeing to this was a mistake.

"I can't do this. I just... argh!" growled Jon, pushing away the board and charcoal he was using to keep track of the vocabulary he was learning. "I don't understand how in the hells I'm supposed to learn another language like this. It's fucking frustrating, and I'm seriously getting sick and fucking tired of your condescending—"

"Jon," Baltsaros warned.

Rubbing his hand over his eyes, Jon let out a slow sigh. Counting to five in his head before he spoke, he forced his tense shoulders down.

"I'm sorry. It's just... all muddling around in my brain. I think this might have been a mistake. Maybe I'm just not cut out to learn another language," he said, wincing at how peevish he sounded. When he heard the first mate's chuckle from the doorway, he scowled. "Don't you start on me too... How many languages do *you* know?" He'd been amazed to learn that Baltsaros was fluent in five and conversant in a handful of others; Jon hadn't even known that many languages existed.

Tom walked up to the table where Jon sat and pressed his knuckles down on the wood. With the warming weather, the first mate had gone back to being barefoot. However, as there was still a deep chill in the air, Tom had taken to wearing a simple linen shirt when out of doors. It hung open at the neck as he leaned forward, and Jon could see the curling, dark-blond hair covering his muscular chest and the swirling lines of his tattoos meandering over the left side of his body.

"I can speak three and swear in six," grinned the first mate, pulling the splinter of wood out from between his teeth and winking.

"I'm not sure the mangled Common you speak passes for a language," laughed Baltsaros, his dark eyes crinkling at the corners.

Tom glowered at the captain in mock offence for a moment, but his pink lips curled up in a smile. He turned back to Jon and pulled the board closer, peering down at the scribbled words on its surface.

"Maybe what ye need is a little motivation, aye, lad?" grinned Tom, a sparkle of mischief in his ocean eyes.

Jon flicked through the jumble of words in his head. Five correct words in a row had Tom move down to tease and lick along the inside of his thighs; ten correct meant the first mate would start to work on Jon's cock with slow strokes of his hand and a soft tongue; fifteen words, and he would swallow down Jon's length... Twenty, and Jon would finally get relief. Any mistakes and Tom would stop what he was doing and go back to the beginning.

Shivering as Baltsaros's hands caressed his neck and chest, Jon let out another soft, needy sound; on top of Tom's gentle fondling, the captain's hard cock was buried deep inside Jon as he sat back with his thighs spread over the captain's lap. In near despair, he opened his eyes and watched Tom grin against the side of his shaft, his tongue leaving wet trails along the taut skin but never quite touching the head.

Seeing the hopelessness on Jon's face, the first mate chuckled and pulled his mouth away for a moment, the scratchy stubble of his cheek scraping at sensitive flesh; Jon gasped.

"It's like the word for 'build'," murmured the big man, his gorgeous sea-green eyes amused.

"Tom, stop cheating!" laughed Baltsaros, reaching forward to swat at the first mate's head.

The movement caused the captain's cock to move inside Jon,

and he let out a whimper. However, the first mate's prompting was enough to jog his memory, and he blurted out the correct word. When Tom's hot mouth closed over his cockhead, the groan that burst out of Jon's chest was equal parts relief and bliss. When his shaft began to slide deep down Tom's throat, Jon furrowed his brow and turned his head, burrowing his face against the captain's neck, his mouth open in a slow pant.

"Almost there, Jon," said the captain, a smile in his voice. "I must admit I was skeptical, but Tom was right about motivation. Now come on... just five more. You're doing so well. And Tom... let's have no more cheating, shall we?" Baltsaros's hands scratched soft lines over his chest, and Jon arched his back slightly with a moan.

The next three words were relatively simple, but the fourth gave him pause. Tom's tongue slid smoothly along the base of Jon's cockhead, a firm yet teasing touch, before he opened his mouth again to take in his whole length. It was frustrating how perceptive the first mate was when it came to bringing Jon close; every time Jon started to skirt the edge of climax, the big man quickly pulled away with a smile.

It occurred to Jon then, as he was desperately seeking the word for "cat" (*why in hells would I ever need to say "cat"?*), that this was probably a novel experience for the first mate, as he was normally on the receiving end of such torture. It was no wonder Tom kept chuckling every time he brought Jon to a panting mess.

Jon blurted out the word when it rose out of the tangle in his mind and let out a long sigh, bringing his hand forward to push his fingers through Tom's short, dirty-blond hair. One more. However, when Baltsaros murmured the next word, Jon's eyes opened in dismay.

"Heart?" he gasped, lifting his head. "You haven't even taught me that one yet!"

Tom frowned, his lips brushing the tip of Jon's cock softly as he looked at the captain.

"Aye, Da. That ain't fair to the lad, dont'cha think?" he said, his deep voice sending vibrations through Jon's cock.

Jon felt the captain move behind him, and Baltsaros's long fingers tapped against his breast, right over where his heart was skittering like a hunted rabbit.

"Close your eyes, Jon," murmured the captain, his mouth touching the rim of the younger man's ear. "You've heard the word from my lips before. Just think."

Jon felt dizzy. The fingers thrumming against his chest opened a strange pit in his belly. Panic. Struggle. A knife. Jon let out a sharp gasp and trembled as Tom's warm, wet mouth enveloped his cock once more. A devil with a knife to carve out his heart. A sharp pain... darkness... then Jon sighed in relief as the strange thoughts were eclipsed by the answer.

"*Haeken*," he said, opening his eyes with a smile. "*Min haeken* is what you call me when you're feeling particularly sentimental. It means 'my heart', doesn't it?"

When Baltsaros let out a low chuckle, Jon grinned wide and let his head fall back again on the captain's wide shoulder. Shutting his eyes, he expected the first mate simply to finish the job he started. However, Baltsaros's arm quickly came around Jon's waist, and he was hauled up and pushed forwards onto hands and knees and entered again so that he could be fucked slowly from behind. Groaning softly, Jon fell thankfully into the shallow rhythm that the captain liked to use on him to make him cum from within.

Tom sat back a moment just watching the two with an amused look on his face as his rough hand squeezed and pulled at his own cock. Then, with an impish grin, the muscular first mate pushed under Jon headfirst to continue using his mouth while Baltsaros's thick cock thrust into the dark-haired young man.

Jon let out a deep moan; it was a feverish, exquisite feeling, and he let himself ride on the wave of it, panting and moving his hips wantonly as both men worked at him. When he lowered himself to his elbows to rest against Tom's hard stomach, he felt the first mate's cock touch his lips. With a pulse of desire, he quickly opened his mouth and sucked softly at the head of it, working along the flared edge of the glans and dipping the tip of his tongue into the salty slit while Tom's hand stroked the shaft, his hard fist bumping up against Jon's wet lips.

Beneath him, Tom let out a low moan and shifted his head back so that Jon's cock slid more easily between his lips. A moment later, the first mate's big hands came up to hold Jon's waist as the three of them moved slowly together.

J on was the first to cry out; having been brought to the edge so many times already, he was nearly feverish with his mounting pleasure when Baltsaros quickened his pace. He pulled his mouth away from Tom with a sob as he came hard. The pleasure crashed through him, making his body pulse in a hot, sweet wave that wrung mindless gasps and moans from him. Pressing his forehead against the man beneath him as he rocked his pelvis, Jon whimpered as the first mate's lips and tongue milked his cock, and Baltsaros's thrusts stroked the throbbing, sensitive spot inside him.

Eyes closed, he panted against Tom's hip for a few seconds, his lips spreading into a wide grin as he tried to catch his breath. When he was able to lift his head, Jon took Tom into his mouth again, and the first mate released him with a gasp. Tom's fingers tightened around his waist as Jon forced his jaw wide around the first mate's cock, taking in as much as he could before working at a fast rhythm.

It seemed like only a few moments before Tom went rigid beneath him, a strangled cry heralding the yolky, bitter cum that pulsed hot over Jon's tongue. Jon groaned around the cock in his mouth, swallowing down quickly as Baltsaros began to pound into him, his sharp growl loud over Tom's panting as the captain shuddered with climax.

. . .

With his head comfortably against Tom's shoulder, Jon slid one finger across the broad, sculpted chest and flicked his nail against the silver ring in Tom's nipple. Tom let out a soft grunt and moved his fingers sleepily in Jon's hair. The lines that circled around Tom's nipple and fanned out down his left side were decorated with a multitude of dots, but it was to one particular cluster near the base of his ribcage that Jon's fingers were drawn to. He lifted his head slowly. The man who had tattooed the first mate had claimed that they were a representation of the Devil's Isles, and there they were: seven dots, spaced evenly except for the gap through which *Baal's Heart* had passed. Jon frowned.

"Funny. These curling lines mean something now, don't they?" he said softly. Tom made no answer except to twitch slightly in his sleep at Jon's touch.

Baltsaros leaned over and placed his own fingers on the first mate's tattooed side. Lips pressed together, he nodded slowly.

"We could interpret them to mean the mists, yes," he conceded, shifting his dark-brown eyes to Jon.

Jon touched a little swirl that vaguely resembled a figure. He was convinced that was exactly what the lines represented. He slid his fingers further up, along the path that the ship was taking. There, right below Tom's pectoral was something that looked vaguely like a flower made of triangles. It was surrounded by a square and bordered on one side by squiggles that reminded him of a jagged shoreline. He tapped gently on this design.

"I wonder what we're going to find here," he whispered, putting his head back down and staring across at the captain.

Baltsaros's sharp teeth shone white in his wide grin as he stretched himself out next to Tom.

"Adventure? Profit?" he said, lowering his head to the pillow and moving his shoulder in a shrug. "A new language for you to learn?" The last was said with a soft chuckle, and Jon wrinkled his nose at the captain.

"You're funny," he muttered. "You do realize now every time I think of the word 'cat', an image of Tom's mouth around my cock is going to come to mind."

Baltsaros smiled wider and pulled Jon's fingers to his lips to kiss the tips softly before closing his eyes.

When Baltsaros began breathing the slow rhythm of slumber, Jon lifted his head and stared at the collection of dots and swirls again. Right next to the jagged flower pattern, there was something that made Jon's skin prickle in foreboding.

Though he couldn't be sure, and it might have been a trick of the light, the hatched lines brought only one thing to mind: bones.

J on turned the little handle on the pulley wheel, hauling in the thin line that held a struggling fish on the other end. Grunting as he pulled up on the flexible pole, Jon strained with one foot against the gunwale to pull in his catch.

"Tha's it! Now ye don' give 'im too much slack, lest ye let the bugger free now!" yelled Old Calum while he watched Jon fight to bring the fish closer to the ship. The old man's eyes were narrow against the midday brightness, and he chuckled to himself as Jon cursed and strained against the side of the ship. A few moments later, the silver fish popped out of the water, its smooth muscular sides flashing in the sun with its frenzy as Jon reeled it higher and higher. Calum slid off the crate and held a hand up as Jon brought the wriggling fish over the deck, deftly grabbing it beneath its jaw and through its gill with a practiced motion. Jon sagged against the gunwale, panting hard as he watched the old man pull the hook from the fish's mouth and stun it motionless against the side of the crate. With a grunt wrought of old age, Calum lowered himself to his knees to quickly gut the fish before throwing it into the bucket with the others.

Jon wiped his arm across his brow and smiled. He was happy to have found something that made him so useful to the crew; for once he was happy to have grown up in a poor fishing town where even the son of a lawman knew how to jig for cod. With a glance at the bucket, he nodded to himself and pulled in more of the line before wrapping it around the pole and securing it against the side of the ship.

"I think that's enough, don't you?" he asked Calum with a wide grin.

The old man's face crinkled into a smile of his own, his pink tongue visible through the gap of his missing tooth.

"Aye, lad. These'll be proper eats for th' crew. Now help an ol' man on 'is feet like a good boy?" Calum said, lifting a hand up to Jon.

The younger man tried not to let his smile slip as he helped his fighting teacher up. Old Calum could still pin Jon in a few seconds, but being in the cold for so long had not done any good to his aged knees. Seeing the look on Jon's face, Calum chuffed out a laugh.

"Don' ye be lookin' at me like that, yun' Jon," growled the old fighter. "I'm far from bein' dead an' buried yet." However, Calum's face went sober for a moment, and Jon wondered if he was thinking about his venture out onto the treacherous ice.

"Jon!" He turned his head aft at the booming call and saw that Tom was leaning over the quarterdeck railing, motioning at him with a hand. The old man had taken up the bucket full of fish to bring to Cook, so Jon waved and jogged towards the stern, climbing up the black and red steps to join the first mate. Tom's brow was furrowed over his ocean eyes as he ran his thumb along the edge of his jaw, lips moving as he chewed at the bottom one. When Jon came to his side, Tom handed him the binoculars and cocked his chin slightly portside.

"Tell me," he murmured. "What do ye make of this, love?"

Jon put the binoculars to his eyes and trained them to where Tom had pointed. For a few moments he saw nothing. However as he made a second pass, Jon saw a distant, dark shape floating in the water. He pulled the double-spyglass away from his face and rubbed at his eyes before lifting them again.

"It… looks like a ship?" he said and frowned. "With two hulls and only one mast. I'm… not sure." Jon passed the binoculars back to Tom, and the first mate looked through them again, letting out a short grunt.

"Ye think it's a boat? I ain't never seen a boat like it, but I guess we're in new waters, aye, ducky? What d'ye think? Do we try to make like we're long lost friends or do we take the first plunder in this gods-forsaken sea?" chuckled Tom, putting the binoculars down and plucking the cheroot out from behind his ear. After pushing it into the corner of his mouth and cupping his hand to shield the match against the wind, Tom looked up at Jon curiously and puffed on the cigar to get it lit.

Jon shook his head. The one thing that had never sat easily with him was the utter ruthlessness Tom had in regard to plunder and pillage; as far as the first mate was concerned, anyone who was stupid enough to stray into their path was fair game. However, when Jon stared back at Tom, he thought he was witnessing a small crack in that cold-blooded facade as the first mate honestly seemed to be asking his opinion. He allowed himself a small smile and shrugged his shoulders.

"You know me," Jon said, taking up the binoculars again. "I'm less of a kill-first, ask-later kind of guy than you are."

Tom chuckled and slung an arm around Jon's waist, pulling the narrow cigar away from his lips to breathe out a plume of acrid, blue-grey smoke as his hand stroked up along Jon's ribs.

"Aye, lad," Tom agreed, leaning companionably against him as Jon swept the binoculars over the distant ship again with a worried look on his face. "That ye are… and that ain't a bad thing."

5

SACRIFICES AND SCARS

The ancients recommended us to sacrifice to the
Graces, but Milton sacrificed to the Devil.

—VOLTAIRE

Though the strange ship was swift, the pirates had an overwhelming advantage in firepower. When *Baal's Heart* had succeeded in getting within range of the fleeing vessel, Captain Baltsaros had ordered his gunners to send a shot across the other ship's bow.

Jon had been hugely relieved when the men aboard had had the good sense to surrender.

With the other vessel tethered to *Baal's Heart*, the three strangers now stood on the pirate ship's deck staring around in outrage as their boat was ransacked.

Standing next to the captain, Jon forced himself not to cringe when the hot glare of the biggest of the three raked over him. He met the stranger's eyes with what he hoped was a stony expression.

Owing to the resemblance between them, he assumed they

were kin; the three men were tall and bronze-skinned with crinkly, wiry, white hair that was worn in long, matted locks down their backs and almond eyes that were bright blue like the waters of Madierus. They were, like the crew of *Baal's Heart*, bare chested in the warm midday sun, and Jon stared curiously at the rings of raised scars that circled the necks of the two older men and continued down their backs in parallel lines. That the youngest of the three had none made Jon think that it was probably part of some coming-of-age ritual.

His eyes flicked up to the captain, and he gritted his teeth when he saw the admiration on Baltsaros's chiselled face as he looked at the willowy youth. The strangers had an exotic beauty but none more so than the fierce boy who glared a challenge back at the captain. Jon turned his head and met Tom's eyes. The big man was chewing the side of his thumb with a thoughtful expression on his face as he stared back at Jon. When Tom raised his eyebrows and crossed his arms across his broad chest, Jon could see the muscles work in the first mate's jaw as his lips twitched down with painfully obvious dismay; Tom was equally unimpressed with the captain's interest in the young man.

"They're just fuckin' fishermen, Cap'n!" shouted one of the pirates from where he clung to the shrouds of the foreign vessel. "There's nothin' 'ere of any worth. Do we scuttle 'er?"

Before Baltsaros had a chance to answer, Nathaniel, who had asked if he could help with the search aboard, piped up.

"I beg to differ," he yelled with a laugh. There was a tube under one arm as he held aloft something that sparkled. After someone leaned over to help him climb the rope ladder, Nathaniel crossed over to where the captain stood and handed him what looked like a water-filled glass globe mounted in a bronze base. In the water floated a wide silver cylinder with etchings on it. "If I'm right, this is some kind of compass, Captain. I'd like a chance to study it to see what the symbols mean."

Baltsaros tilted the base, and the cylinder rotated to stay level in the water. Lips curled into a smile, he nodded.

"What is this?" the captain asked, accepting the leather tube from Nathaniel.

The cartographer narrowed his hazel eyes and tilted his head, his forefinger tapping below his lips.

"They're maps, but I can't figure out what of," he said with a shrug. "Maybe stars? Shall I leave them in your quarters, Captain?"

Baltsaros handed the maps back to Nathaniel, shaking his head.

"No. Take some time with them. There's no rush. Come to me when you find something," he said and walked to the side of the ship where the strange boat was tethered.

"If there's nothing, leave it," he said to the men waiting aboard. "We'll stay here overnight. I'll decide what to do with the boat come morning."

A towheaded, gangly youth with a scar nodded once and called to his shipmates to abandon the fishing boat.

When Baltsaros turned back to the captives, his eyes narrowed. So far the men had not spoken to each other in anything other than a strange, guttural language, and Jon knew it would make interrogating them difficult. Coming to stand next to Jon again, the captain crossed his arms and looked at him appraisingly.

"If I were to keep one of them in the cage in my quarters, which one do you think I would have the most success with? I want to learn something useful from them," he said, his voice low. It still remained to be seen if the captives understood them.

Jon wanted to point out that hauling the men from their boat was probably not the best foundation for trust but instead turned his eyes back to the strangers.

Of the three, the oldest man honestly seemed like the best choice to him. While the other two glared at the pirates in defiance, the third's eyes kept straying to parts of the ship, distinct appreciation on his deeply lined face. There were two rows of raised scars around his neck, and Jon thought it could mean that he was someone of higher standing. Although, he admitted to himself, the extra markings could as easily be a simple indication of advanced age.

"The grandfather. I think you have a similarity of tastes that could be useful in gaining his trust," he murmured. *And you're far less likely to try to fuck him,* he added silently. His eyes slid to Tom for a second and saw that the first mate's lips were pressed together in a tight line.

Baltsaros frowned slightly, his head tilting.

"Not the young one? Wouldn't he be easier to break?" the captain asked, his eyes locked on Jon's. The younger man could feel suspicion colouring the captain's tone, and Jon shook his head.

"Too headstrong. Too proud. I feel like the old man has seen his share of heartache and loss… and I'm betting that the young one is his grandson. If you can't reason with him based on logic, you could always use the threat of harm to his grandson." Jon felt a little ill as he spoke.

He sincerely hoped that the old man was reasonable.

S miling graciously at the old man in the cage, Baltsaros pulled up a chair. He then reached for the beaten metal cup and filled it with cold water, taking a sip of it in front of the old man before holding it out to him. The white-haired fisherman waited a moment, his eyes wary, but he reached out for the cup.

The captain sat down in the chair and watched curiously as the man quickly drank down the water and held out the cup for more. The stranger was well muscled and smooth skinned despite his age, and his eyes were lively with intelligence. The raised scars that circled the older man's neck were long healed, and the captain guessed that they were part of some ritual to mark lifetime milestones. He was interested to know how they had been created.

The most interesting thing was that, though he was wearing nothing but a pair of sun-bleached, loose white pants rolled at the knees, the old fisherman had a gold bracelet with intricate, knotted designs halfway up his forearm.

Baltsaros pointed to it, and the old man's eyes narrowed in suspicion.

"It's beautiful," said the captain, his words genuine. He wondered how a fisherman had come to have something so valuable. Frowning, he realized that perhaps on this side of the mountains, gold was not considered treasure. That would certainly make trade interesting… especially on their return trip.

When the captain made no move to confiscate the bracelet, the old man let out a short grunt and nodded his head.

"Do you understand my speech?" Baltsaros asked the man, surprised, and watched the clear blue eyes that regarded him thoughtfully. After a long pause, the old man pressed his lips together and then let out a slow sigh.

"Yes," admitted the man in the cage. "Some." After another pause, the corners of his mouth quirked up. "Most."

Relieved, the captain reached forward to fill the man's cup again.

"Welcome to my ship," he smiled, sitting back. "My name is Baltsaros."

Jon realized that he had tied the knot wrong a third time and huffed out an exasperated breath. As he pulled the rope to wiggle loose the other end, he furrowed his brow. He was distracted and tense. The captain had spent all afternoon locked away in his quarters with the stranger, and the only instructions he had given anyone were that he was to be left alone and that the other men be locked in the brig but treated kindly.

Jon had obediently seen to the men's supper, which they had refused, unsurprisingly, and had left the plates within reach if they changed their minds. Now he was wandering around aimlessly in the dark, making a mess of rigging that hadn't needed retying to begin with, trying to keep his mind off the fact that he would be bunking down with Tom tonight.

At least Baltsaros's not bedding the boy, he thought angrily to himself, trying once again to loop the rope around in the right configuration. His supper of fish and root vegetables sat heavy in his stomach as he finally managed to tie a proper midshipman's hitch. Letting his eyes stray to the quarterdeck, he could see the cherry from Tom's cheroot where the first mate was sitting behind the ship's wheel. Jon thought for a moment about joining him but felt like he would be intruding; the first mate was probably enjoying his solitude. Besides, he would be seeing a lot of Tom shortly. Jon licked his lips and swallowed, turning away.

As he walked towards the bow, Jon decided to make another circuit of the ship before finding a place to wait for Tom to invite him into the closet that served as his personal quarters.

He let out a slow breath through his nose and tried to ignore the tightness in his chest. Jon had spent time alone with Tom before—many times, in fact, since the reconciliation between the captain and his first mate. Just... never overnight. But that wasn't what was fuelling his anxiety.

Yes, it is.

Frowning, Jon nudged a coil of rope out of the way with the toe of his boot as he made his way along the side of the ship. He knew he shouldn't feel so annoyed about the fact that he had been barred from the captain's bed for the night—what Baltsaros was doing was important for the success of their expedition—but it was the first time it had happened, and it stung a little. Laughing a little bitterly under his breath, he thought about how he and Tom were like orphans tonight.

He stopped and looked out over the water, the sky black and sparkling with stars above him. As he rubbed a hand over his face, he grudgingly let himself admit that he was nervous about spending the whole night alone with Tom. It was stupid. After all, most nights he fell asleep against the big man's warm chest or... at least on nights when Tom wasn't in the hammock nearby.

Jon sighed and climbed a crate, loosening his belt so that he could relieve himself over the gunwale. The hammock... As Tom had stood that day with the awl, making holes for the thick metal hooks that would hold the colourful hammock in place, he had explained that he sometimes felt crowded in the bed with Baltsaros and Jon and just liked the option of sleeping alone. Jon had seen the lie immediately for what it was: diplomacy. He had a feeling that, given the chance, Tom would hold him close every night. Instead, the first mate chose to distance himself so as not to interfere with the captain's affection for Jon. A sacrifice.

He didn't want to think about why that made him ache, or why, when the three of them were together, he often went out of his way not to do anything with Tom that could be construed as tenderness or deeper devotion; he never kissed the first mate in the captain's presence. In fact, it was rare that they kissed at all...

Holding the taut rope above his head, Jon could faintly hear his stream hitting the dark water below. As he was mulling over his complicated feelings for the first mate, he heard a soft step behind him. Startled, he turned his head; Jon had chosen a spot between the hanging lanterns for privacy and so initially saw nothing in the dark. After tucking himself back into his pants, he jumped down from the crate and frowned.

"Who's there?" he asked, squinting into the gloom. When he heard a chuckle, Jon clenched his jaw; stepping out from behind the stacked crates, followed by two of his cronies, was Anslaw. The gangly, blond youth grinned wide at Jon, the knife scar on his cheek stretching grotesquely.

"Oh, it's just me, cabin boy," drawled the young man. "Takin' a stroll with me mates." The mates in question were two others that had come aboard with Anslaw during their stopover at the *Jewel*. It was these three that were responsible for the majority of the teasing and cutting remarks about Jon being nothing but a bedwarmer for the captain and first mate.

"My name is Jon, and I would thank you to remember that," said Jon through clenched teeth. He was in no mood for their nonsense tonight and made to pass them to head back towards the stern. However, Anslaw's hand shot out and blocked Jon's way before he had a chance.

"Aww, *cabin boy*. Are ye sad because yer daddy's too busy to 'ave 'is tallywhacker sucked?" sniggered the gawky deckhand, the other two laughing along with him.

Jon's heart sank. The boys reeked of something that reminded him of *char*, probably some drug they had brought aboard with them when they joined the crew.

"What's goin' on here, lads?" said Tom's gravelly voice from the darkness beyond. The first mate walked towards the group with a dangerous expression on his face.

While Jon was relieved to see him, he couldn't help but feel his reputation would not be improved by the first mate coming to his aid.

"I've got this, Tom," he muttered, balling his fists.

"Aye, we was just talkin', mate," said Anslaw, his dark eyes round as he looked at Tom. "And Jon 'ere threatened to tell ye and the cap'n we was thieves unless we let 'im suck our cocks."

The lie was spoken with such little credibility that no one in their right mind would have believed it; adding to the ridiculousness of the claim was the fact that one of the boys had collapsed in tears of laughter at Anslaw's accusation.

The corded muscles of Tom's neck stood out as he tensed, his blue-green eyes staring hard at the grinning deckhand. The first mate took a step forward, but Jon put a restraining hand against his chest before Tom could show Anslaw just how badly he had misjudged the effect his slander would have on the brawny pirate.

"I said I've got this," Jon repeated, and without a pause, he simply pivoted on the ball of his foot to let the momentum carry all of his weight behind the fist that connected with the smirking deckhand's jaw. The force of it was enough to snap Anslaw's head back; the tall, blond deckhand tried to catch his balance but fell to the deck, his head smacking down on the smooth wood with a loud thump.

Behind him, Tom let out a surprised chuckle.

Fist smarting and teeth bared in a fierce grimace, Jon stood above Anslaw, just daring the younger man to stand up. There must have been something in Jon's eyes that gave the bullying deckhand pause; Anslaw just sat up slowly and wiped his wrist over the blood leaking from the corner of his mouth, making no move to retaliate. Jon stared at him a moment longer before he turned on his heel.

"C'mon," he muttered to Tom as he walked away. With another laugh, the first mate followed Jon as he made his way to the trapdoor that led to the decks below.

altsaros chuckled and nodded, raising his cup of wine to Polas again. The old man grinned wide and lifted his own cup.

"Your health," said the man in his native language, and Baltsaros repeated after him.

The root of the language Polas and his kin spoke was not so far from Baltsaros's northern tongue. The main difference lay in the way the words were pronounced; otherwise, the sentence structure, use of neutral nouns, and lack of indefinite articles were the same. However, the captain's quick mind simply worked to file away the subtle variations as he was not yet ready to string together a sentence on his own, and the wine was doing nothing to help matters. He smiled. After spending so much time in the company of two who were over a decade his junior, it was a nice contrast to interact with someone older than he.

"Should we not let your son and grandson out of the brig?" asked Baltsaros, lifting his brows.

Polas shook his head then took a long swallow of wine before answering.

"They have, ah... hot heads. Jail makes them cool for now, yes?" said the old man, setting his cup down on the table. "Good for now," he repeated with a smile.

Baltsaros inclined his head. It was true—the men in the brig were no worse off than his own crew; the brig was comfortable enough accommodations, and Jon would make sure that the two were fed and warm. He grinned back at the man across the table from him, pleased that he had found a source of information in this new world. His lively yet stilted conversation with Polas was working to keep his mind off the fact that Tom and Jon were cloistered away together for the night, far from his watchful eyes. Swallowing his concern along with another mouthful of wine, Baltsaros began to question the old fisherman about the lands to the west.

Jon flexed his fist, the knuckles red and swollen from where they had met with Anslaw's lantern jaw.

"Did ye see the look on his face when ye clocked him?" chuckled Tom, holding out a rag with a chunk of ice wrapped in it. "I don't know who was more surprised... him or me."

Jon accepted the ice pack and winced as he placed it on his hand; he now understood why Tom's knuckles were so scarred. Watching Tom pull the linen shirt up over his head and wad it into a ball to throw in the corner, Jon began to feel the anxiety begin to creep back under his skin. When Tom unknotted his belt and began to pull his pants down, Jon turned his back.

"Jon?" asked Tom. "What's wrong, love?"

Shaking his head, Jon had no idea how to answer. His heart was hammering in his chest and his mouth had gone dry. The room was too small... it was too intimate.

"Don't tell me yer scared of my cock all of a sudden, ducky…" When his words failed to garner a response from Jon, Tom reached out and touched his shoulder.

Jon barely kept himself from flinching and let out a shuddery breath.

"Aye… oh Jon, hush, lad," muttered Tom, forcefully turning the smaller man around. When Jon saw that the bigger man had kept his pants on after all, he let out a shaky laugh.

"What in hells is the matter, love?" murmured Tom, his gorgeous eyes wide with worry.

Jon stared back at him, trying to find his voice. He watched with dismay as Tom eyes went flinty to cover the hurt that had flashed quickly across his handsome face.

"Ye don't have to sleep here if ye really don't want to," said Tom and dropped his hands. "I just thought—"

"I feel like this is… dangerous." Jon's whisper was hoarse.

Tom's brow creased and his head shook slowly.

"Ye've fucked and abused me every which way yer fine, perverse brain could cook up… and ye think *this* is dangerous, love? And, 'sides, he's the one who put us out in the cold, Jon," he muttered, reaching for Jon again. He plucked the ice pack from his fingers and dropped it. After he'd pulled him towards the low sleeping pad on the floor, Tom slid his hands beneath Jon's shirt and drew it up.

With eyes closed, Jon let himself be undressed, first his shirt and then his boots and pants. Standing naked in the tiny, lantern-lit room, Jon shivered slightly.

He sensed Tom's nearness a second before the first mate stepped forward to take him in his powerful arms, his furry chest warm and soft against Jon's skin, and his smell comforting and arousing at once. The achingly tiny shift of the big man's naked pelvis against his brought a breathless thrill that ran through Jon's skin like crackling fire and made him whimper at the sheer sensuality of being held this way by Tom.

The first mate let out a laugh, the sound just a low rumble.

"Aye, love," he said softly. "Dangerous. Ye had the right word after all."

Jon opened his eyes and looked at Tom in torment.

"There are... words I want to say to you," he breathed.

Tom's brow creased deep, and he let out a soft groan as if he were in pain; Jon could feel the rapid thrum of the big heart that beat beneath the brawn and scars of Tom's broad chest.

"Don't, Jon," said Tom quickly, his voice sounding ragged and weak. "Hush."

He reached for the lantern and turned the cover so that the light from the flame was blocked. After pulling Jon down on the bed, Tom fumbled for him in the dark with gentle hands that shook.

Jon let out a low moan as Tom covered his face with impossibly soft kisses before finally meeting his lips with breathless passion.

T he kiss was endless, staggering. It was as if a dam had broken between the men as they strained against each other on the hard mattress. They were raw with desire and truths unsaid, both wanting to draw the moment out as long as they could, knowing that it might be a very long time before they had a chance to shed their skins and press their scarred hearts together again.

6

DANGER AHEAD

Tom lay on his back and watched as the subtle grey of dawn filtered into his room from the porthole above his bed, his fingers stroking through Jon's long dark-brown curls. The serious young man from the midland isles sighed in his sleep and started snoring lightly, his head tucked beneath Tom's chin, body sprawled on top of the first mate's.

Tom smiled. Jon felt small in his arms, and he liked that. He liked a lot of things about Jon. Closing his eyes, Tom could feel a delicious ache in his cock, and for once it wasn't from some clever abuse.

No… he had fucked Jon.

Tom frowned. "Fucking" was far too crass a word for what had happened between them: Jon coaxing Tom on top of him, his thighs slick with sweat around the first mate's muscled waist, mouths locked together as Tom moved slowly within Jon… so very, achingly slow until Tom couldn't hold back, the two cresting the wave of climax as one, their muffled cries intertwined as they clutched at each other in the dark. His heart had beat so fucking hard…

Tom breathed slowly, trying to keep his erection down so not to wake the man sleeping on top of him. Grinning suddenly, he wondered if Jon realized he had never been on the giving end of sport with a man before. Plenty of women, sure, but he'd never been invited, or allowed, to put his cock in another man.

Despite the lack of sleep, Tom felt good. He pulled the coverlet up over Jon's shoulder and tilted his head to lean his cheek against the soft, dark hair that slid like silk through his rough fingers.

Mine, he thought and mulled over that idea for only a few seconds before another word replaced it.

No. *His.*

Sick to death of the fears and fools' desires that were rattling around in his head, Tom closed his eyes and sighed. The beast inside the captain would eventually try for Jon again, and Tom would have to protect him from it. However, letting himself even think about a permanent solution was just… impossible.

Dangerous.

As if summoned by Tom's covetous thoughts, the door swung open, and Baltsaros stepped in. Tom tensed and, flooded by hot guilt, he almost pushed Jon away. He watched the captain's eyes sweep over the tiny room, Baltsaros's jaw clenched tight at the sight of them entwined.

"Get up, Tom," growled the captain as he turned to leave. "I need you. We have a situation."

Tom let out his breath at the sound of Baltsaros's boots receding in the distance, and he carefully eased himself out from under Jon, pausing to ruffle the lad's hair and pull the blanket up high to cover him. He'd see to it that Jon would be left to sleep… and tan the hide of any who disturbed him.

Scratching his chest, he looked around for his clothes. Brain fuzzy from a night of little rest, Tom pulled the wrinkled linen shirt over his head and left the room while still tying up his belt. With a last look behind him, he closed the door and hurried down the corridor to the stairs.

Above deck, Tom heard the commotion before he saw it. Jogging towards stern, he realized that the shouting was coming from the captain's quarters. The door was ajar and when Tom let himself in, his eyebrows raised at the scene before him.

The three strangers were pointing and yelling at the captain who was holding his hands out to his sides, motioning for them to sit. When Baltsaros looked to Tom as he entered, his face was a mask of restrained anger.

Tom scowled at the fishermen and cleared his throat before letting out a bellow.

"Will ye bloody calm yer shit? Hells, a man can't fuckin' think with this racket!" His loud voice startled the group into silence, and the three of them turned as one to look at the first mate standing in the doorway. Despite the captain's ban on him smoking in their quarters, he pushed a cheroot into the corner of his mouth and lit it; his hands were shaking from fatigue, and he needed a little pick-me-up.

As he walked to the captain's side, he glared at the strangers.

"What the fuck is goin' on, Da?" he grunted. "Who let them out of their cages?" He turned to Baltsaros and was startled to see the captain looking haggard and far older than he normally did.

"I did, Tom. They're to be our guests, and for longer than I had intended," murmured Baltsaros, barely meeting Tom's eye before he turned his face back to the three men who stood in simmering silence. "Someone stole a crate full of supplies and left with their boat sometime in the night. I want you to find out who is missing while I try to mend relations here... and Tom? I can barely stand the smell of you. Please take a minute to clean up before you come back."

Tom bit back a retort, instead ducking his head in acknowledgement and leaving the captain to deal with the furious strangers. As he made his way to the crew bunkroom, he sniffed at his shirt.

J on blinked sleepily and turned onto his back, confused for a moment by his surroundings. When the events from the previous night came back in a rush, Jon grinned wide, his fingers sliding down to tug at the crinkly hair above his cock. Tom's body had trembled so hard as he had buried his thick shaft deep inside him, and Jon had realized in shock that it was a new experience for the lusty first mate. It made him happy that he had decided to share his body with the big man in the moment of heat; the memory brought a warmth to his skin, and he smiled softly.

His bladder full, Jon soon sat up and looked around for a chamber pot. After he'd finished using the one he had found in the corner, his eyes were drawn to the little wooden box he'd noticed before. Jon picked it up from the crate and rubbed his thumb over the inlaid wood design. He'd never seen anything quite like it. The craftsmanship was exquisite; it was simple yet beautiful, and the wood felt like soft satin under his fingertips.

As he sat down cross-legged on the mattress, Jon furrowed his brow and looked at the box in his hands. He was invading Tom's privacy by touching what had to be a prized possession, but he couldn't stop himself. He wanted to put the box back—he really did—but, instead, he watched his fingers flip up the small bronze catch and lift the lid slowly.

At first Jon was puzzled by the contents. There were only two things nestled against the ruby-red silk lining. The first looked like a fragment of a thin steel circlet, the edges of which were sharp and shinier than the rest of the metal, like it had been force-fully cut apart. The second item was a piece of yellowed parchment folded in half at the bottom of the box. Carefully, Jon lifted out the document and opened it. When he saw what it was, his eyes went wide: it was a bill of sale addressed to Captain Baltsaros for one slave… Tom.

Suddenly he understood what the broken circlet was. Taking up the fragment in his fingers, he looked along the edge until he found a stamp in the metal that matched the symbol on the document. This was a piece of Tom's slave collar, obviously cut off of him by Baltsaros when the first mate was brought aboard.

Jon's eyes brimmed with hot tears, and he tried to blink them away before they fell. In his hands, he held the concrete evidence of Tom's decade of slavery, and it suddenly made the big man's past painfully real to him. Pressing the collar to his lips, Jon thought he could sense the fear and pain of a little boy ripped away from his life to suffer years of cruelty at the hands of his master.

No... that first collar would have been much, much smaller to fit his young neck, and it would have needed to be replaced multiple times when it got too tight as Tom grew to the thick-muscled man he was today.

He quickly fumbled the paper and piece of metal back into the box, closing it before he was overwhelmed. How did Tom live with the memories?

After placing the wooden box back carefully on the crate, Jon curled up on his side on the mattress. Running alongside the guilt he still felt about what he had done to Tom and Baltsaros's relationship was the worry that he could be doing even more damage.

With the blanket over him and fisted in his hands, he closed his eyes and breathed in Tom's smell, trying to slow his speeding heart.

When Tom returned to the stateroom, the mood was slightly less strained. The men were seated, digging into bowls of Cook's spiced, yellow porridge as they conversed in low voices.

Straightening his shoulders, Tom hoped that his quick, open-air scrub was enough to mollify Baltsaros as he made his way to the captain's side. It was still cool outside but, seeing as the other men were bare chested, he had finally discarded the stained linen shirt.

A big part of him didn't understand why the captain was bothering with placating the white-haired savages; why not just toss them overboard and forget about their damn queer boat?

Clearing his throat, Tom pressed his knuckles to the table and leaned hard on them.

"Ok. We're missin' three," he reported, annoyed that the captain's eyes slid quickly away from his again.

*It's yer own damn fault, Da. If ye weren't so fuckin' ornery about yer bloody fuckin' possessions, maybe ye wouldn't be so fuckin' sore that I fucked yer—*Tom's inner monologue stopped when he realized that maybe Baltsaros knew *exactly* what had happened between him and Jon. Maybe he had somehow smelled it on him or could see the truth in Tom's eyes. Maybe he was furious and would toss Tom aside again. Fear scrabbled through the cracks in the first mate's heart, and his mouth went dry. As Tom stilled his sudden, guilt-fuelled panic, he tried to ignore the old fisherman staring openly at him.

"Tom?" asked Baltsaros, frowning at his first mate.

Tom huffed out a small breath. The captain's eyes were locked on his, but, thankfully, all the first mate could see was a man who had not had enough sleep, who was worried about peace aboard his ship, and who *needed* him. In the corner of his vision, Tom could see the white-haired stranger still staring at him, and he rolled his shoulder slightly at the uncomfortable attention.

"Uh... well, Da, it's the fuckin' pack of brats ye picked up when ye came for me," he explained. "See, Jon knocked one of them on his arse last night—"

"Is Jon all right?" asked Baltsaros, alarmed.

Tom barked out a laugh and nodded, running the tops of fingers against the stubble on his cheek.

"I think ye'd have been proud, Da," he said with a slow smile. The image of Jon's fist connecting with the deckhand's jaw was one that would stick with him a long time—as would the image of

Jon's head thrown back, mouth open in a soft groan, as Tom moved above him. Tom felt heat in his cheeks, and he let out a small cough to cover his momentary lapse. "Er—Anslaw and the other two cocksuckers never went back to their bunks last night. Cook says he was up late playin' cards an' would'a seen them boys take the crate of supplies. I'm guessin' they waited until past midnight before sneakin' away, the bloody bilge rats... *And will ye quit bloody starin' at me, ye fuckin' savage!*" The last was addressed to the stranger whose eyes hadn't ceased boring into Tom.

The old man blinked at Tom slowly, apparently undaunted by his anger. Instead, he pointed to the first mate's chest.

"Now where have you get these, boy?" he said, his blue eyes narrow as he looked at Tom.

The first mate glanced down at his chest and frowned.

"Why is that any of yer bloody business?" Tom growled back, staring hard at the old man. No one called him "boy".

"Tom," murmured Baltsaros, and the first mate shot the captain a peeved look; none of this was helping his mood. Tom wished he were back in his room with Jon in his arms.

Turning to the white-haired fisherman, the captain raised his stark brow.

"Polas, what do Tom's tattoos mean to you?"

T om let out a small groan as he sunk down to his haunches and pulled up the coverlet so he could slide in behind Jon. The sleeping man woke with a start and then sighed as Tom's arm came around his waist.

"Hey," whispered Jon, pushing back against the bigger man so that they fit together like spoons.

Tom pressed his face against the back of Jon's neck and let out a small, pleased noise from deep in his chest. Despite how tired he was, his cock had begun to get stiff at Jon's movements, and now it was a growing, hardening ridge between them.

Fuck it.

"I want ye again," he said simply, and pushed his hips forward, testing. When Jon shifted back again and nodded quickly, Tom felt nearly breathless with the lust that shook him.

After a sorely needed bath, Jon pulled open the door to the captain's quarters and peered inside. Baltsaros raised his head at the sound and looked over at Jon.

"Come in. It's ok," said the older man, putting aside his book.

Jon frowned and stepped inside, raking his fingers through his still-wet hair.

"What's ok?" he asked warily, eyeing the captain.

Baltsaros laughed and held out his hand. Jon hesitated a moment longer before dropping his shoulders and approaching the captain. Looking up at Jon, Baltsaros shook his head slowly.

"Listen to me, Jon," said the captain, lifting Jon's palm to his lips. "It's *ok*. I won't have you and Tom acting like you're sneaking around behind my back. We've gone over this; I can deal with this *fascination* you have for Tom. I have been fair to you, have I not?" Baltsaros's dark-brown eyes searched Jon's, and the younger man pressed his lips together and nodded. "Tom's fond of you, and he'll keep you safe when I'm not able to—What is it?" The captain furrowed his brow at Jon.

Jon shifted his weight to the other foot and lifted his chin slightly. The captain *was* trying; the fact that Tom and he had remained unmolested for the duration of the morning was testimony to that. But how far was Baltsaros willing to share Jon? Were he and Tom wrong in their assumption that the captain would zealously guard Jon's affections for his own? With a long sigh, Jon realized it was time to put that theory to the test.

"Baltsaros, what if I told you that Tom meant a great deal to me?" he asked quietly, moving his hand out of the captain's grasp to rest it against the older man's cheek. Baltsaros's eyes closed momentarily, and he leaned into Jon's touch, looking wearier than he had ever seen him.

"I expect that he does," muttered Baltsaros, raising his gaze again to Jon's. The older man's big hand covered Jon's hand, the palm smooth and dry over his sore knuckles. "Jon..." Baltsaros's brow creased but smoothed out almost immediately.

Jon tilted his head and frowned at the captain. It was his turn to ask the question.

"What is it?" he asked softly.

The captain let out a slow breath and pulled his face away from Jon's hand.

"I don't want to hear the word 'love' from your lips regarding Tom, but I fear that's the direction this conversation is going," sighed Baltsaros with a bitter smile. "You are my redemption, Jon. You are my soul. You are the hope that I never knew I needed. If that means that I have to share your heart..." The captain's shoulder came up in a small shrug. "So be it. Just don't leave my side, promise me that."

Jon let out a low sound, quickly moving forward to press his lips against the captain's as Baltsaros's hands came up around him. Breaking the kiss a moment later, Jon looked hard at the captain.

"I won't leave your side," he smiled, his fingers twining in the captain's hair. "I promise." The relief he felt completely overshadowed the niggling doubt in his head at the rash promise.

Baltsaros's face creased into a pleased smile, and he nodded once before growing serious again.

"Good. Now... in the next few days, spend as much time with Tom as you can," he said, his brow furrowed. "You both will have to get everything out of your systems before we make land."

Jon frowned, confused.

Baltsaros rubbed a big, sun-darkened hand over his mouth, stroking down on his white-streaked beard. "Go wake Tom and bring him here. I have to explain a few things."

T om sat straddling the chair, his arms folded across the top and his head down against them as he swore softly under his breath.

Baltsaros felt for the big man, knowing that this was possibly the worst thing he had ever asked of him.

He turned to Jon who sagged back in his own chair, staring up at the captain.

Earlier, he'd sent Tom away when Polas launched into his stilted explanation of the first mate's tattoos. As soon as the old man described them as slave tattoos, Baltsaros had been glad he had dismissed the first mate. Now he was unkindly forcing Tom to adopt the role that he swore he would never be in again. He frowned at Tom.

"Polas said that the only way we could pass within the city walls without drawing attention is with a slave. I'm sorry, Tom, but you're going to have to come to terms with this. It's just an act… It's not like you're going to have to bow and scrape to me, and I will do everything in my power to keep you from facing any abuse."

Tom grunted against his forearm and raised his sea-green eyes to Baltsaros's.

"Fine," he muttered, his jaw tight and brows creased.

Though surly, Tom's answer would have to do. The captain nodded, and then let out a short sigh.

"Now, the other problem is this: where we are going, it is illegal for a man to lie with another," he said slowly, looking between Tom and Jon. "Punishable by death."

Tom lifted his head and let out a short laugh with no humour. Next to him, Jon just gaped at the captain with horror plain on his face.

Baltsaros lifted his hand.

"When Polas assumed you were my son, Tom, I told him the truth, and he was, I'm sorry to say, absolutely horrified. However, he admitted that different cultures had the right to different customs. I may have exaggerated somewhat when I told him that in our lands it was normal for men to lie together, but it was necessary for him not to see our arrangement as an aberration," explained Baltsaros, running his finger along the edge of his cup. At the time he had felt nothing but a shocked sort of curiosity at the discovery that they were in a realm of strict moral values that made his uncle Romas' faith look like a bunch of idol-worshiping whoremongers.

Jon's strained voice broke the silence.

"Why do we have to go to this city at all?"

Baltsaros lifted his eyes.

"The city is rich... There's gold inlaid in the very streets themselves. Perhaps we can set up trade once I figure out how to counteract the effects of the spores," he replied with a smile. "Polas speaks of other wonders. They have harnessed lightning... I want to see this with my own eyes." It was *nearly* the whole truth.

The captain thought that Jon and Tom needn't concern themselves with his primary motivation: the deep fascination with a city that was governed by gods who demanded constant human sacrifice. In Baltsaros's esteem, the streets were coloured by something far richer than mere gold.

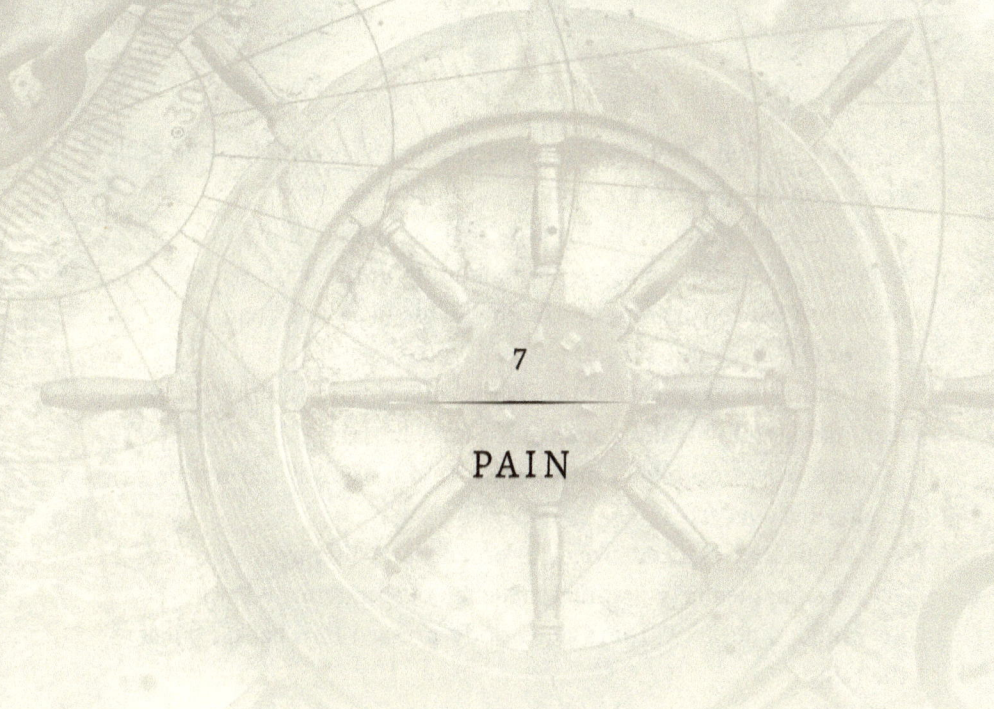

7

PAIN

The only antidote to mental suffering is physical pain.

— KARL MARX

Jon watched the tall, white-haired young man approach the captain to say a few words, Oren's head tilting gracefully as he gestured out to the water with a slender arm. However, when Calum walked up a moment later holding something in his hands, the captain turned his attention towards the old pirate. Oren stood uncertainly for a long minute, staring at the captain's back and shifting his weight slowly from one foot to the other, before turning to walk away.

"That's it. Go bat yer eyes at someone else, ye little cunt," growled Tom under his breath, leaning over the quarterdeck railing next to Jon. The first mate had a deep scowl on his face as he plucked the toothpick from the corner of his mouth, his blue-green eyes trained on Polas's grandson as the young man wandered towards the bow.

Jaw clenched, Jon turned around, leaning back with his elbows resting on the glossy black railing.

"You don't think Baltsaros would actually fuck him, do you?" he asked, frowning up at the flag snapping in the brisk wind; the black lion danced, its mouth stretched wide in a silent roar.

Tom let out a short laugh.

"I didn't think Da would fuck *you*, lovey," said the first mate, leaning to bump his shoulder against Jon's.

Jon's frown deepened into a scowl; Tom's words did nothing to allay his concern.

When Tom glanced over a moment later, his eyes softened. With a sigh, the burly first mate reached over and tugged at Jon so he would slide over. Tom's hard body pressed him back against the railing.

"Listen... as much as he likes to use what's hangin' between his legs, Da's not given to thinkin' with his tarse, lad," said Tom gently, his deep voice a low rumble. "Can ye imagine the shit storm we'd have if he stole that little cunt's cherry? Nah... I just don't like that skinny, white-haired fishmonger sniffin' around Da like a bitch in heat is all. Matter o' principle."

Watching Tom's face as he spoke, Jon had to smile. Tom was, at times, still intimidating; cheerfully brash and bluff, the first mate was almost aggressively masculine. Everything about him screamed of dominant, dangerous virility—from his swaggering gait and his hard, scarred fists to his unrepentant abuse of intoxicants and taste for brutal violence. Yet, less than an hour ago, those grinning pink lips had been wrapped around Jon's cock as Tom knelt submissively in front of him in the stateroom, hands tied behind him as he opened his throat to the abuse Jon inflicted on him. Reconciling the two images of Tom had become easier with time, but it still made Jon a little dizzy. He lifted a hand to Tom's cheek, the dark-blond stubble sharp against his palm, and watched the first mate's eyes grow dark. Jon suddenly felt flush with desire for the big man again.

"Would you like me to take over so you two can do that somewhere a little more private?" asked the captain as he walked up the stairs. "I know that our guests' views on sex are primitive, but there is no need to push it in their faces. A little tact would not go amiss, hm?"

Jon turned his head to look at Baltsaros, still feeling residual guilt about all the attention he'd been paying to Tom despite the captain's assurances.

Baltsaros's dark eyes locked on his, showing no hint of what was going on in his mind. However, when Tom pulled Jon's hand to his lips to slide his fingers into his mouth, Baltsaros's nostrils flared slightly and his lips twitched. The captain reached for Tom, quickly snagging his fingers in the first mate's short hair and yanking him away from Jon, a frighteningly cold expression on his stark features.

"Tom, that's quite enough," growled Baltsaros, tightening his fist and causing the first mate to wince as his head was pulled back.

Jon couldn't keep himself from smiling. Months ago, had he seen the same display, he would have been slightly worried for the first mate; however, he'd long ago learned to recognize what the two men considered foreplay.

Baltsaros dropped his hand and, after a pointed look at the first mate, descended the staircase quickly. Tom took a few steps to follow and paused, a somewhat sheepish expression on his face as he narrowed his eyes at Jon.

"Come and get me if there's anythin', lad," he said gruffly before turning to jog down the stairs.

Jon let out a slow breath and sat down on the bench behind the ship's wheel, feeling abandoned. He ran his hands through his hair and tried hard to stifle the jealous feelings that arose in him every time the captain and Tom excluded him. It wasn't fair of him and he knew it. It would just take a while longer for his brain to stop throwing scenarios at him where the first mate and Baltsaros decided they didn't need a third wheel anymore and dropped Jon off at the nearest uninhabited spit of land to fend for himself.

Grinning at that scenario, Jon imagined himself trying to catch something to eat using only the knife at his belt. The image was preposterous, and he smirked, leaning forward to correct the ship's wheel when it turned slightly off course. A moment later he fancied he could hear the smack of something hard against flesh, and he frowned, licking his lips before tightening his jaw. Despite the exclusion, the thought of Tom being "punished" sent a surge through him, and he shifted on the bench, his face hot.

It hadn't always been like that.

J on stood staring at Tom, a sick feeling in the pit of his stomach. The first mate knelt with his thighs spread for balance, his big arms bound tightly behind his neck by a length of red hempen rope, his muscles bulging and straining. Jon remembered how the captain had tied him up with the same rope and beat him with a slim rod before pleasuring himself. Jon had been in pain; the captain had pushed him to his very limits. However, in the end, it had been a revelation—something staggering and utterly freeing.

But this? This was shocking in its brutality.

Tom's head hung below his shoulders as he panted, his chest and back covered with a crisscross of red lines, some weeping blood down over his tawny skin, long wet streaks that followed the curves of his muscles. Slowly the first mate looked up, his eyes red and wet; he licked the cut on his top lip and let out a shaky breath. Without warning, Baltsaros lashed out and backhanded the first mate hard, a loud grunt bursting out of Tom as his head whipped to the side.

"Fuck... Baltsaros stop it," gasped Jon, reaching out for the older man's arm. The captain, eyes wild, turned to Jon. Baltsaros was breathing hard, and his bare, sweat-soaked chest heaved. He looked confused for a moment, as if surprised to see Jon there, and pulled his arm away.

Swallowing, Jon shook his head.

"Please. He's had enough..." he said, praying that Baltsaros could hear him through the savagery that had turned him into something cold and heartless. He only hoped that he wasn't too late and Tom wasn't badly hurt.

Jon started when Tom let out a hoarse laugh, and he frowned. The first mate's face was creased in a gory grin as he shook his head, his breath coming in short gasps between his clenched teeth.

Baltsaros's hand closed softly over Jon's shoulder, and he turned the younger man towards him. The captain's expression had softened; he looked at Jon with a touch of amusement in his dark eyes and a slight curl of his lip.

"Jon, it's ok," he murmured, his fingers squeezing him gently.

Jon frowned and looked back at the first mate. In amazement, he watched Tom press his lips together and dip his head once in agreement. However, his eyes spoke louder than his nod when Jon realized then that the big man's pupils were wide with desire and not fear.

Jon's chest constricted and he felt weak with confusion. How could anyone *like* this, let alone Tom of all people? Jon thought back to the night a few weeks ago when Baltsaros half-carried the first mate into his quarters, Tom's face bleeding from a deep cut and his pants strangely ripped. Had that been... play? Gritting his teeth, Jon shook his head again.

"I just... don't understand," he said quietly. He liked it well enough when he had Tom on his knees and the first mate let him get a little rough; but, that wasn't anything like this. This was pure abuse.

Baltsaros let out a slow sigh, his palm warm against Jon's shoulder before he let his hand drop.

"It's complicated," he murmured. However, after only a moment, the captain's face creased into a smile, and he pressed his fingers against Jon's back.

"Go kneel in front of him, Jon," coaxed Baltsaros, his voice amused. "Please. Trust me."

Jon's brows pinched over his eyes a moment, suspicious of the captain's motives; but, he wanted to trust the man. Watching Baltsaros take his place behind Tom, Jon let out a slow sigh and sank to his knees in front of the first mate.

Tom looked curiously at him, and Jon felt a little pain in his chest at the bruise blooming over the man's stubbled cheek. He lifted a hand to it and felt the heat against his palm.

"I can probably make him stop," he murmured to Tom. The big man's brows furrowed over his gorgeous eyes, and he gave a little shake of his head.

"Jon, unfasten Tom's trousers and pull his cock out," ordered the captain. Jon licked his lips and quickly did as he was told, eager to bring Tom at least some pleasure in all of this.

What he discovered confounded him even more. Once freed, Tom's erection was a rock hard curve pointing upwards, the head of it bobbing with his breathing. In amazement he saw precum glisten at the tip, beading over to run down the dusky-rose head, and past where someone long ago had cruelly cut away the loose covering of his foreskin. Slowly, Jon reached for Tom, his fingers brushing the hot shaft. It was only then that Tom spoke.

"Da, if he touches me, I'm like to cum," he gasped, closing his eyes.

"No you won't, Tom," said the captain, his voice cold and quiet. "If you do, you won't for a week."

Something about the exchange triggered a soft pulse of lust inside Jon, and he felt curiosity begin to eclipse his doubts. Jon lifted his eyes and saw that Baltsaros had picked up the thin flexible rod again; the captain bent it between his hands. As he placed his palm against Tom's chest, Jon decided to test something.

"The captain's going to hit you again," he said softly. Eyes flicking up to Baltsaros's, he saw the older man smile. Beneath Jon's palm, Tom's heart began to beat faster.

When the rod cracked against the first mate's left buttock, Jon felt Tom's grunt through his hand, the thumping of the great organ beneath his ribs racing at a hard gallop. After Tom sucked in a quick, pained breath, he exhaled with an unmistakable groan of pleasure. There was suddenly no doubt in Jon's mind that Tom was enjoying every minute of this. In response to that realization, his own cock was hardening against the inside of his thigh. That was when Jon decided to leave the "why" for later and concentrate on the "how".

Jon leaned forward to brush his lips over Tom's and felt the man's heart stutter against his palm. The switch came down hard again, twice this time, with a deep grunt from the captain as he put more force into it.

Tom let out a sharp cry and ducked his head under Jon's jaw to bury it against his neck, the first mate's breath hot against his skin. With his fingers curled around Tom's shaft, Jon let his hand slide over the turgid flesh softly, careful to avoid the sensitive flared edges of its head; there was teasing and then there was torture of not being allowed any release for days. As he shifted his other hand to slide through the soft hair at Tom's nape, Jon locked eyes with the captain.

Baltsaros's face was flushed, his lip curled into a slight sneer as he stared back at Jon. He felt a rush of adrenaline as he realized what the captain wanted from him.

"Hit him again," Jon said. "And don't hold back this time."

Against his neck, Tom let out a long, muffled groan.

"The wind is good today," said an accented voice.

Jon started and frowned, quickly turning his head. Oren stood on the top step looking out at the water with one hand on the railing. With a scowl at the lithe, white-haired youth, Jon got to his feet.

"You're not supposed to be up here," he said, gesturing to the main deck. "You need permission before you can climb those stairs."

Brow furrowing over his limpid blue eyes, Oren looked at Jon but didn't reply. With an annoyed sigh, Jon took a step towards the young fisherman, intending to herd him back down the stairs. It galled Jon that he had to look up to address him; Oren stood at least a hand's width taller than he did.

"Please," urged Jon. "Go back down. It's not for you to be up here."

Oren frowned at him, lifting a shoulder in a slow shrug.

"I was looking for Baltsaros," he replied, his Common sharply flavoured with the accent of his people.

Baltsaros. Where does he get off not calling him Captain? thought Jon peevishly. There was nothing overtly unlikable about the young man. Any of his transgressions could be chalked up to misunderstandings and a difference of culture, but still...

"*The captain* is otherwise occupied with the first mate. I'll tell him you were looking for him," replied Jon, crossing his arms over his chest. At that moment, an unmistakable groan of pleasure could be heard from the quarters beneath them, and Jon clenched his jaw.

Oren's blond eyebrows lifted, and his cheeks took on a subtle blush. Blue eyes flicking to the planks beneath their feet, Oren pressed his lips together and glanced again at Jon.

"I... will wait. Below, as you say," said the young man softly. Jon nodded, and watched Oren descend the stairs; he didn't like the way that the young man's breathing had quickened at the sound of Baltsaros and Tom at play.

Sitting cross-legged beside Tom, Jon dabbed a little more salve onto the first mate's back. Next to him, the captain was sprawled out on his stomach, deeply asleep and completely oblivious. Still reeling slightly from the part he had played in Tom's punishment, if that's what it really had been, Jon chewed the inside of his cheek as he tried to soothe the damage done to the first mate's skin. His hand still stung from how hard he had clutched the leather belt wrapped around the first mate's big neck as Jon had savagely fucked him from behind, and the memory made him feel a little ill. However, Tom just let out a pleased sigh, his muscles soft and relaxed beneath Jon's gentle touch.

"Ye 'member the first time ye did this for me?" murmured Tom blissfully, his cheek pressed against his bicep as he looked up at Jon with a smile.

Jon smiled a little thinly; he had applied salve to the first mate's back when Tom had been whipped to unconsciousness by the captain.

"I'm not likely to forget that," he said, shaking his head.

Tom frowned at the look on Jon's face.

"What's eatin' at ye, love? Ye look like ye've been chewin' lemons."

Jon pressed the stopper back over the squat earthenware jar and shrugged before stretching out next to the first mate with his fingers curled around Tom's forearm.

"I just don't understand how you get off on being so... mistreated," he whispered. "And I don't like that I liked... doing those things to you." He slid his fingers gently over Tom's skin, the dark-blond hair on his arm soft against his fingertips. "Didn't you get abused enough when you were a slave?"

A slight crease appeared between Tom's brows, and he closed his eyes, lying motionless for a while. For a moment, Jon thought he had gone to sleep but, after a long sigh, his deep voice broke the long silence.

"It's like this. When ye have no choice, ye can either let it claim ye, or ye can claim it as yer own. The beatin's tore a good lot outta me, lad. But the pain... well, the pain, it helps to fix me back up. I dunno, love. Maybe I been knocked about and taken so many beatin's after fuckin' that my daft brain's got the two o' them mixed up?" Tom laughed softly and opened his eyes, the irises dark like deep, still seawater. "Now since I'm my own man, I get to choose who lays into me, see? It's my *choice*. No one else's. If some bloody asshole tries it with me, and he ain't got my say-so, he's like to die by my fuckin' hands. Right? But the captain, and *you*, ye silly worried thing... it's like heaven's come callin' full o' angels to suck my cock," grinned Tom, wrinkling his nose in amusement at Jon.

Nodding slowly, Jon tried to process the information.

"The captain once told me that you were broken, and that you knew it, and that it was ok," murmured Jon, pushing himself up onto his elbows to look down at the first mate. "And that you were better at coping with it than he or I would ever be."

"Da said that?" asked Tom, a smile creasing his cheek. When Jon nodded again, the first mate chuckled. "Well, fuck me." Placing his big, scarred hand over Jon's, Tom's face slowly went serious.

"Ye once said ye'd kiss me better after a beatin'," murmured Tom. "Can I hold ye to that, love?"

As he squinted into the distance with one hand on the spoked wheel, Jon grinned wide at the memory. How times had changed.

From below he thought he could hear the low, repetitive sound of Tom begging. It took a lot to get the first mate to break down, and Jon wondered with a pang of apprehension whether it meant the captain was working through some internal conflict about the fisherman's grandson. Pushing the petty worry away, Jon leaned back on the bench and sighed.

Warm in the sun, Jon closed his eyes and waited. He knew that after the captain was through with him, Tom would seek him out, and that thought alone was enough to put a soft smile back on Jon's face.

8

A SNAKE IN THE BED

Baltsaros passed a rag behind his neck, wiping away the sweat that ran down between his shoulder blades. When the cloth came away black, the captain realized that he was just as filthy as the others. The three men stood in the small room that housed the trundlehead below the drum of the capstan, covered in grease and grime and bleary-eyed from exhaustion. Smiling tiredly at Malik and Polas, the captain leaned against the wall with a groan; if he were to sit down on one of the crates, Baltsaros truly believed he would not be able to get up again.

It had been a long night. Since the crew's numbers had dwindled, it was all hands on deck merely to keep the ship running, and many small repairs had fallen by the wayside. The previous day, Baltsaros had decided to drop anchor to take care of some much-needed repairs before continuing on. However, as if to make the captain's concerns manifest, the mechanism that allowed the capstan to turn had seized halfway through lowering the anchor, leaving them in a precarious position. They could neither stop from drifting nor could they flee if they found themselves in danger. While the double-headed design was advantageous for the extra-long cables required to anchor in the deep waters that *Baal's Heart* found herself in yearly, the failure of the aged mechanism had been a constant worry; the captain had known it was bound to break down sooner or later, and he was glad it had given out when they were not in any danger.

Thankfully, with Malik's and the old fisherman's help, they had been able to take the whole apart and, rather than just realign the drums, they had meticulously cleaned every piece of it before putting it back together. It had taken almost the entire night but, in Baltsaros's opinion, it had been time well spent. Once again, Polas had proved himself to be a worthy ally; a lifetime at sea had given the old man hard muscles and a deep well of patience, as well as the humour to make a long night of labour go a little faster.

After scrubbing his hand tiredly over his eyes, Baltsaros nodded to the old man and watched him leave the room with Malik close behind. Yes, Polas had proved his worth; Baltsaros was considering asking the old man if he wished to stay on as part of the crew. Once the captain had wiped the rag one last time over the tarnished copper that bound the wood of the trundlehead, he reached up to bang on the boards above his head and stepped back. As he watched the cable begin to wind itself around the drum, Baltsaros thought about the other two strangers.

Unlike Polas, his son Migri was simply a drain on the ship's resources; despite being tall and strong, the big fisherman was more interested in dicing or drinking with the less savoury individuals that lived and worked aboard the pirate ship than doing anything helpful. Baltsaros couldn't wait to be rid of the laggard. Migri was both lazy and dangerous, a bad combination that had landed him in the brig twice in less than a week.

With his arms crossed, Baltsaros kept his eyes on the spooling cable as the drum rotated to the sound of boots above his head. After it had wound all the way, saltwater dripping into the narrow gutter that encircled the mechanism, Baltsaros heard the men stop and turn around. Once more the drum began to rotate but now in the other direction to finally lower the anchor to the seabed.

Satisfied with the repairs, Baltsaros picked up his discarded shirt and ducked through the small door. After a quick stop in the galley to pick up one of the edible red-skinned fruits they had found on one of the small, uninhabited islands they continuously passed, the captain then made his way wearily up the stairs. Once up on deck, he waved a hand in thanks to the men who had roused themselves before dawn to work the capstan. When he noticed the willowy, white-haired youth standing apart, Baltsaros clenched his jaw, staring back at Oren for a moment before turning to his quarters.

On quietly entering the stateroom, Baltsaros's tense frown left his face at the sight of Tom sleeping with Jon clutched to him like a child's toy. It was getting easier for the captain to see the two boys together like this; they offered each other the solace that Baltsaros just wasn't capable of, and their relationship was a much-needed bridge for the gap that had always existed, unbeknownst to him, between Tom and himself. He had decided that he simply needed both of them to feel whole; it worked to soothe his possessiveness somewhat.

After pouring a little water into the shallow basin, Baltsaros quickly wiped his face, staring at his own shadowy eyes in the glass mirror that hung on the wall.

The grandson has to go, he thought.

His mind's eye painted him a picture of the white-haired youth with his unblemished golden skin, and long, lithe muscles. Oren's bright blue eyes seemed to follow Baltsaros everywhere, and it was beginning to make him feel restive. He was fully aware that bedding the boy was a fool's wish, but there wasn't a doubt in his mind that the fisherman's grandson would come to him willingly. Baltsaros scrubbed at the grease on his shoulder with a sigh and wondered how long Oren had known he preferred the company of men and whether he had attempted anything on his own despite the terribly restrictive society he was part of. The boy would probably be a virgin.

Jon had been a virgin, and it had been a heady thing to experience.

With the cloth pressed to his eyes, Baltsaros stood still for a moment, remembering that strange day at the *Jewel* when Jon had forced a promise of fidelity out of him. That promise had changed, of course, to include Tom, but the captain knew he couldn't kid himself into thinking that an indiscretion with the beautiful stranger would go well with either of the young men. Besides, there was the respect for Polas to think of.

Baltsaros dumped the rag into the basin and, longing for a bath, he padded quietly to the bed. As soon as he placed a warm hand on Tom's broad shoulder, he felt the first mate tense as he woke up, Tom's blue-green eyes blinking up at the captain with concern.

"What's the matter, Da?" asked Tom quietly, his voice hoarse from sleep.

"Can you take over? I am dead on my feet, and I need someone to split the men into work groups early before they start to wander off. I want all the repairs done by this evening, if possible. We'll leave for the mainland at first light tomorrow morning," murmured the captain, smiling as the muscular first mate untangled himself from Jon and got to his feet, naked and gorgeous.

When Tom saw the look in Baltsaros's eye, he did something that still tended to take the captain by surprise. Instead of his usual slightly surly "Yes, Da", the first mate reached out and curled his hand around the back of the captain's neck, pulling the older man in for a quick kiss before nodding and looking around for a pair of pants to wear. His eyebrows high in astonishment at the affectionate gesture, Baltsaros smiled at Tom and shook his head in amusement.

As he crawled into bed behind Jon once Tom was gone, the captain frowned, hoping that this new gentleness infecting Tom did nothing to diminish the cold brutality that he so depended on in the first mate.

J on peeled the banana and took a bite, chewing with a smile. The fruit wasn't quite ripe, but it had been months since the last time he'd had one, and it tasted wonderful to him. Craning his neck, he squinted up at Tom, balanced barefoot on one of the yardarms to replace a pulley that had become stuck. After pulling the line out of the old one, Tom whistled at Jon before dropping it. Jon caught it and, taking another bite of banana, he tossed the broken brass-and-wood pulley onto the deck below where it joined three others. At the furious pace they were working, the minor repairs would definitely be done before sundown.

While he watched Tom climb down the shrouds, Jon finished his fruit and tossed the peel overboard, wiping his hand on the side of his trousers before jumping down from his crate. With the pulleys replaced, he and Tom were to tackle rehousing the starboard carronade together. The big gun's wheel had rusted solid, making it impossible to aim, but Tom thought he could get it working with enough oil. The problem was that the elevation thread was also thick with rust and getting the whole thing loose was going to be a hassle. It was worth a try though. Jon tried not to think about the fact that it was the gun that had burst free of its moorings and crushed a man to death the night Tom had been swept overboard.

As he stood braced against the side of the gun watching Tom try to wiggle the base of it back and forth, Jon caught a glimpse of Oren walking towards the stern. When the young fisherman glanced around him quickly, Jon straightened, his eyes narrowed.

What are you up to? he thought, wary of the youth's suspicious behaviour.

"Bloody hells! Will ye keep yer hip on the gods-damned bloody gun, love? D'ye think I'm doin' this for my bloody health?" panted Tom, smacking the back of Jon's calf as he knelt with his shoulder against the wooden pedestal. The big man grinned up at Jon.

"Keep yer fuckin' mind on the job, and I'll give ye somethin' to smile about after, aye? Now heave, mate!"

Oren momentarily forgotten, Jon put his back to the side of the big gun and pushed back as hard as he could, his thoughts on what Tom might have in mind once the work was completed.

Baltsaros sighed as the warm body behind him moved closer, Jon's hand stroking slowly down his flank and coming to rest on his hip. Smiling, the captain pushed back against him; though he was half-asleep and sore from the night's work, there was nothing better than waking up to Jon's touch. The younger man behind him moved slightly, going up on one elbow to begin kissing the side of Baltsaros's neck and over his shoulder, fingers tracing meaningless patterns over the captain's naked thigh.

"Mmm," murmured Baltsaros, tilting his head with his eyes closed. "That's nice." The hand on his thigh moved lower, nails scratching softly as they came back up again. The sensation was incredibly pleasing, and the captain let out another soft moan. His cock, half-hard already from sleep-arousal, lengthened along the curve of his pelvis, and he rocked backwards a little to free it and bring it into Jon's grasp. Behind him, the boy let out a small sound, and his fingers stilled momentarily.

That should have been the first indication that all was not what it seemed.

However, Baltsaros just arched his back sleepily against the young man, pulling Jon's hand down to where the captain's cock lay waiting for warm fingers to close over it. After wrapping his own hand around Jon's fist, he moved his hips to fuck his cock through their grasp, sighing again with pleasure as the head brushed against Jon's palm. Groaning as his hunger began to mount quickly, Baltsaros was gratified to feel Jon's cock hard against him. He let go of the hand on his length and reached back to touch the young man moving slowly against him, to pull Jon closer... and opened his eyes in confusion when the hip his hand encountered was slimmer, far slimmer, than Jon's. Baltsaros turned his head quickly and frowned up into the sly blue eyes of the fisherman's grandson.

For a moment he was shocked into inaction; the boy's hand continued stroking along his hard shaft, but Baltsaros's mind finally registered the unpracticed way Oren held the captain, and how the younger man smelled absolutely nothing like Jon did.

The captain opened his mouth to tell Oren to remove himself but instead found himself kissing him, his fingers tangling in the long white dreadlocks as he continued to move in Oren's grasp. Heart beating a dizzying rhythm, Baltsaros turned onto his back and reached for Oren, crushing him against his body, a low growl in his chest. It was completely absurd to take such a risk, but his lust was a crazed thing that would not release him. When the long-limbed fisherman moved against him hesitantly, pushing his cock against Baltsaros's pelvis, soft little whimpers of need came from his graceful throat. With another growl, this time fierce, the captain tugged Oren's head back and leaned up to bite hard into the side of his neck.

"Fuckin' bloody hells!" yelled Tom, and Oren pulled quickly back in shock, a guilty expression on his face.

Baltsaros just closed his eyes slowly and lay panting, disappointment and annoyance warring with the self-reproach he felt.

Stupid.

Oren quickly climbed off the captain, and Baltsaros could hear him scrabbling about for his trousers before the door slammed shut.

"Have ye lost yer bloody mind, Da?" asked Tom, his gravelly voice low and furious. "I just finished tellin' Jon that ye'd never be so fuckin' stupid as to put yer cock in that little piece o' shit, and here ye are, about to heave the bloody cunt down and give him a good, deep ploughin'..." Baltsaros opened his eyes and watched as the first mate continued his tirade, pacing back and forth across the thick rugs. When Tom put one of his slim, black cigars between his lips and lit it, Baltsaros just frowned and said nothing.

The first mate stopped and turned to Baltsaros, his blue-green eyes narrow with anger as he pointed at the captain.

"There's somethin' bloody *wrong* with ye, Da. Ye can't keep just replacin' folks when some little slut shakes his hips at ye," spat the first mate. "And not to fuckin' bloody mention that yer the one who said we'd all be dancin' the hempen jig for stickin' our cocks in mates instead of skirts—"

"That's enough, Tom," warned Baltsaros sitting up, his eyes on burly young man. He rubbed a hand over his face, feeling suddenly twice his age and so very tired. With a sigh, he tilted his head at Tom.

"You're not going to tell Jon," the captain said softly.

Tom's brows pinched together as he chewed on the end of his narrow cigar, his big arms crossed over his chest. However, after a moment he shook his head once.

"Good," said Baltsaros, stretching his sore shoulders as he stood slowly. "That little 'slut' as you so aptly called him stole into my bed... not unlike the way someone else I know did."

Tom blinked and then looked down at the floor, pulling the cheroot from his mouth and wiping his lips with the back of his hand. When he looked back up, there was a wry grin on his face; the first mate chuckled softly and shook his head.

"Ye were half-asleep," recalled Tom. "And ye weren't about to pull away once I got my hands on ye." Tom smiled a little wider with the memory, but he quickly sobered and frowned again at the captain.

"I know. Not an excuse," agreed Baltsaros, walking up to the first mate. He felt ridiculous for letting himself be chastised by Tom, but he needed his full cooperation in the days to come; making a show of contrition to mollify the first mate was something he could do. "I'll keep my hands to myself," he continued, and reached up to cup the back of Tom's head, the younger man's short hair slightly coarse against his rough fingers. "I promise."

Tom's eyes softened slightly at the gentle touch, and the big man let out a slow sigh. After pulling the cheroot from his mouth and stubbing it out quickly in the empty cup on the table, Tom closed his eyes and leaned his cheek against Baltsaros's wrist.

"If I find him in here again, Da, I'll cut the bloody balls off o' him myself," swore Tom softly.

Baltsaros smiled. Still ruthless after all.

J on looked up from the crate he was tying when the door to the captain's quarters banged shut. In disbelief, he watched the young fisherman hurry away, a hand hastily working the fastenings at the front of his pants. Bitter bile rose up in his throat, and Jon clenched his jaw in anger, dropping the rope to the deck as he stood. A tightness in his chest made it hard to breathe as he tried to make sense of what he had just seen. Then, he saw the door open again and Tom step out, the first mate scanning the deck until he found Jon. Brows furrowed, Tom shook his head slowly.

Don't worry, said the first mate's eyes, and Jon swallowed, wanting to believe him. With lips pressed together, he nodded and started walking towards Tom. However, before he got halfway there, he spotted Oren sitting on the gunwale, his blue eyes trained on Jon as he made his way sternward. Jon wanted to avert his gaze but found that he couldn't as he watched the golden-skinned sylph's face split into a slow, wicked smile.

9

THE METTLE OF A MAN

Truth, like gold, is to be obtained not by its growth,
but by washing away from it all that is not
gold.

— LEO TOLSTOY

Jon flattened his hand on the tabletop and stared down at it, jaw tight with anger.

"Tell me again why I can't come with you?" he asked, his voice quiet and furious.

"Because it's dangerous," said Baltsaros and Tom, speaking as one.

Jon raised his eyes to the first mate; at least Tom looked a little shamefaced as he lifted his shoulders.

"What am I to do, then?" Jon said, turning his eyes to the captain.

"You'll do what you normally do, and obey Calum as you would me. He'll take over while we're gone," replied Baltsaros softly, frowning down at Jon.

Staring up at the older man, Jon breathed quickly through his nose.

"You really have no idea how insulting it is to have the both of you acting like nursemaids," Jon growled. "I'm not a wilting flower, for fuck's sake. I can hold my own! I didn't come all this fucking way to just sit in the ship while you two go gallivanting off to gods-know-where."

Tom's face had creased into an amused grin as Jon spoke, but Baltsaros's eyes had grown darker.

"My decision is final, Jon. This is only the first trip into the city. I need Tom with me, not only because I know I can count on him not to lose his head, but because he's acting the part of my slave," the captain said in a low voice. Leaning forward with his knuckles pressed to the mahogany table, Baltsaros stared hard at him for a moment. Jon watched the captain's expression begin to soften, some humour returning to his chiselled face.

"No, you're not a wilting flower, Jon. I'm honestly concerned with the safety of the whole crew—that's why we're anchoring so far from the harbour. I am going on the word of a man whose boat was stolen out from under him by my crew and, as much as I like the old man, I have no idea if anything he says is true. Polas is not even from the city; his people just do business in the fish markets. It's a different culture, Jon; one that is extremely wary of strangers. There are new rules to follow... harsh rules, from what I understand." The captain rounded the table and reached out to stroke Jon's dark curls back. "Patience, Jon. All right?"

Jon almost flinched at the touch, unable to forget the sly smile that had spread over Oren's elfin face. Instead he forced himself to close his eyes and lean into the captain's hand like he normally would.

As if I didn't know what you were up to, he thought bitterly. The previous day had been spent watching Oren as the young man made his way around the ship. Twice, the tall fisherman had approached the captain, both times his body language that of a fawning sycophant as he hung on Baltsaros's every word. It was enough to make a man sick. When the captain had quickly sent the boy away with a few harsh words, Jon had been childishly pleased; perhaps he had been imagining things. However, as Oren made his way belowdecks, Jon had raised his eyes and seen the captain's gaze following the willowy youth. When Baltsaros noticed Jon watching him, the older man's face had gone still, wiped of expression, before the captain had turned and walked away.

Jon opened his eyes and pulled away from Baltsaros's hand.

"Why are *they* still here?" he asked, looking up at the captain. He didn't want to say the boy's name.

Baltsaros narrowed his eyes at Jon, and he felt sure that his suspicions were grounded in *something*; it galled him that the first mate was once again covering for the captain.

They deserve each other, Jon thought, looking over at Tom. The big man's brow was furrowed in concern, his sea-green eyes on Jon's.

"I asked Polas to join the crew this morning," replied Baltsaros, dropping his hand. "He's mulling it over and will give me his answer before long. Migri and Oren are staying on until they can find a replacement boat or some other suitable accommodation." With a tilt of his head, he lifted his hand again, this time to Jon's cheek. "Don't worry, I want both of them off my ship," he said softly.

The words did nothing to appease Jon. They only showed that Baltsaros was aware that he had concerns, but Jon nodded anyway and bent his lips into a smile. The captain, satisfied with his response, smiled back and leaned in to kiss him quickly.

"I have things to take care of before we leave," said Baltsaros, straightening. "Tom, be ready to go in an hour."

Tom watched the captain depart then turned back to Jon, the same anxious expression on his face as before.

Jon folded his arms on the tabletop and rested his chin on his wrist, staring back at Tom.

"You hate lying to me," murmured Jon. "Yet, you fucking do it

139

anyway." He watched something flit across the big man's features, the first mate still frustratingly unreadable when he wanted to be.

"Not my secrets to tell, love," said Tom softly. "I ain't really lyin'... " The hard muscles in Tom's jaw moved under his short stubble as his eyes lost a little focus. "Like Da said: patience. Have a little patience and... I'll straighten him out for ye."

Tom sounded distracted, as if he was thinking of something else. With a sigh, the first mate leaned back in his chair and rubbed at the tattoos on his skin.

"A fuckin' slave again," Tom muttered, and Jon realized that the first mate was feeling some strain about revisiting the role. He remembered the slave collar in Tom's room and felt a sharp twinge; with shame, Jon realized that his jealousy was the furthest thing from the first mate's mind. Tom needed to be fitted for a new collar today. It seemed that some customs were strangely universal. Watching Tom touch the marks on his skin, Jon felt almost sick with the thought of how that would affect the normally fearless first mate.

Abandoning his petty grievances for the moment, Jon slid out of his chair, padding around to Tom to put his arms around the big man's shoulders from behind. With a sigh, he laid his cheek down on the first mate's short, dirty-blond hair.

"The other day Polas told me that your tattoos aren't *slave* tattoos per se," murmured Jon, his hands stroking the marked skin, fingertips skimming over the slightly raised lines as he spoke. "They're tattoos that belong to a nomadic people, a warrior people, strong and proud."

When Tom remained silent, Jon decided to push on with the tale.

"See... about a hundred or so years ago, there was a great war between tribes, one that lasted for nearly a generation. One tribe stood out in bravery and strength of heart, and they were completely unbeatable. But, the other tribes banded together and got help from powerful warlocks from this 'golden city'. To the lords of the city, they had promised the spoils of war: the women and children.

"In the end the strong were almost completely destroyed by the weak. Afraid for the fate of the tribe, the elders sent the women and children away in secret, scattering them like seeds to the wind, before the lords of the golden city could enslave them. Each child was given a tattoo that would show them the path back to their homeland so that they could one day find their way back… if the golden city fell. But, the lords of the city had many allies, and lots of the children were caught and brought back as slaves. The practice of tattooing their children continued… The 'marked' slaves, as they're called now, are the most valuable slaves because of their great strength and fortitude. They're also said to be fiercely loyal." Jon decided to leave out the part about skinning the slaves and tanning their decorated hides for souvenirs; Tom was worried enough as it was.

The first mate sat quietly for a moment and then let out a short grunt.

"Nice story," he said, his deep voice a low rumble against Jon's fingers. "Doesn't explain why I got them though." Tom lifted a hand and stroked his thumb along the inside of Jon's arm, a touch that brought out goosebumps on his skin.

"You said you got them from an old man, didn't you?" asked Jon as he straightened, an idea forming in his head. Tom nodded, and Jon continued. "Did he have tattoos himself?"

Tom looked up, his brow deeply creased in confusion. After a moment his eyebrows rose.

"Are ye sayin' ye think the ol' codger was one of them kids? He *did* have a mess o' lines like the ones he did me. Shit, and he was really fuckin' old." Tom's eyes were wide as he shifted to see Jon better.

"Maybe he saw something in you that reminded him of the warriors he was descended from: fierce and proud," said Jon with a grin. He thought it was *possible* that the old man was one of the children from the story—how he had wound up in the southern peninsula was a complete mystery, but where else would he have gotten the tattoos? However, Jon knew that even if he *was* a child of these nomadic warriors, the old man probably tattooed people for money and not out of some bestowment of honour; the little lie didn't hurt if it soothed Tom's worry somewhat.

Jon almost laughed out loud at his hypocrisy.

T om closed his eyes tight, remembering all too well the half-dozen times that he had been fitted for a collar. Granted, this time it was different; no one was holding him down nor was he tied up. Plus, Malik had been kind enough to put something between the metal and Tom's neck while he clamped the rivets and fastened the collar so it couldn't be taken off except by metal shears. The last time he'd had a collar put on, Tom had been so bruised that he hadn't been able to swallow for nearly a day.

The metal felt cold against his skin when Malik removed the rag, and Tom licked his lips and shivered. When his mouth filled with the thin spit of nausea, he quickly stood and spat over the side of the ship, knuckles white as he clung to the metal cleat, his breath heaving through clenched teeth.

"Hey, big guy, you going to be ok?" asked the dark-haired ship-wright, putting a hand lightly on Tom's shoulder.

Tom let out a short grunt and nodded his head quickly, closing his eyes again as he listened to Malik put his tools away. However, the first mate stayed pressed up against the side of the ship for another few minutes until the dizziness passed completely.

. . .

Half an hour later, outfitted in just a pair of shortened pants belted at the calf, Tom climbed down the rope ladder after the captain and settled between the oars of the small rowboat they were using to get to land. Though he had bragged to Jon about his proficiency in languages, Tom was still running through a few key phrases—"Yes, Master" being the one that stuck most in his craw—and feeling a little nervous as he fiddled with the metal band around his neck.

Polas and Baltsaros had explained that no one of any means went about Ereme'ia Balor, the "golden city" of Jon's story, without at least one slave. Since the captain wanted to fit in and be granted access to numerous establishments, the presence of a slave in his company was necessary; that Tom bore the tattoos of a highly valued one would only work to their advantage. With Polas's help, they had concocted a credible backstory about being travellers from somewhere the old fisherman, now a full member of the crew, called the Badlands. When Baltsaros had originally asked why they couldn't just speak the truth about being from the other side of the black mountain range, Polas had made the same strange sign across his chest that he made every time they mentioned their origins: an up-and-down movement of his fingers that touched spots on both shoulders and his sternum.

Tom smiled to himself, remembering the way the man had almost shat himself the first time they had explained where they were really from. Legends told here about the Devil's Isles were far more elaborate than back home, including stories of giant eels that could steal a man's soul by kissing him while in the guise of beautiful fish-bottomed women. Why anyone would want to kiss some tart with a tail was beyond him, but it had made for some pretty interesting listening. The part that had made the old fisherman the most nervous though was that, supposedly, a man could not cross through the Devil's Isles—or the Gods' Claws as they were called on this side of the mountain range—with his soul intact. Anyone caught sailing out of there was immediately deemed a ghost or a *duppy* and had their boats burned, and any men aboard were tossed into the sea.

So the Badlands it was. Baltsaros's northern accent could just pass for a rich Badlander, as long as he remembered to use the correct words. Both languages were similar and, while that was handy when it came to learning it quickly, it was becoming a pain in the ass to remember which one was the right word. Tom hoped he wasn't called on to speak too much. Still, despite all of his misgivings, he was pretty damn curious about this golden city, especially the "warlocks" that Jon had spoken of in the story.

As he curled his hands around the oars, Tom looked up and scanned the side of the ship for Jon. When he found him standing up on the gunwale with one arm through the shrouds and a deeply worried look on his face, the first mate chuckled a little and winked.

Be good, he thought. *Be safe.* Tom hoped he would be back real soon to coax some smiles out of the serious young man.

Feeling like a country bumpkin, Tom tried not to stare up, mouth agape, at the colossal doors that led to the walled city. He had never seen anything like them and had no idea what to expect when they finally made their way inside. Soon, he hoped. Weapons were allowed within Ereme'ia Balor, but visitors had to pay a tax for the "privilege" of wearing them on their persons, so Baltsaros and he were standing in a long line waiting for admittance.

Chafing a little at the long wait, Tom glanced around at the folks milling slowly around them. Standing amongst a pretty normal-looking bunch of peasant-types were a few of the tall, white-haired fisherfolk. Interestingly enough, none of them seemed to be sporting the double-ring of scars that Polas had, and Tom wondered if the old man wasn't telling them something.

Tom scratched his nose and quickly ducked his head to avoid

meeting the eyes of a fat man wearing blue silks; Tom was a slave, and slaves didn't have the *right* to look at anyone directly, he kept reminding himself. He gritted his teeth, his fists clenching and unclenching at his sides.

"Tom, you look like you're about to break something," murmured Baltsaros. "Or someone."

Tom let out a slow breath and nodded; straightening his shoulders, he glanced up at the captain.

Baltsaros was wearing a long black tunic, belted at the waist with a red sash. Tom recognized it as something he wore often when at home in Madierus, but the embroidery had been picked out of the hem. The captain's hair was tied back and braided in a long queue down his back, and his beard was oiled and tamed into a neat spade shape. Around one bicep, the older man wore what looked like a braided length of black leather, which Tom knew was just an oiled piece of black sailcloth. To finish the outfit, the captain wore a steel cuff over one wrist that had been stamped by Malik with the same symbol found on Tom's slave collar: the silhouette of a lion's head. It was a quickly cobbled-together outfit, but Polas thought it would pass muster.

The line inched along, and Tom nearly groaned from impatience. It seemed to him like the men at the gate were purposefully doing everything at a snail's pace. As he let his eyes wander again, Tom found himself staring once more in the direction of the fat man in blue, but this time, he looked curiously at the slaves standing with him.

Like Tom, the tall dark-haired man was tattooed. It was a slightly different configuration of dots and swirls from his own but definitely done in the same style. The other slave was a slight blonde woman, pretty enough to look at but with such a forlorn expression in her bright blue eyes that Tom had to look away.

As he glanced around himself, he met the eyes of another muscular, tattooed slave. The man's head was shaved on both sides, the short hair in the middle sticking up like a brush, and he had two silver rings in one nostril. The slave looked incredibly fierce because of it, and when the man nodded solemnly to Tom, the first mate was quick to return the gesture. Maybe the slaves here were better treated than he had been; this marked one certainly looked well fed, and he held his head high. However, when the other turned away, Tom saw that the man's back bore layers upon layers of scars just like his own.

With his heart beating a swift rhythm from the sight of the lash marks, Tom shuffled closer to the captain, embarrassed by the weakness that made him wish to bury his face against the older man.

Sensing Tom's discomfort, Baltsaros stared at him, his eyes a clear golden-brown in the bright morning sun.

"Stay a pace behind me, stop fidgeting, and stop looking around you like you want to start a fight. You were a slave long enough, start acting like one," said Baltsaros in a low, harsh whisper.

Tom clenched his jaw and looked down, nodding.

"Aye, Da," he murmured. Even at the best of times, Tom had made a lousy slave... but the captain was right; he was behaving foolishly. There was gold to be had here and maybe something even more valuable. He had to get a hold of himself. After all, it was just a bit of play-acting.

Following slowly along behind the captain, always a pace behind like a good little slave, Tom wondered if the city had taverns and whether they served beer on this side of the mountains. It had been far too long since he'd held a nice foamy dark beer in his hand. When he found himself grinning at the thought, Tom quickly sobered, letting out a frustrated huff of breath.

He doubted very much that slaves were given pints of beer to enjoy.

J on sat cross-legged on the planks, eating his lunch off of a metal plate. It was a gruel mash that Cook had flavoured with some nuts and berries they had found on a little spit of an island. Though it was far from inedible, Jon couldn't wait to eat something that wasn't gruel or fish; he hoped that while the captain and first mate were out scouting about the city, they had the presence of mind to pick up a few supplies. As he scraped at his plate with his wooden spoon, Jon narrowed his eyes at the man below who was pacing from one side of the ship to the other.

"What do you make of him?" he asked, looking up at Calum, who was lounging back on the quarterdeck bench.

The old man blinked at Jon in confusion a few times, and he passed a gnarled brown hand over his face before he squinted down at the main deck.

"Ye mean Migri, lad?" replied Calum, frowning down at Jon. When Jon nodded, licking his spoon, the old man shrugged. "Well, 'e ain't much fer words, that's fer bloody sure. Mean as a pinched badger. Broke Timmy's nose last night, ye hear? Over a claim o' bad dice. Big lout was loaded t' th' gunwalls. Took three o' 'em to haul 'im off t' the pokey."

Jon nodded again. That was the third time that the big fisherman had landed himself a night in the brig. The crew was on strict orders to leave the three strangers unmolested, but Jon knew that, left to their own devices, the pirates would have cut Migri to pieces and tossed him overboard by now. Watching the beefy, golden-skinned man cross the width of the boat again, Jon was reminded of a wild boar he had seen at a fair once. It had paced back and forth in its tiny cage the whole time the fair was in town, half-mad with the need to escape. Watching Migri made Jon just as tense.

After scanning the deck for the son and not seeing him, Jon looked back up at Calum.

"What about Oren?" he asked, the name bitter on his tongue.

Calum's mouth turned down at the corners as he thought, his dark eyes narrowed to the midday sun.

"Tha' boy better watch 'imself," muttered Calum after a long silence. " 'E's got trouble in 'is soul, like 'is ol' man. Do 'imself a favour if 'e were t' look up more to 'is grand-da. There's some fine mettle in Polas. A shame 'is kin's such trash."

Jon had to agree. He found it odd that a man so level headed and affable could have spawned such an unlikeable character like Migri... and grand-sired such an ass-kissing, little twat. Jon grinned softly to himself; life with pirates had done wonders to his vocabulary.

With a sigh, he turned to look back across the water to the jungle through which Baltsaros and Tom had disappeared a few hours earlier.

"Don' worry, lad," chuckled Old Calum. "Them's been up t' worse. Tom'll see 'em home safe. 'E always does."

Frowning, he wondered if Calum was wrong—at least this time. Jon hoped that Baltsaros had the sense to realize that what he asked of Tom would be completely traumatizing for a lesser man. As it was, Jon had never seen Tom look so unnerved as he had earlier, his pallor noticeable even under his deep tan.

After placing the plate down beside himself on the wooden planks, Jon drew up his knees and wrapped his arms around them, resigned to wait for their return come nightfall.

10

FEAR AND BLOOD

Fear is pain arising from the anticipation of evil.

— ARISTOTLE

Beneath Baltsaros's boots the cobblestones were smooth and even, and the street was well maintained. To his left, he could see what looked like swampy farmland within the city walls with a handful of slaves bent over or kneeling in the water among tall, green shoots. To his right there was a series of paddocks holding horses of various breeds, some of which he did not recognize. Behind them were other enclosed areas, and Baltsaros could see slaves feeding cattle and goats beyond. In a little field next to the fences, the captain spotted children working between rows of what looked like potato plants; all of them wore the thin metal collars of slaves.

Brow furrowed, Baltsaros picked up his pace slightly, trusting Tom to follow. In the distance, at what would probably be the end of the arrow-straight thoroughfare, was a stepped pyramid. Far off to the right and left of the squat structure were two more and, when Baltsaros looked back towards the city walls on either side, he saw yet another pair. Five pyramids arranged in a circle within the city walls; Tom's triangles-within-a-square tattoo made more sense now. Narrowing his eyes at the stone pyramid ahead, Baltsaros wondered what they were for.

The throng of people became thicker as they approached a large paved space that held a thriving marketplace. To avoid being jostled, the captain moved to the side of the street and stopped to watch the crowd pass by. Tom, on alert as always, stood at his side with his head ducked, eyes shrewdly scanning everyone who came near. Baltsaros turned and watched the first mate' hand lift slowly to his ear as he looked for the cheroot he usually had perched there. Finding none and obviously remembering why, Tom let out a rapid string of curses under his breath. The first mate clenched his jaw, rounded his shoulders, and let out a long slow exhale. Baltsaros pressed his lips together and looked back towards the market. Tom wasn't holding up as well as the captain had hoped. It definitely didn't help that the big man was probably beginning to feel the withdrawal from the mild narcotic that was found in the slim black cigars he habitually smoked. It was probably good that they not stay in town for long... at least not today.

Chin raised, and with a haughty expression on his chiselled features, the captain pushed his way back into the crowd, shadowed by the first mate. At first glance, the wares that were for sale were not much different than those that sold on the other side of the black mountain range. However, upon closer inspection, there were items that were baffling to Baltsaros. Turning a small earthenware bowl in his hands, he frowned at the corked hole in its side. Was it a serving vessel of some sort?

"Da, take a look at this," murmured Tom, pointing to a big cast-iron pot.

Baltsaros frowned, confused by the first mate's interest in the normal-looking pot. He then saw the manufacturer's mark: a double anvil with a circle around it. There was no mistaking it— the cast-iron pot had been made in the mainlands, not far from the mining and smelting town where he had found Tom.

Curious, the captain went from stand to stand, his eyes picking out familiar items at each one: watered silks from the southern peninsula, pottery from the midland isles, even an elk-bone throwing game from his own homeland in the north. Obviously, trade was flourishing with the east, but how?

Lifting a small silk scarf with a smile, he caught the merchant's attention.

"How much for this?" he asked in the foreign tongue.

The merchant grinned wide, showing off gold eyeteeth.

"Half a *dokscha*!" said the man. "Very cheap for something so beautiful!"

Baltsaros made as if to look for flaws in the brown- and copper-dyed fabric, curling his lip in a doubtful sneer.

The merchant, seeing the captain's hesitation, let out a pained sigh.

"The price does not please you? It is such exquisite work! An unusual colour! Straight from the silk makers of Jalon T'sek!" exclaimed the man, his eyes wide and guileless. "But... for a discerning man like yourself, I suppose I could part with it for four *rukscha*. No less or my family will starve. Please!"

Baltsaros continued to bargain with the seller until they agreed on one fifth of a *dokscha* or two *rukscha*—the equivalent of ten pieces of silver. In the southern peninsula where it had been made, not in this Jalon T'sek that the man claimed, the scarf would fetch a price of three or four pieces of silver and no more. It was exorbitant.

Polas had explained that gold was plentiful but hard metals scarce; the conversion rate was one steel *dokscha* to three standard gold pieces or forty-eight silver. Not having any of these steel coins—Polas's meagre, hidden stash having been stolen along with his boat—Baltsaros had had Tom beat some gold coins with a hammer to obscure the stamps on them.

The merchant stared down at the damaged gold coin in his palm for a long time before he looked back up at Baltsaros, his brown eyes narrowed in suspicion.

"Where did you say you were from, stranger? I don't recognize your accent," said the man, all pretence of camaraderie dropped.

Baltsaros tensed; *stranger* was synonymous with *intruder* here. Letting his lips curl into a sheepish smile, the captain touched the medallion on his chest, a trinket he knew would mean absolutely nothing to the merchant.

"I *was* worried my accent would give me away," he said, tapping the little silver disc. "I'm from the Otak clan. I needed to get away from the heat for a while, so I decided to visit your beautiful city!" Baltsaros grinned wider when the salesman nodded, his eyes on the medallion. The man, not wanting to seem ignorant, made as if to suddenly recognize it. According to Polas, the well-known clan rarely ventured beyond their walled compound in the Badlands and, while they did have a sigil, very few would have seen it firsthand.

"Of course!" said the man. "I hear that the Badlands are most oppressive this time of year! How silly of me to not notice the Otak clan's sigil! It must also be so nice for you to be around civilized folk for a change." The last was said with a wry grin and a laugh, a friendly gibe about the far-off Badlands. Polas said that the citizens of Ereme'ia Balor—or Balorians as they called themselves—viewed anyone from outside the city as uncultured. The old man was proving to be an invaluable source of information though it made Baltsaros wonder again whether Polas was more than just the simple fisherman that he claimed to be.

Chuckling at the merchant's words, Baltsaros accepted his change of a single *rukscha* and bid the man farewell. After fingering the slim, oval piece of bronze thoughtfully, he tucked it into the pouch at his waist. At this rate he would be a poor man before long. He would ask Polas later whether he would raise suspicions if he tried to trade broken steel swords.

Across the square, Baltsaros could see a number of food stalls. Curious to see what they served and feeling peckish, the captain and first mate slowly made their way over to where a man was selling what looked like meat and vegetables on long skewers.

"It must cost you a fortune to feed that brute," said the tall, dark-haired merchant good-naturedly as he handed over two skewers to Baltsaros.

The captain was momentarily confused until he realized that the man meant Tom. Instantly he wondered if he had made a blunder by buying his "slave" some food from the market. Laughing in response, Baltsaros nodded to the man before he turned away. Glancing around quickly, the captain tried to see whether slaves ate near their masters or if there was some other convention he was meant to follow.

It was hard to discern which slaves belonged to the patrons and which to the merchants; everywhere Baltsaros looked, he saw slave collars. Finally deciding that it seemed safe enough just to share his food, the captain handed over one of the sticks of meat over to Tom who accepted it gratefully; the first mate's face was set in serious lines, and Baltsaros couldn't remember ever seeing Tom so anxious.

"It'll be ok," he murmured to Tom in Common. "You'll feel better when you've eaten." It was everything he could do not to place a reassuring hand on the young man's shoulder.

Tom nodded as he chewed, his green-blue eyes darting around him.

"So many fuckin' slaves, Da. Seems like too many, don't it?" asked Tom in a low voice, wiping his lips with the back of his hand.

It was true; Baltsaros had never seen such a high number of slaves in one place before. Looking around him, he calculated that there were probably four or five slaves for every free man. It was bizarre... Why were there so many, and how were they being kept from rebelling in force? What were they used for? Most seemed to be simply following their masters around the square, arms laden down with purchases. Some were obviously bed slaves; a tall man in a scarlet tunic walked by with two nearly naked slave girls trailing behind him, their high breasts painted or tattooed with flowers that matched the embroidery on their master's clothing.

Others seemed to act as bodyguards; Baltsaros could see marked slaves that walked behind their masters holding tall spears, the powerful young men all sporting interestingly shorn hair with their fierce eyes often ringed with black. Some slaves, employed by the merchants, did nothing but stand around or package purchased goods.

"Status symbols," guessed Baltsaros, taking another bite of the savoury meat. When the captain turned his eyes to a pair of marked slaves waiting for their master to finish a transaction, he saw that one of them was staring intently at Tom's tattoos. In dismay he watched the man nudge his companion and point his chin at the first mate, tilting his head to murmur something to the other. Belatedly, it occurred to the captain why Tom's tattoos would stand out.

"Put a hand over your ribs," he whispered quickly to Tom, catching the big man's eye. Frowning, the first mate crossed his right arm across his ribs, his big hand obscuring the tattoos that swirled down his ribcage... the ones that showed the path home past the Devil's Isles.

J on peered at the maps that Nathaniel had unrolled on the crate, confused by all the dots and lines that joined everything.

"See, I knew they were maps, but I wasn't sure what of," said the middle-aged cartographer, using a cup to hold down the edge of the curling paper. "I was thinking stars at first, but it didn't explain why everything was superimposed on what looks like a shoreline. Polas here was kind enough to educate me." Nathaniel smiled wide, showing the slight gap between his front teeth. "It's like a calendar and a map at the same time. It shows the fisherfolk where they're supposed to be fishing on each day of the month according to a complicated set of rituals. It's absolutely fascinating."

Holding down the other edge of the map, Jon nodded and furrowed his brow.

"These dots are... rituals?" he asked uncertainly.

Polas nodded and placed a calloused finger on one of the dots, slowly tracing one of the thin lines to the next dot over.

"Yes. This is, ah... blessing of *soft*. If it is well received, we go along this path. If it is not, we go to this," said the old man, tapping another dot. "This is the blessing of *hard*."

"Blessing?" asked Jon, confused by what Polas meant by soft and hard.

The old man nodded again and moved his finger, tapping dot after dot.

"Light, dark, young, old, one, two, barren, virgin..." he listed.

"Wait, what? Virgin?" asked Jon, looking at Polas in confusion. "What do you mean by virgin? What are we talking about here? *People*?" Something about this "blessing" business was filling Jon with a feeling of extreme dread.

"Yes, people. Well... slaves," agreed Polas with frown. "They are blessed, and if gods are happy, then is good. If not, more blessings until they are."

Jon's mouth was dry. Nathaniel was staring down at the map, jotting something down on a piece of paper, lost in thought. Obviously, the man had not come to the same realization that Jon had.

"Polas... by *blessing*... do you mean *sacrifice*?" he asked quietly. When the old man stared at him blankly, Jon realized he didn't understand the word.

Nathaniel looked up with his forehead creased and hazel eyes on Polas.

"Do these people die?" asked Jon quietly.

"Yes," said the old fisherman with a bitter laugh. "With much blood for the gods."

After moving quickly away from the tattooed slaves, Baltsaros and Tom made their way out of the market-place and back onto the main thoroughfare. They ducked behind a small structure, and Baltsaros rubbed the silk scarf in the dirt to dull the colours to an almost uniform tan. He then draped it over the first mate's shoulder and under his arm, turning it into a sling; the fake injury would work to hide the map of the spires on Tom's rib cage.

From this close, the big man smelled of nervous sweat, and it *pulled* at something inside Baltsaros. As they stood hidden from view, the captain placed a hand over Tom's heart, dismayed by how fast it was going. Tom leaned into his touch and let out a shuddery sigh.

"I'm sorry, Da. There's just so many," whispered Tom. "I'll be ok. I just need to stop..." The first mate shook his head, his sea-green eyes unfocused. "Did ye see their backs? Da, if somethin' happens to ye... an' I'm here..." A shiver ran through Tom's body, his heart racing beneath Baltsaros's palm.

"Listen to me, Tom. Nothing will happen to me. To us. Nothing, do you understand me?" murmured the captain, reaching up to touch Tom's cheek, a brief, soft caress before he adjusted the sling and stepped back. "Now... get a hold of yourself." Without warning, he smacked Tom across the cheek he had cupped tenderly only a moment earlier.

Tom's head snapped to the side with a grunt. When he turned back to the captain, the first mate's eyes crackled with blue-green fire.

"That's better," said Baltsaros with a nod.

With a soft chuckle, Tom knuckled the red mark on his face and nodded back.

"All right. I'm ok. I've got yer back, Da," said the first mate, straightening his shoulders. "Head on the prize... Let's find out where the gold's at an' get the fuck outta here, aye?"

Baltsaros's eyes turned to the closest pyramid.

"Yes," he said quietly. "Gold."

Head aching and reeling with the knowledge that they were dealing with a civilization, if it could even be called one, that relied on the death of dozens of people a week just to plan their activities, Jon made his way numbly down the stairs. Not only was fishing dictated by human sacrifice, but harvest, beer-making...

Laundry days for fuck's sake! he thought angrily, pulling open the door to his quarters. The most distressing part of all this was that the captain *knew* about the blood rituals and hadn't said anything to anyone.

There was a soft noise and Jon's head turned. Standing next to the open chest at the foot of the bed was Oren. The boy was frozen in place, a guilty flush on his face.

"What the *fuck* are you doing?" growled Jon, balling his fists. "Get the fuck away from there!"

Recovering quickly from his surprise, Oren straightened and smiled coyly.

"Oh, I thought I leave something in here the other day," said the tall youth, his clear blue eyes narrowed at Jon. "When I was *with* your captain."

There was no doubt in Jon's mind what the young fisherman meant when he had sneered the word. Before he had a chance to warn Oren that he was in no mood to be fucked with, the younger man continued.

"Oh, yes. Your captain, he did me. Did me hard and good," cooed the willowy youth. "He says I was like a perfect one."

With a strangled cry Jon leapt forward, intent on grabbing Oren. The young fisherman darted backwards with a laugh, evading Jon's grasp.

He couldn't understand why Oren was purposefully baiting

him like this, but he was suddenly past all caring; the anxiety and anger of the past few days gave life to a crazed demon that took over Jon's body. When he lashed out to hit Oren, and the fisherman tried to jump backwards again, Jon let out a dark laugh as the youth's head hit the wall behind him. Oren was trapped, and his blue eyes widened with that realization. Hands up in supplication, the tall young man shook his head at Jon.

"It's… ah… it's joke," said Oren, his Common failing him as his predicament began to infuse real fear into him.

Jon's fists connected with the younger man's abdomen, first the right, then the left, doubling Oren over in a pained gasp. Fingers snarling in the fisherman's long white dreadlocks, Jon dragged the other forward and kneed him solidly in the face. Oren collapsed on the floor with a groan, curling into a ball. Jon could hear him whining softly in his native tongue, the only word that he understood being "please".

"Shut it," yelled Jon, his chest heaving and eyes burning. "Shut the fuck up, you little shit. You think the captain would want *you*? Do you? I will break your godsdamned hands if you ever fucking touch him. Did you touch him? *Did you*?" He delivered a hard kick to the boy's side, eliciting a satisfying grunt. Kicking Oren again, Jon smiled. He was glad that he was wearing boots.

"I think I changed my mind," Jon said, his voice a low growl. "I want you to beg. Come on, boy… beg for your life."

Below him, Oren began to sob.

T he open square that fronted the stepped pyramid was empty save for a few slaves that carried bundles on their heads as they made their way to one of the side streets. Baltsaros stood looking up at the stone structure for a long time, his arms crossed over his chest.

With interest, the captain saw that the pyramid, wider than it was tall, had gutters running down its steps that disappeared under the flat stones at the base of it. When he leaned down to peer thoughtfully at one of the gutters, he could see that it was stained dark brown; in fact, everywhere the paving stones met across the square, there was a thick, dried residue. He spied holes placed in the ground at regular intervals, and a fascinating picture began forming in Baltsaros's head.

"It reeks like the bloody pit o' hells, Da," said Tom nervously, his nose wrinkled. "What the fuck is this place?"

"I'm not sure," lied Baltsaros, looking around. It didn't seem like any sacrifices would be performed today, unless they happened after dark. Dusk was falling, and it was a shame that they had to leave so soon.

"I don't like this," muttered Tom, rubbing his thumb against the side of his jaw. "Not one bloody bit."

With a nod and a sigh, Baltsaros motioned for Tom to follow him. They would come back tomorrow; tonight he would ask Polas more about the sacrifices, specifically about when they normally happened.

As the captain and first mate made their way slowly back towards the main gate, Baltsaros was surprised to see that not many were walking in the same direction as they were.

"Ye'd think the street would be packed with folks leavin'," said Tom, echoing the captain's misgivings.

When they reached the gate, the reason was instantly apparent for the lack of foot traffic: the giant doors were closed and barred.

"Excuse me," Baltsaros said, stepping over to one of the guards. "Why is the gate closed?"

The tall man looked the captain up and down before answering, his mouth hidden behind a black cloth.

"Curfew."

After thanking the guard for the curt answer, Baltsaros turned to Tom. The first mate was staring at him with a distraught look in his eyes; the sight of such weakness in the big man brought about a strange twist of worry in his own gut.

"What d'he say, Da?" asked Tom quietly, his jaw tight and nostrils slightly flared.

"The gate's shut for the night, Tom," replied Baltsaros, wishing he could put his arms around the big man to reassure him; the tremors that shook Tom at the captain's words were noticeable even from a distance in the failing light. "Come, my boy. Let's find somewhere to sleep, shall we?"

J on was about to kick Oren in the side again when he was pulled backwards by hard hands. With a yelp, Jon landed solidly against the corner of the heavy table and fell to his knees on the rug. Before he had a chance to bring a hand up, a big fist connected with his jaw, and his world exploded in a flash of light and pain. The whimper he let out was followed by a retch when his mouth filled with blood; opening his eyes in confusion, Jon saw that Migri stood above him, his face distorted in fury.

"My son," said the big fisherman, pointing a thick-knuckled finger at Jon. "My son!" repeated Migri with a shout when Jon made no reply. The man's Common was extremely poor; Jon knew that he couldn't communicate beyond a few simple words here and there. However, he quickly realized that even if he could explain the situation, it wouldn't make the slightest difference to Oren's father. All he cared about was that someone was attacking his son.

Oren spoke rapidly to his father as he slowly got to his feet. With some fatalistic satisfaction, Jon saw that the younger man's face was a mess of bruises, and his nose was a swollen, squashed-looking thing that leaked blood down Oren's chin. At least if he was going to die at the hands of Migri, he had done some permanent damage to the son. Served the little bastard right.

Gods, who am I becoming? he thought in alarm.

Body singing with the buzz of adrenaline, Jon crouched low trying to gauge whether he'd be able to take down Migri with a leg-sweep and grapple. It could be a thoroughly pointless endeavour; even if he managed to get the upper hand on Migri, it would leave him open to retaliation by Oren. Gritting his teeth, Jon tried desperately to come up with a plan of attack.

"Oi there," said Calum from the open doorway. "Let th' boy alone." The old pirate limped into the room, his eyes darting from Migri to Jon with his face set in serious lines. After staring hard at Jon for a moment, Calum motioned with a gnarled hand for him to stay down.

"It's my fault," said Jon between clenched teeth. "I should have kept my head."

"Should'a, would'a... lad," said Calum, holding his hands up as he approached the big fisherman. "Migri. Stop now... peace, aye? D'ye understand that? *Peace*? C'mon, let's all be takin' a breath o' fresh air, aye, mates? Get yer hot heads out in th' open t' work things out—" Before Calum could finish, Migri stepped forward with a roar and smashed his fist into the old man's nose with an audible crack.

Even before he dropped to the ground, Jon somehow knew that Calum was dead.

With a hoarse sob, Jon sprang to his feet, his hand darting to the knife he kept at his belt. In an instant he was on Migri, knocking the bigger man to the ground and straddling him as bucked and struggled. In an almost dreamlike state, Jon watched his hand come down, strange and slow, and drive the knife point-first into the fisherman's eye; there was little resistance when it sunk into Migri's brain right down to the hilt.

Jon went numb as the body beneath him twitched twice and went still. There was a loud keening noise in his ears, and he blinked slowly trying to clear his head.

Calum is dead.

The room spun and darkened. Jon stared at the blood on the hand still wrapped around the handle of the knife.

Calum is dead and it's my fault.

The keening had stopped, and Jon looked around in confusion.

After getting to his feet shakily, he walked over to the basin. It would be ok. It would be all right. Maybe Calum wasn't dead. Maybe he hadn't just killed a man. Maybe he was asleep in his bed, safe against Baltsaros or Tom's side. He leaned over the basin and vomited, the bile burning the shallow cut in his mouth. Maybe if he closed his eyes, everything would go back to normal, but he gagged again, remembering the way the blade slid into the man's brain like a hot knife into butter.

Breathing deeply, Jon pulled himself away from the basin, wiping his mouth on his wrist. The front of his pants was wet where he had pissed himself.

Calum is dead and this isn't a dream. And, oh gods, I killed him.

Jon walked unsteadily to the crumpled form of the old sailor and sank to his knees on the rug. The motion caused him to realize that he was in extreme pain; his ribs throbbed with his heartbeat and screamed with every breath. He wouldn't be surprised if one or more were broken. With a shaky hand, he touched Calum's neck, searching for a pulse. However, the way that the old man stared sightlessly at the ceiling was enough to kill any hope of finding one.

When he heard someone approach, Jon froze, instinctively knowing who it was. With his heart redoubling its already frantic pace, he raised his eyes and met the wide, wet stare of the man standing above him.

With a shudder, Jon held out a hand to Polas, the word "please" on his lips.

11

A WILLING SLAVE

Tom followed the captain in the direction of an inn that someone had been kind enough to point out to them. Eyes on his feet, the first mate breathed in time to his walking: one inhale for every three steps, one exhale for every four. His jaw was clenched so tight that his back teeth had started aching, but he couldn't relax. The collar felt like a noose around his neck, like it was tightening, but there would be no reprieve tonight since he'd have to sleep with the fucking thing on.

Stumbling against Baltsaros when the man stopped suddenly at the door of the inn, Tom clutched at the captain to steady himself and let out a pained grunt when his hand was grabbed and twisted. Wrist bent at sharp angle, Tom looked up at Baltsaros, his chest so tight he could barely breathe.

"Watch where you're going and don't touch me," Baltsaros hissed quietly. "People are looking at you. Say 'Apologies, Master'."

"Apologies... Master," repeated Tom in the Balorian tongue, the words like broken glass in his mouth. He shuddered and almost let out a groan when the captain released him.

I need a bloody drink.

Baltsaros's dark eyes held his a moment longer, not a shred of

163

sympathy on his chiselled face, before turning to open the door. Miserable, Tom passed through the doorway behind the captain with his head held low.

The room they walked into was brightly lit and the hewn boards smooth and clean under Tom's bare feet. All around him, the first mate could hear the sounds of talking and laughing, but he didn't dare raise his eyes. The last thing Tom wanted to see were free men enjoying themselves. The big man swallowed back his ire and just stood quietly by Baltsaros's side, chewing on the inside of his cheek while the captain waited to speak to the proprietor.

It was as if, by putting on the collar and stepping into this gods-blasted world of slavers, Tom was taken back to the hells that five years with the captain had finally started erasing from his soul. All the anger, frustration, pain and fear... yes, fear, was creeping back under his skin like stinging poison, but here he could not spit in his master's eye. He couldn't crack his fist against any slave-lover who stared at him. No... He had to play the part of the obedient slave, and it was making him physically ill.

Not *once* in the decade he had served as a hard labourer in the mines, as an unwilling bed slave for anyone who could pay, or as a bare-knuckle fighter in the pits, had Tom bowed or scraped to any man. They had beaten him senseless over and over, but the only thing that had kept him going was his refusal to submit willingly. He had fought them every step of the way, and he had never broken.

No—that was just the lie he kept telling himself.

Tom felt nauseous.

It was a whip—a thick, black leather bullwhip—that had finally made him beg and weep. His flesh had been torn over and over into gory ribbons. He remembered the way his master had cracked the whip beside him, pausing, laughing, taking his time like he was courting a lover; Tom had been kept on edge, never sure when it would slice into him, and it had become the living fear that poisoned him still. Sometimes, he had been tied up for days, the smell of his festering wounds ripe in his nose.

Tom licked his lips and swayed slightly, remembering the way he had screamed until his voice was no more.

"Is your slave ill?" asked a man from somewhere close by.

Tom slowly glanced up, frowning.

Eyes down ye fuckin' worthless piece of shit, so help me gods, I'll cut yer cock off at the root, said his master, standing over him, pants undone.

He blinked the memory away.

"I don't want him contaminating the other slaves in the barn if he's sick," continued the fat man with the curly beard and dirty apron. The proprietor stared at the first mate with a worried look on his ruddy face, and Tom quickly looked back down again, glaring at the floor between his feet.

"The barn?" asked Baltsaros. Tom could hear a smile in the older man's voice, and he could see the captain's look of polite confusion in his mind's eye.

"Yes, sir, we have a sturdy barn out back where we keep the slaves for the night. They're all chained apart so there won't be any damage to your goods. Though with this fella... Well, he looks like he could take a lick and not be worse for wear, hey?" said the fat man with a chuckle. "Do you fight him in the ring ever? I'd put good money..." The man's voice droned on cheerfully.

Tom's head spun.

Sleepin' in the barn chained to the wall like a dog surrounded by slaves chained to the fuckin' wall like bloody dogs...

"I'm afraid I have to insist that he stay in my room," said the captain, cutting off the proprietor as the man started quoting prices for slave accommodation.

Tom closed his eyes.

"That's... an unusual request," said the man slowly. "I assure you, sir, your chattel will remain unmolested if that's what you're worried about. My personal guarantee."

Tom balled his fists and held his tongue.

"It is a question of the quality of my sleep," replied the captain, his tone amicably apologetic yet firm. "I rest better with him in the room. I hope you understand. It is by no means a slight to your establishment; I am simply accustomed to having him watch over me while I sleep. I hope this won't be a problem? He is fiercely loyal, I assure you."

Tom heard the sound of money clinking and let out a slow, quiet breath. Spared. Saved. But not free yet.

After the captain made arrangements for some food to be sent to the room, he beckoned for Tom to follow him. They went up the narrow staircase and down one side of a long hallway to a wooden door marked with a symbol that Tom didn't recognize. Following Baltsaros into the room, he looked around. A narrow bed, a wooden chair next to a low shelf mounted on the far wall, and a chamber pot in the corner.

Shitty accommodations, but at least they were away from prying eyes. He pulled off the makeshift sling, flexing his arm as he watched Baltsaros walk over to sit down on the edge of the bed. The captain looked hard at him, his face set in serious lines.

Now that they were alone, Tom felt a little better. It was just an act, after all. Just a stupid piece of metal around his neck. Jaw clenched tight, Tom rubbed the back of his head; when his fingers made contact with the slave collar, he felt his skin crawl.

With a grunt, Tom dropped down to his knees and put his knuckles to the floor; straightening his legs behind him, he began doing quick press-ups.

"What are you doing?" asked the captain.

"What does it look like I'm bloody doin'?" replied Tom curtly. The exercise felt good; his muscles were stiff from tension, and he was full of nervous energy. He wanted a drink or a smoke, but he figured this would have to do.

"Tom, I'm sorry," said Baltsaros quietly.

The words stopped the first mate in mid-lift, and he looked up at the captain. Baltsaros was staring at him with a thoughtful look on his face, his stark brows low over his eyes, hooding them in shadow.

Tom frowned and nodded, looking back at the floor between his hands as he continued his press-ups with a grunt. *Sorry...*

"I didn't know it would be so hard on you," said the captain matter-of-factly.

Tom felt a flash of anger and let himself up on his knees, glaring at Baltsaros in disbelief.

"What fuckin' part of 'I don't fuckin' want to do it' did ye not understand, Da?" asked the first mate, shaking his head. He stared wide-eyed at the captain a moment longer; the older man was silent and expressionless, a sun-darkened hand slowly stroking his greying beard.

Tom fell back on his ass to start doing some sit-ups, the boards hard against the knobs of his spine. Baltsaros was the smartest person he knew, yet he blew Tom away with how frustratingly bloody *clueless* he was at times. Breathing deep as he felt his stomach muscles begin to burn, Tom closed his eyes and worked on clearing his mind.

There was a knock at the door, and Tom heard the captain get up from the bed to cross the room. When Baltsaros kicked softly at the first mate's shin a moment later, Tom opened his eyes and saw that the older man was holding a plate with two trenchers in one hand and an earthenware mug in the other.

"I'm not hungry," Tom lied, sitting up.

"Now you're acting like a fool, Tom," said the captain with a small smile as he sank down gracefully to the floor next to him.

When his stomach growled in response to the sight of food, Tom jutted out his bottom jaw and accepted the trencher from the captain with a scowl. The hard loaf of bread was hollowed and filled with some meaty stew; it smelled absolutely bloody delicious.

"Here," said the captain, handing the mug to Tom. "Have it all. It's yours."

Tom let out a derisive snort and took a deep swallow of the dark beer.

"Ye are, are ye?" he asked, taking a big bite of the bread and stew. "Yer *sorry?*"

Though his eyes were narrowed at the captain, Tom's anger and frustration had begun to dissolve as the food and beer worked their magic on him. He sighed and shook his head.

"Hells… Listen… This is just doin' some really shitty things to my head. Can't think straight. Rememberin' things," he explained, gesturing with his mug as he chewed a savoury mouthful. After washing it down with some more beer, Tom licked the side of the bread to catch a drop of gravy before it fell. "Somethin' about this place gives me the bloody willies. I got ants in my skin. This ain't helpin'." Tom flicked a nail against the side of the collar. "Keep yer bloody sorrys to yerself."

The captain remained strangely quiet as he sat cross-legged beside Tom, his dark eyes just watching the first mate as he ate.

"Aint'cha eatin', Da?" asked Tom, licking his fingers when he had finished his trencher. The captain looked down at the bread in his hand and broke it in two, careful not to spill any of the stew that was soaked into it. After handing one half to Tom, Baltsaros took a bite out of his.

Tom frowned. Maybe this place was doing weird things to the both of them.

"Why're we even here, Da?" he asked quietly. "Why'd we come? I mean… adventure is grand, gold is better, but is that really why?"

Baltsaros blinked slowly, chewing the last of his meal carefully.

"I need to be here," said the captain after he had swallowed, his eyes losing focus for a moment as he stared off across the room. The older man's brow creased again, and he lifted his hand to brush the crumbs out of his moustache before turning his eyes back to the first mate. "Jon's dreams, your tattoo, the similarity of the language to my mother tongue." Baltsaros accepted the mug from Tom and took a small sip before handing it back. "I'm not normally given to fanciful thoughts, but doesn't it seem like too much of a coincidence?"

The words poured a cold trickle of dread down Tom's back,

but before he could think of an answer, Baltsaros waved away the question and rose to his feet.

"It's not important. Ignore me, Tom," muttered the captain, looking down at the first mate with a frown. "There's something else we need to take care of."

Curious, the first mate watched the captain stride quickly to the door to pull the lock and, after a moment's hesitation, drag the chair over to wedge it under the latched handle.

Baltsaros then crossed the room back to the bed where he sank down and folded his hands in his lap. For a few heartbeats, the captain just stared back at Tom, his face unreadable.

Then he spoke in a soft voice.

"Slave, stand and strip," said Baltsaros.

The words were like a stinging slap. Frowning at the captain, Tom shook his head slowly.

"Da, that ain't fuckin' funny," he said.

Baltsaros tilted his head slightly and raised an eyebrow.

"You're wearing a slave collar, aren't you? So stand and strip, *slave*," repeated the captain, his voice now a low growl.

"I said that's not funny," growled Tom back. However, somewhere buried in his annoyance was a soft pulse of lust, and he felt disgusted at himself.

"I fail to understand how this differs from what I normally ask of you, Tom," murmured Baltsaros. The older man's eyes were dark chips of glass in his stark face. "You *are* my slave, are you not?"

"No... what?" asked Tom in growing alarm. What in the hells was the matter with the captain?

"Call me Master," sneered Baltsaros. "Now strip. Your body is mine, *slave*. Do as you're told."

The words... a familiar command... twisted. Tom felt dirty and betrayed.

"Don't call me that," snarled Tom. "An' I sure as shit ain't callin' you 'Master.'"

At this, Baltsaros's expression shifted, the cold glare replaced instantly with curiosity.

"Because I am *not* your master?" asked the captain softly, raising his eyebrows. Baltsaros's bowed lips quirked up at the corners in something that was not quite a smile.

Tom let out a short grunt in reply, eyes fierce as he stared up at the older man.

"Yet you call me 'Da', and I am no more your father than I am your master."

"That's different," was all that Tom could think of saying.

"Tom, come closer," said Baltsaros with a sigh.

The first mate looked at his captain suspiciously before climbing to his feet. He took a step forward and crossed his arms over his chest, not understanding what in the hells was expected of him.

Sure he called Baltsaros "Da" but... He cleared his throat and shook his head.

"Listen, I call ye that because yer good to me. It started as a lark to get under Abetha's skin, aye, but... yer..." Tom closed his mouth, crushing his lips together tight as he breathed quickly through his nose. This was harder to explain than he had expected. "Ye mean... uh... to me—bloody hells, Baltsaros... there's no higher word I can think of... so yer my Da. And... since ye've never minded..."

He looked desperately at Baltsaros; he knew it was a ridiculous thing to call the man he'd been fucking for years. It sounded more than a little perverted but, really, who cared?

"Tom... you'd do *anything* for me, wouldn't you? Even pose as a slave though it's obviously hurting you to do so?" asked Baltsaros softly. "Come closer and kneel."

Tom stepped forward and went down on one knee and then the other. Baltsaros reached out a hand and touched his hair, the captain's hand then sliding down the side of Tom's face. With a sigh, the big man leaned into the touch and frowned. The new gentleness that Jon had brought out in Baltsaros pricked at the scar tissue in his heart, but he clung to it like a man drowning.

"Aye, Da," said the first mate with a small nod. "Ye know I would."

"Then, how are you *not* my slave, if you obey me so?" asked Baltsaros, stroking his thumb along Tom's cheek. "Why, when I set you free, did you decide to pledge your body and soul to my happiness? You bind yourself to me... Tom, I need you, but *why do you need me?*"

Tom's eyes had closed slowly with the captain's caress, but at the renewed slave talk, he stared up in dismay at the man he loved. The captain sat quietly with his warm hand against Tom's face, a deep crease marking his smooth brow. The first mate let out a slow breath and placed his hands on Baltsaros's thighs, lowering his forehead down to the man's knee. He lay there just breathing quietly as Baltsaros's fingers tickled gently through the hair at his nape.

E ven in the early days when Tom was no more than a miserable bastard with fresh scars, a limp, and something to prove, he had stayed. He had obeyed. He had watched the captain and learned that he was beholden to a man like no other. The iron fist that Baltsaros led with was tucked into a satin glove lined with the softest fur. Men looked up to the captain; they praised his fairness and feared his anger. They emulated his grace, refinement, and unshakeable self-confidence; they bowed their heads in loyalty and vied for his attention.

Then, when Tom had stolen into the captain's bed of his own volition, he had discovered that the man expertly mixed pain and pleasure in a way that had left him stunned and breathless.

From that day forward, Tom was simply Baltsaros's.

. . .

"Ye don't need to ask me that," Tom murmured against the captain's leg. Baltsaros's fingers paused in their tickling caress for a moment, one soft finger tracing the edge of the metal collar that bound him before sliding beneath it, pulling the metal tight against Tom's throat. Suddenly, it was like the captain was touching a raw wound inside him, and he felt himself shudder. Fear and anger bloomed. *Humiliation.*

The touch was possessive, and it felt more cruel than anything Baltsaros had ever done to him.

"Don't..." choked Tom. *Stop touching it.* The hand didn't move, and Tom balled his fists to either side of the captain's thighs.

"I've never thought of you as a lesser man for submitting to me, Tom," said Baltsaros, tugging harder on the collar.

Tom groaned softly, his eyes clenched tight. His heart hammered, and he felt a trickle of sweat make its way down his spine. Despite himself, Tom realized he was getting aroused, and it confused him. Why was Baltsaros doing this to him?

"It pleases me to no end that you indulge and actually *enjoy* my predilection for violence. The problem is that it never occurred to me that I failed in freeing you completely. I left the job unfinished," continued the captain almost conversationally.

Tom opened his eyes and watched as Baltsaros pushed aside the hem of his tunic, long fingers deftly undoing the laces at his groin.

"This," said the older man, slipping a second finger between metal and skin, "is not a cage. Nor is it a sentence. You have nothing to fear from it." The captain yanked Tom's head up using the collar, Baltsaros's face oddly serene as he freed his cock from the confines of his leather pants.

"Ye want my pride? Ye want to strip me of that?" breathed Tom hoarsely, his eyes on the captain's hand stroking the thick, veined shaft. Baltsaros's hold on the slave collar felt obscene, but it did nothing to slow the desire that had begun to unfurl inside him.

"I already have your pride, Tom," asserted the captain, staring down at the younger man. "Look at you. I have you by the throat, but you can pull away from me at any time. I've never forced you to do anything. Everything you do is freely offered. Tom, do you *know* what this collar symbolizes?" Baltsaros tugged softly at the metal tight around Tom's throat with a smile. "This is your trust in me."

Tom opened his mouth to deny it but shut it a second later, mute with bewilderment. Testing Baltsaros's words, the first mate pulled back out of the captain's grasp easily and sat back on his heels, his head spinning. Baltsaros's hand had stopped moving over his length, and he laughed at the expression on Tom's face.

"You laid your head and heart at my feet, my gorgeous brute, and I broke your trust. But here you are, wearing your trust for me, plain as day," murmured Baltsaros, his dark eyes fond as he watched Tom.

"Trust?" said Tom softly, one hand turning the metal around his neck. His thoughts touched briefly on the day he had been lashed to the mast. It felt like a lifetime ago. "Aye, Da, I trust ye."

"All right then, so trust me, listen to my words," replied the older man. "You are mine, and you are free..." He motioned for Tom to stand.

"*Slave*, stand and strip," said the captain again, his face serious.

This time, however, the words carried less sting. *Trust.* Tom narrowed his eyes at the captain and then let out a quiet laugh.

He could scarcely believe it. In the middle of this godsforsaken slavers' city, surrounded by men who would see them dead for sharing a little spit and cum, the captain was unambiguously inviting him to play... using the collar and some meaningless words as props. It was ridiculous, and it was freeing.

"Ye mean to break me?" asked Tom playfully, testing the waters. "*Master?*" No, not yet meaningless; the word still felt sharp on his tongue, but he understood what Baltsaros intended now. It was time to give new meaning to the words he'd carried for so long like burns etched into his heart, time to make them mean something positive, like the deep trust that he knew existed between the two of them. Hells, it was worth a shot.

"I mean to have your hide if you don't obey me," sneered Baltsaros as he leaned back on the bed on one elbow, his hand sliding once more along the half-hard cock jutting from his unlaced pants.

Eyes following his master's hand, Tom nodded and unbuttoned his trousers, a *willing* slave.

And he grinned.

Baltsaros looked down at Tom, sleeping on his side on the hard floor next to the bed. Their union had been quick, satisfying, and completely necessary. The captain only hoped that it had been enough to reassure the stubborn first mate and dull some of the negative associations he had. The whip would be a harder one, but, in time, Baltsaros thought he could cure Tom entirely of those fears. He needed the first mate to be his normal, capable, ruthless self.

Until Jon manages to make the both of us soft, he mused with a frown.

Lying flat on the narrow bed, Baltsaros stared up at the ceiling, thinking of his own past. How strange that the three of them, all essentially orphans, had wound up on the same path. Not only that, but Tom, Jon, and he himself had suffered one type of abuse or another for a long period of their lives. Closing his eyes, Baltsaros wondered if their scars would ever totally disappear and whether there was a physical aspect of them somewhere hidden inside their bodies that would match up if pressed together. It was one of those thoughts that often drifted through his head in the last minutes before he fell asleep. Absurd thoughts.

. . .

At the sound of a loud commotion in the hallway, Baltsaros sat up, tense and fully awake. He looked over and saw that the first mate had risen into a crouch, his eyes trained on the door.

"Fire!"

Boots thundered by their room, and Baltsaros quickly pulled on his own before lacing himself up. Tom stood with his back against the wall next to the door; he slowly opened it a crack and peered out. There were more calls of fire, and some angry yells as more men ran down the narrow hallway.

"Do you smell smoke?" asked Baltsaros quietly, tying the sash around his waist.

Tom frowned, nodding his head as he kept his eyes on the corridor. A moment later, the big man let out a startled grunt and pulled away from the door as a figure burst in. In seconds, Tom had the intruder down on the floor, one hand wrapped in the man's cloak, the other balled in a fist above his head.

"Tom! It's me, you idiot."

"Jon?" Tom dropped his hand and blinked in surprise.

Jon pulled the bunched fabric out from Tom's fist and tried to sit up, pushing back on the stunned man's chest.

"C'mon. Let's get out of here," said Jon, brushing himself off as he stood assisted by a grinning Tom. "We've only got about ten minutes before the guard at the side gate changes, and the next one's not amenable to bribes."

"You started a fire as a diversion?" asked Baltsaros, confused. The younger man nodded.

"I needed the cover to get you out," explained Jon quietly.

"That-a boy, Jonny!" said the first mate, playfully punching him on the shoulder.

However, when Jon pulled the hood away from his face, the captain felt a burst of fury erupt in his chest. The young man's jaw was mottled with fresh bruising, and his eyes were red-rimmed.

"Something's happened," said Jon in a faint voice, his eyes

sliding away from Baltsaros's with an expression the captain couldn't read. "I'll explain on the way. Let's go."

B altsaros and Tom shared a look before they took off after the young man in the cloak, the same apprehension mirrored on their faces. Unfortunately, in their hurry to follow Jon through the panicking crowd, the men missed the figure that watched them closely, clear blue eyes narrowed in keen interest.

12

WEAKNESS

Baltsaros stared down for a long time at the two bodies lying on the deck. Both men had been placed on pieces of unbleached sailcloth, waiting only for the shrouds to be sewn shut. Jon knew that the decision to give Migri a proper sea burial wouldn't be a popular one, but he didn't care. He was responsible for the man's death.

"I screwed up, and it cost Calum his life," he said softly. In death, Calum looked small and shrunken, the fire and good humour of life leached out of him by one well-placed punch. "If I had kept my temper. Shit—" Jon looked down at his feet and rubbed his forehead, unable to finish. He could hear Tom's low curses as the first mate paced back and forth behind him. Baltsaros had long ago warned him that rash actions had deadly consequences. If only he had stepped back. Taken a breath. If only…

The captain knelt slowly and touched the old man's face. Turning it to the side, Baltsaros let out a sigh and shook his head; it was obvious even to Jon that the bridge of Calum's nose had been forced into his skull.

"At least he probably didn't feel it," said Baltsaros, standing up.

"What an absurd way to die. That punch was pure chance; Migri's a drunk, not a skilled fighter." The captain's face was devoid of expression, but Jon thought he could detect sadness in the way Baltsaros's eyes swept over the corpse of the old man again. The captain put his hand against Jon's back; it felt gentle and warm through his thin shirt.

"Stop beating yourself up over this," the older man said softly. "What's done is done. I, for one, am incredibly thankful that Calum was there. Had he not stepped in, Migri would have undoubtedly hurt you further. Now," Baltsaros turned to him, his dark eyes on Jon's. "How long has Oren been gone?"

Jon furrowed his brow. The past few hours felt surreal, like a waking nightmare.

"Two, three hours. Maybe more. I... I don't know if he took off right after—" ...*after I sank a blade into his father...* "After everything," he continued, his voice hoarse. "The ship's been scoured, and men went out to the jungle to look. No trace of him."

Baltsaros's lips worked against each other, a curse unspoken, and he nodded.

"Why the *fuck* hasn't 'e been chucked off the side like the piece o' shit 'e is!" growled Tom, jabbing a finger towards the fisherman's body. The first mate's shoulders were high, and he rocked forward on the balls of his feet, fury and anguish barely contained. Tom's eyes were wide and red-rimmed as he rubbed his nose, the muscles twitching in his strong jaw.

"I *killed* him, Tom. I killed him for trying to stop me from beating the shit out of his son," said Jon in anguish. "This is so fucked up. I just... with Polas—" Jon pressed the back of his hand against his lips, holding back the sob that was threatening to erupt from him.

"Aye. Where is that sack o' shit? I'll cut 'im down like I'm gonna cut down tha' bloody l'il fawnin' twat when I find 'im so 'elp me fuckin' gods," choked Tom, his agitation further roughening his accent.

The captain placed a calming hand on Tom's shoulder, leaning in to say something quietly to the first mate; Tom pressed his lips hard together and nodded stiffly in response, sniffing once and wiping at his nose again before turning to walk away.

Baltsaros's eyes were gentle when he looked back at Jon.

"Where is Polas?"

Baltsaros stood next to Jon in his quarters, watching the old fisherman through the bars of the cage. Polas lay on the narrow cot, fast asleep.

"You locked him in here after he attacked you?" asked Baltsaros frowning as he turned to look at the young man beside him. Jon's face was drawn and pale, and he held onto his biceps as he stared forward. "Jon?"

Blinking quickly, Jon turned his head to the captain; Baltsaros could see that Jon was in pain by the way he winced as he took a deep breath.

"What? No, he's not locked in," said Jon, and he pulled on the door to demonstrate; it swung open silently on oiled hinges. "He just wanted a place to... mourn. Alone. I guess. I gave him some sleeping powder. I hope that's all right? I didn't know where else to put him."

With a nod, Baltsaros reached out for Jon's arm and pulled him back towards the bed so they would not disturb the old man.

"I was sure he was going to kill me, Baltsaros. He was crying. But... he just lifted me up and hugged me. I killed his son, and he was comforting *me*," said Jon, shaking his head in a dazed way. He lifted his arms up obligingly when Baltsaros pulled up on his shirt, breathing out a soft groan as he did so.

The captain let out a sound of dismay as he saw the damage to Jon's side. Over his ribs, like a dark splash of paint, was a large contusion. Pressing on the area brought out a pained gasp from Jon, but Baltsaros thought only one rib might be fractured, with a few more badly bruised.

"Did he say anything at all?" asked the captain, referring to Polas. Jon turned his head back towards the cage, his face grey-tinged with pain and exhaustion.

Jon's brows came together over his stormy eyes.

"He said something about not being able to save Migri after all and that I shouldn't feel bad about doing the work of the gods," said Jon, wincing when Baltsaros touched the bruise on his jaw.

"Are you hurt anywhere else?" The captain pulled back his hand and turned to the armoire to get some salve and something to wrap around Jon to protect his ribs. With Migri dead, Oren missing, and Polas seeking no vengeance, his immediate concern was making sure that Jon was all right.

"No. I don't think so, no," said the dark-haired young man quietly. "Baltsaros, it *is* my fault. I just lost it. The thought of Oren *insinuating* himself into your arms…"

Baltsaros's eyes widened as he watched Jon blink back tears and turn to him, his pale face taut with sudden anger.

"Gods, tell me there is no truth to his claims," breathed Jon.

Head tilted in thought, the captain unrolled the wide piece of silk in his hands; would the truth serve him, or was he better off with a lie?

"Yes, and no," he replied, deciding on a partial truth. "I didn't seduce the boy, Jon. He came to me while I was sleeping and, thinking it was you, I kissed him. That was all. I sent him on his way once I realized the mistake. Now, hold your arms away from your sides so I can bind your ribs."

Though Jon moved to obey, Baltsaros didn't like the way that the sombre young man stared at him. He frowned and passed the stiff silk around Jon's ribs, his hands smoothing the material as he went.

"That's not the whole truth," whispered Jon, watching Baltsaros closely. "What aren't you telling me?"

The captain paused. Anger flashed through him, swiftly followed by a finger of unease. He resumed wrapping Jon in silence.

"What is the *whole* truth?" Jon asked, reaching up to stop Balt-saros's hand. "Tell me all of it for once in your damned life."

After pulling his fingers out of Jon's grasp so he could fasten the bandage, the captain straightened. The younger man stood looking at him quietly, waiting for him to answer.

It was infuriating. It was unnerving. It was also fascinating.

"How do you know I'm not telling you the whole truth, Jon?" he asked, pulling the stopper out of the small jar of salve.

Jon let out a short, bitter laugh.

"When have you ever?" said Jon. "No, that's not it. Call it a gut feeling. Call it the fact that Tom isn't as skilled a liar when he's covering for you. But you know what? Never mind. I don't even care about the substance of the lie. As sick as it makes me to think of you and that... that—no, the thing I care about is why you feel the need to lie to me at all. Do you think so little of me?"

Gods be damned, Jon. Baltsaros felt uncomfortably like he was being cornered. But... why *was* he lying? What would happen if he started telling Jon the truth? The *whole* truth, as Jon had put it. Would Baltsaros lose him?

It occurred to him then that he would lose Jon regardless if he continued to lie; the boy was starting to see through him more easily. It would only get worse with time.

The captain nodded to himself then cleared his throat.

"Weakness," Baltsaros said finally. He reached out to dab some salve on Jon's face. When he saw that Jon was blinking at him in mute confusion, he continued while smearing the ointment gently over Jon's jaw. "Weakness is the answer you're looking for. And I would thank you not to accuse me of disinter-est." He frowned when he saw the tired skepticism in Jon's eyes. "Oren snuck into my bed. I was sure he was you. When I real-ized he wasn't, it was my intention to push him away; but the truth is, Jon, that I didn't. You have Tom to thank for the inter-ruption. I'm honestly not sure how far it would have gone otherwise."

The truth.

Jon's face had pulled away from Baltsaros's hand as he spoke, blue-grey eyes wide with chagrin.

"It is weakness in that I didn't even try to control myself. It is weakness in that I am affected by your opinion of me. You matter very much to me, Jon, and I didn't want to lose you for a stupid mistake," the captain said softly. Leaning his hip on the edge of the table, he watched Jon curiously.

Jon stared at Baltsaros for a moment, his hands coming up to test the stiff material that bound him from nipple to navel before he turned away, shaking his head. When he looked back at the captain, his eyes were glassy.

"Maybe if I had known that, Oren's words would have meant less to me," whispered Jon.

Baltsaros almost groaned as he reached for the young man. Jon let himself be pulled forward, and he leaned into the captain with a slow exhale, his body tense with obvious pain.

"Oren was out to make trouble; it's as simple as that. He had no business being in our room and had I been the one to find him, he would have spent the night in the brig with my boot print decorating his backside," Baltsaros laughed bitterly as he gently stroked Jon's back. "Be angry at me for betraying your trust, but my honesty, or lack thereof, is not the cause of anyone's death. Not today. Put that out of your mind. Yes, Calum is dead. It is a sad thing indeed. I was rather fond of the old man; it's in great part because of him that I am who I am today. However, his death was an accident, and your reaction, involuntary. That is what I believe."

Baltsaros closed his eyes, remembering the muscular, dark-skinned man who had befriended the frail orphan that he had been. As always, there was no rhyme or reason to death. The thought made him frown again, his chest tight as he put his cheek against Jon's hair.

"Do you realize that you're lucky to be alive?" he whispered, tightening his fingers in the dark curls that hung past Jon's shoulders. "You mean so much to me."

Jon raised his head, his face wet with tears but his eyes serious.

"Do you really think it's a weakness to be affected by me?" he asked, his voice barely audible.

Baltsaros nodded.

"It *is* a weakness. A weakness that might one day be my undoing." The captain leaned forward to brush his lips over Jon's and was gratified when Jon sighed into the gentle, brief kiss. "I left you here to keep you safe and, by doing that, nearly lost you. You'll come with Tom and me when we go back tomorrow."

"We're going back?"

"Yes. If for nothing else, I'd like to see if we can find Oren. There's no telling what sort of trouble he could cause for us on the loose," said the captain, stroking Jon's uninjured cheek. Some of the colour had come back into Jon's face, an easing of his tension, but Baltsaros knew that he needed something to kill the pain and some uninterrupted sleep.

"Thank you for telling me the truth," said Jon, closing his eyes to Baltsaros's caress.

"Truth, Jon, is what you will get from me from now on. I promise. Ask me anything and I will tell you... but only ask me questions you want to know the answers to."

Despite the throbbing in his side and the way his jaw clicked sometimes when he moved it, Jon felt a tug deep inside him at Baltsaros's touch. The warm hand moved down his cheek to his neck where the captain's long fingers tickled the sensitive skin at his nape. At Baltsaros's words about truth, Jon had opened his eyes. The captain's starkly chiselled face was soft with emotion, and his dark-brown eyes looked at Jon as if he were a sacred object and not just a weary, beaten young man with too much pain in his soul.

Heart pounding high and swift in his throat, Jon realized that he believed Baltsaros. The man would tell him the truth.

The thought frightened him suddenly.

Sagging against the table when Baltsaros pulled away, Jon watched the captain mix up some sleeping powder with something he'd given Tom after one of his many fights with the rougher denizens of the *Heart*. Jon accepted the cup and peered into it curiously.

"It will lessen your pain," explained Baltsaros with a grim smile. "Sleeping on broken ribs is not a pleasant experience. I will lock the cage door on the off chance that Polas has a change of heart when he wakes up, but I'll leave a note explaining. If I know the old man, he will understand my reticence to have him loose given the circumstances. Now, drink."

Jon lifted the cup to his lips and drank down the bitter potion in a few swallows. Yes, sleep; hopefully dreamless. Baltsaros took the cup and helped him onto the low bed before covering him with the dark-red blanket. Almost nauseous from fatigue as the last of his adrenaline left him, Jon closed his eyes.

Jon walked down a long marble hallway. The stone felt ice cold on his bare feet. To his left was the giant, black lion; to his right, the tawny wildcat. The two bracketed him like guards, and he was glad for their presence. At the far end of the corridor was a set of red and gold doors, the shape of a human heart burned into the painted and gilded wood. There was danger on the other side, Jon could feel it. Breathless, agonizing suffering.

But not for him.

In terror he watched the golden snakes slither from beneath the door and rear up to quickly bind the legs of his companions with their muscular, sinuous bodies, pulling the lion and cat down to the ground. Jon cried out as the snakes reared back and bit, working to bleed his protectors dry...

Jon jerked awake and let out a grunt as the motion caused his ribs to twinge. He felt disoriented and hot, and he pushed the blankets away. The spot next to him was empty, but he could hear Tom's snoring close by. As he eased himself up carefully, Jon looked around the darkened room. The door of the empty cage was ajar, and Polas was not in the room. Jon rose to his feet and felt around for the shirt hanging from the back of the chair nearest the bed. After pulling it on slowly, he approached the hammock that hung in the corner of the room.

Tom was passed out in a drunken sleep, his broad chest rising and falling slowly in the light of the moon. Jon reached out to place his hand on the first mate's warm skin, and he furrowed his brow, noticing that the man still wore his metal collar. Tom would have to keep up the ruse of being a slave for at least one more day. He hoped that when they had accomplished whatever it was the captain had set out to do, Tom would not have any new scars, emotional or otherwise. The first mate frowned and muttered something under his breath, turning his head away from Jon.

"Don't touch," mumbled Tom and let out a long, shuddering breath.

At first, Jon thought the first mate was talking to him, but when he said a few more unintelligible words, it was obvious he was still fast asleep. With a pang of sorrow, Jon wondered whom Tom was talking to in his dream. The captain? His former master? Someone who had abused him? With a sigh, Jon pulled the thin sheet over Tom's body, pressing down softly on the big man's shoulder before turning to go.

. . .

Outside, it was quiet, not a soul to be seen. Jon knew that if he were to walk from stern to bow, he might find a sailor here or there, passed out atop gunny-sacks or slumped against a crate. After weeks of frigid weather, the warm summer nights drew the men outdoors; it was a welcome reprieve from the stuffy bunkrooms.

With a pang, Jon realized at that moment just how much he missed Katherine. While he was friendly with much of the crew, Jon had yet to spark up a close friendship like he'd had with the wisecracking pirate. Many a night like this, he and Katherine had sat, thick as thieves, passing a bottle back and forth just enjoying each other's company in the warm night breeze. He wondered if he would ever see her again.

He heard muffled voices from above and turned to look up at the quarterdeck. Side by side on the bench behind the ship's wheel sat Baltsaros and Polas talking quietly. Jon watched them for a moment, loath to disturb the two men. He had decided to return to bed when he heard the captain's voice call to him.

"Jon, come up."

He climbed the staircase, a little nervous to be in the old fish-erman's presence again. However, when he reached the top, Polas just smiled at him sadly. No, the old man did not harbour any bad feelings about his son's death. In fact, to Jon's keen senses, it seemed as though Polas was glad that something was over.

After lurching tiredly to his feet, the old fisherman patted Jon on the shoulder before he bid the captain and him goodnight.

"How are your ribs?" asked Baltsaros, watching Polas descend the stairs.

Jon put a hand to his side.

"Sore as hells. But I'll live," he said with a small smile. "Why are you still awake?"

The captain's brows pinched together, and he looked down at his hands, his lips parted in a slow exhale.

"I could not sleep, Jon," said Baltsaros softly. "I tried, briefly.

But I find my mind unable to rest. Polas woke up, and we came up here not to disturb you or Tom." He raised his head, and Jon was alarmed to see that Baltsaros wore an expression he had never seen on the man before. The captain looked lost. "What have I done by bringing us here, Jon?"

Jon felt a sliver of fear pierce his heart at the captain's uncertainty; it was disturbing to see the man's confidence shaken. However, before he could answer Baltsaros, the moment had passed, and the crack in the captain's mask closed.

"Ah... listen to me. Tonight is a dark night, isn't it?" chuckled Baltsaros, reaching for Jon. "Come here, I have to take off that silk. You need to breathe deep for a while or else you'll wind up with congested lungs."

Jon held up his shirt while the captain swiftly unwound the silk from his ribs. His side hurt when he breathed, but the painkillers in his system dulled the ache. The breeze was cooler up on the quarterdeck, and he could hear it rustling the leaves of the trees on shore. Turning to watch the dark jungle, he wondered what dangers lay beyond for them on the morrow.

When Baltsaros's hands glided softly up his back, Jon let out a startled gasp. The captain moved close behind him, his chest pressed to Jon's back, arms wrapped gently around him.

I'm honestly not sure how far it would have gone otherwise.

Baltsaros's words had hurt, but not as much as he had feared. Jon's own weakness was that he forgave the man, again and again. He ran his fingers along the captain's strong forearm as Baltsaros pressed his lips to Jon's neck. There was a question he wanted to ask.

...only ask me questions you want to know the answers to.

Jon closed his eyes. He would ask it one day, but he feared that he already knew the answer. The captain was fond of him... but love?

Baltsaros murmured something against his skin.

"*Min haeken*," whispered the older man, sliding his hands down to the waistband of Jon's pants and pulling apart the knot on his belt. "I don't want to hurt you when I take you, but take you I shall."

Jon shivered at Baltsaros's words. The captain's hand was cool when it slid into his pants to cup him softly. Already his cock was a throbbing thing, lengthening and hardening in Baltsaros's deft fingers. Was this also a weakness? Jon was virtually the captain's slave when it came to his body; in the midst of pain, sorrow, and fear was this burning, compulsive desire. It seared through Jon like a cleansing fire. He groaned, heedless of the pain in his ribs as he leaned forward to grasp the ship's wheel and push himself back against the captain.

Quickly, the captain tugged down the waist of Jon's trousers, exposing him completely in the dark of the quarterdeck. The hand around his cock tightened, stroking him quickly and firmly as the captain freed his own hard length from the confines of his pants. Jon felt the heavy organ rub up against the furrow of his ass, warm and hard against him. He heard the captain spit into his palm, and Jon's side ached as he panted with his need.

"Baltsaros," he whimpered when the older man pulled back. The head of the captain's cock pressed against him, pushing slowly into his body. Saliva was a poor substitute for oil, but it was enough. He would be sore later, but he needed to feel something other than the terrible guilt and fear that had hounded him all day. With a low moan, Jon gripped the wooden spokes of the wheel as Baltsaros's cock opened him up, and he shuddered when he was filled, the captain's pelvis tight against his buttocks.

Baltsaros began fucking him with short, quick thrusts, his hand stroking Jon's cock in time with his movements. Though his ribs twinged in pain with every jolt, Jon was soon sobbing his breath out, Baltsaros's cock hurtling him towards climax with every fast plunge. With a low grunt Baltsaros quickened his pace suddenly, and Jon let out a soft, ragged cry, letting himself go over as the captain spilled his seed inside him. Jon's orgasm was a sweet, aching, breathless thing that made his heart beat light and fast in his chest. His knees felt weak, but he held onto the wheel and tried to catch his breath as the captain rested his forehead against his back.

After a long, panting moment, the captain slipped wetly out of him, and Jon felt Baltsaros's seed slide down his thigh. With a small, pained groan, he turned and pushed himself into Baltsaros's arms. Warm hands slid gently down his sides as Baltsaros leaned his head against Jon's, his body a comforting, solid presence in the dark.

"Come, my love," murmured the captain, pulling up Jon's pants to cover him. "I think I can finally sleep."

Jon nodded wearily against Baltsaros's neck and let himself be led to the safety and warmth of their shared quarters, trying desperately to keep thoughts of their future at bay.

13

ONCE MORE UNTO THE BREACH

Jon winced as he pulled the shirt over his head, his ribs tender to the touch. Tom sat sideways in the hammock, one foot kicking slowly to make it rock, as he watched Jon dress.

"Well?" Jon asked when he was done, holding his arms out. Jon was outfitted similarly to Baltsaros, in tunic and sash, in an attempt to mimic the dress style of the Badlanders.

"I think ye look lovely," said Tom with a grin. "Really lovely. Now come give us a kiss." The burly first mate pushed himself up out of the hammock and reached for Jon, his usual bluff cheer having been restored by the catharsis of a late-night brawl. Amazed as always by Tom's ability to shrug off hardship, Jon kissed the bruise on the first mate's jaw with a soft smile.

"That ain't a kiss, lovey," laughed Tom, and the man bit at the corner of Jon's mouth before kissing him hard. Jon closed his eyes and opened to the kiss, shifting in Tom's grasp so that their hip bones touched. When the big man started kissing down the side of his neck, Jon's hands slid around Tom's back, his palms flat against the scar-layered skin. Tom let out a low growl and tightened his hold on Jon; but, with a gasp at the sharp pain in his side, Jon pulled back.

"Careful of my ribs," he complained, letting his hands drop to Tom's waist. The first mate nodded as he gathered up handfuls of Jon's shirt to avoid his ribs altogether and leaned forward again to recapture Jon's lips.

With a soft laugh, Baltsaros walked over to them and pressed himself against Jon from behind, ducking his head to kiss the back of his neck. Tom pulled away from Jon and grinned over his shoulder, his ocean eyes both amused and dark with desire.

"While I would love to see where this leads, we need to get going soon. I want to avoid another lengthy delay at the gate," murmured Baltsaros. "Finish up whatever it is you need to do in here, and meet me up top in a few minutes." Nudging his pelvis against Jon before turning away, the captain picked up the curved sword from the table and left the room.

Jon stepped back from Tom and tugged on the hem of his shirt to smooth it out. His earlier excitement at visiting Ereme'ia Balor had been eclipsed by the tragedy of Calum's death, but they needed to go, and quickly. Polas had told them that the city was the first place Oren would run to. Though the old man thought it more likely that his grandson would simply be hiding out and licking his wounds, they had to assess the damage the young fisherman may have caused in telling anyone about the ship from beyond the spires. It was for this reason that *Baal's Heart* would sail out to the safety of open water without them, returning two days hence to rendezvous at the same spot where they were currently anchored.

Jon felt a flutter of dread in his stomach, and he breathed deep, trying to clamp down on it before it became something worse.

Tom frowned at the look on Jon's face.

"It'll be all right, my dove," said the first mate as he untied his belt and passed it over to Jon. After Jon fastened it around his own narrow hips, Tom's knife sat in the small of his back, so he turned the belt to wear the knife more comfortably at his side. Since Tom was a slave, he couldn't carry weapons unless he was registered specifically as a bodyguard—something that required wading through bureaucracy to obtain stamps and signatures—so Jon had offered to wear it instead.

His fingers closed over the bone handle, and he pulled the blade out. It was longer than his own and sharp on both edges. As Jon rubbed his thumb over the notches in the handle, he remembered thinking that he would never have a chance to ask Tom about them.

"What do these mean?" he asked, tilting the handle towards Tom. "How many men you've killed?" It didn't seem far-fetched. There were over two-dozen notches in the yellowed bone.

Tom chuckled and looked down, his hand rubbing the back of his head. When he glanced back up, his blue-green eyes were sheepish.

"Aye. With that blade," he said with a wry grin. "Completely daft. Don't know why I'm keepin' track."

Jon felt a chill and wondered if he would ever feel so callous about death. The thought made him feel a little ill. Migri had *twitched* beneath him as the blade entered his brain. Jon licked his lips and swallowed back his unease.

Tom stared at him for a few heartbeats, his brow wrinkling at the effect his words had on Jon.

"Shit... sorry. Look at me bein' a heartless bastard," said Tom quietly.

Jon forced himself to laugh, and he shook his head.

"Don't worry about me. I'll get used to it," Jon said with a rueful twist of his lips. "I'm becoming more and more like you every day."

"Don't ye ever say that, lad," Tom growled, quickly reaching out to grab Jon by the shoulders. "Don't ye *ever* become like me! Yer good, Jon. Ye are. If any of us has a chance of escapin' the pits o' hell, it's *you*. Keep bein' good... for me. Aye?"

Jon felt his chest tighten from the urgency in the first mate's voice and leaned in to press his lips to Tom's in a brief kiss.

"I'm changing..." he whispered, pulling back to look sorrowfully into Tom's worried eyes. "What I did to Oren—Tom, I feel like I'm being consumed by all these *base* desires. I have to learn to embrace the violence or else I'm going to get lost in it."

The muscles in Tom's jaw worked for a second before he replied in a choked voice.

"Ye don't need to embrace it... I'll be yer sword, lad, and I'll be yer shield. The blood's already on my hands—don't dirty yers for hells' sake! I'll keep ye safe or die tryin', I swear to ye."

The exchange was so earnest that Jon didn't know whether to cry or to laugh at the raw pathos of it. Instead, he grabbed Tom's wrist and turned it, leaning down to kiss the tanned skin of the first mate's forearm before placing the blade against it. Tom watched, curious.

"I did this with Baltsaros before the battle at Madierus. I want to do it with you now. Before anything else goes wrong," Jon said in a rush, pressing the edge of the knife hard enough to make a cut; the big man didn't even flinch as the blade drew blood.

J on had explained to him about the pledge before, when Tom had noticed that a new scar on Baltsaros's arm matched Jon's. It was a ritual, Jon had said, a mingling of blood to pledge loyalty to one another. At the time Tom's guts had twisted painfully in jealousy over something that bound Jon and the captain so tightly together; he had hidden his feelings and tried to accept the fact that the relationship he had with Jon was simply on a different scale than the one Jon shared with Baltsaros.

T om's heart beat fast and light in his chest as Jon pressed their bleeding forearms together.

There are... words I want to say to you, Jon had said to him not so long ago as they lay entwined on the mattress in Tom's tiny room.

Fairy-tale words. Words for maidens and knights. Words for those without stones in their hearts. Sacred words.

Tom had stopped Jon from saying them for fear that it would bring down the wrath of the captain on the both of them. He realised he was no longer afraid.

"I love you," said Tom, speaking slowly. He knew they weren't the words to the ritual, but these were far more important. He frowned at Jon. It hurt to say them; his chest felt like it was on fire. Jon's eyes were wide and blue like dusk as he stared at Tom. Tom tried to slow his breathing and clutched at Jon, the blood warm between them. "I love you," he repeated.

For a moment he thought he had made a mistake; Jon stood motionless, silent. Tom was confused and felt his face start to burn. Then everything righted itself, and his heart started beating again when Jon pulled him in for a fierce kiss.

"I love you too, you big idiot," said Jon with a smile. "I've loved you a long time, it feels like." His fingers were cool against the back of Tom's neck, confident and strong. Jon was the one person who could understand the feeling of relief that coursed through Tom; the sombre young man who touched him tenderly had also been devoid of love for most of his life.

Tom's tears had long ago dried up inside him, but he thought he might just start to cry if he didn't say something. He cleared his throat and kissed Jon's temple, forcing his lips to curl into an easy smile.

"Now, just because I love ye, don't think it means ye get out of doin' grunt work," he said gruffly. Jon laughed, and Tom squeezed him softly, careful not to hurt his ribs, before pulling away. He had to get a hold of himself. There would be time to explore this later; at least he hoped so. The thought sobered him. "Now, let's shake a leg, aye?"

Jon nodded quickly and walked to the armoire, gathering some strips of cloth and the small pot of salve to attend to their wounds.

Tom waved off the bandages.

"Nah, leave it, lad," he said with a smile. "It's only a scratch. Who'd bother to bandage a slave—" He grinned wider; he'd just come up with a great idea.

J on watched Baltsaros peer curiously at the bandage around Tom's ribs, his eyebrows raised.

"Elegant solution, Tom," said the captain with a smile. The bandage neatly covered up the fact that Tom originated from the other side of the Devil's Isles.

Tom chuckled.

"Aye. I ain't walkin' around with my arm done up again," grinned Tom. "Just tell any who asks that ye stabbed me for bein' smart with ye."

Jon watched the exchange quietly. He was still reeling from Tom's words and the staggering realization that he had probably never spoken them before. At least not out loud. He watched Tom grin and throw a length of rope over his shoulder as he joked with Baltsaros, and Jon wondered what had happened between the captain and the first mate in the city. Gone was the fear and uncertainty that had plagued the first mate the previous day, and Tom even made a wisecrack about Baltsaros being his master as he settled down between the oars to row them to shore. He was back to his normal, aggressively cheerful self.

No. Not quite.

Jon knew Tom was a changed man from the brute who had kidnapped and knocked him senseless almost a year and a half earlier. The sadness that had come to the surface had left its mark on Tom; but, now that he had confessed his feelings, Jon thought he could see a new sort of confidence flowing through the first mate.

When he'd felt Tom's slight tremble, Jon had also felt his relief and understood immediately that the first mate was trying to get himself under control. Now watching with a smile as Tom rowed,

Jon realized that this was the first time he was getting a real sense of what went on behind Tom's gruff exterior.

Tom's eyes were fond when he turned to look at Jon, and the first mate winked, grinning wide as he pulled the oars. Unlike his love for the captain, what Jon felt for Tom was rough-edged, almost painful. Oddly protective.

When Baltsaros placed a hand on his shoulder, Jon turned, noting with dismay that though the captain smiled, it was a little thin-lipped.

"You two will have to stop grinning at each other like newly-weds," said Baltsaros, his dark eyes narrow. "Tom's a slave and you're my nephew. Act accordingly."

With so many slaves, the Balorians had no need for things like squires or valets, and the Badlanders supposedly eschewed such things anyway; Jon needed to play a different part. Neither Tom nor Baltsaros would even consider letting him be a slave for fear of him getting separated. So, since Jon looked nothing like Baltsaros, the captain thought that "nephew" would be the best fit. Polas had felt that the family connection would also seem less suspicious when it came to two men sharing a room.

The thing that worried Jon the most was that the old man had strongly advised against departing from the norm if they did have to remain in Ereme'ia Balor overnight should there be another unexpected curfew, and the captain had agreed; the first mate would stay in the barn with the rest of the slaves. Jon hoped it wouldn't come to that and that they would find Oren quickly. Though Tom had shrugged it off when it had been decided that he sleep apart, Jon thought it would be a strain on him.

· · ·

J on turned his head to watch the *Heart* recede in the distance, the crew already weighing anchor. It was unfortunate that they could not bring Polas with them; the man would have been a welcome help. However, after hearing his story that morning, it was obvious why that would not be possible.

J on blinked at the old man.

"You were the headman of your tribe?" he said in amazement. Polas looked up at Jon and smiled his craggy smile.

"Yes. Headman. So hard to believe?" asked the old fisherman. Polas turned his bright blue eyes to Baltsaros who tilted his head thoughtfully.

"I had thought as much," confessed the captain. "At least someone with a much higher standing than you led us to believe."

"I am sorry," said Polas, turning the intricate knot-work bracelet over in his hands, the gold glinting in the morning sun. "It was necessary. I think? But I am sorry."

T he man explained that over the years, his son Migri had found his way, over and over again, to a jail cell. Not a good man to begin with, the death of Oren's mother had killed the last of Migri's restraint, and the burly fisherman had descended into a spiral of self-destruction fuelled by drink and gambling. Migri's behaviour and Polas's refusal to give up on him had begun chipping away steadily at the tribe's esteem.

Then, after Migri had wounded the son of a lord, he was put behind bars for the last time. As the fisherfolk were considered barely above the status of slave, his life was proclaimed forfeit, and he would receive, as Polas put it, a "blessing" that would feed the gods and help the Balorians to stay on the sacred path.

By this, Jon knew that the old man meant a blood sacrifice that would dictate anything from that year's harvest to whether or not it was prudent to bake bread in the middle of the week.

However, the night before the sacrifice was meant to take place, Polas and Oren had incapacitated the guards and freed Migri. By that act alone, had they been caught, Polas and his grandson would have been sacrificed alongside Migri. They left the golden city via the same gate that Jon had used the previous night and fled for the water where their catamaran waited for them.

"It was a matter of time before gods took Migri," said Polas sadly. "But he was a bad man. Oren is good. You need to find him. Make sure he is safe; make sure you are safe. If you bring him back, and he is not welcome on your ship, we leave." Polas glanced at Jon before holding the bracelet out to the captain. "Take this. Show to my people and they will help."

Baltsaros frowned at the gold bangle.

"They will help even though you stole the gods' offering?" he asked quietly.

Jon frowned and turned his eyes to Tom; there was something in the captain's manner that spoke of profound curiosity, and it troubled him.

The first mate leaned back in his chair, cleaning his nails with his knife as he listened. He affected an air of indifference, but the way his eyes were trained on the captain instead of on Polas was enough for Jon to suspect that the first mate was also concerned about something.

"Yes. They will help. They have no love of the blessings. No love of the slavery. Pah... these blood gods. We are kin to the old gods. Please... my people, they will help," repeated Polas and closed Baltsaros's fingers over the bracelet with a nod.

After the trek through the jungle and the wait at the front gates, Tom could barely keep the grin off his face when he saw Jon take in the first view of Ereme'ia Balor. Though he himself had goggled like a fool the previous day, he couldn't help but be amused by the way Jon's head turned every which way. Tom worried that he'd get a cramp from all of his gawking.

On Polas's advice, they made their way to a second, permanent marketplace located between the dense buildings of the city-proper. Called the *madina*, this market was not in a square but crawled its way through the belly of the city like a narrow, winding maze. Behind buildings and in alleyways, the business that took place there was somewhat less scrupulous than that of the open market. If Oren was in the city, the denizens of the *madina* would know... for a price.

As Tom looked around curiously, he caught the eye of a woman in a red sarong who stood in a doorway, beckoning to passers-by. She was tall and dark-haired, and the flimsy material barely covered her. Before he was able to stop himself, Tom grinned. When he was rewarded with a coy smile in return, he realized that life in the *madina* was probably a little less cut-and-dry when it came to what slaves could and couldn't do. The thought heartened him a tad, and he winked at the woman as they passed her.

When he could smell fish, Tom knew they were close to the fish market that Polas had said was run by an old friend. This was where they would begin their search. However, before he turned down the alleyway to follow Jon and Baltsaros, Tom noticed a cloaked figure watching him from the other side of the narrow street. Bright-blue eyes stared hard at him for a moment before the slight figure turned away and was lost in the crowd. It wasn't Oren; that much was clear. The figure wearing the purple cloak wasn't nearly as tall as the young fisherman.

After a thought, Tom decided to keep the stranger's behaviour to himself, at least for the time being. They had more important things to take care of, and there was no need to bother the captain about his concerns when they might turn out to be shite. However, as they made their way to the small fish market at the edge of the *madina*, Tom kept his eyes on the crowd.

14

A BLESSÈD RITUAL

The sprawling, covered marketplace was overwhelming. The sights, the smells… Jon had never been anywhere like it. Some of the alleyways and streets were wide enough to walk four abreast even with stalls lining each side. Others were so narrow that they had to walk single file. And the people! There were so many people swarming the *madina* that Jon started to feel a little nauseous from the constant movement of the crowd. As much as his general discomfort around people had decreased over his time aboard the *Heart*, the teeming *madina* was threatening to send him into a panic. Finally, Jon resorted to watching Baltsaros's boots as he walked, his head down in an attempt to insulate himself a little against the throngs of people around him.

Before long, Baltsaros turned down a relatively empty alley-way, and Tom increased his step to match Jon's, bumping him gently on the shoulder when he caught up. Jon lifted his eyes and saw that Tom looked worried. Thinking that the first mate was concerned for him, Jon shook his head.

"Don't worry, I'll be fine," he said with a strained smile. "Once we get out of this crowd, anyway."

Tom's brows dipped in confusion, and Jon realized that the first mate's mind was on something else; he frowned.

"What is it?" he asked as a cold finger of unease slipped beneath his skin.

Something had the big man on high alert. Tom's eyes darted to the side, narrow with suspicion.

"I think we're bein' followed," he said quietly, turning back to Jon. "There's a bloke in a hood that's been dartin' in an' out of sight. A purple cloak... ye seen him?"

Jon waited until a group of men passed them before answering.

"I've been too busy trying to keep sane with all these people around," he murmured. "Are you sure? It's awfully crowded."

Tom's lips pressed together, a crease appearing between his brows as he nodded.

"Aye. Blue eyes is all I seen of him other than the cloak," Tom replied. He lifted a hand and squeezed Jon's shoulder quickly. "Listen, love... if I ask for it, give me my knife and run like hell. I don't want ye to ask any bloody questions... Just get outta here. Savvy?"

Jon swallowed, his heart thumping quickly in his chest. After a second he nodded. Tom had better instincts than he did; he had to trust that the first mate knew what he was doing.

"Shouldn't you tell the captain?" he asked, turning his eyes to Baltsaros. The tall man was peering at the stalls as they made their way towards the wharf, looking for the symbol that Polas said would mark the one belonging to a friend.

Tom shook his head.

"Nay—not yet, lad. Don't need another bloody thing to bother Da. I'll keep my eyes out. Ye lemme know if ye see him. Listen, it's naught to worry about yet, Jon. I'm just bein' careful, aye?" The first mate smiled reassuringly then slowed his step, trailing once more behind Jon and the captain.

With a frown, Jon kept his head up, eyes moving over the crowd. While he saw no one matching the description of the man following them, Jon noticed something odd: despite the brilliant silks that were on sale all around them, the Balorians all seemed to favour sombre clothing. Something about the dark colours bothered him… it was funereal.

After a bit of backtracking when they had reached the water with no sign of the symbol, Jon spotted the stylized seashell on a sign above a tiny stall. There were thick boards that made up a long table to one side of the stall, and it was here that they found the man they had been looking for. Bare-chested, the stocky fisherman was covered up to the elbow in blood as he methodically gutted and chopped fish from a large bucket at his side. Baltsaros stopped in front of the stall, and the man looked up; Jon could see that one of his eyes was milky white. The man's name was Ertos, and he was kin and close friend to the old fisherman. When folks had begun turning against Polas as headman, Ertos had stayed a staunch supporter. His eyes widened at the sight of Polas's golden cuff on Baltsaros's wrist, and he nodded curtly before asking a question.

Jon listened to the captain and the fishmonger exchange words; though the language was similar to the northern tongue that Baltsaros spoke, Jon could not understand more than a few words.

"What are they saying?" he asked Tom quietly, leaning towards him.

Tom laughed softly.

"Ah, Jon… do ye need another lesson? Hm?" joked the first mate; Tom's eyes twinkled in merriment as he smiled at Jon.

Jon's cheeks burned and Tom's grin widened.

"They're talkin' fish, but not about *fish*, if ye know what I mean. Da says there's a special little white fish he's lookin' for. The big white-haired bastard thinks he's seen him. Spot o' good luck that, I think? Maybe we'll be beddin' down in the bushes, waitin' for the *Heart* to come back instead of lurkin' about in this fucked up place, aye, mate?"

. . .

T hey soon made their way to the part of the city where most of the fisherfolk lived, following the lead that Ertos had given them. There was a possibility that Oren had sought out a cousin of his.

When they turned yet another corner, Jon saw furtive movement from the corner of his eye. Turning to look at the alleyway, he saw nothing. However, a moment later, he spotted a figure in a burgundy cloak ducking into what looked like a bakery.

"Tom," he murmured. "I think I just saw the man you noticed earlier."

The first mate's expression turned dark, and he moved closer to Jon, protective and alert.

"Aye... There he is," said Tom, and Jon saw the figure keeping up with them across the wide street. He curled his fingers around the bone handle of the blade in his belt. Then the cloaked stranger quickly turned up a narrow side street, and Jon caught a glimpse of crystal-blue eyes in a pale face. He frowned.

"Fuckin' hells, I'm not likin' the attention," spat Tom. "Next time I see the bastard, I'm goin' to grab him."

"Her," corrected Jon.

Tom's eyes widened.

"Ye sure, love?" asked the first mate, and Jon nodded.

Jon wanted to let Baltsaros know about the woman following them, but the captain had stopped ahead and stood looking up at a small wooden building. When Jon and Tom caught up, Baltsaros curved his lips into a genteel smile and smoothed down the front of his tunic as he began quickly climbing the steps.

"All right. Let's see if luck is on our side."

T wo hours later, Jon was thoroughly sick of searching for the brat. The first lead had turned out to be nothing; Oren's cousin hadn't seen him in some time and had no answers for them. However, a neighbour had sworn up and down that she had seen Oren at the open-air market that morning. That had proved to be fruitless too, and now Jon's feet ached from circling back through town a third time.

Over the shouts of the stall keepers hawking their wares, he heard bells ringing in the distance and turned towards the sound. Suddenly the *madina* was eerily quiet. Glancing around him, he saw that the other market-goers had all stopped to face in the same direction: towards the big stepped temple that rose above the city. Jon felt a prickle of fear.

"Now what in bloody hells…" murmured Tom, looking at the crowd. His jaw jutted out as he scanned the marketplace, blue-green eyes searching for any sign of danger.

"Come on. Let's go," said the captain, passing between Tom and Jon.

Jon glanced back at the fishmonger and saw that the man was hastily closing up shop. By the looks of it, the entire city was making its way towards the pyramid.

H eedless of the how it looked, Tom put an arm across Jon's back, pulling him close so that he wouldn't be jostled by the crowd. Baltsaros was ahead of them, getting further away as he lengthened his strides. Tom frowned at the captain's back, uneasy about how eager Baltsaros was acting. While searching for Oren was ultimately the reason for being back in the city, Tom was beginning to suspect that it was far less important than what had drawn Baltsaros here in the first place, something that the first mate was finally starting to piece together.

The captain's first priority was to himself, and Tom knew that there was one compulsion that Baltsaros rarely ever tried to curb.

The first mate looked over at Jon who was once again staring down at his feet as the crowd grew more dense; Tom had hoped that the strange influence that Jon was able to exert on the captain would have made Baltsaros a little less... *hungry*.

With a small curse, Tom set his teeth together grimly and pulled Jon along after the captain, wondering bitterly why he wasn't leading the two of them away to safety instead.

T he crowd slowly spilled out from the narrow street into the large square that they had investigated the previous day. Looking around, Tom saw that on the lower steps of the pyramid, men juggled red balls while a woman played a stringed instrument about the size of a fiddle.

Now that it was filled with people, the square no longer reeked of death, and for that, Tom was glad. He wanted to get closer to the captain, but Baltsaros was halfway across the square, and Tom did not want to leave Jon's side nor did he want to drag him further into the crowd. Instead, he crossed his arms over his broad chest and stood there glowering, hoping that they were not about to witness what he thought they would. Thankfully, the stranger tailing them hadn't made another appearance.

When two more musicians joined the first a few moments later, Tom started to doubt his suspicions about the reason behind the gathering. The mood in the square was one of merrymaking, with people laughing and mingling as they ate spicy, brittle cakes wrapped in banana leaves. Finding himself beginning to relax, Tom saw that Jon had raised his head and now looked around him curiously.

"What's going on? What is this?" asked Jon, his blue eyes wide.

The woman standing next to them peered at the dark-haired

young man suspiciously, and Tom frowned. He manoeuvred himself to stand in front of Jon and leaned in to whisper.

"If yer gonna speak Common, keep yer voice down, Jon. Ye don't sound right to them."

While in the city, Baltsaros and Tom conversed in the captain's mother tongue, knowing that it was close enough to Balorian and to the harsher dialect that the fishing tribes spoke that they could pass it off as a Badlands variant. Though Common *was* spoken freely in the city, the accent in Ereme'ia Balor had nothing like the flat-sounding vowels that marked Jon's midland origins. Tom kept his own voice down to a bare whisper when he spoke to Jon for the same reason.

Jon pressed his lips together and nodded stiffly, a deep comma between his brows. When he spoke next, Tom could barely believe his ears.

"How do you think they get wares from our side of the mountain range?" asked Jon. He spoke Common still, but with the guttural accent of the fisherfolk. It was absolutely flawless, and Tom stared at Jon for a moment, his face slack with surprise.

"How did you..." he started.

Jon's face creased into a smile, his unease forgotten for a moment because of Tom's reaction. He shrugged his shoulders and pushed a stray curl away from his face.

"I might not have a talent for languages, but I seem to have a gift for mimicry," said Jon, managing to look both sheepish and proud. "I can do ye too if ye'd like, lovey."

The last was a perfect replica of Tom's rough mainland accent; the first mate let out a surprised bark of laughter. It was simply amazing. Tom grinned like a fool.

"Can ye do anyone?" he asked, thinking of the outrageous accent Old Calum spoke with that put his own to shame. Then he remembered the man was dead and sobered.

Jon shrugged again.

"Maybe? I used to do it when I was a little kid. I had no friends, so I just pretended to be different people and acted out all the parts. I... I think I just picked up accents from the soldiers and servants. We had folk from all over the place," replied Jon, switching back to Polas's guttural accent.

"Well, it's a mighty fine talent, lad," said Tom with a soft smile. He thought it was a crying shame that the boy had been so utterly friendless; even Tom had had friends among the other slaves. He was almost overwhelmed by his desire to touch Jon, just skin to skin, fingertips to the clean-shaven curve of his strong jaw for a single moment to reassure him. However, he held back. There were too many eyes on them. "Ye know... I used to sound like my ma. Upper crust. Sometimes I think the reason Abetha was so scared o' me when I came back to her was that I sounded like a bloody peasant. What'cha think?"

Jon stared at him, his face drawn and stormy eyes locked on Tom's. After a second, he looked away, blinking quickly. As he rubbed a hand over his face, Jon sighed and then let out a low chuckle. When he glanced back up at Tom, Jon had a wry grin on his face.

"How pathetic are we?" he asked, the corners of his eyes crinkling.

"Bloody fucking miserable bastards," said the first mate with a wide smile.

Tom started when a loud cheer went up in the crowd nearby. He raised his head to get a better look.

Standing in a cleared area were two muscular slaves holding a long spear between them. At first glance, Tom couldn't figure out what they were doing; however, when the smaller of the two let out a loud cry, twisting the spear out of the other's hands, the crowd roared again. Tom could see money changing hands, and he grinned. It was obviously some contest, a feat of strength. A way to earn a few coins...

"Jon, I want ye to enter me," he said, cocking his head towards the cleared space where two more men now stood, holding the spear between them.

Jon tilted his head and watched the men fighting to gain control of the spear. After the short struggle was over and the bets collected, Jon nodded slowly.

"Aren't you afraid of drawing attention to us?" he asked quietly.

"Naw—them's that take up with this sort of sport ain't the kind to go lookin' too close at the details. What'cha say, love? I can blow off a little steam and make some coin at the same time."

When Jon turned to Tom, his blue eyes held a note of amusement in them.

"You sure you can win?" he asked, his tone a challenge.

Tom chewed on the side of his thumb for a moment. It seemed easy enough; he certainly had both the strength and the balance to pull it off. He nodded.

Jon narrowed his eyes in response, reaching out to squeeze Tom's bicep and prod his shoulder. The touch was both rough and strangely impersonal, and it took Tom a second to understand what it meant.

The master was sizing up his slave to see if he was fit to participate.

A thrill ran through Tom, and he held his breath for a moment, fascinated by the sudden shift in Jon. Mimicry indeed; it bordered on sorcery. He'd seen glimpses of it in their play before, when Jon took on his coldly dominant role, but this felt utterly genuine. There was nothing in the sombre young man's eyes except professional concern for his chattel... Then Jon winked, and the illusion was shattered. Tom suddenly wished that they were somewhere that he could fall to his knees and have Jon transform himself into that indifferent creature again.

"Stop staring at me and get to it," said Jon as he pointed. "I'd like to make some good money off of you before the sun goes down. Plus," he added quietly, tugging at the bandage around Tom's ribs to make sure it was secure, "if we have to stay here instead of looking for Oren, we might as well unwind and have a little fun, right?"

Tom blinked at Jon before grinning wide.

"As you wish, *Master*." The word was getting easier to utter every time.

J on tried to rein in his anxiety as he bantered with the two men who were running the impromptu competition. The rules were simple: two men had to stand with the toes of one foot touching while they tried to twist and wrench a staff or spear out of the other man's grasp. The first one to have both hands off the spear was the loser.

As he looked over at Tom, Jon could see that first mate was bouncing on the balls of his feet, eager to begin. Jon smiled and shook his head, taking a bite of the spiced bread he held in his hand. There were two more bouts before Tom's turn, and Jon watched the men struggle for control of the long staff, finding himself getting caught up in the action.

Jon realized that his earlier reservations about being in the city were starting to fade, and somewhere in the back of his mind, there was a small voice murmuring words of worry.

As he had told Tom earlier, Jon knew he was changing. It was taking less and less effort to shrug off things, and he feared that he had no control over it. Despite Tom's pleas that he stay "good", Jon suspected that he would continue to shed morals the longer he stayed aboard *Baal's Heart*; he felt it was inevitable.

Jon took another bite and chewed thoughtfully; was he having a crisis of self or going through a metamorphosis? Why was he worried? It's not as if he had particularly liked the pale, weak thing that had scurried about Portsmouth doing Reginald's bidding. A sad, pathetic little worm working underground, he had been. Friendless and ignorant of the heady, addictive thing that love had turned out to be. He watched Tom flexing his large, scarred hands in preparation for his bout, and he smiled.

The first mate's short dirty-blond hair stuck up in a few places, and his thick stubble was at least half a week old; Jon thought he could make out a streak of dirt on the big man's cheek, and he laughed softly to himself. Overall, Tom looked rumpled and unkempt, and utterly gorgeous in the bright morning sun with his sun-bronzed skin and easy grin. The sparkle in Tom's sea-green eyes gave him a mischievous, dangerous air, and Jon thought again about how the man *was* most assuredly dangerous, in more ways than he was prepared to think about. Standing bare-chested, the brawny first mate made most of the other contestants look small in comparison, yet this ruthless brute often curled against Jon like a tame wildcat, his kisses ardent and tender. It made his chest ache just looking him.

A hand closed over Jon's shoulder, and he glanced up. The captain peered curiously at Tom as the first mate walked forward to take his place opposite a great, swarthy bear of a man.

"What's going on, nephew?" asked Baltsaros, his brows high.

Jon smiled blandly. *Nephew.*

"Just making a little money, *uncle*," he replied.

Baltsaros's eyes widened at Jon's assumed accent, but he didn't comment. Instead, he turned to focus on the two men in the ring.

Tom and the dark-haired brute placed their hands on the spear as the crowd counted down. When the cheer went up, Jon saw Tom's muscles bulge as he struggled to pull the spear out of the other man's hands.

"They're a little mismatched, aren't they?" murmured Baltsaros.

Jon frowned; Tom's opponent stood a few finger widths taller than the first mate, and his shoulders bulged with great corded muscles under the dark hair that covered his torso. Jon felt a momentary pang of worry.

When Baltsaros saw the look on Jon's face, he laughed and pointed at Tom.

"No, I meant the other way," he grinned. "Watch." As he spoke, the first mate let out a grunt and pulled while twisting away. As easy as taking a sweet from a child, the spear was plucked from his opponent's grasp.

The crowd roared.

Jon let out a cry and pumped a fist into the air. He was, he suddenly realized, thoroughly enjoying himself.

Tom's lips spread in a cheeky grin, and he spread his arms to take a quick bow, twirling the spear lazily in one hand as he straightened and stood waiting for the next man to step forward.

Beside Jon, Baltsaros collected the winnings: a handful of *doksha* and a few ingots of gold. The captain smiled at him, the strange preoccupied look that he'd worn all morning replaced by amusement that mirrored Jon's own.

The captain shouted something, and the crowd cheered; Jon saw Tom dip his head at Baltsaros before stepping forward to hold out the spear to the tall blond man who was to be his next opponent.

"What did you say?" asked Jon.

"I doubled the wager," said Baltsaros, and his lips curled into a pleased grin. "Now let's hope that Tom's up for the challenge."

Tom won three more bouts before the bells sounded again a half hour later. Jon and Baltsaros stepped quickly to the side as the crowd went quiet and hurried to put away the makeshift seats and stalls. Tom, his torso slick with sweat, frowned in confusion as he walked up to Jon and Baltsaros.

"Good job, Tom," said the captain, placing a hand on the first mate's shoulder. "Though I think that last one almost had you beat."

Tom scowled, but Jon could see that he was pleased with the captain's compliment.

"Do you think the bells mean that whatever this was is over?" asked Jon quietly.

The question was answered for him a moment later when a great drum boomed, a giant heart beating over the square. In confusion, Jon heard soft weeping around him, and he realized with dread that the mood of the crowd had become permeated with fear and something *savage*; a corrupt, electrifying tension like a howling storm stoppered in a bottle. Dismayed, Jon looked up at the temple and saw that there were men standing on the wide platform, sharpening knives.

A blessing for you, a blessing for me, a blessing for slave, a blessing for free.

Jon's heart took a swift plunge, and he turned to the first mate.

Tom's eyes had narrowed as he stared hard at the captain. The glare was accusatory.

"Da," he said angrily. "This ain't right. Let's get the bloody hells out of here. Ye don't have to fuckin' do this. I'll find ye a place to hunt later, Da. Promise. But just... please, Da. Jon ain't gonna want to see *this*, and I ain't so keen meself. Please, Da."

Jon barely followed what was being said, so great was his shock at the change that had taken place in the captain when the drum started beating. The man's eyes glittered with a frantic excitement that made Jon's blood run cold.

"We don't have a choice now," said Baltsaros dismissively. The captain took a few steps into the crowd, and Tom reached out for his arm to pull him back. When Baltsaros swung around to Tom with his teeth bared, Jon recoiled in fear.

"I *need* to see it, Tom," growled the cold thing that wore the captain's face, and he turned back towards the temple, his eyes like shards of glass.

Jon's breath hitched in his chest at the confusion and terror that welled up in him, and he let out a startled cry when a horn blast rent the air.

The crowd went completely silent, and a man's voice rose up above them.

Clutching at Tom's arm, Jon whispered hoarsely.

"What is he saying? Translate. Now."

The muscles in Tom's jaw bulged, and his nostrils flared as he stared down at Jon.

"I can try to get ye out of here, love," Tom said, his eyes sorrowful.

Jon shook his head.

Tom's lips pressed together, and he nodded once. Quietly, the first mate started to translate, his voice a low rumble in Jon's ear:

"…the gods are wise… good. The gods call on blood. Call on ye to feed them so the crops can grow and the sun come up in the sky. Let the blessin's commence…"

Jon's stomach took a tumble when he saw that there was a line of people that stretched along one side of the huge square and up the near side of the temple; there had to be over a hundred of them. In horror, he watched the first sacrifice take her place at the top of the temple. Strapped onto a device that reclined, the woman let out a shriek as the two men above worked on her. When the pallet was righted, Jon pressed the back of his hand to his lips. The woman had been stripped. Even from this distance he could see that the woman's chest heaved in terror as she strained against the restraints.

"…with this blood we ask the gods…"

The man to either side of the woman made swift cuts to her inner thighs and down the inside of her forearms. A rivulet of red ran down the channels on either side of the device she was strapped to.

"…to bless the house of the… uh… *something*… lord for his comin' child…"

The woman's struggles grew weaker and finally stopped. Her

blood was joined by that of a second sacrifice's as he was strapped to another reclining stretcher and hastily cut.

"...to bless the weddin' of the son and daughter of..."

The blood oozed down the open gutters that ran down the sides of the temple. Jon watched in horrified silence as a third and then a fourth were strapped and cut, the previous sacrifices pushed aside to tumble down the far side of the pyramid. He couldn't look away.

"...to bless the—"

"Stop it, Tom. Enough. I've heard enough. Oh gods, I've heard enough," choked Jon. He put out a hand to steady himself against the first mate.

There was a low gurgling sound, and suddenly, from the small holes that nestled between the paving stones of the square, founts of blood erupted high into the air, falling down warm and sticky on the crowd.

In the middle of it stood the captain, his face a mask of serenity as the blood rained down upon him.

15

BLOOD SICKNESS

Jon felt dazed as he stood waiting for his turn to rinse off in the river, his skin coated and tight with dried blood. He knew he would be sick without the iron hold he had on his mind.

Float above it.

The water downriver was red as he stepped down the bank and waded up to his knees. Next to him, the captain scrubbed his arms and face, scooping up handfuls of the cool water nonchalantly as if performing his morning ablutions.

Jon splashed further in and sank down to his chest, eyes lowered.

It's just blood. You've washed blood off before, he thought.

Not the blood of a hundred men and women... whispered a small voice inside him; Jon felt it should have been a scream.

Unnerved, he reached down to the riverbed and brought up a handful of coarse sand. As he rubbed it against his skin, he watched the red drift down current. It was a strange sort of detached hysteria that he felt, his pulse quick and feathery light as he methodically cleansed himself.

John lifted his head to look for Tom. The first mate stood on the riverbank with the other slaves, waiting until the free folk were finished before taking their turns. Feeling Jon's gaze on him, Tom turned to look at him, his lips pressed together and nostrils flared. The blood on the big man's face made a striking contrast with the brilliant blue-green of his eyes; Jon thought the first mate looked a little pale beneath the gore.

Tom's eyes slid to the captain, and Jon read a deep worry coming off the first mate in waves.

What have you not been telling me? he thought.

Jon took a deep breath. After lowering his face to the water, he ducked beneath the surface to rinse his hair as best he could. When he emerged, the captain reached out a hand to help him up. Water dripped from Baltsaros's beard as he smiled at Jon, and Jon smiled wanly back, accepting the help. Lurching to his feet with pink-tinged river water streaming from his clothes, Jon finally understood why everyone in the city wore dark colours.

Silently following Baltsaros up the sandy bank, Jon saw that most citizens rushed away after cleaning up. The festive mood from earlier had been replaced by one that Jon read as equal parts relief, shame, and fear. He noticed that the Balorians carefully avoided looking at a woman who was on her knees in the river, crying brokenly.

How do they live with themselves?

Jon's mind touched briefly on the horror he had just witnessed, and he shivered despite the warmth of the late afternoon sun. In contrast, Baltsaros looked more relaxed than Jon had seen him in a long time. The man seemed refreshed, the tiredness that had lined his face washed away by lifeblood falling like warm rain.

Jon turned to watch Tom take his turn in the bloody river. The first mate quickly ducked underwater to rinse off and made short work of the blood on his arms and chest. Jon wondered how many times Tom had cleaned blood from his skin. A hundred times? A thousand? How many times before someone started washing away parts of their soul in the process? When he looked down at his hands, Jon saw that he still had blood under his fingernails and wondered about the state of his own soul; already the disgust and shock were starting to recede.

He lifted his eyes to the captain's.

"This," he said in a low voice, gesturing to the temple behind them, "it means something to you, doesn't it?"

Baltsaros frowned and tilted his head. For a moment Jon thought the captain was going to evade the question or lie.

"Yes... and no," replied Baltsaros slowly. "I know nothing of their gods."

"What of your gods?" asked Jon. "Do they demand blood as well?"

The captain laughed.

"I have no gods, Jon. God is a word men use to hide the truth of their desires," the older man said, turning to watch Tom climb out of the river. "I have no such need. What is a god to you? A rule maker? A judge? A parent? Behind every god there is the very mortal hand of man, trust me."

"Then why, Baltsaros? Why do I feel like what just happened resonates very deeply with you?" whispered Jon.

"It does, lad," said Tom, his eyes locked on Baltsaros. "And yer goin' to tell him every last bit, Da, so help me. But this ain't the place for it, aye? Let's get gone. We need a place to eat and bed down so we can get lookin' again tomorrow mornin'." Tom's irritation and disappointment were obvious; Jon saw the first mate's jaw muscles twitch under his dark-blond stubble as he stared hard at the captain.

Baltsaros nodded and squeezed the water from the braid hanging over his shoulder as Jon stepped back into his boots, retying Tom's belt around his hips. Though the hot sun was quickly drying their clothes, Jon was cold; the thought of a warm meal hurried his strides. It also took his mind off the taste of blood in his mouth.

The trio made their way back to the city centre, skirting the edges of the *madina*, and Tom was glad for the nearly empty streets as he followed Baltsaros. Quietly trudging by his side, Jon kept his head down, seemingly lost in thought. There was a soft curve to his shoulders that projected a deep weariness, and Tom frowned in concern for the sensitive young man; he had witnessed the shock and horror that had filled Jon's eyes when the sacrifices had begun, and it had made him sick with fury. Chewing on the inside of his cheek as he followed the captain down streets hazy with the falling dusk, he wondered what would happen when Baltsaros came clean to Jon about his obsession. Would it be the end of everything?

Tom glanced again at the tall, elegant man at his side and remembered his own feelings upon the discovery of the captain's grisly hobby.

Tom grinned wide at the woman in Baltsaros's arms, his fingers quickly undoing the buttons that held the flap up at the front of his pants, and wondered again whether the captain did this with all of his lovers. Sharing a woman with another was something that Tom had never considered before and, despite his preference for men, the thought of it made him horny as hell.

The captain let out a low chuckle and then a soft hiss when the pretty young whore bit his nipple with a smile. As her tongue licked a wet trail across Baltsaros's furry chest, Tom could see the woman's hand working quickly below the waist of the captain's pants. Tom's heart thudded in his chest, and he crawled forward, intent on freeing the captain's cock.

"What are you doing?" asked the woman, pulling her hand away in dismay when Tom reached out to untie the captain's laces. The first mate hesitated and looked up at Baltsaros.

The captain's eyes narrowed, and he stared at the whore with a blank expression that Tom knew hid a very dangerous temper.

"Continue," nodded Baltsaros without shifting his eyes from the woman.

Moving quickly to obey, the first mate pulled the leather laces apart and eased his fingers into the opening. The captain's cock spilled out into his hand, and Tom let out a pleased sigh before ducking his head to pull it into his mouth. He moaned softly around the cock between his lips, the simple act of putting his mouth to the captain making his own erection bob up eagerly. He tongued it slowly for a moment, savouring the feel and taste of the wide, smooth head before opening his jaw to take Baltsaros deeper.

The captain let out a low growl of pleasure, and his hand cupped the back of Tom's head, pushing him further. Baltsaros liked being rough with him, and it drove Tom wild to be used by a man who knew exactly how to control pain and pleasure to suit his needs; it was freedom like no other to give himself over completely to the captain.

Above him, the woman let out a sharp sound of disgust. Tom closed his eyes and ignored her, the edges of his mind blurring as his awareness narrowed down to the movement of his tongue and lips. Baltsaros's long fingers slid down around his nape and squeezed, exerting a painful pressure. Tom obeyed without pause, relaxing his throat and rationing his breath until his lips reached the base of Baltsaros's cock.

Tom's shaft throbbed, wrapped tight in his hard fist as he pulled back and slid the captain's thick cock back down the cradle of his tongue. Right here and now, his mouth's sole purpose was for fucking... for pleasing Baltsaros. The thought made him ache; a warm drop slid from the head of his cock down over his knuckles.

"That's sickening," hissed the woman. "You should be branded and your dicks torn o—" There was a squeak, and Tom lifted his eyes, startled. He saw that Baltsaros had wrapped his hand around the woman's neck, her face contorted with shock and fear as she began to struggle.

Tom pulled quickly out of the way. Sitting on his heels, his cock in hand, Tom watched with morbid curiosity as Baltsaros simply suffocated the woman to the point of unconsciousness and lay her back on the bed as if this were a common occurrence. The captain then rose up on his knees and slid the long hunting knife from its sheath by the bed. With the point of the blade hovering over the woman's heart, Baltsaros murmured something under his breath.

The blade sank so easily into her chest.

Tom blinked slowly. It was perplexing and slightly worrying; though the captain was certainly ruthless and had a deeply sadistic side to him, Tom hadn't seen him do something so... inhuman before. In a daze, he watched the captain pull the knife out to place his hand on the heart's blood that rose out of the wound in a thick, dark puddle; Baltsaros licked his dripping red fingers and smiled at him.

Somewhere in the back of Tom's mind was the thought that he should be more concerned about the captain's actions, but there was something so primal, fierce, and alive in the man's eyes that Tom felt nothing but awe. Maybe the *char* had something to do with it, but before his eyes, the captain had become a gorgeous, bloody, fallen god. Tom trembled.

Baltsaros spat into the palm of his hand, and he stroked the rigid, thick cock jutting from the opening in his pants, the smile fading from his face as he stared at Tom with eyes dark with lust.

With a growl, Baltsaros shoved him hard so that he fell back on the bed. The older man was on him in an instant, his teeth sharp and lips sticky and hot against Tom's throat as he quickly pushed his spit-and-blood covered cock deep inside him in one brutal thrust. Tom grunted from the pain, both in his neck and ass, and brought his hands up to the captain's waist to hold on as he was fucked hard and quick. His own cock sat heavy against his stomach, each stroke of Baltsaros's wide head inside him firing nerves that sent waves of pleasure to his groin. Tom let out a sharp cry as the captain bit him savagely, his thrusts vicious and jarring. It was almost too much for a moment, almost overwhelming, but then the adrenaline crested inside him and Tom let go, falling into the bliss of surrender.

That was the first time he'd seen Baltsaros sacrifice someone. The next time it had happened, it had taken a different form; the captain had pulled the young man's heart from his body to take a bite of it, but the result had been the same: Tom was fucked into oblivion. Initially, Tom had begun to find himself getting hard at the mere suggestion of a "hunt" as Baltsaros called it, but over time he'd started to grow concerned about the captain's state of mind.

It was an obsession, and a deeply disturbing one at that.

Tom didn't believe in sorcery, but the way that the blood renewed Baltsaros was something that worried him. It spoke of a dark power that Tom had no wish to be part of.

Glancing over at Jon, he wondered whether their shaky, three-part arrangement would survive the truth of Baltsaros's compulsion. He scratched the back of his head, turning the metal collar as he thought. If it did spell the end, would he be made to choose? The thought sobered him, and he drifted closer to Jon's side as they walked towards the brightly lit inn.

Tom reached out and let his knuckles graze Jon's arm, a hidden touch just to ground him for the span of a heartbeat. Maybe Jon would turn a blind eye. Maybe they'd continue to live in denial that they both loved a fucking monster.

Jon smiled at the brief caress, and Tom felt his chest get tight.

Love was a bloody, fucking headache.

16

LAID BARE

The tongue like a sharp knife... Kills without drawing blood.

— BUDDHA

Jon watched money change hands as Baltsaros secured a spot in the slave quarters for Tom. The first mate would be given adequate food (an extra charge for Tom's bulk) and a comfortable place to sleep (chained to the wall, atop bedding that was changed weekly). Jon was furious, and fanning his anger was guilt; he had knowingly used slave-forged pots made from slave-mined ores in the past and had thought nothing of it. "Slave" had once held almost no meaning for Jon, and he had felt only a vague sense of pity over the plight of the faceless and nameless toiling away in the mainlands. Now, having had spent the day wandering through a city literally steeped in the blood of generations of slaves, Jon felt ill. How anyone could treat another human being with so little regard was utterly... shameful. Deplorable. It was everything he could do not to openly glare at the innkeeper and his casual cruelty. Jon tugged down on the edge of his tunic, fingers purposefully brushing the handle of the long knife and shifted his gaze from the inn's proprietor to the first mate.

Despite Tom's assurance that he would be fine sleeping with the other slaves, Jon could feel that the big man was anxious. He stood stock-still as the transaction took place, staring off over Jon's shoulder, his expression a little lost. Then, as Baltsaros discussed a last few details with the tall man behind the bar, Tom leaned towards Jon and muttered something that made his heart skip.

"If… ye need me," said the first mate, his eyes purposefully flicking to the captain, "run and find me. I'll keep ye safe, love."

Jon's reply caught in his throat. What in the hells did Tom mean? He thought he picked up on something unexpected in the man's tone and tried to focus on the emotion before Tom buried it.

Baltsaros caught the end of Tom's words and frowned at him. There was anger there, a sense of betrayal… Then it was gone, and the captain's eyes softened.

"He'll be fine, Tom," said Baltsaros quietly with the hint of a smile.

"He better be," Tom growled in response. There it was again: fear. This time Jon was sure of it. Tom was more than just anxious over sleeping locked away from him and the captain; he was *afraid*. But what of?

The innkeeper looked between the captain and the first mate with a bored sort of curiosity. Baltsaros nodded to the man, and Tom was led away, turning his ocean eyes to Jon again before he left the room.

Find me.

J on was dismayed to learn that the captain had arranged for them to eat their meal in the main room. Almost nauseous from the constant crowd and distraught over Tom's words, Jon sank down onto the hard wooden bench and stared despondently at the bowl of fish stew in front of him. He breathed slowly through his nose, hoping the spicy smell of the dish would whet his appetite.

Jon was impatient to be alone with Baltsaros; he wanted to be somewhere where the only voices he could hear were theirs, and the desire for privacy was almost overwhelming. Jon was weary in mind and body; the search for Oren was fruitless, Tom's fear was ominous, Calum's death was senseless, Baltsaros's nonchalance over human sacrifice was... Well, he didn't even know. Didn't want to think about it. With a sigh, Jon lifted the bowl to his lips and took a sip of broth, barely registering the taste.

The captain dug into his own meal with gusto, dipping hunks of bread into the fish stew and drinking deep from the mug of malty brown beer. He peered curiously at the silent Jon as he ate, and when he had finished his stew, Baltsaros wiped the corner of his mouth with the heel of his hand. With a nod towards the door, the captain finally spoke.

"The woman who's been following us just made an appearance," said Baltsaros quietly. "But don't turn around; she's already gone."

Jon stared at Baltsaros a moment.

"How did you know there was a woman following us?" he asked, astonished.

The captain grinned wide before taking another bite of bread, chewing it thoroughly and swallowing before answering.

"Do you think that I am such an old man that my eyesight is feeble? I would wager that she's watching us on behalf of someone, but I cannot tell whether there is any malice in it. For the moment, I am content just to let her be; to confront her might put something into motion prematurely. Besides, I am curious to see whether she will approach us on her own." Baltsaros tore off another chunk of bread and held it out to Jon, his eyes amused. "You know, I did *somehow* manage to stay alive before you and Tom decided that shielding me from pertinent information was in my best interest," laughed Baltsaros, his smile creasing his sun-darkened face.

Despite everything, Jon felt a little tension go out of his shoulders at the captain's good-natured chiding. He took the bread and followed the older man's lead, dipping it into his stew.

"I wanted to tell you," he said with a shrug. "Tom thought it was a bad idea."

"Tom is overprotective," replied the captain, some of the humour leaving his eyes. A touch of weariness returned to his face a moment later, and he looked down. In one large hand he held an eating knife, and he tightened his fist around it, knuckles whitening. Baltsaros's face went blank as he stared at the blade, motionless.

Unnerved, Jon put down his bread and watched the captain. When the older man finally lifted his head, his pupils were wide in his dark eyes, trapping Jon in an unblinking gaze that was menacing, self-possessed, and cold.

Run and find me.

"Tom is worried that I am going to kill you," said Baltsaros slowly.

He wanted to laugh, the words were so absurd. However, Jon's mouth went dry as he stared back at the creature of ice who looked at him through Baltsaros's eyes. He licked his lips.

"Why... would he think that?" whispered Jon. Something chuckled inside him. *Foolish boy,* it crooned. The scar on his back twinged as Jon hunched his shoulders. He remembered dreams of blood, of terror, of a black night, of Tom's strong arms, and the captain bleeding on the rug. Dreams? He realized that Baltsaros watched him closely, and he shivered as the captain smiled, his brown eyes once more warm and amused.

"Because I came very close once already," said Baltsaros, and he speared a thick chunk of fish from Jon's bowl on the end of his knife.

Jon stared at the fish and felt the bench beneath him sway as if he were at sea.

S itting cross-legged against the rough-hewn wall, Tom stared down into his bowl. With a sigh, he sopped up the last of the stew with the hard heel of black bread, softening it lest he pull loose his teeth trying to gnaw the end of it.

The back building was little more than a long structure with four walls and a roof, each slave separated from the other by a low stack of wood that acted as a divider. The floor was earthen and covered in old straw that was infested with all manner of vermin. As he ate the rest of his supper, Tom noticed a tiny, fawn-coloured mouse watching him from under a clump of dirty straw, and he smiled. After working loose a crumb of bread, he reached forward slowly and held out his offering with a steady hand. Bit by bit, the tiny mouse came forward, its eyes black and shiny, its nose quivering.

"That's it, mate," he murmured to it. "Ol' Tom won't hurt ye. Come and get it; ye know you want it."

When the mouse finally stood on its hind legs and reached hesitantly for the crumb, Tom held his breath. He felt its little claws touch his skin briefly before the mouse plucked the bread from between his fingers. Without a backwards glance, the mouse scurried away and disappeared beneath the straw. Tom laughed.

"Without a bloody bit o' thanks..." Tom grinned wide and leaned back against the wall, the chain hooked to his collar clinking with the motion.

"If you're so full that you're up for sharing your meal, I'd prefer you share with me, friend," said a deep voice to Tom's left.

Startled, the first mate turned his head and saw a young man about his age looking at him over the low woodpile with an amused smile. The man's skin was the same deep walnut that Calum's had been, but his pupils were a surprising pale-amber colour. For a moment, Tom wondered if the man could see, so strange were his eyes.

"Tom," he said, gruffly by way of greeting.

The stranger grinned and tilted his head slightly in acknowledgment.

"So I gathered. I'm called Jarrod," he replied, placing a hand on his chest.

Tom noticed right away that the slave was missing a few fingers. He looked at Jarrod's other hand and saw that it too was short at least one digit.

Jarrod's eyes followed his gaze, and he let out a short laugh.

"I've got an unfortunate habit of running away," said the young man, holding up his hands for Tom to see. Despite his cheeky grin, Tom saw a man who was only a few fingers shy of losing hope. The slave was incredibly skinny, his ribs outlined clearly under his dark skin. Tom looked down at the bread in his hand.

"Here," he said, tossing it to Jarrod. The slave caught the heel of bread and set to work at it right away.

Curious, Jarrod looked up at Tom.

"*You* look to be intact," he said, chewing the stale bread and wiggling the stumps of his fingers. He gestured at Tom. "You marked ones sure get the lion's share when it comes to food, don't you? Look at the size of you! I don't see how you don't just break your master like a twig. Is he good to you?"

Jarrod seemed friendly enough, and Tom had nothing but time on his hands; the company was a welcome distraction from the worry he felt at being so far from Baltsaros and Jon. He smiled and shook his head.

"A real bloody tyrant," he replied and shifted in place so Jarrod could see the scars on his back. Jarrod whistled appreciatively.

They sat in silence for a few minutes while they finished eating. Then Tom had an idea.

"What say ye to a game o' dice?" he asked, reaching for the pouch sewn into the side of his trousers. He pulled out two carved-bone dice and held them up. For a second he wondered whether it was a gaffe to suggest the game, realizing suddenly that maybe they didn't have dice this side of the black mountain range. However, Jarrod's face split into a wide grin at the suggestion.

"Sure, my friend," said the young slave, rubbing his palms together. "What shall we wager? Imaginary wealth? Make-believe women? Our eternal souls... Ohh, wait... I know! The morning meal! What say you?"

Tom laughed and nodded, crawling as far as his chain would let him. When Jarrod pulled a rolled cigarette from a pocket in his rust-coloured vest, Tom's eyebrows lifted. Though the physical withdrawal was still gnawing at him, it was the simple, comforting act of smoking that he missed the most.

"Can I get ye to share that with me, mate?" he asked with a grin.

Jarrod chuckled.

"I'll roll you for it..."

J on sat on the edge of the bed and rubbed his face.

"I honestly don't know how much I want to hear," he said quietly. He looked up at the captain standing in the centre of the room, his arms crossed. "Nothing I hear from you today will endear you to me, will it?"

Baltsaros shook his head slowly but then lifted a shoulder in a slow shrug.

"It's the last of it, Jon. The very last of it, I promise," said the older man. "No more secrets between us."

Jon laughed and pinched the bridge of his nose.

"Do you even hear yourself? How many times have you said what you were telling me was the last secret?" he asked. "Does it occur to you that maybe you've burned me out? That I no longer care whether what you spout is truth or lie?"

Baltsaros's lips pressed together.

"If that were true, you wouldn't have begged off the end of your meal and forced us to take to our room early, Jon."

After taking a deep breath, Jon wiped his palms on the knees of his pants and sat up.

"I'm sorry. You just confessed to trying to kill me. How else was I supposed to react?" he asked, annoyed.

Baltsaros stared hard at him, and Jon's eyes widened as the silence dragged on. Though the captain's face was set in stony lines, it was glaringly obvious to Jon that Baltsaros was conflicted about what he wanted to tell him. That alone made his heart beat a little faster.

"Just... tell me," he said gently. For a split second he saw something in Baltsaros's eyes that gave him pause. The captain was confused; Jon blinked and Baltsaros was younger, much younger, and afraid—keenly human.

Then the vision was gone, replaced by the self-possessed stare of a man in control.

"I kill people," said Baltsaros with a grim smile.

Jon frowned.

"That's not news to me," he said. "I've seen you kill, what... dozens of people now?"

The captain shook his head.

"No, Jon," said Baltsaros, stepping forward and going down on one knee in front of him. "I *enjoy* killing people. It gives me great pleasure. It gives me power."

"Power?" Jon searched Baltsaros's eyes as the older man looked up at him.

"Blood gives me power, Jon," Baltsaros's hands curled around Jon's forearms, fingers digging painfully into his muscles. "It... speaks to something inside me and grants me strength. It grants me peace." There was an odd cast to the man's eyes; Jon thought he could see desperation in Baltsaros's face, and it clashed with his words.

The blood on the captain's shirt, the heart in the icebox, the whore in the brothel that fateful day. Hands that had held him down and pressed the blade into his skin. The man that has no heart taking the hearts of others.

Baltsaros, what have you done? he thought weakly.

Run and find me. Run and find me. Run.

Jon felt dizzy, the two images of the captain overlapping: one charming and gentle, the other a blood-thirsty murderer. He let out a slow breath, his pulse thrumming in his ears. The monster holding his arms stared at him while the seconds ticked by.

Baltsaros was crazy.

Tom knew it and had hid the captain's insanity from him. Jon had to get away, now. Before it was too late. Before Baltsaros finished the job he had started the night they passed the spires. Before he went crazy himself. He had to go. Had to.

Jon didn't move. He simply closed his eyes.

The captain loosened his grip on Jon's arms, and his fingers stroked Jon's skin softly. He turned Jon's forearms in his hands and laughed quietly. Jon let out a small gasp as the captain ran a fingertip along the fresh knife wound.

"I'm not crazy, Jon," whispered Baltsaros. The captain touched the healed scar on the inside of Jon's other forearm, the one that had been made in a tiny room above a tavern half a world away. "You believe in blood magic too, after all."

Jon's eyes snapped open, and he growled at Baltsaros.

"Don't you *dare* equate the pact we made with your damned perversions." He yanked his arms out of Baltsaros's grasp and pulled himself backwards on the bed.

You are a liar too, Jon, said a little voice inside him. The voice of his innocence.

What have I lied about? he thought miserably.

You've always known the truth.

His head swimming, Jon watched Baltsaros stagger to his feet. The older man balled his hands at his sides, his eyes crackling with cold fire as he glared down at Jon; and then, as if a light went out, the captain's posture turned to defeat, and Baltsaros let out a low sound.

"Jon," said the captain in a strange voice as he sat down slowly on the edge of the bed, "when I thought I had killed you, it was as if I had killed hope itself... I couldn't bear it. I would never do anything to harm you. Never."

Jon closed his eyes tight and leaned his head back on the wall; he didn't need his gift to know that the captain was speaking the truth.

"I know," he murmured. The craziest part of it all was the glowing feeling the captain's words gave him.

Baltsaros's hand touched his calf, warm through his thin pants, and Jon shifted his leg away.

"Then what is it?" asked Baltsaros.

Frowning, Jon sat up. He looked at the captain, his eyes wide with chagrin.

"What about the others?" he hissed. "You're a murderer, Baltsaros. What about all the innocent people you *murdered?*"

The captain's graceful lips worked against each other for a second, the lines of his face taut and his eyes flinty.

"Innocent? Were they innocents, Jon?" asked Baltsaros finally. He sounded angry.

"They were guilty of what, then? The whore at the *Rose Garden*... tell me, what had she done except be born into poverty and sold into a life of prostitution? Or the one at the *Jewel*? Do you only kill whores? Is that some kind of sick shame for your total lack of self-restraint when it comes to shoving your cock into any willing hole?" Though Jon wanted to yell, he kept his voice down to a seething growl.

"They were degenerates who held ignorant beliefs, Jon. Little lives that would only serve to pollute others."

"Oh? And who told you that you could act like a god and take lives at a fucking whim just because you disagree with them? And... oh gods, we ate her heart, didn't we?" *...the heart in the icebox...* Jon's mind finally addressed the horror of it, and he pressed his hand to his mouth.

Liar. You knew.

He felt nauseous over the truth of his complicity.

Baltsaros watched him warily.

"You had *no right* to make me a party to your murdering ways," Jon said when his nausea began to recede. "You're sick."

When the captain made no response other than to continue staring at him with that same strange expression, Jon clenched his teeth with a frustrated groan and raked his hands through his hair. Death, death, and more death. Tom's knife with its grisly tally, Baltsaros's penchant for outright murder. There was a scream buried deep in his chest, trying to claw its way out. He buried his face in his palms, pressing against his eyes so hard he saw starbursts in the dark.

The bed shifted, the cords creaking as Baltsaros moved closer. When the captain's hand settled gently on his head, Jon cringed. Baltsaros's fingers stroked him slowly.

"I… wish I had words to make it better for you," said the captain in a small voice. He trailed his fingers down the side of Jon's throat, raising goosebumps as his touch always did. "There's nothing left of my lies. You know all of my secrets. You know *me*, Jon, more than anyone alive."

"Tom knows you better," Jon muttered against his hands. "He's the one who cleans up your messes and pretends like all is right with you." Baltsaros's warm palm slid across his shoulders, the captain's fingers caressing him softly.

Jon lifted his face and looked at the man on the bed next to him.

Baltsaros had a pensive expression on his chiselled face, his eyes far away.

"The first time it happened, I was seventeen years old. We had stopped at a port town, and my men had scattered among the four brothels there. I myself hadn't yet…" Baltsaros frowned and then laughed a little sheepishly. He looked over at Jon with a shrug. "Other than the few times I was put to, ah… servicing my uncle, there had been but a few kisses here and there, and some naïve fondling in the dark. I was, for all intents and purposes, a virgin." As he spoke, Baltsaros reached for

Jon's hand and turned it palm up against his knee, tracing the lines there with the tips of his fingers.

There was something in Baltsaros's manner that automatically put Jon at ease, and he found himself wondering whether it was an act. However, despite his misgivings, he could feel himself being lulled into complacency by the captain. He was tired of fighting.

"She wasn't much older than me, pretty in a painted sort of way. After the act, which was largely forgettable despite it being my first time, she confessed that she had been afraid of being paired with one of the "animals". I had no idea what she meant at first so I pushed her to explain. She said that men like Calum and Peter, my former first mate, were so dark-skinned because they were less than human," Baltsaros laughed grimly. "I was instantly angry, but a coldness descended upon me, moving my hand to my sword. I knew what I had to do. I made her beg for her life before I cut into her like an animal for slaughter. I made a terrible mess, Jon."

Jon watched the captain's eyes grow distant again, his fingers ceasing in their motion. Through the crack in Baltsaros's walls, Jon could see a man who was searching for answers.

"But... why did you *kill* her?" asked Jon despite his horror and folded his fingers over Baltsaros's. "Make me understand."

Baltsaros pressed his lips together and shook his head once.

"Jon... You can't understand. If you ever come close, I think I would never forgive myself for killing the innocence in you..." The words were spoken in a rush, and there was a catch in Baltsaros's voice. In wonder, he watched the captain lean forward until his head touched Jon's thigh. Jon let out a slow breath, confused and concerned. He threaded his fingers through the captain's hair as the man curled up on his side on the narrow bed, resting in Jon's lap with his eyes closed.

"I killed her because she angered me. I killed her because I felt she deserved it. I killed her because something *told* me to. The reason is always so clear at the moment when my blade meets skin. When my hands are red and my tongue tastes the rich copper flow. I feel powerful. My thoughts clear... It's as if I can finally *see*. But the reason? I kill because I am a killer, my love. It's that simple. But... seeing that fact reflected in your eyes? It confuses me. It wounds me, Jon."

There it was. The captain's truth laid bare.

Jon pulled on Baltsaros's shoulder until the man turned, staring up at him with troubled eyes.

When he placed his palm against the captain's broad chest, Jon felt the regular, strong beat of the heart within and closed his eyes. Baltsaros was wrong; there was one more thing he needed to know.

"Do you love me?" asked Jon quietly.

...only ask me questions you want to know the answers to...

When the silence stretched on, Jon opened his eyes and looked down at the captain. Baltsaros looked weary, and he pulled Jon's hand to his mouth to kiss his knuckles softly.

"No, Jon. I don't."

17

BROKEN BODIES AND SOULS

Baltsaros watched Jon's eyes lose focus. He could almost feel the confusion and hurt that ran through him, so plain were the emotions on the younger man's face. When the captain tried to press Jon's hand to his lips again, Jon pulled it slowly out of his grasp, shaking his head a little. Baltsaros almost groaned out loud, frustration spiking his blood and making him want to lash out, when what he really *needed* was to hold Jon close. It was important that Jon understand him, how he had been foolish in his hopes for the future, and how the knife wound on Jon's back was testament to that naïveté.

Now there was no way of telling Jon the rest of it without first addressing this futile question of love.

There was a knock at the door: three hard blows against the wood.

Startled, Baltsaros sat up, his hand reaching immediately for the dagger at his waist. He slipped off the bed and strode quickly across the room, casting a look over his shoulder at Jon who sat motionless as if in a trance. Baltsaros pressed his lips together; everything he was, everything he believed in, was cast into doubt by the look in those stormy grey-blue eyes. He clenched his jaw with annoyance at the interruption; damn Jon for his ill-timed question.

"Yes?" he asked, opening the door a crack. The innkeeper, a scowl on his face, stood on the other side.

"You have to come with me," said the man.

The captain frowned.

"Is there a problem?" Baltsaros's hand tightened around the dagger's handle.

The man on the other side of the door looked past Baltsaros's shoulder, his eyes narrowed in suspicion.

"What's wrong with him?" asked the tall man, pushing the door open.

The captain stepped back, resisting the urge to sink the point of his dagger into the crook of the man's neck; he felt strange and tense, off balance. As he straightened his shoulders, he took a calming breath. His eyes went to the bed where Jon still sat in a daze. It was as if he had not even registered the intrusion.

"He's had a spell. It's none of your concern," Baltsaros said curtly. He turned back to the innkeeper and made a show of sliding his blade back into its sheath. "Now what do you want?"

"It's your slave," said the man. "He tried to burn down my inn." When the innkeeper looked at the captain, Baltsaros realized he was sporting a fresh bruise just visible above his wiry black beard.

Gods be damned Tom, what have you done? The rejuvenating effects of the blood sacrifice had all but faded, and Baltsaros felt brittle.

"What happened to Tom?" Jon's voice was hoarse, and he sounded lost; Baltsaros wondered if he could be counted on to keep up the charade in this state.

"Nephew, stay here and get some rest," he said slowly. "You're unwell. I will be back as soon as I can."

Jon stared at him, a deep furrow between his dark brows. The worry in Jon's eyes loosened something in Baltsaros's chest, and his own concern for Tom reared up inside him, its intensity taking him by surprise.

"No... I'm coming with you," said Jon, pushing himself off the bed. The captain stared hard at him for a moment, but he knew there was nothing he could say that would change Jon's mind now. Not when Tom was involved. With a sigh, he nodded to Jon and then motioned for the innkeeper to lead the way.

"This had better be worth my time," growled Baltsaros at the man, following him out of the room. "I had your express assurance that my slave would be secure in this back building of yours."

They went down the back steps two at a time.

"He was smoking with another slave," said the man gravely, looking over his shoulder at Baltsaros. When he saw the puzzlement on the captain's face, the innkeeper threw up his hands in exasperation. "It is absolutely forbidden to smoke in the slave quarters! I said as much... I know I did. There is dry straw on the ground; what would happen if the building went up in flames? It is connected to my inn!" The bearded man gesticulated angrily as he went on with his rant, leading Baltsaros and Jon down a dark, narrow corridor. "Worse, he attacked two of my own slaves when we tried to restrain him! I don't know how you do things in the Badlands, but this is Balor, gods bless! He is a complete savage and should be put down. One of my slaves has a broken nose; the other, a broken arm. I even caught a fist to the face when pulling them apart! I've dealt with the other slave, but since yours is *marked*... and you seem to be a man of standing and, ah... means... I thought perhaps a little minted steel could remedy some of the situation"—the innkeeper shot a shrewd look at Baltsaros before continuing down yet another short staircase—"and you could handle the punishment of your own slave. We did subdue him, however..."

Baltsaros's jaw tightened as they went through a low doorway into a room that appeared to be used for the sole purpose of detaining or punishing slaves.

Tom lay curled on his side, chained ankle and wrist to a metal ring in the stone floor. When the men stepped closer, the first mate slowly lifted his head. Before Baltsaros could stop himself, a low sound escaped from his open lips from the sight of the damage wrought.

One of Tom's eyes was swollen completely shut, and blood ran freely down the side of his face from a deep cut on his scalp. His lip was split on one side, and a string of blood and saliva hung from the torn edge. His one eye stared angrily at Baltsaros; the captain ground his teeth and took a step towards his tomcat, horrified. Outraged. No matter what the cheeky mainlander had done, Tom was *his* to punish. That someone had taken it upon themselves to lay hands on Tom sickened Baltsaros.

You weren't there to protect him.

Baltsaros's heart hammered against his ribs, raw anger burning through his chest making it hard to breathe.

Tom was his responsibility. Baltsaros had let him down, and the beautiful, broken young man who had given him his loyalty and love had suffered for it. The captain pushed away the strange, terrible guilt that shook him and opened his mouth to chastise the innkeeper for his treatment of Tom when Jon stepped forward and spoke up.

Jon's voice was cold, his words flavoured with the sibilance of Baltsaros's own northern accent.

"How *dare* you? Who gave you the right to damage my property?" growled Jon. Baltsaros's eyebrows shot up, and Tom's one good eye widened in surprise. "I should have you whipped like a bloody cur for presuming you had authority to exact *any* sort of punishment on my chattel without my leave... *you piece of shit.*"

When the innkeeper started to respond angrily about the possible fire, Jon cut him off with a motion of his hand and an icy glare.

"Unchain him *now*, you worthless pig. I had hoped to fight him in the cages tomorrow, but you have robbed me of that with your mishandling of the situation. If... so help me gods, *if* my best fighter is permanently damaged, you can sure as hells expect me to come seeking payment." Jon stood a few inches shorter than the lanky innkeeper, but the haughty fury he projected had the other shrinking back in dismay.

"But what about *my* men? What about the damages your beast caused? I use those slaves to keep out the rabble—" stammered the man; his anger had a weakened edge to it.

Baring his teeth, Jon took another step forward, and Tom's long blade came out of its sheath slowly as he stalked the innkeeper. *"Unchain him, or I will flay the skin from your bones."* Jon's words were a low, deadly hiss, and in the wan, flickering torchlight, his lips seemed to curve into a bloodthirsty smile.

Stunned, Baltsaros watched the innkeeper fumble at his belt for the keys. The man tossed them at Jon, his eyes darting to Baltsaros's and back again.

"Take him and leave. I don't want to see you here again. Just go." Though he sounded irate, the innkeeper was pale, and the vein in his neck jumped visibly under his skin.

Jon quickly unlocked the shackles binding Tom and helped him to stand. Baltsaros saw that Jon took in a sharp breath when the big man leaned against him for a second, his ribs still obviously painful to the touch, but to his credit Jon's expression never changed from one of imperious outrage. Baltsaros's own fury and sharp guilt had sputtered to nothing over the astonishment at Jon's acting.

Without sparing a glance at the innkeeper, Jon turned and left the room. Baltsaros placed a reassuring hand against Tom's lower back, the first mate's skin warm against his palm, and gently pushed him to follow Jon.

Once they were outside and far away from the door of the inn, the summer night warm and scented with night blooms, Jon finally broke character. He turned, and Baltsaros saw that his eyes were full of pain as he took in Tom's injuries.

"Are you ok?" he asked in a hushed voice.

In contrast, Tom's face had creased into a gory smile. Wincing as he touched the cut on his lips with the tips of his fingers, Tom let out an amused chuckle.

"Jon, that was bloody brilliant," said the first mate, accepting Baltsaros's handkerchief. He dabbed at his mouth with it then pressed the white square of cloth to the cut on his scalp. "That cocksucker nearly shat himself when ye pulled out the ol' knife. I take back all the things I ever said about ye bein' soft, lad." Tom shook his head, his one blue-green eye narrowing in mischief as he looked up at Baltsaros. "Jon put ye to shame, Da. Shit, I got stiff jus' hearin' 'im talk like he was a right scourge."

Baltsaros smiled wryly. Despite the beating he took, Tom seemed no worse for the incident. The captain knew there would be no hard feelings there. Jon, on the other hand... The younger man's eyes were closed off to him, his shoulders high and tense when he finally met Baltsaros's gaze. Quashing his dismay, the captain let his features soften as he looked at Jon.

"He was certainly something," he said warmly. Jon had not only saved Tom from further molestation, but he had also kept their coin purse full. They were now short of lodging for the night, but that was a minor thing. They could try to find beds in the *madina*. "Thank you, Jon, that was very well done."

"Yes, that was quite the display," said a woman's voice. Out from the darkness at the side of the road emerged a hooded figure. Baltsaros's hand went to his sword, and out of the corner of his eye, he saw Tom take a step to place himself between the shadowy figure and Jon.

Gloved hands reached up to pull back the burgundy hood, revealing a woman about the same age as Tom and Jon. Her large, limpid blue eyes were set wide over a snub nose, and they narrowed in amusement as she looked at the three of them.

"Oh, you won't be needing that," she said, gesturing to Baltsaros's sword, her cupid's-bow lips quirking into a small smile. "I assure you that I am nothing if not friendly."

Baltsaros loosened his grip on the pommel but did not move his hand away. The woman's smile widened at his suspicion, and she shook her head, her springy, orange curls brushing her cheeks with the motion.

"So distrustful! I know who you are, Captain Baltsaros, and I give you my word that I mean you no harm. Not to you or your associates," laughed the woman. Her gaze slipped back to Tom, and Baltsaros frowned as she took a step towards the first mate. Tom looked down at her with a slow grin; however, Baltsaros knew that the potential for immediate violence lay behind his impish smile.

She placed a gloved finger on Tom's chest and ran the tip of it downwards, over the first mate's hard stomach.

"My, my... You're a big boy, aren't you?" she said in a husky voice.

To Baltsaros's complete surprise, Tom flushed visibly. The muscles in the first mate's neck twitched as he shifted his weight slightly, and the woman's lips parted in a low chuckle at his discomfiture, her teeth white and even in a smile that could only be called predatory.

Jon's face had darkened to a scowl, his upper lip curled in distaste.

Interesting. Baltsaros wondered what Jon's gift was telling him about the woman before them.

"See... I know that Jon is not your nephew," continued the woman, her eyes on Tom, "and this gorgeous creature here, despite obviously having *been* a slave, is certainly not one now." The woman winked at Tom before turning and tilting her face up to Baltsaros.

The captain cocked his head, both curious and wary. The woman exuded a brazen self-confidence that she wielded like both sword and shield; Baltsaros wondered what truths lived behind that hard exterior.

"You know who we are," he said with a smile as he ducked his head in a shallow bow. "However, you have us at a distinct disadvantage."

"Charming, well-spoken, handsome. I like you, Captain Baltsaros," said the woman with another bright smile. Once again, the captain noticed that it didn't reach her eyes. "Tonight, I am but a

247

simple messenger, here to invite the three of you to the emperor's palace. He has taken an interest in you and would like to offer you a place to stay while visiting our golden city."

Baltsaros looked at Tom and Jon and saw that the latter was slowly shaking his head, his face drawn. Tom seemed equally leery, but Baltsaros knew the first mate would follow his lead.

"What if we refuse?" asked Baltsaros.

The woman laughed and snapped her fingers.

"Now why would you refuse? I took you for an intelligent man, Captain. The emperor, gods bless him, does not extend such invitations every day."

They were quickly surrounded by tall, muscular slaves, each armed with a spear.

Tom let out a low string of curses, his scarred fists white-knuckled at his sides. Baltsaros knew that the first mate was more wounded than he let on, and with Jon's injured ribs, they didn't stand a chance against so many.

With a graceful smile, Baltsaros extended his hands in a gesture of supplication.

"My dear, I was simply asking a question," he chided her. "There's no need to force the issue. We would be pleased to accept the invitation." In truth, he was extremely curious about the man who ruled Ereme'ia Balor through fear and blood. Polas had called him a "collector of broken bodies and souls", and Baltsaros had a keen interest in finding out what that meant. Maybe this man was what he needed...

The young woman's lips curled in amusement.

"In that case, *my dear*, we can be on our way. The emperor is anxious to make your acquaintance," she said. She tilted her head, her blue eyes wide as she regarded the captain. "I wonder what he'll make of you... I have a feeling that you and he share some common... interests."

Baltsaros smiled wider, his eyes crinkling at the corners.

"And what role do you play when you're not a 'simple messenger'?" he asked, keeping his tone light.

"Why, I'm the emperor's spymaster, of course," she said with crooked grin, staring at him a moment longer. "You can call me Ceara."

The slight woman pulled the hood back up to cover her hair and turned to lead them up the wide street towards the brightly lit pyramid that rose up above the city centre.

18

FATHER OF THE RITE OF BLOOD

Each player must accept the cards life deals him or
her: but once they are in hand, he or she alone
must decide how to play the cards in order to
win the game.

— VOLTAIRE

Flanked by armed slaves, the pirates followed the woman closely as she led them down one street and then another. Jon walked next to Tom, the big man's quiet presence a comfort. Though Jon desperately wanted to reach for him, he couldn't. Not in this world of slave and master. Not where a man was barred from offering succour to another man. Instead he kept his head down and trudged along, doing everything he could to keep his mind from returning to that terrible, hopeless moment in the inn.

The street was dark, lit only by firelight that spilled from doors and windows open to the cool night breeze. He could hear voices raised in laughter, anger; a child's cry rang out once and then went silent as a woman began singing quietly. Down one street, the scent of spices mixed with the salty sea air. Then the wind shifted as they crossed an open square, and Jon could faintly smell animal dung. He turned his head and saw that there was a series of pastures far off to their left; humped shapes dotted the fields, and Jon heard the lowing of a cow as they passed by.

Despite the terrors of the day, the city felt peaceful around him, the citizens safe in their homes. The night was quiet and pleasant; he could almost forget where they were.

Almost.

When they passed a post with a set of shackles bolted into its side, Jon looked quickly away in disgust. Next to him, Tom let out a low curse at the sight of the whipping post. This was what Jon could not understand about the captain's fascination with Ereme'ia Balor. Pushing aside the horror of human sacrifice, Jon couldn't believe that Baltsaros was so blind to the human suffering around him. Baltsaros had freed Tom. He cultivated freedom and equality aboard his ship... Yet it didn't seem to bother the captain that the blood feeding the "gods" came from the vast leagues of enslaved. That he didn't seem to care disturbed Jon.

He *didn't* care, did he? Jon was once again in the room, Baltsaros staring up at him with eyes dark and unreadable.

No, Jon. I— Jon felt the hollowness inside him again and shook his head, trying to force the memory away.

—I don't. On the edge of a precipice and pushed over, no one to catch him as he fell... He stumbled slightly, and Tom's arm shot out to steady him. The first mate's hand rested on his shoulder a moment, concern lining his bruised and bloody face.

"I'm ok," said Jon quietly. He had to be. What other choice was there? Nothing had changed... everything had changed.

Tom nodded, dropping his arm.

No, Jon. I don't.

Had he *really* expected a different answer?

This was Baltsaros... The man had no heart. And yet, when Baltsaros had frozen in reaction to seeing Tom beaten and bloody on the stone floor, Jon had seen nothing but pain and fury through the cracks in the captain's mask. It was then that Jon had jumped in, afraid that if he let Baltsaros speak, more blood would end up pooling on the cold ground. The captain was fiercely protective of his first mate... But was it love? It certainly seemed like it.

No, Jon. I don't.

Jon's pain was slowly evaporating, disappearing into the fissures of his growing anger. After everything, was he still an interloper? A pathetic third wheel that dragged behind Baltsaros and Tom as they lied, cheated, and murdered gleefully together? He knew it was a petty thought—especially when he met Tom's eye again and saw that the first mate's forehead was creased in worry—but he preferred anger to the aching dejection that soured his stomach. Fuck Baltsaros. Fuck Tom.

Being loveless and alone had not hurt nearly as much. Jon hitched his shoulders higher and glared at Baltsaros's back.

When they turned yet another corner, the pyramid loomed up high above them, lit on every tier with blazing white light. After walking through the darkened city for so long, Jon's eyes watered from the sight. As he lifted a hand to partially shield his vision, Jon tried to see how the effect was accomplished, but he could not see any flickering of flames.

"Bloody hell," muttered Tom from behind his own raised hand.

They followed the woman past a pair of marked slaves standing guard outside red and gold double doors.

Jon frowned. There was something extremely familiar about the doors that made his heart beat a little faster as they passed through them. He tried to shake away the feeling of unease, telling himself that he had probably seen other doors like this in the city. It didn't explain, however, why his palms felt damp as his eyes slid over the carved silhouettes of snakes that decorated the walls to either side.

When they came to a stop in a vestibule that was lit by the same brilliance as the exterior, Jon rubbed his eyes, peering around him at the bewildering white globes that shone bright.

"Phosphorus?" asked the captain, his features alive with curiosity.

The woman lowered her hood again and chuckled, shaking her head.

"Something much more interesting," she said with a wry grin. "I assure you."

Jon scowled at her. He didn't trust the spymaster in the least; his senses screamed at him that she was thoroughly duplicitous, someone capable of sinking to great depths to advance herself and her cause. When she turned her clear blue eyes to Jon, she smirked at the look on his face.

"You don't like me very much, do you, Jon?" Ceara asked, arching a shapely brow at him.

"You haven't exactly given me much cause," he replied tersely.

Her girlish laughter echoed in the small stone room, and she made a shooing motion with her hands. At once the slaves bowed and filed out of the room. The moment they were gone, the woman's smile disappeared, and her expression became serious, almost fearful.

"I don't have much time to explain, but listen to me carefully," she said quickly in a hushed voice, her gloved hands clasped together nervously as she looked up at each of them in turn. "You will have to keep playing your roles... for the time being. Do nothing to make him suspect you are anything but what you claim to be."

Jon blinked, remembering something she had said.

"You said 'I know who you are', not 'we'," he said slowly.

"I did, didn't I? Such a perceptive boy," she said, a touch of wry humour returning to her face. "Yes, our Most Exalted Emperor knows you come from beyond the Gods' Claws, as they are known here. However, I have kept the other truths from him. It's... for the best."

As she spoke, she pulled a small earthenware bowl with a cork in its side from an alcove in the stone wall. She motioned to Tom.

"Give me your hand," she said. "Quickly."

"The hells I will," growled Tom, crossing his arms.

"Tom," warned the captain, his brows low over eyes flinty and black. The first mate shot a dark look at Baltsaros but extended his hand, a scowl on his damaged face. Ceara pulled a needle-thin dagger from her sleeve and jabbed it quickly into the meat of Tom's thumb. The first mate flinched but didn't take his hand back, watching with wary curiosity as she turned his hand over the bowl and let the drops of blood flow into the vessel.

"We don't have much time before he sends someone looking for us, and this is the only place where we can speak privately," she explained. "I'm sorry about the cut, but the emperor demands a personal blood sacrifice from those who seek audience with him." When she was satisfied that enough blood had fallen, she dropped the first mate's hand and reached for Jon's.

Jon narrowed his eyes at her, bracing himself against the prick of the blade.

"What will keep you from holding the truth of who we are like a knife over us?" Jon asked. "Why should we trust you?"

Ceara lifted her gaze, and again he was struck with the impression that she was thoroughly unscrupulous; however, there was real fear in her wide, sky-blue eyes and that disturbed him even more.

"Because I'm going to help you get out of here alive," she said, holding his stare a breath longer before frowning down at his bleeding thumb.

Jon's heart froze in his chest, skipping over itself in dread. Mouth dry, he watched numbly as she squeezed another drop from his hand and then reached for the captain's.

"Why would you help us, Ceara?" asked Baltsaros quietly, watching her pierce his skin with her knife.

"Because you're going to take me with you when you go," she replied. She straightened her shoulders and stared a challenge at the captain, her face pale and lips pressed together in a grim line.

In the stark light of the small room, the captain's angular profile was a series of planes and shadows as he looked down at the woman holding his hand. Two predators: one fierce, the other devious.

After a moment Baltsaros nodded.

"If you truly think we are in danger, we shall do as you say, Ceara," he murmured, "though I do not like being a piece in a game that I am not familiar with."

She pulled away and smiled tightly.

"The game of survival is one that we should all know…" She turned and held the earthenware bowl over a golden urn to one side of the doors. "Do what I say, and we will survive. I give you my word."

Jon felt an icy touch of foreboding. What was her word worth?

After she pulled the cork out of the side of the small bowl, she let the mingled blood within it drip into the urn. A moment later, the gilded doors parted soundlessly.

"Please follow me," said the slight woman brightly, her veneer restored. She turned on her heel and led the way through the open doors.

Tom sucked on the ball of his thumb as he followed the others down a long corridor towards a raised, curtained platform in the distance. Beneath his feet, the stone was surprisingly warm, and he was glad for it. He'd lost quite a bit of blood in the fight with the innkeeper's bodyguards and felt cold and a little weak. Losing another few drops of it just to get through a bloody door hadn't helped any, he was sure. At least here it wasn't as bright as it had been in the other room; he was having problems focusing the one eye he could open and had felt nearly blinded by the glowing orbs. Touching the cut on his scalp gingerly, Tom wondered if there wasn't something a little wrong with his head; when the bigger of the two slaves had started in on him with hands the size of hams, Tom had seen some crazy flashes of light. The captain would know... though who could guess when they would next be alone.

He looked curiously at the woman leading them. His gut told him she was a real piece of work and probably a hellcat in the sack. He scratched his chest, remembering how her gloved finger had snaked its way down, following the line of hair to his belly. He grinned to himself, imagining her tiny, gloved hand wrapped around his thick cock.

"What are you smiling about?" asked Jon softly, a bewildered look on his wan face. "Aren't you the slightest bit worried that we're being led to our deaths?"

Tom smiled wider.

"Naw," he said. "Horny, maybe..." He shook his head when Jon's eyes widened in disbelief. How to explain to him that danger always made him feel a little randy? Now that they were no longer tip-toeing around the bloody back alleys like some cloak-and-dagger amateurs and finally facing some real fucking danger, he felt excited.

"Listen, love. There ain't nothin' to worry about yet. Don't be afraid of what ye don't know; that's a bloody waste of time. I'm thinkin' the little lady's puttin' on a bit of a show, aye? Don't tell me ye ain't seen it. A snake that one—" He frowned when he saw Jon's face go a shade whiter. "What's the matter?"

"A snake... The doors..." whispered Jon. "I had a dream where you and Baltsaros were attacked by snakes. You were a wild cat and he was a giant lion, and—"

"We were what? Was there fuckin'? Shit I'd love to see—"

"No! Tom, what the hell is the matter with you?" hissed Jon. They were quickly approaching the platform.

"It was a bloody dream, ducky," said Tom, shrugging. "Not a fuckin' prophesy."

Jon's face fell, the muscles working in his jaw as he looked hard at Tom.

That's it, lad, he thought. *Pissed is better than afraid.*

However, Jon's talk of dreams had unnerved him too. He didn't normally put any stock in dreams—ten long, bloody years of his own had been false visions of freedom—but this was Jon, and Jon had seen them coming to this land long before Tom's tattoos had healed.

T here was a sudden blast of horns, and the red and gold curtains parted. Beyond them was a series of low couches on the carpeted platform with colourful floor cushions strewn haphazardly between them. The air was redolent with incense, and it reminded Tom of the church he once attended with his mother. Gods and prophecies... he didn't like either of them one bit.

In the middle of the platform was a couch larger and more elaborate than the rest. Reclined on it was a dark-haired man wearing loose, sand-coloured robes. At their approach, he sat up and looked down at them over the bridge of his hooked nose, his head tilted back arrogantly. He had blue eyes that bulged slightly in his sallow face, and his mouth was small and mean over a weak chin that bore the dark shadow of a beard; Tom thought he looked a little like a rat or a weasel and struggled to keep the sneer from his face.

Look at the good little slave I am.

The redhead stopped with a low bow and then turned to address the men with a smug smile.

"Please bow before the Pillar of the Gods, the Master of Sacred Blessings, Father of the Rite of Blood, our Most Exalted Leader... Emperor Ah'puch," she said with a flourish.

For a moment the pirates stood motionless. Jon looked dazed and a little frightened, and the captain stared at the man on the couch with a blank expression; Tom was almost certain that Baltsaros's brain had simply dismissed the request that he bow and was instead storing away all his little observations about the man. He himself had no desire to bow or scrape, but he was damn sure that if no one did, it would probably look bad for the three of them.

After taking a small step forward, Tom bowed low with a hand on his chest, the same way he'd done it as a child when his family had visited the king and queen. Following Tom's cue, Jon quickly bowed also. The captain took a moment longer, but when it finally occurred to him to show a little respect, Baltsaros ducked into a graceful bow that put both his and Jon's to shame.

"You may rise," said the emperor in a nasally voice.

Tom lifted his eyes and straightened, watching the man shift himself off the couch and stand using the aid of a gilded walking staff.

"Welcome to Ereme'ia Balor, Captain Baltsaros!" said the emperor with a small smile. "It was so good of you to accept Our invitation!" The man approached the captain and held out his hand. Tom was confused for a moment until he realized that the emperor meant for Baltsaros to kiss his ring. Laughter threatened to bubble out of him at the thought of the captain kissing someone's ring; he rubbed a hand over his face to hide his smile, glancing sidelong at Jon as he lowered his head.

Jon's expression was the same distracted, lost look that he'd been wearing since leaving the inn. Tom grazed his teeth along the cut on his lip, wondering what was going through his mind. One moment Jon could sound like the evilest bastard this side of the black hells, the next he was a frail wisp with eyes that showed the depths of his soul. Tom wished he understood Jon better, but it didn't change the fact that he truly loved all versions him.

Tom quietly clicked his tongue once to get Jon's attention. Face bleak, Jon turned, and Tom sighed, wishing he could take away some of his anxiety; with a tiny smile, he slowly tapped the fresh cut on the inside of his arm.

I have your back.

With his eyes on Tom's forearm, Jon's lips curled in a humour-less grin as he thumbed his own thin scar. When he glanced back up at Tom, all the big man could see was despair.

What does it matter?

Tom shifted his gaze to the others and saw that Baltsaros and Ah'puch were exchanging pleasantries, ignoring the rest of them. He turned his eyes back to Jon but saw that the serious young man had resorted to staring at his feet.

This was going extremely well so far.

Tom shifted his weight, realizing just how tired and sore he was. As a slave, he would never be offered a seat, and he wondered how long they would be made to socialize with the rat-like emperor. As he looked around, Tom caught the spymaster's eye. The woman stared blatantly at him, and he found himself returning her coy smile. Certainly not meek, this one.

"Why don't we have a seat and get to know one another?" asked Ah'puch, motioning to the couches and cushions around them. "We would love to hear stories from your lands."

"I was led to believe that those coming from beyond the spires were assumed to be ghosts," said Baltsaros, seating himself slowly with a smile.

"Suspicious nonsense... But an utterly necessary ruse," replied the emperor with a conspiratorial grin. The man sat himself down on his gilded couch and pointed to Tom as if he were an object.

"Does he understand what we're saying?" he asked.

Tom stared blankly forward, feigning ignorance.

"No. What value is there in teaching a slave another language?" laughed Baltsaros. "But unfortunately," he said, switching to Common, "neither does my nephew."

"That is a shame," said the emperor with a moue. He tapped the side of his jaw. "We find Common tedious to speak. Never mind."

The captain glanced over at Jon, who still had not taken a seat. Astonished, Tom saw a flicker of something on the captain's face that he had rarely, if ever, seen. It looked suspiciously like shame.

"My nephew is unwell," said Baltsaros. "He should get some rest. Can he be shown to a room where he can sleep? When Ceara extended your gracious invitation, it was quite late, and the walk has exhausted Jon."

"Of course!" said the emperor, motioning to his spymaster. "Ceara, would you be so kind? You can also take the slave to the slave quarters—" Ah'puch turned back to Baltsaros. "If you don't mind, of course?" When the captain shook his head, the emperor smiled. "Also... please return with some more wine, Ceara, if you may? We are in for a late night."

Turning back to Baltsaros, the emperor dismissed the lot of them.

19
___

DESPERATE MEASURES

Desperation is the raw material of drastic change.
Only those who can leave behind everything
they have ever believed in can hope to escape.

— WILLIAM S. BURROUGHS

Tom peered around the bathhouse and whistled quietly to himself in amazement. After being dropped off at the slave quarters by Ceara, he had asked the burly slave master whether he might get cleaned up. This is where he had been brought to.

From where he stood at the entrance, he could see that there were various pools of water spaced out between thick, intricately carved pillars. Steam rose from some but not others, and he grinned; it meant that both hot and cool waters were available to the bathers, and that was bloody fantastic. He shook his head. If this was the slaves' bath, he wondered what the emperor's looked like.

He took a step forward, the sandstone under his feet heated like the rest of the palace, and saw that along one wall was a vast scene picked out in small stones. It depicted a multitude of scantily clad men and women frolicking in dance. Or at least it looked like dance; amused, Tom squinted at a pair of "dancers" and took another step to get a better look just as loud voices erupted on his left.

Tom swivelled quickly, all of his senses focused on possible danger, and let out a frustrated sigh. *Almost* all of his senses; he still couldn't see out of one fucking eye, and the lack of depth perception was starting to get to him. The room was dimly lit, and it took him a few seconds to see the figures at the far side. Two men and a woman stood next to a row of stone benches, and at first glance it looked like a friendly argument between three slaves. However, when the woman kept shaking her head and stepping back as the two tall slaves stalked forward like cats cornering a mouse, Tom realized something felt bloody wrong. Tom scratched his cheek, wondering whether he should step in, when one man gave the young woman a quick shove that landed her hard on the bench. The other man barked an ugly laugh, and Tom's instincts took over.

The woman let out a small whimper; Tom could see that one of the men had his hand on her shoulder holding her down, while the other yanked up the hem of her dress, the bulge at the front of his loose linen pants evidence of his intent.

"Aye, mates," Tom called out as he approached the group.

At the sound of Tom's voice, the two men started and looked up, frowning at him as he came to a stop on the other side of the bench.

"What do ye think yer doin', mates?" he said with a friendly grin. He felt naked without his blade nestled in its usual spot at his lower back. Without it, he'd have to use his fists, and he was damn sore from his earlier fight.

"None of your business... *mate*," sneered the man holding the woman's dress up. He was tall and muscular with a thin face and hair that stuck up over a peaked forehead. Tom pegged him as the top dog, the one he needed to rattle. The slave's dark eyes narrowed at Tom with suspicion.

"Well, ye see… I was about to take a bath, and I can't be doin' any sort o' relaxin' with this sort of foolery goin' on," Tom said slowly, staring hard at the slave. "She'll be all screamin' and cryin' and carryin' on… puttin' off my bloody *requiescence*, if ye know what I mean? But! ye say. But! Oh… I know what yer about to say, matey: *they always get quiet after a few dozen thrusts*, aye? Well I ain't got that sort o' patience." Maintaining eye contact, Tom leaned slightly forward and crossed his arms across his broad chest. Flexing his shoulders, he curled his lip at the man in front of him. "So ye'd best be off, peaceful-like… What d'ye say, mate?" He saw from the corner of his eye that the other hadn't yet moved, and it seemed he wouldn't until his companion decided what he made of Tom.

Across the bench, Tom and the slave stared at each other, unblinking. He was beginning to think that maybe he would actually have to fight the fuckers, when the man restraining the slave woman slowly pulled his hand away from her shoulder.

"Laz, look at his tattoo," said the shorter man in a strangled voice. "He's the one that broke Saban's arm at the Stone Inn tonight."

Tom chuckled.

"So ye heard?" he said, smiling wide again. News certainly travelled fast in Balor.

The thin-faced slave blinked, an edge of uncertainty creeping into his expression. He glanced down at Tom's chest.

"It's true then," said Laz, looking back up at Tom. His voice was strangely hushed. When the slave released the woman's dress, she quickly pulled away, covering herself.

Tom glanced at her, and she stared back at him fearfully, her green eyes wide. She probably wondered if he meant to take her himself.

"Shoo," he murmured. "Run away little mouse." If there was one thing that Tom could not stomach, it was rape. "Hells, of course it's bloody true, and I'll break yer fuckin' arm too if ye don't stay out of my fuckin' way..." he growled, narrowing his good eye at Laz as the young woman fled.

The slave shook his head, hands up in supplication.

"No, *friend*," said the man gently. "I meant... that you're kin from across the mountains."

"You know that it's heresy to even think that," said Ceara, stepping into the light. "Now leave us, or I will make damn sure your names are in the drawing for the next round of blessings..."

Laz blanched and dipped his head quickly, crashing backwards into his companion in his haste to leave the room.

Tom watched the two men leave.

"Fuckin' dogs. Ye'd think they'd respect their own... but it ain't never like that, aye love? What's to keep 'em from preyin' on the weaker?" he asked with a frown.

Ceara lifted her hand, waving his question away.

"Despite what I generally lead them to believe, I have little influence over their discipline," she said. "My job is information, not punishment."

Tom shrugged. Life was a mess of shitty things; he wasn't out to save the world.

Turning his head, he looked longingly at the water, hoping whatever it was that she wanted wouldn't take up the rest of the bloody night. He ached everywhere, and the warm bath called to him.

"Don't let me keep you from it," said the woman with a wry twist of her lips.

Tom didn't need any coaxing. His hands went to the laces holding the front of his pants together, and he quickly loosened them.

"Ye here to give me a bath then?" he asked with a cheeky grin. He let his trousers drop. The woman's eyes stroked down his body, her eyebrows lifting as she took in his nudity. Her cheeks reddened noticeably, and she quickly raised her eyes back to his, her smile coy.

"Ah... no. I came to talk to you about getting us to your ship," she said softly.

Tom nodded and crouched next to one of the steaming baths. He dipped his hand into the water and found it to be so hot that it nearly burned. It was perfect. He slowly eased himself into the bath and let out a low, pleased groan as the hot water enveloped his aching skin. It was just the thing he needed.

"So... talk," he said, closing his eye as he leaned back against the marble edge. "I'm listenin'." He heard her soft step as she moved closer.

"The emperor is being gracious to you for now, but I don't see it lasting. He'll eventually separate the three of you, and I'm not sure what he'll do with your captain, but he's the real interest here. Ah'puch will put you to work in the mines or the leather pits, and you'll eventually wind up as a sacrifice, I have no doubt of that. With Jon... It might be execution for something petty if he can't find a use for him," she murmured.

At the mention of Jon, Tom opened his eye, his heart thrumming hard against his ribs.

"But he's safe for now?" he asked.

The woman nodded.

"Safe for now, yes. Perfectly safe... and I can *keep* him safe as long as you can convince him of something," she said. She knelt down at the edge of the bath next to Tom. He watched curiously as she took off her glove and put her hand into the water; cupping her fingers, she scooped some up to trickle it over his shoulder.

Tom frowned, but it felt great. Sensual. When she did it again and let her fingers trail along his collarbone, he felt himself stir.

"Why don't ye convince him yerself?" he asked gruffly. Her fingertips brushed the side of his face, her skin hot from the steaming water, and he closed his eye again, just letting her touch him. He breathed slowly, the motion sending delicious eddies against his sensitive, submerged cock.

"He doesn't like me," she replied, a smile in her voice. Her lips were so close to his ear that he felt her breath against him.

"Mmm...kay?" muttered Tom. "What do ye want me to tell 'im?"

"Just this: when the accusation comes, he has to say he was *forced*. It's extremely important for my plan to work," whispered Ceara, her mouth brushing the rim of his ear.

Tom flared his nostrils, concentrating on her words. Forced?

"Sure," he agreed. He didn't trust her, but what choice did he have? "He was forced. Got it." He shifted slightly in the hot water and turned to look at her. "Now can ye do somethin' for me, doll?"

Ceara smiled coyly, her cheeks a pretty pink.

"Of course," she said huskily. "Anything you want..." She slowly stroked one fingertip down the side of his neck, and he reached up to take her hand.

"Can ye go get Jon for me? See that we have some privacy, aye?" he said with a grin. "There's a good girl."

She looked confused for a moment and pulled her hand away. When she grasped Tom's meaning, her face fell slightly, but she quickly hid her disappointment with a smirk.

"And if I don't?" she asked, getting to her feet. Tom looked up at her and forced the corners of his mouth down, shrugging.

"I've been told that sleepin' abovedecks in the rain isn't *so* bad when ye don't have a bunk to call yer own," he drawled, watching his bruised hand flex below the water. "At least ye get to feel at one with nature... savvy?" He looked up at her and gave her a sudden, wide smile.

Ceara rolled her eyes at him.

"Yes, fine. Savvy," she muttered.

"Aw lovey, yer a fine-lookin' woman, it's not that," Tom said apologetically. "All jokin' aside, if it ain't the captain, or it ain't Jon..." He shrugged again. "There just ain't anyone else."

J on jerked awake, hands out to push away the dark form that loomed above him.

"Ouch," said a woman's voice. A moment later, the room lightened as the emperor's spymaster tapped the globe on the wall.

"Oh, it's you," said Jon, annoyed. "What do you want?" He stretched his shoulders and winced as the movement twinged his ribs. He hadn't meant to fall asleep, but the bed was unbelievably soft and the room dark.

"I've been sent to fetch you," said Ceara with an ironic smile.

"By whom?" asked Jon, rubbing his eyes.

"By the big tattooed bastard that you've got wrapped around your finger," she said, turning to leave. "Come on... before he threatens to not only give me no place to sleep aboard your ship but forces me to swab the decks too."

Jon slid off the bed and padded quickly across the room to follow her. Before they turned down the corridor, she gave a short laugh.

"Wait... he's the first mate, isn't he?" she said, looking up at him with wide, blue eyes. "Come now... If we're going to trust each other, I should know more about you."

Grudgingly, Jon nodded his head.

"Yes... Tom's the first mate," he replied.

"Interesting," replied Ceara, a curious frown narrowing her eyes. "And what does that make you? The shipwright? The taskmaster? What *is* your role aboard?"

Jon suddenly had the feeling that she wasn't as ignorant as she was making herself out to be—the too-quick response, the flicker of satisfaction that had passed over her face. It was as if she was just confirming facts that she already knew. Jon's tired brain didn't know what to make of it.

"Me? I'm nothing," he said faintly.

Ceara stared at him a moment longer and then nodded once, turning to lead him down the hall without another word.

J on pulled his shirt off, dumping it onto the ground before working loose his belt. He glanced to the side where Ceara stood watching, and he felt himself redden.

"Are you sure we won't be caught?" he asked, his brow furrowed.

"Yes," she said simply.

He felt too tired and too soul-weary to do anything but believe her. His senses told him she was telling the truth, though he was beginning to question just how reliable those senses were these days.

Tom beckoned to him from the water, and Jon hopped on one foot, taking off his boots and pulling down his trousers while trying to ignore the fact that Ceara had not yet left. Was she planning on watching them?

Jon wondered if he even cared.

He let himself down into the pool with a gasp; the water was hot and, though it was a shock to his system, it felt good. He walked forward, propelling himself with his arms until he reached Tom sitting on the submerged ledge. Exhausted and so sick of feeling the dull ache in his chest, he sagged gratefully against the big man; Tom let out soft sound and curled his arms around Jon. He closed his eyes tight, pressing his face against Tom's neck for a few breaths. This was good. This was right where he was meant to be.

When he looked up, he saw that the woman was watching them with a look of distaste on her face. She quickly smoothed her expression, but Jon shook his head.

"Let me give you some advice: never, ever let Baltsaros catch you looking at him like that. Ever," he said softly. "Now... please?" He motioned with his head towards the door.

Ceara, with a slightly mystified look, nodded slowly and left silently.

. . .

J on's hands slid over Tom's slick back as he pushed himself against him, and he felt the first mate kiss the side of his head.

"Ah... So he told ye..." murmured Tom.

Jon nodded with his jaw clenched tight. All the outrage and betrayal he'd felt at Tom's silence and possible complicity over Baltsaros's murders had fallen to the wayside following the captain's rejection of him. However, with the big man's words, he felt a resurgence of bitter anger. He hooked his fingers around the edge of the metal collar Tom wore, causing him to let out a quiet grunt. The sight of the slave collar digging into the first mate's skin gave him a sense of satisfaction. He pressed his lips to the side of Tom's face and shuddered, his eyes squeezed shut.

"I am so *fucking angry* at you for keeping Baltsaros's secrets," he growled against Tom's stubbled skin, crushing his nose into the hollow of the big man's cheek. Baring his teeth, Jon pushed his forehead against Tom, his whole body tense. He wanted to tear into him, hurt him, *punish* him. He wanted to gather all of his anger, fear, and pain and bury it into Tom like a lance. He slipped another finger beneath the collar, and this time when Tom made a sound, it was a strangled little gasp.

"Not my secrets," whispered Tom, his voice hoarse. When Jon pulled back, he saw that the big man's face was turning red. For a second he felt sorry, ashamed of what he was doing to Tom. The first mate was bruised and battered, one of his eyes only able to open in the barest of slits. However, when Tom's thighs squeezed Jon's hips, his legs wrapping around him to pull him closer, the thick, hard cock that touched Jon's belly blew all of his doubts away.

"You are never to keep anything from me again, Tom," he whispered, yanking on the collar. "Never again." He ground his own half-soft cock against Tom's groin, suddenly filled with an aching *need*. He grimaced, fury and desire throbbing in his gut. "Never... Say it."

"Never," choked Tom, his brow furrowed. The big man kept his hands loose around Jon's ribs, gentle despite the fact that Jon was slowly strangling him.

"Say it again," growled Jon.

"Ne... ver," came Tom's response, a little weaker.

With a low, malicious laugh, Jon pulled the collar just a little tighter, gratified when he felt Tom's hands twitch ever so slightly. Just as it seemed like the big man was about to lose consciousness, Jon finally pulled his fingers out from under the collar.

Tom coughed and took in a big lungful of air, his eyes watering.

"Never," he croaked.

Jon grabbed Tom's jaw hard in his fingers, not caring about the bruises and the cuts.

"And why is that?" he asked softly.

"Because I'm yers, love," breathed Tom, his hands sliding around to grab Jon's buttocks to pull him even tighter against him.

Jon thought he would shake himself to pieces from the frantic desire that tightened his muscles and put a low growl deep in his chest. Yes, Tom was his. He wanted to mark him, carve his name in Tom's skin. With a moan he tilted Tom's face back and spat into his open mouth. Tom blinked in surprise, but the sound he let out was rough with lust. He dug his fingers into Jon's buttocks, and Jon let out a strangled cry; mashing his lips against Tom's, he savaged him with a brutal kiss.

Breaking away, Jon panted and took his cock in hand, stroking himself quickly. Again he looped a finger around the back of Tom's collar, yanking it tight against Tom's throat. He spat again, and Tom licked the saliva from his lips, a fervent glaze in his eyes as he panted against the constricting metal ring.

"I'm going to fuck you, you godsdamned bastard. I'm going to bury my cock in you and fuck you hard... you lying *asshole*," Jon's words were part growl, part sob, and he bent his knees, fumbling with desperate fingers between Tom's legs until he found his opening. "I don't care how much you like licking the captain's boots. You will never betray me again. Not for *anything.*" This time his voice broke. His love for the big brute was a vivid, pulsing thing in his chest. He needed Tom so much—for his strength, his loyalty, his fierceness, his submission... cock in hand, he pushed the head of it into Tom, almost frantic. Jabbing himself hard into the big man, Jon let out a sharp cry. Water was a poor lubricant, but after a only few slowly-deepening thrusts, Jon's whole length slid tight into him. He leaned into Tom with every plunge, one hand curled around the bigger man's back, the other slowly cutting off his air supply.

"I want to feel you cum. Make yourself cum," he snarled. Forgiveness was couched in the permission for release; he was learning a new language after all. Leaning forward, he growled against Tom's lips. "Do it. Now."

Despite the fact that every breath Tom took whistled as he choked against Jon's hold, he obediently took his thick, curved cock in hand and quickly stroked himself. With a moan, Jon slowed his thrusts, realizing belatedly that he wasn't going to last long enough. However, as he skirted the edge, each push into Tom's body a panting breath closer to culmination, he felt the big man finally go rigid against him, his voice just a low, strangled hiss as his body jerked with the force of his orgasm. Jon released the big man's collar and grunted as he let himself go, the sound echoing against the stone walls of the bath house as his cock pumped and throbbed inside Tom. With a desperate cry, he brought his mouth to Tom's as the very last of his pleasure ebbed sweet and deep inside him, sharing his breath to replace that which he'd taken.

T om's hands came up slowly, painting soft caresses on Jon's skin. His chest heaved with each laboured breath, and he pulled away from Jon with a hoarse chuckle. "Holy shit," he wheezed with a grin. "Bloody fuckin' hells, Jon."

Jon shifted his hips so that his softening cock slipped out of Tom, and he groaned, feeling chafed. He wrapped his arms around Tom's back and pressed his lips to the dark red line that circled the first mate's neck right above the metal collar. He felt a little ill from exhaustion and from the heat of the water, and his ribs ached with every breath, but he didn't want to move. He wanted to sink beneath Tom's skin and hide there, forget his fears and pain and curl up in the first mate's solid warmth. He clenched his eyelids shut.

"Tell me you're mine again," he whispered. "I need to hear it."

Tom's hands ceased in their movement, and Jon could see the frown on his face painted against his eyelids by memory.

"I'm yers, Jon," said Tom slowly. His hands closed over Jon's shoulders, and he gently pushed him back.

"What's wrong?" asked the first mate, his voice low and gravelly. Tom's ocean eyes darted over Jon's features, worry plain on his face. "What happened?"

Jon shrugged.

"I asked Baltsaros if he loved me," he said quietly.

The surprised laugh that burst out of Tom was the last reaction he had expected.

2 0

THE MENAGERIE

Tom was incredulous.

"Ye can't have figured Da would answer different," he asked, shaking his head. When Jon's grey eyes slid away from his, Tom realized that the sombre young man still held onto some innocent notion that Baltsaros was something that he wasn't. He squeezed Jon's shoulder. Fucking Baltsaros... what a bloody time for the captain to start telling the whole truth. "Why don't ye be glad that he's tryin' to be honest with ye? That's a bloody miracle, aye?"

Jon turned to look at Tom again, a scowl on his face.

"Yes. But where in hells does that leave me? Tom... I don't even know what to think anymore. He's insane. He kills people and gets off on it. The most fucked up part is that, despite that fact, I'm sitting here wondering how I can make him love me. It's sick. He's a fucking murderer, and I feel like it's something *I've* done that keeps him from loving me." Jon pulled out of Tom's grasp with a sigh and took a step back in the warm water.

"Aye, that's a fucking path ye don't want to go down, love," said Tom quietly. "Ye ain't done a bloody thing. Trust me. He's just...

well, yeah, he's a black-hearted madman when it comes down to it; but he does love ye in his own way, lad. Ye gotta believe me. Just because he doesn't *think* he does…" He rubbed a hand over his face, not knowing what to say. "Hells, ye know what? It's all shite, but would ye rather he'd lied to ye?"

Jon shook his head; he was starting to seem less lost, but Tom knew that look. It was important to make him understand that it wasn't the words that mattered; Tom could see something in the way Baltsaros's eyes constantly turned to Jon, the way he touched him all the time, the care he took with the meals he prepared for the two of them. It was enough to make Tom cold with envy from time to time, but it was evidence that the captain felt more than he let on…

"Do you think that he loves you?" asked Jon.

Grimacing, Tom scratched the back of his neck where a thin welt had come up. Sometimes Jon was so frustratingly naïve that he wanted to shake him. Why was this so important to him? Tom clenched his jaw rhythmically as he thought.

"He needs me. And sometimes I think, aye, maybe he even loves me, lad. But with the captain… it's complicated," he finally muttered. "Listen, he's told ye he can't live without ye, aye?"

Jon nodded.

"Well, he ain't never said the same to me—" Tom waved away Jon's soft sound of dismay. It was honestly a sore spot with him, but how could he make Jon believe him if he couldn't believe his own damn words? "That he ain't said it, don't mean it ain't a fact. He's a bloody, stubborn tyrant who knows shite about being a decent, bloody person without makin' all that cares about him bloody insane." Tom smiled a little sadly. "I get what I can from Da, and fuck the rest. This fuckin' *word* between us… 'love'. Hells, some people just don't know how to make the word work for 'em. Da's one of them.

"Jon, I love ye more than I can say, but I think ye might be a damn fool when it comes to the cap'n. If ye can see past his murderin' ways, just… Look at his doin's with you… Don't wait for his words, lad."

Some of the tension that held Jon shoulders high had leached out while Tom struggled to explain himself, and he nodded slowly at the end of it.

"Do you think he will change ever?" asked Jon, his blue-grey eyes shrewd.

Tom lifted his shoulders.

"Maybe? Hells, years go by without a single 'sorry' from the bastard and, since ye been around, I heard it more times than I can count on one hand. That's somethin'," mused Tom with a crooked grin.

"Maybe you're right. It just… hurts," replied Jon.

With a sigh, Tom nodded.

"I know, love."

The heat of the water was starting to get to Tom, and he lurched to his feet, intent on getting out. He was about to comment that just being with Baltsaros was a recipe for pain, when he saw Jon's eyes drop to his abdomen and his nose wrinkle slightly.

Tom glanced down and saw that his seed had become a gluey mess that stuck to his chest and belly hair in pale clumps.

Tom let out groan and pulled at the mess.

"Fuckin' hells…" he muttered. When he looked up, he saw that Jon was smiling again, dispelling some of the gravity caused by their words a moment earlier.

"It's not bloody funny," scowled Tom, hamming it up slightly to further lighten the mood. He pointed to the line of fine, dark hair on Jon's belly that rose above the water. "And ye can wipe the bloody smirk off yer face, lad. It's not like ye came out clean…"

Tom stroked Jon's hair while he sat deep in thought. They had moved to a different pool after cleaning up, and Jon snoozed against Tom's chest in water that was warm like a soft kiss against their skin.

Jon wasn't stupid, and he was no longer the wide-eyed innocent that Tom had accosted at the *Rose Garden*. However, the way that Jon's face turned so bleak when he spoke of Baltsaros… Tom frowned, shifting slightly to press his cheek against Jon's soft curls. It was never going to be easy for him to accept what the captain was.

And what is he? he thought to himself. Was he truly loyal to a madman, as he had called him earlier? He closed his eyes. Before Jon, it had never been this complicated, but Tom wondered if that had been wrong. Perhaps he should have been questioning all along. Jon's hand twitched slightly against his side in his sleep, and Tom pressed his lips together and frowned.

He was furious that Baltsaros had purposefully hurt Jon. Would one more little lie have been so fucking hard? However, Tom *was* happy that he would no longer have to keep secrets from Jon to protect the captain. It was all out in the open, and maybe, just maybe, now that Jon had taken a good look into the belly of the beast, he knew a way of… bloody fixing things. The last few days had made Tom realize that things with Baltsaros were worse and far stranger than he had assumed.

Jon had done something to the captain to make him capable of being sorry; could Jon's influence make Baltsaros whole?

Then there were the woman's strange instructions. What did she mean by Jon having to say he was *forced*? Neither of them liked the sound of it.

Tom was tired of pushing his weary brain through convoluted thoughts; he needed to get some sleep. Just as he was thinking of waking Jon up, he heard the soft footfall of someone approaching.

"It's only me," murmured Ceara. "I have to get you two back to where you belong. There's only so long I can maintain the ruse that there's an interrogation taking place in here."

Jon blinked sleepily when Tom shook him, and he sat up looking disoriented. Tom helped Jon out of the water, and they dried off while the spymaster looked on impatiently.

"Is... uh... the captain back?" asked Jon groggily as he handed her the bath sheet back and moved to get dressed.

Ceara shook her head.

"No, he and Ah'puch have called for another jug of wine. There's no telling how long they'll be," she said. She lowered her eyes for a moment, a crease appearing between her brows before she looked up again. "Do you trust me now? I took a big risk letting you two in here together."

Tom couldn't help but wonder how much of her earnest expression was complete pig shit. He nodded anyway, though Jon shot him a sidelong glance. At least Jon wasn't fooled.

"Aye, lass. Ye've proved ye can be useful. Now when d'ye plan on tellin' us the rest of it?" he asked, lacing up his pants. "We've got our own woes to deal with, lovey. Can't be holed up here. We'll take ye with us, but it's gotta be soon."

Ceara smiled a little wanly.

"Yes, I understand that you're anxious to rejoin your crew, but I know for a fact that they won't be back to fetch you for another day, so we still have plenty of time. I can't tell you more than what I've already said," she shifted her blue eyes to Jon. "You're on board with this?"

The lines next to Jon's mouth deepened as his jaw worked.

"I don't like agreeing to something without knowing what it is," he said quietly, fixing her with a steely glare.

Ceara's smile had an edge to it as she stared back at him.

"I'm sorry you feel that way, Jon," she said. "But what choice do you have?"

B altsaros suppressed a sigh, maintaining his air of interest despite the fact that Ah'puch's idea of an intellectual discussion was an hours-long, detailed, egotistical, and mostly one-sided account of everything wonderful that had happened since he took the throne. If even half of what he related was true, then Baltsaros would have been sitting in the presence of an innovative and exceptional man. It was not the case.

The captain was disappointed. The emperor of Ereme'ia Balor had turned out to be a strutting little cockalorum who had not, as of yet, provided any insight at all into the mysteries of sacrifice or of the blood rituals that literally kept the golden city running. Baltsaros had expected a man who understood the power of holding life and death in one's palm, a compelling sovereign who ruled with an iron fist, and a stimulating match for the captain's intellect... someone with answers. He had instead found a man so wrapped up in himself and his so-called accomplishments that he had little room for what he called the "day-to-day bloodletting" that went on at the hands of his warlocks. Ah'puch was nothing but a figurehead it seemed, and one that was grasping and desperate for the admiration he felt he was owed. The man had no respect for the life-giving ichor that flowed down the sides of his temples, and it was utterly frustrating.

After lifting the golden cup to his lips again in a mimicry of imbibing his wine, Baltsaros smiled as the man launched into yet another account of some lord that grovelled at the emperor's feet only to be shown great mercy and understanding. The captain was wondering if he could claim great exhaustion and retire for the night when his eyes strayed to the lights that hung over the raised platform where they were comfortably seated. Narrowing his gaze, he tried again to see whether there was any movement inside the globes. There was no hiss or smell of gas, and he was completely baffled as to how the light was created. Forgetting himself, Baltsaros spoke up, interrupting the emperor.

"What makes the illumination so bright?" he asked. He turned his eyes to Ah'puch and saw that, though the man looked a tiny bit annoyed at the interruption, having his magical lamps noticed and admired was enough to forgive the captain's rudeness.

"Ah! What is your guess?" asked Ah'puch with a smile, looking down his hawk nose at Baltsaros.

Stifling his irritation, Baltsaros smiled blandly and shrugged.

"It is a complete mystery to me," he said graciously, and then he blinked, remembering something Polas had said. "Wait, perhaps not... Is it harnessed lightning?" He sat up a little straighter, wondering if he was in fact looking at the product of somehow trapping the electricity of lightning within glass.

Taking another sip of his wine, Ah'puch looked almost coyly at Baltsaros over his cup, pleased to have yet another reason to show off.

"Not quite lightning, no. We fabricate electricity here, and it is channelled through the building on copper wires to filaments inside these blown glass bulbs. It is extremely complicated; I'm quite sure that I would lose you in all the details," said the emperor, smirking. "Suffice it to say that We are very proud of this invention."

Baltsaros felt a tiny buzz of excitement.

"You fabricate it? Can I see?" he asked. Before the emperor had a chance to turn him down, Baltsaros smiled graciously and bowed his head in reverence. "I would be so honoured to bask in Your Excellency's ingenuity." When he looked back up, the emperor was nearly preening with delight over Baltsaros's words.

"Yes, yes. We shall show you tomorrow," said Ah'puch with a generous smile, and Baltsaros gritted his teeth; so much for a change of venue. He tried to rein in his irritation, and taking a big swallow of wine, braced himself for another long-winded account of the emperor's accomplishments. However, the captain was surprised when the man changed the subject.

"The young man you travel with, your... *nephew*. Tell me about him," said the emperor, his eyes locked on Baltsaros's.

A touch of apprehension suddenly soured the wine in Baltsaros's mouth. He frowned. There was no mistaking the emperor's inference. Ah'puch knew *something* about his relationship with Jon, but Baltsaros decided to play it safe and feign ignorance.

"He is my sister's son by marriage," Baltsaros lied smoothly. "He works aboard as my advisor helping me to secure honest deals with dishonest men. He is particularly adept at detecting lies and foul intentions." He thought that perhaps if he spoke of Jon's gift, the emperor would be more inclined to share his secrets.

Ah'puch sat up and peered closely at Baltsaros.

"What do you mean? How does he do this?" asked the emperor, looking intrigued. "What is involved?"

"There's nothing mystical about it," replied the captain. "He is just extremely good at reading body language. Far more than any other I've seen. Sometimes it seems like he senses or detects the emotions of others even before they feel them themselves."

A drastic change had taken place in the emperor's demeanour at the captain's words. The man was wide-eyed and interested; gone was his haughty, half-lidded, self-important slouch. Baltsaros smiled, curious at the dramatic shift.

"I'm a keen study in the realm of the human psyche," said Ah'puch with a broad, toothy smile, discarding the royal "We" for the first time in their conversation. "Is he aware of what cues he is seeing? Can he explain to you how he comes to his conclusions?"

Baltsaros shook his head and held out his cup for more wine. This time, Ah'puch poured it from his own hand, and when the captain sat back in his couch, he smiled behind his glass.

Another evening of conversation, and he would have the man eating out of his hand.

"Jon can't explain, no. It's unfortunate, as I would love to better understand what he sees," he said sadly.

"Perhaps you're asking the wrong questions," replied Ah'puch with a raised eyebrow.

Baltsaros felt a sharp spike of anger at the man's suggestion and nearly sneered at him.

"I don't think so," he answered quietly instead. With a thin smile, he leaned towards the man across from him. "Why? What questions would *you* ask, if I may?"

The emperor had obviously missed the captain's reaction; he furrowed his brow and tapped a finger once against his bottom lip in thought.

"Perhaps it isn't the questions that are wrong, but the way you are asking them..." he said thoughtfully.

"What do you mean?" asked Baltsaros.

"Have you tried to force his brain to answer? Have you tried to hypnotize him?"

Baltsaros's brows rose slowly.

"Ah, you haven't. I can see that," responded the emperor with a smug grin. "Would you like to see what my own experiments in the mind have yielded?"

Four levels beneath the main floor were the palace dungeons. At least that's what they had been before the emperor had them converted into his own private laboratory. As they walked through the thick wooden door, Baltsaros was immediately assailed by a series of overlapping smells. Some he recognized, like urine, camphor oil, and valerian root. Others were not so familiar. There was something that smelled of the flowering plant he knew as monkshood, but it was subtly different. Same with the waxy, green scent that he associated with the aloe plant, and the tang of the snow-in-summer bush. Close, but not identical.

His nostrils flared as he turned his head like a hound scenting the air. It was everything he could do not to delve into the herbs and toxins that were neatly arranged on shelves along the back wall.

"Impressive," he murmured.

The emperor smiled and spread out his hands, making a show of looking humble.

"Alas, I am but an amateur. These are only the very basic of ingredients. But that is not what I wanted to show you." The emperor made his way across the dark room and hit a switch. A long corridor was illuminated, each of the dozen cells on either side fronted by gilded metal bars that gleamed in the stark light. Frowning, Baltsaros walked slowly to the first cage. Within it, blinking sleepily, was a man of about his own age. He was curled up on a mound of blankets in one corner, having eschewed the narrow cot bolted to the wall. When the man noticed Baltsaros staring at him, he opened his mouth wide, baring his teeth. A low growl emerged from his throat. Fascinated, Baltsaros took a step closer. The noise coming from the man became higher pitched at his approach.

"What is wrong with him?" he asked the emperor.

Ah'puch looked pleased with himself.

"He thinks he's a house cat," replied the emperor, grinning conspiratorially.

"*You* did this to him?" When the emperor nodded slowly, Baltsaros frowned and looked back at the cage. The man had retreated against the wall, his back rounded like that of a cat, his face in a tense rictus of fear. A small tongue flick... and still that low growling noise. It was mesmerizing.

"Does he understand us?" he asked quietly.

"Not anymore," said Ah'puch. "Not in this state. If I set up my apparatus and put the right drugs in his system, I can coax him through hypnotism back to a level of, ah... human-ness, as it were, where he can understand speech. Otherwise he just cleans himself and shits in that sandbox," the emperor said with obvious amusement.

Baltsaros nodded slowly, his mind stumbling over itself in waves of fascination, excitement, and a delicious sense of horror. He turned his head to look down the corridor at the other eleven cages; he could hear the inhabitants beginning to stir.

"Would you like to meet the rest of my menagerie, Captain Baltsaros?" asked the emperor, leaning forward on his golden cane, his eyes sparkling with enthusiasm.

"Yes. Yes, I would very much like that."

A few hours later, his mind reeling from the possibilities shown to him by the emperor, Baltsaros followed the weary slave to the chamber he had been given to sleep in. Before the woman turned to go, he touched her arm. The slave girl jumped at the contact, looking warily at him a moment before touching the strap on her simple dress.

"Do you want me to stay?" she said in accented Balorian, her meaning obvious.

"No, my dear," responded Baltsaros with a tight smile. "But thank you for the offer. I simply would like to know where the other man I came with is sleeping. Is it nearby?"

The slave woman nodded and pointed to a door across the hallway. A brief, timid smile lit up her face.

"Your slave was very kind to me, sir," she said quietly. Her eyes darted to the side, obviously feeling reckless for speaking up. Before Baltsaros could respond, she sketched a quick bow and scurried down the corridor.

Surprised, the captain watched her leave, wondering what the woman meant. Random acts of kindness weren't in Tom's usual repertoire. He just hoped that whatever he was up to, the first mate didn't catch some foolish disease. The thought kindled a strange feeling in the pit of his stomach, and the captain frowned. Jealousy? Over Tom? Baltsaros shook his head to clear it. He was more tired than he realised.

After waiting another minute in the dark to make sure no one was watching, he crossed the hallway to the door the slave had pointed to. He pulled up on the latch and let himself into the room silently. Though it was nearly morning, Baltsaros wanted to curl up with Jon for just a few minutes before they had to be apart for another long day; he needed to ground himself.

As the captain navigated the small room in the dark, he put out a hand and found the bed at the far side. As soon as he put a knee up onto it, he heard Jon stir in his sleep. Careful not to startle the young man, he lay down slowly behind him and put an arm around his waist, pushing aside Jon's hair with the other hand so he could press his lips against the back of his neck. He felt Jon wake up, and he smiled before touching his tongue softly to the sleep-warm skin of his nape.

In dismay, Baltsaros felt Jon go rigid against him.

"No," said Jon, his voice hoarse. He pushed at Baltsaros's hand and moved away from him. Baltsaros frowned.

"Jon..." he whispered, skimming his fingers over his young lover's shoulder and tracing them down the defined muscles of his bicep and forearm, looking to link his hand with Jon's.

"No," repeated Jon a little louder. Baltsaros wondered for a second if Jon was actually awake and was aware of what he was saying, but when Jon continued after a few heartbeats, his voice was calm in the inky darkness.

"I'm not interested in sharing my bed or my body with you, Baltsaros," continued Jon. "Not here, not now."

The captain sat up slowly, just breathing deeply for a moment. He should have been angry, but he wasn't for once. There was something in Jon's tone that spoke of great pain... pain that *he* had put there.

No. He felt something akin to shame.

"Sleep, Jon," he said quietly. "I will see you in the morning."

When Jon didn't reply, Baltsaros slid off the bed and made his way out of the room.

S tanding at the window of his own accommodations, facing the new dawn, he felt even more determined to go ahead with his plan.

The captain looked down at the blood on his hands that only he could see, blood that never washed away, and he closed his eyes, reaching for the calm that was ever further with every passing day. He'd found something better than the magic of blood sacrifice to make him whole:

If Ah'puch could put an animal in the body and mind of a man, could he not just as easily take the beast out of Baltsaros?

21

A LOYAL MAN

Jon watched the light move across the ceiling as he lay on his back, hands behind his head. Sleep had eluded him once the captain had left, and he had spent the early morning just drifting, lost in thought.

He was alone for once, and it felt odd. It wasn't often that he got to lie in bed without Tom coming to seek him out. Though the big man's companionship was never quite smothering per se, it was almost constant. Jon smiled softly; sometimes the first mate reminded him a little of Brutus. The thought instantly sobered Jon; he didn't like thinking about the small, jewel-like island of Madierus. The good memories only served to cause him more pain.

Jon closed his eyes and curled onto his side, the sound of his slow breathing the only thing he could hear. After a moment, he opened them and looked at the pillow in front of him, a soft divot to one side of it where the captain had laid his head a few hours earlier. Jon wondered if he pressed his face into the soft silk, would he smell the sweet almond oil that Baltsaros used in his beard? Or the subtle, musky cologne that always reminded Jon of the first time the captain had touched him?

He stretched out his hand and patted the pillow flat, erasing the evidence of the man's presence. With a sigh, he stretched out on his belly, taking up the entire width of the bed, his arm cradled against his side to take the pressure off his ribs. Tom was right: he *was* a fool. When Baltsaros had pressed against him earlier in the cool dark of the bedchamber, his body had crackled with electricity; when the man had gone, he had been filled with a deep aching want that reached his very bones. It had taken everything for him not to call out to Baltsaros before he left to say that he had changed his mind. As the captain had quietly shut the door, Jon's chest had constricted, and he had buried his face in the covers to muffle his quick, pained breath. Pushing Baltsaros away had left him feeling hollow.

Right in the midst of a dangerous, desperate situation was not the time to have a crisis of the heart.

It felt foolish.

It also felt like the most important thing in the world.

With his eyes closed once more, he tried to steer his mind away from the downward spin it took every time he thought of the way Baltsaros's lips had brushed his skin so softly.

altsaros stood next to Ah'puch, watching what it took to create electricity. Behind the stepped pyramid that the emperor used as his palace was a large spoked wheel, not unlike the capstan of a ship. Turning it round and round at a constant, never-ending pace was an army of slaves. During the ten minutes Baltsaros stood there, mesmerized and disturbed by the sight, two men had fallen, collapsing from exhaustion. Instead of stopping to help their fallen mates, the slaves turning the wheel just stared forward with hollow eyes as they stepped over them. Slave drivers with long metal rods quickly looped the ropes at the end of them around the feet of the insensate men. The slaves were dragged out from under the machine as two new men were brought in. It was unending. It was utterly wasteful.

"Can't the wheel be turned by other means?" asked the captain, looking askance at the emperor.

Ah'puch, his eyes red-rimmed from little sleep and too much wine, twitched his upper lip into a small disdainful sneer as he shook his head.

"Why bother? Animals are too costly. Setting up a water wheel to turn it would require too much effort. With wind, it is too unpredictable. These"—he pointed to the slaves—"are plentiful. Cheap. Easy to replace."

Another slave fell, a woman this time, and was hauled out by her arm. The man with the staff bent low over the woman's body and, even from where Baltsaros stood, he could see the slave driver shake his head. A brawny brute in a harness was called forward to carry the woman's corpse away, and the captain grimaced. The casual cruelty to so many left a bad taste in his mouth.

Baltsaros decided right then that he would kill the emperor once he was through with him.

"Come! You must taste this coffee..."

Baltsaros curved his lips into a courteous smile and nodded, following the self-important little man off the balcony and back into the large sitting room. He was irritable this morning; not enough sleep and Jon's rejection made every attempt to seem gracious that much harder. Worse, the emperor wasn't interested in speaking about his "subjects" in the laboratory, nor was he forthcoming with any information about how they managed trade with the east. Despite seeing the creation of electricity in action, the morning had proven to be an exercise in patience.

With a quiet sigh, he let his eyes roam while the emperor directed a slave to place a tray of coffee on the low table between the cushioned *récamier* couches. Gold was everywhere, from the thick rods that held up curtains and tapestries to the very thread that wove those fabrics. There was an entire life's fortune just in the little statue of a bear-like creature that sat upon a pedestal near the captain's knee.

Baltsaros looked again at the two large slaves who stood to either side of the door, eyes trained on nothing. Tattoos swirled and meandered down their left sides, and Baltsaros felt an oddly anxious pang as the markings brought Tom to mind.

"My slave… when can I have him back?" asked Baltsaros with another courtly smile.

"I assure you that you do not need him while you're here, Captain. He's in good hands," smiled Ah'puch as he poured coffee into two golden mugs. "If you're worried about his physical conditioning, I would be happy to put him to work. We have many—"

"That won't be necessary," replied Baltsaros, accepting a cup, "as we unfortunately don't plan on staying very long."

"Of course," replied the emperor glibly. "It will be a shame to see you go."

Anyone watching the conversation would have thought that the two men were friends, and not captor and captive.

Baltsaros smiled blandly. He would continue to charm the emperor and feed into his need for intellectual legitimacy; as much as he hated the thought of such an inferior meddling with his mind, he had to persuade the man to take him back to the laboratory where he would pry loose the beast from within him. Then, he would kill Ah'puch… with his bare hands if he could.

Baltsaros brought the cup to his lips, hiding his look of sudden apprehension. *Would* he be able to kill when the procedure was done? He took a sip of the bitter coffee, swallowing it down along with his trepidation. It was his *obsession* that he wanted to remove, not his ability.

While the emperor chattered away about copper wires, slaves, and the expense of maintaining such a lavish palace, Baltsaros let his mind go back to the night where he had made the decision to travel beyond the spires.

J on lay trembling on the pillow. His face was flushed with fever as his body tried to fight the infection that had taken root within the wound that Reginald had given him. As Jon moaned and tossed his head, Baltsaros clutched his hand, wishing that he could do something to help him. Nothing was working; not a single one of his medicines had effected even the slightest change in his condition.

Baltsaros was going to lose Jon.

All the suffering inflicted upon him in his life didn't even come close to the pain he felt at that single, horrifying realization. Each breath squeezed past a throat choked with emotion into lungs that burned and was exhaled between teeth clenched in helplessness. This wasn't rage. This wasn't anger. This was anguish, pure and overwhelming.

With a soft groan, he pressed his lips to the weak pulse in Jon's wrist.

The chain of events leading up to this moment was entirely his fault. He'd chastised Jon for rash reactions when his was the most rash of all. Burning the castle... what kind of man did that?

He was no man at all. He was inside the barrel again, staring into the frigid black, and the beast with evil in its heart stared back at him, a smug smile on its face.

Suddenly Jon twitched, the breath rattling in his pierced lung... and then he was silent.

With a low sound, Baltsaros fumbled at Jon's neck, desperate to find any sign of life. His hands shook, fingers sliding down Jon's chest to the edge of the sucking knife wound he had covered in waxed linen, searching for his heartbeat.

There was none.

In that moment, Baltsaros was lost.

He bowed his head, mind numb.

"Anything," he whispered, kissing the clammy hand he

clutched. "I will give up anything." He closed his eyes tight against the raw hopelessness he felt.

"I will give up anything for you." Prayers to gods he didn't believe in.

He let a long, slow exhale and pressed his face to Jon's shoulder.

At Baltsaros's touch, Jon jerked on the bed. He took in a strangled gasp of air and coughed a few times before letting out a hoarse moan. Astounded, Baltsaros quickly grabbed the cloth in the bowl of water by the bed, pressing it to Jon's lips to get moisture to his mouth.

"Balt... saros," wheezed Jon. "Baltsaros."

"Don't speak, Jon," said the captain, brow furrowed. His mind reeled. Hope. A second chance. He would redouble the medication. He would cure Jon.

"Devil's Isles..." whispered the younger man, his eyelids fluttering open though his eyes roamed from side to side as if he still dreamed. "Your... heart!" Jon's hand scrabbled over the captain's arm, his touch insistent. "Baltsaros, Tom and I found your heart! I know where it is. We have to go. Promise me..."

Baltsaros frowned. Someone had spoken to him. He blinked.

"I said, are you all right, Captain?" asked the emperor. Baltsaros looked up at the man, his heart thudding against his ribs at the memory.

You are my everything. I will give up anything for you.

He saw movement out of the corner of his eye and looked over Ah'puch's shoulder to the young man standing hesitantly at the door.

"Yes, I will be," Baltsaros said quietly.

Jon stared back at Baltsaros, struck motionless by what he read in the man's expression. The captain looked relieved and determined, proud and fiercely possessive as his dark eyes held Jon's, but the thing that made Jon's breath catch in his throat was the naked *want* he saw... Want that came from the soul. He frowned, and it was gone when Baltsaros turned away to smile at the emperor.

He took a few steps into the room, feeling dazed. He wondered belatedly if there was some sort of protocol he was supposed to follow on entering an emperor's presence, but the man swivelled in his seat and grinned wide at him, gesturing.

"Don't be shy, Jon," said Ah'puch in heavily accented Common. "Come. Join us for coffee. Your uncle was telling me last night that you have an exceptional gift. I would love to hear of it from your lips."

Jon glanced at Baltsaros in surprise. It wasn't like the captain to volunteer that kind of information; he wondered what it had been bartered for. However, Baltsaros's expression was a strange one and offered him no explanation. With a tight smile, he took one of the straight-backed chairs and accepted a cup of coffee from the sallow, dark-haired emperor. With another quick look at the captain, Jon wondered what had been said.

"What can I tell you about it?" he said softly, adopting Baltsaros's northern accent.

The questions that the emperor asked were straightforward. How had he learned to read people? How did he use it?

As Jon gave the man a faltering, semi-truthful account of his talent, his eyes kept turning to Baltsaros. The captain's face was pale, and he had dark smudges under his eyes. Jon wondered if Baltsaros had slept at all. Refusing to allow himself to feel bad about any part he played in that, he forced himself to adopt a cold look when he met the captain's eye again. However, what he was rewarded with was completely unexpected, and it sent a trickle of unease down his spine. The captain's lids had lowered quickly to stare down at the coffee in his hands, but not before Jon caught a look rife with pain. When Baltsaros looked up again a moment later, his expression was resolute. Pulse skipping along rapidly, Jon stumbled over his words and apologized to the emperor.

His brain on fire, Jon wished Tom were at his side to offer insight, strength... anything. He'd just had the distinct impression that the captain was planning something crazy.

om paced. Back and forth he went across the roughly cobbled square of the atrium. Though sleep had quickly found him on his narrow cot, he had woken at the crack of dawn with the other slaves. Unlike them, he had no work to take part in and thus was left to pace impatiently like a wildcat trapped in a cage, waiting to be summoned by Baltsaros or Jon. His lip was already on the mend, surprisingly not made worse by Jon's fervent kisses, and he could open his eye completely. He was sure that he wasn't pretty to look at, but at least he was not as sore as he had assumed he would be.

When he turned to make another trip through the sparse greenery, Tom was surprised to see Ceara watching him with an amused expression.

"Bored?" she asked.

He grunted in reply and stopped, crossing his arms.

"I need to see the captain," he said. "I don't feel right not bein' able to keep an eye on him or Jon."

Ceara shook her head at him then tilted it to appraise him.

"You're loyal man, I'll give you that much," she said. "Tom, they're fine. Trust me. But, if the emperor says you're to stay here, you stay here. The slave driver who overlooks this place is also a loyal man."

She took a few steps forward until she was close enough to touch him. Looking up into his eyes, she smiled.

"Can I get you anything?" she asked, her cheek dimpling.

"My blade," he replied with a wry grin. "And a smoke... and a bottle of somethin' that'll warm my belly."

"I can't give you your knife, but I'll see what I can do about the other two," Ceara replied blithely, but Tom heard a distinct "no" in her answer and scowled.

"Don't ye play games with me, love. Ye'll find that I ain't the cuddly kitten ye obviously take me for."

The spymaster's smile faded at the danger in Tom's eyes, and she took a deep breath as if steeling herself. He understood why a second later.

"Tom... What if I told you that I may only be able to get Jon and you out?" she said slowly.

Before he could stop himself, he had backed her against one of the wide pillars surrounding the atrium, his hand around her slender throat. When her head hit the stone, her fingers came up, trying to pry him off of her. Ceara's sky-blue eyes were wide and scared.

"No," he growled. Already his mind was putting together a simple plan to break his way out of the slave quarters and find the captain and Jon. He had seen at least a half-dozen items along the corridors of the palace that would do for a weapon in a pinch. "No!" he repeated. "Ye fuckin' said we'd all make it out if we listened to ye, ye cunt." He brought his mouth close to hers and felt her shaky breath on his lips. "I can squeeze the bloody life out of ye here and now..."

"Tom, no..." she gasped, digging at his hand with her nails. "Let—let me explain!" The woman stopped struggling all at once. "Please."

Tom loosened his grip slightly and curled his lip into a sneer.

"Talk," he grunted.

"The emperor is not a stupid man, despite how he seems. He's cautious. He's moved up his plan to incarcerate the captain—" she wheezed.

"What do ye bloody mean *incarcerate*? That wasn't part o' the bleedin' plan was it?"

"Yes... yes, it was. I was hoping to get the captain and Jon to the dungeons where I could spirit them out... but he's also now taken an active interest in Jon. I'm not sure how that will affect things. My whole plan relied on him waiting until tomorrow... and now I'm not sure he will. He knows something. Has something. I don't know, Tom. I haven't been able to find out anything —" she stammered.

"Try harder," spat Tom, squeezing her neck again.

The redhead let out a rasping breath and pulled on his hand.

"Please, Tom," she coughed. "Maybe—probably get Jon out... but not Baltsaros—"

With a roar he threw her down onto the ground and stood over her, fists balled at his sides.

"You fuckin' planned this... Yer a lyin' bloody cunt," he growled. "Ye never cared if it was us three or jus' the one ye thought would be dumb enough to think with 'is cock. All ye cared about was gettin' yerself a free ride out o' here, aye?" He wasn't Jon; he had no idea if the woman was lying, but he was furious. He was also on the verge of panic.

The woman held up a hand.

"It's ok, Mikon," she said in a tense voice. "I merely fell. This slave was just helping me up."

Tom's head swivelled quickly, and he saw that the big, bald bastard who kept the slaves in line stood at one of the doors. His blood ran cold instantly, crushing out the fire in his anger when he saw that the man held a big, coiled, shiny, black bullwhip in his huge hands. Time stood still for a moment, Tom's pulse loud in his ears.

Then he reached down slowly and curled his hand around the fallen woman's wrist, helping her up gently. His eyes remained locked on the slave driver.

"Thank you," murmured Ceara, dusting off her dark-grey dress.

Mikon wasn't fooled. Tom could see that. Despite the fact that the man made no move, Tom was certain that his flesh would feel the bloodthirsty kiss of that whip once the spymaster left.

"Take me with ye," he said urgently in a soft voice as he leaned closer to Ceara. "I don't care what bloody excuse ye use, but I'm comin' with ye. Now."

Ceara fixed him with a skeptical look. Then, with a slight pursing of her lips, she looked away, and for a moment Tom wasn't sure whether or not she'd feed him to the dogs.

As she began walking away, she beckoned at him to follow.

"Are you coming or not? I told you the emperor wanted to see you," she said impatiently.

Tom glanced again at the big man with the whip and stepped quickly to follow Ceara out of the atrium and into the corridor that linked the slave quarters to the main pyramid.

"Thank you," he said gruffly.

"Just keep your hands off of me and your godsdamned mouth shut," she muttered as she widened her strides. "So help me if we get caught and bled for a blessing, it'll be your fucking fault."

Without another word, Tom followed the slight woman into the heart of the emperor's palace.

22

PARLEY

Tom balled his fists and hit the big burlap sack filled with rice again, trying to work loose some of the nervous energy that burned through his muscles, making him jittery.

Before pushing him into the storage closet, Ceara had said that she would find a way of getting him to the captain and Jon, but it felt like hours since she had left him there. Tom gritted his teeth and bunched his shoulders, giving the burlap sack a quick double jab with the left and right fist at around waist height. If the sack were a man, the damn scoundrel would be pissing blood tonight. Tom let out a grim chuckle, enjoying the stinging pain that warmed his knuckles.

The door opened behind him suddenly, and he spun around. A woman walked into the small storage room and froze, eyes wide. For a second, the two of them stared at each other. Tom's mind started clicking rapidly through ways of subduing the woman when she spoke up.

"What are you doing in here?" she asked in a hushed voice. The woman quickly turned and closed the door behind her.

Tom narrowed his eyes; she looked familiar. He lowered his

fists slowly but stayed poised for a strike if she so much as hinted that she was looking to yell.

When Tom didn't answer her, she gave him a shy smile.

"You saved me," she said softly. "In the bathhouse?" Her round cheeks dimpled, but she sobered almost immediately.

Tom nodded slowly, relieved. An ally.

"Aye lass, I remember ye now," he said. "Be a good girl, and stay clear of those mates. They seem a peck o' trouble."

She smiled again, fidgeting under his scrutiny.

"I just wanted to thank you," she said, her hands clutched in front of her. "It was... nice of you to step in like that."

When Tom's noncommittal grunt put another brief dimple in her cheek, he returned the smile.

"Why are you in the dry goods pantry?" she repeated, her green eyes wide with curiosity.

"I'm waitin' for someone," he replied with a shrug. When she continued to stare at him in bewilderment, an idea popped into his head, and he grinned wider.

The woman flinched when he reached out and took her narrow shoulders gently in his big, scarred hands.

"Listen, lovey. If ye'd like to thank me, ye can take me to my captain, real quiet-like. Can ye do that, darlin'? Have ye seen him? He's a tall fella with a beard and a face ye wouldn'a forget," he said hopefully.

The woman nodded quickly.

"Yes. He's with the emperor right now. Him and the other man. I was just sent to get some dried figs... I have to go back right away. But if you stay here, I can return in not very long and take you to the room your captain is staying in," she said, looking nervous. "Is that all right? That's all I can do."

"Aye, lass. That'll do." It would have to.

He watched her pick up a small, wooden box from one of the lower shelves, eyeing him sidelong with a flush to her cheek.

"Are they right?" she asked quietly. "Are you really from the other side of the Gods' Claws?"

When Tom nodded, she clutched the box of figs to her chest tightly with one hand. With the other, she tapped out the same warding sign that Polas had used.

Tom chuckled.

"I ain't a bloody ghost or monster, if that's what yer thinking, lass. I'm just a man like any other." He frowned, realizing that it probably wasn't the best thing to say to her. "What's yer name, love?"

"Bettie," she said shyly, and ducked her head. She quickly turned to go. "I'll be back soon."

"It's Tom," he said, "and thank ye, Bettie. Truly."

Jon walked slowly next to the captain, so ill at ease that he was nauseous. They'd been dismissed by the emperor so that he could conduct some state business, but they had been told not to leave the palace. Though it had been couched in gracious terms, Jon had clearly caught the message: if they tried to leave, what little freedom they were afforded would be taken away. They really were prisoners; Ceara hadn't been lying about that.

He glanced at the captain as they were led to the floor where their sleeping chambers were located. Baltsaros had been nearly silent for the remainder of the morning, answering Ah'puch's questions with one- or two-word answers. It was unlike the man to be so terse when decorum was called for, and it fed into Jon's worry that the captain was planning on doing something reckless. When they reached Baltsaros's room, Jon hesitated for only a moment before following him in.

To his utter surprise, he saw that Tom was in the room, sitting cross-legged in the middle of the wide bed with a bright smile on his face.

"Bloody hells, is it good to see ye," said Tom, pushing himself off the mattress. He closed the distance quickly and looped an arm around each of their necks, pulling them in for a swift hug. The move hurt Jon's side, but he pressed his forehead to the bigger man's scratchy cheek, ridiculously happy to see him.

"I'm amazed they let you in here," said Baltsaros, drawing back after a moment. His dark eyes darted over the first mate's face, searching for any new injuries; Jon could see through the captain's worry that he was deeply relieved to see him.

Tom rubbed at the back of his neck, his brow wrinkling as he looked up at the captain, his green-blue eyes amused.

"Yeah... I ain't actually got leave to be here, Da," said Tom grinning. His face went dead serious in the next instant. "Listen, we have to get the hells out of this bloody place. Now. The redhead says there's plans to jail ye. I figure we can get—"

"We're not leaving, Tom," interrupted Baltsaros.

The silence that followed the captain's words was heavy, and Jon slowly closed his eyes. He felt Tom tense before the first mate dropped his arm from around his waist.

"What the fuckin' hells does that mean?" Tom's voice was rough-edged with anger.

"There is something I require here," replied the captain.

"Bloody hells, Da."

"No, Tom, I need this."

"Are ye fuckin' off yer nut, man? He's gonna put ye behind bars. We have to go!"

"There is something I need to do."

A deep tiredness washed over Jon.

He opened his eyes.

"Let him stay here. I'll come with you, Tom. Leave Baltsaros to his fucking blood rituals and insanity," he said softly. He felt defeated. The captain's dark eyes met his, but Jon couldn't read the man's expression. Didn't care to. "Just you and me, Tom. We'll get out of here. We can get one of those little catamarans and sail out together. We'll be free. Stop thinking you owe him anything..."

He looked over at Tom. The first mate's forehead was deeply

creased, and his eyes flicked between the captain and Jon. Tom swallowed and then licked his bottom lip as he started to shake his head slowly.

"No. Don't you fuckin' do that to me," Tom said hoarsely, the desperation plain in his voice. "Please, Jon. Ye can't ask me to choose."

Listening to Tom plead just made him more weary.

"You know what? Stay here... Fuck you. Stay here with your pain and your lies and your godsdamned twisted loyalty," said Jon evenly. His heart felt heavy in his chest, but his eyes were dry. He didn't even sound angry despite his words. Jon looked at Baltsaros. "I can't keep forgiving you. Stay here... Get your sick fill of murder because that seems to be all that you care about. Otherwise we wouldn't—"

"*I haven't killed anyone,*" said Baltsaros, his voice tight and quiet.

Jon couldn't believe his ears. What did the captain gain by lying now?

"That's bullshit, and you know it," he spat.

"Da?" said Tom. The first mate stared openly at Baltsaros.

The captain's lip twitched, and his jaw was tight as he breathed slowly. Jon realized that the man was struggling with something. A ripple of pain crossed Baltsaros's features before they smoothed out again.

Jon frowned.

"You're lying," he said, but he didn't feel as certain as a few heartbeats earlier.

"No, Jon. It's the truth," Baltsaros said, barely above a whisper. "I haven't killed anyone since I nearly lost you to Reginald."

Tom finally found his voice.

"Ye haven't killed *anyone*? No huntin'?" he asked slowly, his disbelief obvious.

The captain glanced at the first mate and shook his head.

"The only death by my hand since then was to save you, Tom."

Jon's eyes widened, and he looked in alarm at the first mate.

"Tom? What is he talking about?" he asked, but Tom lifted a hand.

"Hang on," said the first mate, his eyes fixed on the captain.

Jon watched his expression shift from skepticism, astonishment, and then once again to confusion.

"That's gotta be a bloody lie, Da. Ain't it been..." Tom looked down at his fingers, counting out on them. "...four months... nearly five since...?"

"Yes."

Jon's heart began to pound in his chest. He felt strange, every sense focused so intently on the words that were being said without really understanding what was taking place.

Tom glanced at Jon, pointing to the captain.

"Is he tellin' the truth, lad?" asked Tom, his ocean eyes wide.

Yes, whispered the tiny voice inside of him. Jon swallowed and nodded; the captain seemed utterly genuine.

Tom looked completely bewildered.

"Then... why? *Why the bloody hells are we here*, Da? If yer not lookin' for a bloodbath... why did ye drag us here?"

Baltsaros let out a slow sigh, his expression wary as he looked between Jon and Tom.

"Because I made a promise to Jon," he said finally.

Jon shook his head.

"I don't remember a promise," he said.

When Baltsaros's eyes met his, the depth of emotion he could see in them startled Jon.

"I never told you... You *died*, Jon. You died from your wounds, and there was nothing I could do about it. You died as a direct result of my actions. I may as well have murdered you myself," Baltsaros murmured. He stepped closer to Jon and reached out. Jon held himself still as the captain's outstretched fingers rested on the twisted scar beneath his shirt, and he shivered at the touch. "It was my fault. I realized it in the terrible moment when I thought I had lost you. So I made a promise to you: I would give up anything for you. Then you woke up, Jon. You lived."

Jon's mouth was dry; he was dizzy from the captain's words. He knew that his survival had been a close thing, but not *how* close.

"But... I don't understand. I thought you lied to us so you could take part in these human sacrifices. Feed into this blood magic you said gave you strength," Jon said helplessly. "Aren't we here because you want to learn... Because you wanted more... ugh. I don't understand. Earlier I could have sworn that you were going to fall in with the emperor... That you were set on doing away with the last bit of good in you somehow..."

Baltsaros laughed in surprise, and his hand moved from Jon's chest to his face. He stroked the ball of his thumb over the younger man's cheek.

"No, Jon. Quite the opposite," he said. His smile dropped a moment later, and he looked to Tom; the first mate frowned at him, suspicion plain on his battered face. "The discovery of a culture steeped in blood sacrifices was serendipitous. The very thing that could feed my fetish without me getting my hands dirty! Of course I needed to come here, but I came here to learn about *myself*. To see if I could trigger the same results that have always calmed my soul. To drench myself so thoroughly in the rituals that I might begin to understand the workings of this obsession. To find answers. *To find a cure so that I could keep my promise.*"

"But, Da... it's been months and ye ain't killed. If that ain't a bloody sign that yer fine to keep on that path..." Tom gestured, looking confused.

"The incident at the Devil's Isles makes it very clear that I am not fine, Tom," Baltsaros said tiredly, his chiselled face pale.

Tom nodded, and he passed a hand over his face, his eyes vague.

Jon was startled when the first mate suddenly stepped forward and grabbed Baltsaros's shirt, yanking him away from Jon. It took him a second to realize that Tom was furious.

"Why the *fuck* didn'cha say a bloody thing? Holy black hells,

Da! Why the bloody secrets, ye daft fuckin' bastard?" he growled, shaking the captain.

Baltsaros wrapped his hands around Tom's wrists, but he made no move to pull out of the first mate's grasp.

"There was no way of presenting my intentions without divulging the truth of my past actions to Jon," replied the captain, his eyes flicking momentarily to Jon's. "I wanted to avoid that at all costs."

Tom shook him again, his rough fists white-knuckled.

"Then why the fuck wouldn't ye come to *me*? Ye godsdamned fuckin' arse... why in the bloody hells wouldn't ye let *me* in on yer fuckin' plans? Ain't I the one who keeps all yer bloody secrets? All this fuckin' time I thought ye was gettin' worse, and now ye tell me that ye been *curbin' yer appetite*? Why the *fuck* did ye let me worry ye were losin' yer bloody mind?"

"Tom, keep your voice down," said Baltsaros gently. "I had no idea you were worried."

"Why wouldn't I be? Gods, yer fuckin' thick, I swear to bloody damnation!" Tom said, incredulous.

"Stop. Just... Stop," said Jon, placing a hand on Tom's shoulder. "Please."

Tom's jaw jutted forward, and he reluctantly loosened his grip on the captain's shirt, but Jon could tell that the first mate's anger had run its course.

Jon shook his head at Baltsaros.

"You realize that in the span of a day I went from learning that you're a blood-obsessed maniac to finding out that you're also a man who is desperately seeking out a cure for his madness," Jon said. "If the latter is true..." He let out a slow exhale, sifting through his feelings. "It's a lot to take in."

The captain nodded mutely.

Jon tilted his head and searched Baltsaros's face for signs that the man was holding something back; what he saw was strength, hope, and determination... and a deep fondness that the captain was unable, for whatever reason, to call love.

"So what is your plan?" he asked finally with a sigh.

Baltsaros smiled.

Tom shadowboxed while Jon and the captain discussed the emperor's twisted hobby. The plan was to use Ah'puch's methods to somehow cure Baltsaros of his own grisly obsession. To Tom, it sounded completely crazy. He couldn't understand why flashing lights and mere words could cause someone to think they were a dog, but what did he know? Who cared as long as this wizardry killed the beast in Baltsaros? He smiled to himself and glanced at Jon; maybe everything was going to be all right.

Tom had felt sick to his stomach for a few minutes when he thought that he'd have to choose between Jon and Baltsaros; he'd die a happy man if he never had to feel that way again. He shifted his weight and bounced on the balls of his feet before neatly breaking the nose of his imaginary foe.

"What if he jails you like Ceara says he will?" asked Jon. He sat at the far corner of the bed, picking at the embroidery on the coverlet while Baltsaros leaned back against the bed frame, feet crossed at the ankles.

"I think I could persuade him not to, Jon. The man's not as clever as he thinks he is. I'm sure I can come up with a reason for why he and I should join forces," said the captain with a thin smile. "What if Ceara's warning was a ruse? Has that woman done *anything* so far to let you believe that she's trustworthy? Has she taken any real risks?"

When Jon glanced at him, Tom winked. He was still annoyed that the captain had kept things from him, so he felt no burning need to tell him about the bathhouse. A shadow of a smile crossed Jon's face before he turned back to Baltsaros.

"She brought Tom to the storage room when she could have just as easily left him in the slave quarters," said Jon with a shrug, neatly leaving out the fact that he and Tom had spent time together.

"Yes, but she left him there for quite a while, and we have no idea where she is now," Baltsaros pointed out.

"Aye, that's true," said Tom. "But she was sayin' that the emperor has something he ain't sharin' with her. I'm no bleedin' mind reader, but she seemed like she was real scared."

"Yes. Which brings me back to my original question: what do we do if he throws you in a cell, Baltsaros?" asked Jon.

"I don't know," replied the captain. He glanced at Tom. "I'm sure you two can come up with a plan. Just promise me one thing: don't die trying to save me."

Tom dropped his fists, the pit in his stomach having opened again at the captain's words.

Seeing Tom's expression, Baltsaros smiled wider.

"I'm hoping, of course, that it doesn't come to that. Believe me when I say that I want to get out of this unscathed as much as you do," laughed the captain, waving a hand in the air. The corners of his eyes creased in merriment. "Tom, come here. Stop looking at me like that." Baltsaros beckoned to him.

Tom chewed the corner of his lip.

Fuck it.

He took a step towards the bed. With a sigh Tom climbed up onto it and crawled across the mattress on all fours like a cat. He sank down onto his belly and pressed his face against the captain's thigh. After a moment, Tom felt the captain's fingers trace the bruises that Jon's rough handling had left around his neck.

"Is this your handiwork?" asked the captain quietly. Jon made no reply, but Tom heard Baltsaros chuckle a second later. "Don't look so guilty. But tell me, did you abuse my first mate before or after you refused my company last night?" There was a distinct smile in the captain's voice.

Jon let out a short laugh, tinged with bitterness.

Baltsaros's fingers begin to draw patterns, and Tom knew that he was following the tattoos that curled and meandered across his skin. It was a soothing touch; he let out a small contented sound.

"I am very sorry for the way I've completely mishandled this. In an attempt to lessen the damage I could do, I seem to have made matters worse," murmured the captain. "You both make me want to be a better man, and that puts me at a loss. I find myself... troubled. I'm sorry that I didn't grant you the trust that you both deserve. I'm sorry I have such a difficult time asking for help."

Tom smiled to himself. So many apologies. The man really was changing. Tom raised his head slowly, propping himself up on his elbows to glance over his shoulder, curious to see Jon's reaction.

Jon remained at the end of the bed, a pensive look on his face as he continued to fiddle with the blanket. After a moment, he lifted his blue eyes and regarded Baltsaros in his quiet, serious way.

"See, this is what comes from believing that what we have together is a weakness. If you understood that it was in fact a strength, we wouldn't be sitting here at odds." Jon's lips quirked into a wan smile before he let out a long sigh. "Yea gods, I was certain this was the last straw. You certainly test the promise I made to you time and time again. I feel crazy, absolutely crazy. Maybe I should have Ah'puch take a look in my mind too while we're here." He chuckled, shaking his head. "What do you think?"

"I think you should come here, Jon," said Baltsaros.

Jon blinked.

The captain's fingers touched Tom's shoulder again, and he turned.

"Why don't you coax Jon to come closer?" asked the older man with a small smile.

Tom was skeptical, but he was also tired of the distrust and miscommunication that seemed destined to forever plague them, so he shrugged inwardly and moved to obey.

When Tom pulled himself up onto his knees, Jon watched him dubiously as he moved towards him.

"I don't think this is the time," Jon said. However, he made no attempt to stop Tom when he lowered his mouth to the hand that Jon had curled limply in his lap.

Tom kissed one knuckle, and then another, opening his lips so that his teeth grazed Jon's skin as he moved to a third. Above him, Jon let out a huff of breath and Tom smiled. He pushed the tip of his tongue into the crevice between two fingers and was rewarded with another soft sound. Using nothing but his tongue, teeth, and chin, he gently turned Jon's hand over and kissed the centre of his palm. In response, Jon's other hand came up to rest on the back of Tom's head. Tom brushed his lips along the heel of Jon's open hand and pressed tongued kisses to wrist, forearm, and into the sensitive crease at the crook of his elbow. When he glanced up, he saw that Jon's eyes were half-lidded, the irises dark as dusk as he watched Tom seduce him slowly.

Tom smiled cheekily before ducking his head to push his face against Jon's abdomen. He knew he wasn't skilled at finding the right words to make things better; but if there was one thing that he *was* good at, it was this. Jon let himself be pushed back on the bed, his head at the edge of it, and cleared his throat as he watched Tom lift up the hem of his tunic to expose his stomach. Tom smiled and kissed the soft, dark hair below Jon's navel.

"What if someone comes in?" asked Jon in a breathless voice.

The bed creaked behind Tom, and the first mate looked up after licking a slow stripe along the line of Jon's pelvis. Baltsaros walked to the side of the bed, and stared down at Jon for a moment before he leaned forward and placed his hands to either side of the younger man's head, his expression strange.

"At this moment, the only thing I care about is that I don't lose you," said the captain quietly. "If love is strength, then let's have no more talk of leaving. I need your strength more than ever." His dark eyes were wide with emotion when they lifted to meet Tom's. "Both of yours."

Tom's chest felt tight; Baltsaros had never sounded this earnest before. Tom stroked his thumbs softly along Jon's skin and felt him shiver slightly.

"Aye, Da," he said gruffly. "Ye know ye have mine."

"I don't know what will happen. I'm in no way sure that my plan will work," said the captain, looking back down at Jon. "It may very well be for naught... But if I am to be dragged away in chains, please let me spend this stolen time here with you. Put away your doubts. Find the good in me so that I might hold onto it a little longer."

Jon stared wide-eyed into the captain's fierce gaze. He doubted the story of the promise; if Baltsaros didn't believe in a higher power, he had no reason to hold true to a vow made to a man deaf to his words. However, that didn't change the fact that the captain was willing to put his mind into the hands of a lunatic to try to cure himself. No, it had little to do with a promise, realized Jon. His pulse sounded loud in his ears in the silence as the captain waited for his answer. No... This was Baltsaros simply and honestly wanting to change himself so that they could be together. If that wasn't love...

Jon nodded once.

Baltsaros let out a little breathless sigh. There was a flush to his face as he leaned down again and pressed his lips tenderly to Jon's. It was awkward at first to kiss Baltsaros back, their mouths reversed, jaws working in opposite ways. However, when he brought his hands up to clutch at him, he felt the captain's pulse racing against his palms, and he no longer cared. He strained up from the bed, deepening the kiss, fingers locked behind Baltsaros's neck. He felt Tom's rough stubble scrape against his stomach before the big man's lips opened over his skin. He gasped. Tom's hand stroked down his side and down between his legs, cupping him warmly through the fabric. The touch was gentle, delicious, confident, and Jon felt himself react to it.

He released Baltsaros, shoving him up and away.

"Tom," Jon said, feeling utterly reckless. "Go push something heavy against the door."

"Aye, aye," replied the first mate.

When Jon raised his head, he saw that Tom was grinning at him.

The burly pirate lifted himself up on hands and knees and slid off the bed; he put his back to the heavy stone table nearest to the door and began to slide it across the floor.

Jon turned over onto his stomach, going up onto his knees quickly to back up. Baltsaros stood and watched as Jon straightened and did away with the sash around his waist, tugging the tunic up over his head with a wince. When the captain made to approach, Jon held up a hand.

"No," he said.

Baltsaros's expression darkened at the command, but Jon repeated himself, tempering the word with a smile.

"Not yet," he added.

Brows high, the captain crossed his arms over his broad chest, but he stayed where he was.

Tom finished sliding the table in front of the door, and when Jon beckoned to him, the first mate obeyed quickly, climbing up onto the bed in front of him. Eyes locked on Baltsaros, Jon undid his pants quickly and pulled his cock out. Without any ceremony, he grabbed the back of Tom's head and forced him forward. The first mate pressed his face against him willingly, his mouth opening over Jon's half-hard cock to quickly suck in its length.

Jon grunted from the sudden, eager contact, rocking back on his knees as Tom's hot mouth enveloped him. He closed his eyes, giving into the sensation for a moment before sparing a look at the captain.

Baltsaros had a smirk on his face, obviously amused by Jon's reaction.

When Tom's hand came up to fondle the soft sack between his legs, Jon let out a shuddering sigh. Maintaining the air of detached dominance he was trying to effect was nearly impossible given

Tom's talented fingers and tongue. With a groan, he bucked his hips, his head down as he watched his wet shaft slide out of Tom's open mouth before the first mate swallowed it back down again.

Jon started when Baltsaros's hand touched his back, and he blinked at the captain.

"I told you not to move," he said, his words ending on a gasp as Tom's tongue dipped into the slit at the head of his cock.

The captain smiled darkly, and he lifted his other hand to run his fingers over Jon's nipple, pinching the bud of sensitive skin between thumb and forefinger.

"Yes, you did," said Baltsaros. He lowered his mouth to Jon's but stopped a hair's breadth away. "But I'm not in the mood for games."

He pinched harder, and Jon's groan of pain opened his lips to Baltsaros. He whimpered into the kiss, surrendering to the captain. His hands left Tom's head, and he scrabbled at Baltsaros's chest, wanting to pull the shirt off of him. The older man broke the kiss and laughed, ridding himself of the tunic swiftly as Jon took care of the laces at the front of his pants.

Tom let Jon's cock slide all the way out of his mouth, and he looked up at Jon for a moment, his lips red and wet. Jon watched as the first mate moved to use his mouth on the captain's exposed cock, his hand shifting from Jon's sack to stroke along his length instead. As Tom gorged himself on the older man's cock, Baltsaros let out a small growl and captured Jon's mouth again, savaging him with a kiss that brought out a keen edge to his desire. When Tom's lips and tongue reclaimed him, Jon felt the heat and hardness of the captain's cock against his own. With a moan, he pulled away from the kiss and saw that Tom held both shafts tight in one hand; the first mate licked and sucked at their cockheads, working his lips over both with a soft moan.

Jon could barely breathe, the ache in his side sharp as he strained to pull in air. Despite the pain, however, he found himself getting close as Tom stroked their shafts as one. He could feel

Baltsaros's wet cock slipping against his; it made the heat in his loins swell and tightened the skin between his legs.

He pressed his face against the captain's neck and sobbed out his mounting passion; another stroke... yet another. Closer. He would soon spill. Baltsaros wrapped his arms around Jon's shoulders, one hand tight against the back of his neck, holding him firmly as he growled deep in his chest. Jon felt the captain's heart race against his chest, his fingers clutching at him almost painfully. With a gasp Baltsaros's body trembled, and Tom let out a small sound.

Jon closed his eyes tight; Tom's mouth was suddenly wetter, more slick, the captain's cum spread back over his own cock... and he fell headlong into his own orgasm, every liquid pulse forcing a helpless sound from his throat.

Shaking, Jon pressed breathless kisses to Baltsaros's neck when his groin stopped throbbing out its exquisite release.

Tom's soft licks were nearly too much for his spent cock, and he let out a shuddering sigh. Blindly, he reached out for the first mate and was rewarded with a soft nuzzle against his palm.

When Baltsaros released him, Jon let himself fall back on the bed, his thighs trembling. Baltsaros tugged his pants back over his hips; the captain's face was serene as he looked down at Jon, his lips slowly bowing in a fond smile.

Baltsaros turned to Tom and stroked his cheek, turning his hands to claws to scratch down the kneeling first mate's back. The sound that came out of Tom's broad chest was a low grumble of pleasure, and Jon could see that the big man's hand moved beneath the material of his shortened trousers.

There was a scraping sound. Startled, the three looked up to see a section of the wall come open.

Tom let out a frustrated noise when he saw the figure emerge.

"Cock and bloody balls, sweet cheeks. Could ye have waited another fuckin' five minutes?"

However, his face fell to stark seriousness a moment later at Ceara's words.

"The guards are coming."

23

THE END OF THE ACT

I assess the power of a will by how much resis-
tance, pain, torture it endures and knows how
to turn to its advantage.

— FRIEDRICH NIETZSCHE

Baltsaros glanced at the door behind him and frowned as he fastened his pants.

"How much time do we have?" he asked.

"Minutes. Enough that you can follow me through here so we can be away," replied the woman in the burgundy cloak.

"Captain, let's go. We can find a different cure," Jon said quickly. "I'm sure there's some other method…"

Tom turned to Baltsaros; the first mate's blue-green eyes were hopeful.

Jon was right. His salvation could not possibly exist solely within this bloodstained citadel. They could leave here and sail from rumour to hearsay until they found something that calmed his soul. He could rely on Tom to protect Jon… Baltsaros clenched his jaw, his eyes on the two young men on the bed. Yes, and hunger would steadily chip away at his resolve until he was unable to deny himself any longer. Murders would follow. He would lose Jon, and he was not as sure as he once was whether Tom would stay by his side. Here and now, *this* was in his grasp. He had to take a chance. The captain shook his head and tensed at the disappointed look on Jon's face. However, Jon set his jaw a second later and nodded once. Tom followed suit.

"Why are the guards coming? What does he know?" he asked, turning to Ceara. Something akin to disappointment clouded her limpid, blue eyes when she realized he wasn't moving to follow her.

"I'm… not sure," said the women with twist of her lips.

A quick glance at Jon told him that she was lying; Jon's face was pinched in an expression of disgust as he stared at her, shaking his head slowly as if in disbelief.

Ceara glared at Jon.

"Listen, do you want to stick around here to find out? You won't be in any danger at all if you come with me *right now*. We don't have time to discuss this," she said, her voice tight and quiet.

"I simply don't trust you," the captain replied. "Jon thinks you're lying to us, and I trust his instincts implicitly. We are not leaving yet; there is business I have with the emperor that has yet to be addressed. Tom, go move the table."

"Aye, Da," said the first mate with a grim nod.

"What?" coughed the woman. "You've got *business* with the emperor? You cannot be fucking serious. I have a way for all four of us to get *out*. Right now. I've already wasted enough time trying to track down this big fucking lout."

Tom snorted in amusement as he slid the heavy table away from the wooden door.

The petite woman took a deep breath and stepped towards Baltsaros, putting her hands together in supplication as she changed tact.

"Captain. Listen to me. You're a man of reason. We can be away and hide in the city until *Baal's Heart* returns tomorrow.

There is nothing for you here, and every second spent debating this is another step towards imprisonment," she pleaded.

"Aren't we already prisoners?" asked Baltsaros, brows high. "Despite not letting us leave the palace, Ah'puch has been nothing but courteous. As far as I can tell, he is simply curious about us. What is the impetus behind this sudden threat of further incarceration?" There was something incredibly odd about the woman's whole demeanour.

Ceara blinked twice, and her lips curved up into a weak smile, no doubt preparing another lie.

"What aren't you telling us, Ceara?" pressed Baltsaros, his voice cold. He could hear sounds coming from down the hallway.

"I wish you had come with me... It's too late now," she said hurriedly, glancing at the door. "I lied to you. He knows. He knows everything, but I will *fix this*. I promise I will prove my worth, Captain. Trust me. But no matter what, say nothing of my help; *he must not suspect me*." Her eyes were utterly guileless, and he doubted she could fake her sudden ghostly pallor.

Baltsaros held the woman's gaze a moment longer. He nodded as the door behind him opened; even a dubious ally was better than none at all.

Smoothly shifting his expression to one of outrage, he turned to the men who spilled into the room.

"What is the meaning of this?" he asked in Balorian, straightening to his full height. Though he was a tall man, the two marked slaves at the fore looked down at him.

"We're to take you to the emperor," one of them replied. "No delay. Come with us."

"And this gives you permission to simply walk into my room?" asked Baltsaros angrily. "Have you forgotten yourself... *slave*? Is this any way to treat a guest of the emperor?"

The guard stared back at him blankly, rendered momentarily uncertain by the captain's words. Behind him, another man spoke up.

"What is he doing in here?" asked a thin-faced slave, pointing to Tom.

"He is in my charge," answered Ceara, stepping forward. "The emperor asked to see the slave too, did he not?"

The man's eyes widened, startled by the spymaster's presence.

"Yes. But... Emperor Ah'puch only now just asked for—" he stammered.

"Do you not think that I know everything that goes on within these walls, slave?" sneered Ceara. "Do you not think that I have the power to anticipate Our Most Exalted Emperor's every wish?" The woman gave a throaty little laugh, her smile wicked. "Or perhaps Our Most Exalted Emperor sent me here to make sure that you performed your duties as quickly as He demanded... Tell me: have you done anything to make Him suspect you of colluding with these men?"

Baltsaros nearly chuckled at how quickly the spymaster was able to completely take apart a man twice her size. The slave was nearly shaking with terror; he would not bring up Tom's odd presence in the bedchamber. It had been neatly done. The captain looked curiously at the woman in the burgundy cloak. Her loyalty was unproven and her motives suspect, but he couldn't help but think that she would make a valuable addition to his crew... if they made it back to the *Heart*.

Maintaining his act of indignation, he motioned impatiently for the guards to lead them to Ah'puch.

J on grunted when the guard hit the back of his knees with his spear. The slave growled a word that Jon didn't understand, but its meaning was clear: *kneel*. Hastily, he got down on his knees. Tom and Baltsaros followed suit to either side of him.

The room they had been brought to was yet another study in excess. Every narrow, fluted column was gilded, and every elaborate cornice glittered with gems. Small, burnished pedestals lined the walls, each holding the solid gold bust of a man. Above them, the ceiling was painted with a detailed scene of satyrs and nymphs playing by a river surrounded in lush greenery. To each side of the thick, colourful rugs on which they kneeled were tiered fountains that trickled melodiously.

Dominating the room was an enormous dais at its centre. It was modelled to look like a miniature of the palace, but each step of this pyramid was inlaid with different coloured gems that formed floral and arabesque patterns. At its apex sat an ornate throne and, unlike the rest of the gilded furnishings, it was painted blood red. It was from this grisly seat that the Emperor Ah'puch looked down upon them. Ceara stood at his side with her hands clasped in front and head down. Dread became a cold finger caressing the length of Jon's spine.

"The time for pretending has come to an end," said the emperor in accented Common, his thin lips quirked in a disgusted sneer. "Our warlocks counselled against bringing forth the accusations against you until the end of this moon phase. However, We feel that even letting you roam free in Our palace risks polluting Our subjects and slaves with your degenerate sins."

"What are we accused of?" asked the captain.

Ah'puch motioned, and the slave behind Baltsaros kicked him hard in the kidneys. Jon flinched as the man fell forwards onto his hands and knees with a pained grunt.

"Do not speak until We have given you leave," scolded the emperor from his lofty seat. He glanced at the arm of his throne and fiddled with something for a moment.

Behind Jon, the doors opened, and he heard a small, choked sob. He turned and watched two marked slaves drag a limp figure past him. When they reached the base of the dais, the men threw their charge to the ground, and the figure remained prone, hands over his head.

"Kneel," barked the emperor.

Immediately, the young man on the floor scrabbled to his

knees. It took Jon a moment to recognize Oren with his hair shorn and face bloodied. The slender fisherman shook as if palsied, and little whimpers escaped his swollen lips.

Jon felt ill; Oren's whole body was a mass of bruises, large burn blisters, and lacerations. Though Jon's own fists and boots had caused some of the damage, it was obvious that the boy had been brutally tortured. Tears made a clear path through the blood on Oren's face as he stared at Jon; he was terrified.

There was a rustle, and a group of masked figures entered the throne room; they walked slowly in single file to the base of the pyramid and turned to face the accused. The eight were draped in heavy red cloaks, and the masks they wore were fashioned to look like horned animal skulls.

"Oren, son of Migri, kin to the Dogfish clan, you are here to give testimony before the Council of the Eight, the Lords of the Knife. May your words match the truth in your blood," the cloaked figures said as one.

Their sepulchral voices made the tiny hairs on the back of Jon's neck stand up. He glanced quickly to his right and saw that the captain had resumed kneeling and stared curiously at the eerie figures. Tom, on the other hand, just looked unimpressed.

Jon turned back to Oren; the young fisherman had closed his eyes and in his terror had begun to rock back and forth.

One of the cloaked figures stepped forward holding a little corked vessel in his hands. Even from this distance, Jon could see that the man's fingernails were crusted with something dark. Without any warning, the man grabbed Oren's arm and sliced his wrist quickly with a small, curved blade. Oren gave a strangled cry as blood poured into the little bowl. When the warlock was satisfied, he turned back to the pyramid and lifted the sacrifice above his head. He intoned a few words, *blood* being the only one of which Jon understood.

Oren resumed his rocking as he clutched his arm to his chest.

"Speak, boy," said the emperor, leaning forward in his throne.

As if jabbed by a red-hot poker, Oren let out a sharp gasp; he began to speak in Balorian, the words fast and so slurred that Jon understood none of it. However, his mouth went dry when he heard Tom's quiet "fuck".

"He's lying," growled Baltsaros. This time, the slave hit him hard in the head with the butt of his spear; the captain went down in a slump and didn't move again.

With a roar, Tom sprang to his feet and grabbed the guard before anyone could react. The sound of the man's neck snapping rang out in the throne room, and Jon let out a startled yell as the guard fell on top of him; in shock, Jon pushed the dying, gurgling slave away and crawled backwards on his knees. He watched in helpless dismay as four guards wrestled Tom to the ground.

At the foot of the dais, Oren wailed like a wounded animal, a puddle of piss at his knees.

"Enough!" roared Ah'puch. The emperor had risen and glared down at them from his lofty throne. From behind Jon came a low groan from Tom. The emperor pointed to his warlock. "What do the gods say?"

The cloaked figure raised the bowl to his lips. When it came away, the man's mouth was red. From between his gory lips hissed a single word, one that Jon understood: *death*.

Jon held out his hand in a panic, as if the gesture alone could halt the confusion and horror unfolding before him.

"Stop! Wait! What did he say?" he yelled, pointing at Oren. "What are we accused of?" He heard a step behind him and ducked as the spear came down. It missed his head but cracked against his shoulder, and he gasped in pain.

"We're fucked, lad," groaned Tom.

The next warlock took his taste of the sacrifice and repeated the verdict.

Jon suddenly remembered Ceara's words. He stumbled to his feet, his hands clutched in front of him.

"I was forced!" he shouted. "Please! I was forced!" His voice broke in his rush to get the words out, and he cried out as the slave hit him across the back with the spear.

"Forced?" rasped the figure with the bowl. The warlock sounded startled, and Jon felt a whisper of hope. He nodded frantically, hoping to the black hells that he wasn't damning them further.

The cloaked warlocks glanced at one another, the sentencing interrupted for the moment. Oren sobbed and gibbered as he lay curled up on the polished floor.

Ah'puch descended a few steps, and he pointed to Jon with his walking stick.

"Take his blood," said the man, but Jon could see that his words had softened the emperor's expression; there was sympathy there. What had Jon just admitted to? He hastily extended his arm when the figure with the blade approached and did no more than wince when a shallow cut was made.

The warlock smelled of fire and blood, and his skull mask was terrifying.

However, when Jon looked into his eyes, what he saw there surprised him. This was just an ordinary man, no demon: a little weary, skeptical... fearful. The masked man averted his gaze quickly, and Jon frowned. His mind spun in confusion and frustration at not knowing what was going on, but the edge had been taken off his panic by the very mortal unease in the warlock's eyes.

After the cloaked figure lifted the sacrificial vessel to his lips, he looked up at the emperor and nodded. Ah'puch's dark brows pinched together over his hooked nose as he stared hard at Jon for several seconds. Finally, he spoke.

"Ceara, since this is now a matter for the gods, please escort Jon back to his room. There's nothing else to be done for now. Guards, bring the captain to my laboratory," Ah'puch paused, his eyes on the first mate. Tom spat a bloody gob on the beautiful carpet and stared brazenly back at the emperor. "You were once a slave, were you not? Shall we make that permanent? What do you think? Yes?" The man on the dais chuckled as Tom started to struggle anew. "Mikon... Give him fifty lashes at daybreak tomorrow. Let's see if we can break this brute and turn him into something useful."

Part of Jon was glad that he was pulled away before he could see the look on Tom's face. He needed to think, to plan a way out of this mess. The panic he knew would beset the first mate at the threat of the whip would only serve to fuel his own abject terror; fear in those fearless blue-green eyes would derail any hope of keeping himself from falling completely to pieces.

J on pulled his arm out of the spymaster's grasp and stepped away once they had reached his room.

"What did I just confess to?" he said hoarsely. "What was I *forced* to do?" He asked only to confirm his suspicions.

Ceara reached up and undid the hidden clasp on her cloak, letting it fall to the floor behind her. She looked fragile without its bulk. Slowly, she sat on the edge of the bed and looked around her.

"You might not know the language, but you're not stupid, Jon," she said finally. "You know perfectly well that you just admitted that the captain forced himself on you."

Jon's lip curled up in distaste, but he nodded.

"Sit, Jon," said Ceara gently. "I'll tell you why."

The last thing he wanted to do was sit, but he sank down on the mattress a moment later, suddenly exhausted and overwhelmed by the enormity of the situation.

Ceara appraised him with her wide blue eyes, and the cupid's bow of her mouth curved into a small, sombre smile before she began to speak in a low voice.

"Two days ago, some of my men found Oren wounded and completely incoherent, wandering in the *madina*," she said. She looked down at her hands and frowned. One shoulder came up in a little shrug a second later, and the lines around her mouth deepened. "Well... at least, at the *time*, nothing he was saying made any sense to me. Stories of a vessel from beyond the Gods' Claws..."

She glanced up at him, her eyes wide. "Jon, you have to understand that even *suggesting* men can cross through there with their lives intact is heresy. To say that there are living men on the other side of that mountain range..." A crease appeared in her smooth brow as she searched his eyes. "Do you have the concept of purgatory in your lands? Where souls wait to get weighed before being sent to the gods or banished to the underworld forever?" When Jon nodded, she continued.

"The black mountain range is the wall that keeps the spirits locked in purgatory, and the Gods' Claws are the gate... That's what is taught. So you can understand why I didn't believe his rantings. I thought he was so wounded that it had enfeebled him somehow; no one in their right mind would speak blasphemy the way he was. If men could escape purgatory..." She shook her head and sat silent for several seconds before resuming with a sigh. "So... I handed Oren over to Emperor Ah'puch," she confessed.

Ceara twisted her fingers together and looked back down again. Jon's gut churned at the memory of the captain's description of Ah'puch's "patients".

"The emperor has a way with the mysteries of the mind. I thought he could study Oren." Another one-shouldered shrug; she glanced up, her features smooth. "It was a little over two hours later that I heard reports from my spies about a strange ship anchored not far away and strange men in the jungle. I began to have... doubts. I know there is no truth behind the stories of the black mountains."

As she talked, the woman kept shifting between a calm coldness born of duty and the appearance of heartfelt regret.

"Why do you know this as a fact?" he asked.

Ceara huffed out a tiny, bitter laugh.

"If you were the emperor, do you think *you* could conduct secret trades without the help of your spymaster?" she asked with a sardonic lift of one eyebrow. "Who do you think makes certain that the citizens of Ereme'ia Balor are none the wiser?"

Jon let this sink in for a moment; he ran a hand through his curls.

"Why then?" he asked, nonplussed and more than a little angry. "Why do you want to leave if you're so fucking cozy with the emperor? Nothing you've said so far makes me want to trust you. You gave what you thought was a—what did you call him? Enfeebled? You gave an *enfeebled* boy to a bloodthirsty sadist... to *study*."

She nodded.

"I'm not asking for forgiveness nor am I trying to justify my actions to you. I'm not even asking you to trust *me*, only to trust my honest, desperate desire to get us out," she said softly. "Let me finish before you judge me completely."

Jon chewed on the inside of his cheek. As far as he could tell, she was being completely honest with him.

"All right. What happened after you got your *doubts*?"

"I went to see whether I could coax more information out of Oren... only to find that the emperor had done it for me using his, ah, methods. However, along with the details of your ship, Oren also let slip that the captain, you, and Tom were lovers," she said. A delicate grimace creased her brow. "Because of this, you three were to be captured immediately and put to death as per the law. However, I stepped in and bribed the Counsel of Eight to dissuade Ah'puch from doing anything before the end of this moon phase; I was trying to buy some time.

"I quickly made my way alone to the inn, intent on approaching the captain, but then you arrived with your fire and your daring rescue and seriously fucked things up for me. I thought I had lost my chance... I wanted to follow you back to the ship, but I couldn't. I've suspected for a long time that Ah'puch has me watched; he doesn't even trust his own spymaster. However, I did manage to keep the truth of your escape hidden from him so that guards weren't sent out to your ship. Imagine my surprise when the three of you came waltzing back in yesterday morning," Ceara laughed, shaking her head. "And you might have thought you were fooling people with your little act, but I was receiving a constant stream of reports about the three strangers in the *madina*. So, I decided to follow you myself until I could find a safe place to talk.

"Before I had a chance to, the emperor, pismire that he is, sent guards to bring you in; he wanted to keep an eye on you despite the warlocks' dire predictions. I intercepted them and took charge, knowing that if I brought you in myself, it would provide us with a chance to speak privately, however brief.

"My plan was simple: when you and the captain were thrown in the dungeons, I would bribe the guards to get you out. And, by you saying you were forced by the captain to submit to his perversions, the emperor would have no choice but to allow for a stay of execution, giving me ample time to get us away. The laws take this sort of thing very seriously; an oracle has to be consulted for the—"

"What about Tom?" Jon asked impatiently.

"Oh, I can get Tom out of the slave quarters any time I want," she replied with a small, dismissive wave of her hand. "No one guards the slaves. The guards *are* slaves, Jon. Anyway, my plan completely backfired when the emperor took a shining to both you and the captain. For different reasons, of course. Instead of a neat escape from the dungeons, I found myself faced with the task of freeing Baltsaros from the laboratory, an area of the palace that I have a hard time accessing. I told Tom that I could get you both out, but perhaps not the captain. He was, needless to say, not very happy with me."

With his mind reeling, Jon could do nothing but stare at the woman. While he didn't doubt her story, he was sickened by the irreverence with which she discussed their plight.

"...though I have to say that I'm not very happy with any of this either. You know, that escape I had planned for the four of us earlier? It cost me every last *rukscha* I had," Ceara said peevishly. "Now I have no clue what to do. What in demons' blood compelled the captain to want to stay here? What in hells is this 'business' with the emperor anyway?"

Jon leaned forward, ignoring her question.

"Why wait until now to tell us all of this?" he growled. "Why all the secrecy, the lies, the running around with cryptic messages?" Jon was exasperated, furious. At that moment he truly believed that he would slit the throat of the next person who lied to him.

"Simple," said Ceara with another little flick of her wrist. "I thought if you knew I was the reason behind your arrests, you would refuse to take me with you."

Despite the glibness of her answer, something in the woman's eyes kept Jon from throttling her right then and there out of sheer frustration; he had seen despair and more than a little fear for just an instant. It was enough to make him set his teeth together and take a slow breath to garner his calm before he spoke again. She looked at Jon curiously as he moved closer, his eyes fixed on her.

"I asked you something earlier and you didn't answer. Will you answer me now?" he asked softly. *"Why do you want to escape so badly?"*

The petite spymaster turned her head, staring off at the blue sky outside the narrow window set high in the stone wall. After a moment she let out a slow exhale and nodded to herself. She glanced at Jon but averted her eyes again quickly as she lifted her hands to the high neck of her dress and began to undo the tiny buttons. When the fabric parted, Jon's breath caught in his throat. Beneath the dress, the woman's pale skin was covered in a gruesome maze of twisted scars. Feeling ill, he hastily reached out and stopped her from undoing any more buttons; he had seen enough.

There was a subtle tic in her jaw as she turned, chin held high, and forced herself to meet his gaze again. When she spoke, her voice was defiant.

"Why do I want to leave? Let's just say that the mind is not the only thing that sadistic asshole likes to experiment with."

24

LAYERS AND LEAVINGS

One, two, they're coming for you;
Three, four, always wanting for more;
Five, six, seven, the red hands, they beckon;
Eight, nine, ten, slaughtered now, feast on men.

— NORTHERN CHILDREN'S RHYME

Consciousness touched Baltsaros's mind like cold fingers slipping through layers of gauzy cloth. He groaned and turned his head, wincing as the swollen bruise on the back of his scalp touched the hard surface beneath him. His first attempt to open his eyes was painful; bright light seared his vision, and he closed his lids quickly. Tears beaded on his lashes and shimmered in his sight for a moment when he tried again. He blinked quickly and saw that right above him were four of the electric illumination globes. He went to shield his face from the harsh light but couldn't move; at wrists, ankles and shoulders, he was strapped down to a table.

"Ah, there you are," said a voice from somewhere to his left.

Baltsaros licked his lips, his tongue barely moist enough to make a difference.

"Where am I?" he croaked. The details were fuzzy. He could remember a farce of a trial, but nothing else.

"In my laboratory," said the man again. The emperor.

Baltsaros rested his eyes again. He was having a hard time concentrating. Suddenly the red-tinged, semi-dark he had retreated to flashed with starbursts, and his stomach roiled in protest. With a choked gasp he opened his eyes again. The lump at the back of his head now made sense.

"I'm concussed," he whispered, trying again with a leather-dry tongue to grant his lips some mobility. His throat stuck on a swallow.

The emperor leaned over Baltsaros for a moment, blocking the light. The captain was grateful for the short respite from the blistering brightness.

"What was that?" asked the man.

It was as if he was registering the man's words on a delay, the meanings lost momentarily in a haze, and it added to his confusion. Not able to see Ah'puch's features, only a dark shadow, the captain frowned and tried to force his thoughts into some order.

"A... brain injury," he said, the words a mere croak. His eyes felt gritty in their sockets as he blinked slowly.

"Ah, is that what you call it? *Concussed*?" asked Ah'puch. Baltsaros thought he could sense the man's dark eyes on his. Nausea rose like a tide within him.

"Sick," he whispered, and Ah'puch shook his head slowly. Baltsaros heard the man click his tongue once against his teeth.

"You're not going to be sick. I've given you a g------," said the man. Baltsaros didn't recognize the word.

An antiemetic? he thought fuzzily. He groaned when the emperor walked away; the lights began burning into him once more.

"How long...?" he rasped, crushing his eyelids together against the onslaught.

"Mm… only about two hours," said the emperor. "But you've woken up to ask me the same questions three times now." The man gave a little chuckle then began to hum softly to himself.

Baltsaros could hear a strange buzzing sound and water running. Slowly, he lifted his head, and his heart stuttered at the sight that greeted him. He was naked, and from his chest, arms, and legs trailed long, stiff ribbons of narrow, white cloth. They were adhered to his skin somehow, and their loose ends fell below the edge of the table to where Baltsaros could not see. He flexed his arms, trying to move, but the straps holding him down were secure.

The emperor stood with his back to him, doing something over a burnished golden counter. When the man heard Baltsaros grunt as he tested his bonds, he turned with a frown. In his hands was what looked to Baltsaros like a glass syringe, but the hollow needle at the end was crude and overlarge; it was nothing like the fine work that the steel craftsmen managed in the north.

It will hurt.

"This won't hurt a bit," said Ah'puch, and curled his thin lips into an eager smile. "Just relax. Don't worry! You're not going anywhere… You and I have a lot of work to accomplish, Captain."

When the thick needle stabbed into his skin, Baltsaros was silent despite the pain. It was only a moment later when the contents of the needle boiled through his veins did he lose control of his voice.

Tom shifted uncomfortably on the hard-packed earth, unable to move more than an inch or so in either direction because of the shortness of the chain. He thumbed the corner of his lip where another fist had opened up the healing cut, and he winced. Thankfully, the beating he had taken was largely just to subdue him. He had a feeling that Laz had pulled his punches on purpose even though Tom had robbed him of his sport earlier.

Must be the tattooed-kin thing, he thought to himself. *That's a bloody laugh.*

Another shift, and he extended his legs out in front of himself. He rubbed his heel on the ground to mark the limit of his reach should anyone approach. It would be quick work to get his ankles around someone's neck and twist; he'd done it before. However, if there was more than one, he was fucked... That is, if he didn't strangle himself on his collar in the process of breaking the neck of the first man.

Tom let out a frustrated growl and rubbed his eyes. No, he had to stay alive. The fear of the whip was slowly seeping through the cracks in his resolve, and he found himself thinking stupid, selfish thoughts. It didn't matter if he was to be whipped bloody, crying out like a suckling babe for his momma's teats while his legs turned to water. He couldn't do anything rash; who would rescue Jon and the captain if he died?

"Fuck you," he muttered to his frightened, chicken-shit guts.

"Fine, I'll leave you be then."

Tom looked up, startled. The figure before him lowered her hood as she crouched down in front of him. Right within his reach. He'd been so caught up in his own fucking panic that he'd let down his guard. *Sloppy. Stupid. Pathetic.*

"The fuck do ye want?" he grunted, scowling at Ceara. "Come 'ere to gloat? Poke me with a stick? Sit on my cock?"

"Hush, you idiotic brute," said the spymaster with a wry smile. "I'm going to get you out of here."

From beneath her cloak, she produced a key; she quickly rose to free him from his chain.

He pulled himself away from the wall and stood a little shakily. Between the beatings and the missed meals, Tom was feeling a mite unsteady on his feet.

"All right, big boy," said Ceara covering her hair once again with the hood. "Follow me, stick close, and for gods' blessings, don't say anything to anyone. Understood?"

Tom nodded.

Silently, he followed her through the back corridors of the slave quarters, past the baths and the atrium, up some stairs and through a number of doors that branched off to other hallways. As they walked, they passed a number of slaves, both servants and guards, none of whom bore them any mind. After a few minutes, Tom felt thoroughly lost even though he'd never had trouble in the twisty warrens of the mines he'd slaved in as a lad. As they ascended another set of stairs only to go down a level a moment later, Tom realized the interior of the palace had been built without rhyme or reason. He frowned; maybe that was the point? How could you easily take over the structure if you got lost five minutes after you stepped through the door?

Suddenly, they stopped at a bare piece of wall. Tom frowned and looked askance at the petite woman at his side. She peered at the wall for a few more seconds, then tapped out a pattern on the sandstone bricks. Instantly, the wall parted on a seam, and he smelled fresh air. The spymaster glanced around quickly and then gestured. Tom followed her through the hidden door.

He looked around him in confusion. They were outside.

"Where's the captain and Jon?" he asked.

Ceara turned to him, her blue eyes narrowed.

"They're still in the palace," she whispered.

Dread squeezed at his chest, and he tensed.

"Yer gonna go get them, aye?" he asked, staring hard at her.

"No," she replied.

He heard a shuffle of footfalls to his right and spun to face the sound. Out of the darkness emerged two veiled and helmeted guards. They were heading straight for him.

B altsaros slowly realized that the sound he was hearing was the emperor talking.

"...find it interesting to see where the languages diverged when my ancestors crossed the mountains during the *year of the thousand snows*. See, what you're asking for right now is called *water* here. See how it's ever so subtly different? This sort of thing absolutely fascinates—" Ah'puch's face wavered into view, and Baltsaros's head swung to the side as the emperor slapped his cheek. "Are you still with me? Pay attention! I'm sure this sort of thing fascinates you just as much as it does me.

"Take your name for instance. Baltsaros. Baal-tsaros. Baal... like your ship, the root of your name. You northerners have the word "Baal" to mean God, correct? Well... *a* god, yes? We have the god *Bal* here! In fact, He is what our golden city is named after: *the eater of hearts*. The name comes from the same root! You and I, Captain, are kin. From a long, long, long time ago. Hang on, this will pinch a bit..."

The captain's entire body jerked against the restraints as another thick needle pushed some chemical into his blood. For a moment all went dark, and noises echoed as if he were in a tunnel. There was a sudden iron taste in his mouth, and he gasped for air as the cold trickled through him. He panted and twisted with agony for a moment, convinced the pain was unending, his mind worn down to a raw, blistered nub. Then, the spasms stopped and were replaced by a strange floating sensation. He couldn't see out of his left eye, but he felt... nice. Part of his mind told him he had just suffered a seizure, maybe even a stroke, but strangely he didn't care.

"Oh, that's better," crooned the emperor. The man's face lacked dimension with only one of Baltsaros's eyes working for the moment. "That's nice. I like to see my subjects happy. Look at that smile! Here, let me help you with the drool..."

The captain's face was entirely numb, but his head moved as the man patted at him with a cloth.

"Where was I? Oh yes... So, you see, the Balorian doctrines—these "blessings" and the nonsense about purgatory—are only a few generations old, twisted from previous beliefs for the single purpose of keeping a population ignorant and the men in charge very, very rich. There are walled cities, just like this one, dotting the entire continent. At the head of each is a man, like myself, who is responsible for maintaining the bloodletting, the slavery, the superstitions, and the intense xenophobia," said the emperor, flapping his hand in haughty disinterest. Baltsaros realized that he must have passed out again; the man's monologue seemed to have jumped topics quickly. "See, all these walled cities share a common problem: a lack of mineable ores and metals. That's where my great-grandfather comes in. He was the first one to create an antidote for the m------ that affects the Gods' Claws—"

"Spores," whispered Baltsaros. The word sounded wrong. Muffled. Inside out. A laugh threatened to bubble out of him, unbidden.

What a helpful child! said his grandmother. *What a sweet boy!* The monsters ate her up in one bite. Little Baltsaros closed his eyes.

Red hands, red feet, sharpened teeth, and fists that beat.

"Spores?" repeated the emperor from a lifetime away. Baltsaros's mind drifted closer to hear him. "All right. *Spores.* Yes, my great-grandfather found a way past the Claws into your lands. Understand that there was not much of a taboo then, just reports of hallucinations and whatnot. Imagine what the people of your lands thought when they saw the shiny yellow metal that he brought with him! That was the beginning of trade. Ereme'ia Balor began to prosper *immensely* because of your metals. Our gold fetches a high price in your lands. The taboo of the Gods' Claws was expanded on afterwards just to hide the trade from the other cities..."

. . .

The emperor's voice droned on and on. The light was replaced by darkness at one point. Baltsaros remembered someone he had lost and began to weep because he couldn't think of his name. The boy with black curls. The boy with eyes like a storm. The boy with scars on his back. The boy with eyes like the ocean. One boy or two? ...dreams?

He jerked awake, the four lights above his head bright as the noonday sun. In his mouth was something he couldn't spit out. There were straps on his face. He could see out of both eyes now, but could no longer move his head. His jaw ached like he had clenched it tight enough to break his teeth. The spots where the ribbons of stiff cloth stuck to his skin burned and throbbed. He could no longer remember his name, and that bothered him. For a moment.

He closed his eyes. Red. Red like the hands that took him from his mother's arms. Red like the feet that kicked his father's corpse. A wicked knife made a weeping, red smile on his mother's chest. Sharpened teeth tearing into the heartmeat *one, two, they're coming for you; three, four, always wanting for more; five, six, seven, the red hands, they beckon; eight, nine, ten, slaughtered now, feast on men.*

"- - - -," said Ah'puch. "- - - -, - - - -"

The man's hands were cold on Baltsaros's cock. Something slipped slowly into him, widening, opening him up. It was an unwelcome pleasure that fought tooth and nail with an alien, surrendering sensation, almost itchy in its intensity. Gloriously strange and suddenly breathless.

Tom would like this, he thought. *But who is Tom?*

The pleasure was forgotten a moment later when the machine behind Baltsaros began to buzz again.

340

"…man of your intelligence. It is sad to destroy such a mind…"

[…]

"…fucking repugnant f----- deviant sex…"

[…]

"…root of the evil inside you…"

W hen the buzzing reached its crescendo, Baltsaros could hear a shrieking noise. He looked around to try to figure out what it was. The body on the shiny table below him jerked and trembled as the machine belched its eye-blistering sparks. The bearded man's eyes bulged, red and black and full of rage. Baltsaros was free of rage now. Gone, gone, gone. No more need for the constant, iron control. No more worrying about Jon.

Jon?

Jon!

T om's hands came up in tight fists, and his muscles bunched to attack when one of the guards raised his arm, palm out in a calming gesture.

"Whoa there, buddy," said a familiar voice. "Peace, friend."

Frowning, Tom hesitated. It took him nearly a second to recognize the amber-coloured eyes that narrowed at him in amusement over the black cloth. In amazement, he let himself relax a little bit.

"Jarrod?" he said, uncertainly.

The man who had been his neighbour in the Stone Inn's slave quarters pulled away the veil with his truncated fingers and smiled wide.

"The one and fucking only," said Jarrod with a little flourish of his maimed hand.

"Of course you two know each other," said Ceara with a short laugh. "The two most problematic slaves in Balor's recent history; why wouldn't you know each other?"

"I thought they'd done ye in!" said Tom with a grin. He had watched the guards at the inn pull Jarrod down the hallway, sure that the oft-runaway slave would finally meet his end before the night was over.

"Naw," said the dark-skinned man, with a cocky smile. "They beat me some, but when you started fighting them, they just dumped me in a side room. Didn't take much to get out of there."

Tom laughed. He'd liked the brash slave from the get-go and was glad that he'd made it out in one piece. Then something occurred to him.

"But... how are ye...?" Tom frowned and looked over at the spymaster.

Ceara had a smirk on her face.

Jarrod laughed.

"Ceara's one of the good guys, Tom. She's been helping escaped slaves for years now. Keeps us safe. Finds us places to live. Does what she can to free more of our kin. In return, we're her ears and eyes," he explained. "And sometimes, we dress up and take away some big fucker who's bound to eat all the food in my house." Jarrod's smile faded at the look on Tom's face when the first mate realised that the captain and Jon hadn't yet been mentioned.

Tom swung around to glare at Ceara. Last time he'd held her neck between his callused fingers, it had felt like a bird's: thin and all a-tremble with a skittering pulse. He didn't kill women often... didn't like it; the two women he'd had killed to get Jon behind bars in Portsmouth sometimes came to him in his dreams. But he'd kill Ceara if he had to.

"Where're Jon and Baltsaros?" he growled.

"I told you," she said, her clear-blue eyes wide. "They're still inside. Listen to me... I can't get to your captain. He's with the emperor right now. I can get to Jon, but I gave him some sleeping powders, and he'll be out until morning."

"Why... the fuck... did ye...?" Tom took a step towards the spymaster, his tone menacing. He needed to get back in. Had to figure out a way of getting them back to the *Heart* and sailing out of this bloody, fucking, loony town.

"He started to freak out when I told him that he had to stay put for now," she said.

"And why did ye tell him that?" he rumbled; anger and worry were fighting for space in his chest, and all he wanted to do was hit something. He clenched his fists harder, the skin taut over his knuckles.

Ceara took a small step back but lifted her chin.

"Tom, please, this is the way it's going to have to work," she said. Her voice was a little unsteady. "If I take Jon out... understand that Ah'puch will *kill Baltsaros*. He will, Tom. I know the man. He's petty, and he hates to lose. You, he cares almost nothing about. He has zero dealings with the slaves. The captain's sword and dagger are more than enough to bribe the folks I need to. But Jon... He's taken an interest in Jon. Instead of sending him to the dungeons, he's letting him stay unfettered in the palace. That is something. *We can work with that something.* We will need to get you to the *madina*. I've arranged it so that you'll stay with Jarrod. But Jon needs to stay here. For now. Do you understand me?"

Tom swallowed and let his shoulders fall. He nodded, defeated and deflated and terribly weary. The woman was talking sense, wasn't she? To get everyone out in one piece was the goal...

"What is the emperor doing to Da?" he asked quietly.

A few heartbeats ticked by as she stared at him with an expression steeped in dread.

"Tell me, Tom," she whispered. "Is your captain a strong man?"

25

THE SACRIFICIAL LAMB

reaction formation • *n.* *psychoanalysis* the
tendency of a repressed wish or feeling to
be expressed at a conscious level in a
contrasting form.

Jon pulled on the cord to let more water flow from the tub
above; it was cool and felt good on his sweaty skin. The
sound of the falling water echoed on the glossy tiles of the
small bathhouse he had been brought to, and he wondered
briefly who else used these guest facilities. Did the men in cloaks
and animal horns strip down naked in these stalls to wash the
blood off? Did they have loved ones to go home to once the
slaughter was over? This morning, Jon was the only one there,
and he was thankful for that.

He had awoken before dawn, gasping and choking for breath
as he frantically struggled with the covers. The guard who had
been tasked to watch over him as he slept had stared at Jon impas-
sively as he fought his way out of bed and collapsed panting on
the floor, soaked in the cold sweat of terror. It had taken him a

few moments to remember where he was and why he felt so frantic.

He had been hounded by nightmares all night. Unable to fully wake, Jon had been plunged over and over into blood-slickened dreams full of demons and pitfalls, held in thrall by the sleeping draught Ceara had given him. All he could remember now was a dream of a giant, skinned lion running him down, its eyes like burning coals. The tawny wildcat had called to him from far away, unable to reach him before sharp claws pierced him through.

As he pressed his forehead to the cool, wet wall, Jon let out a slow sigh. He grimaced as the spymaster's words snaked through his mind, poisoning him slowly.

"Flirt with him," she said, her sky-blue eyes earnest. Jon stared at her, deeply confused and more than a little alarmed.

"Isn't that why we're...?" he asked.

Ceara grimaced slightly and looked away.

"I know, I know. I don't pretend to understand it." When she turned back to Jon, she frowned at his expression. "Listen, I'm not asking you to fuck him, ok? Just... I don't know. Compliment him. Show him your... Fuck, I don't even know how this works for men. Show him your muscles?"

Jon let out a helpless laugh; he couldn't believe what he was hearing. Ceara glared at him and stood. She began to pace in front of him, her gloved hands rubbing and twisting over each other.

"Jon, I don't know what else to say," said the woman. "He has... tastes. But, be subtle! Be charming. I know you can act; I watched you play the master at the blessings ceremony. Just do this! Jon, think of it this way: the less time he spends with your captain, the higher the chance we have of getting your captain out alive. You understand?"

Jon let her words sink in.

"I'm to seduce the emperor, but not let him think I am seducing him," he said faintly. "What do you take me for? I have no... skills at this." He pressed his lips together tight and thought about the teasing, coy creature he could become when the mood struck him; but that was for Baltsaros and Tom. He... couldn't with a complete stranger. Especially one that he wanted to see die a painful death by his own sacrificial blades.

But it seemed he would have to. The thought of it made him nauseous.

"And Tom?" he asked quietly. "What will become of him? Can you save him before he gets whipped?" He remembered the way that the stolid first mate had begged when the captain's long black whip had whistled through the air.

"Yes. I'll have him out before dawn, Jon. I promise you," she said with a resolute nod. "He'll be safe. This will all be over soon if everything goes as planned. I know, I know, I don't have a great track record so far, but this time I have your help. Right?"

Jon clenched his jaw and stared at her before dipping his chin a little.

Jon followed the slave guards to a large open terrace at the rear of the great pyramid. Colourful pillows and throws were scattered on the sandstone, and a large, triangular piece of pale-rose silk was stretched out overhead to create an area of shade. It was beneath this canopy that the emperor was stretched out on his side on a mound of bright cushions. Before him on a low table were dishes filled with various fruits and a graceful decanter with a pale-yellow liquid in it. Jon took a deep breath and stepped forward, his head lowered meekly.

"Jon!" said the emperor cheerfully. "Come! Come closer. Sit with me. Thank you for joining me for breakfast." The man said it like Jon had been given the choice.

Jon took another few steps and sank down onto a thick mauve

cushion with golden tassels; he watched a bead of water slip down the side of a green apple and waited for Ah'puch to continue, his shoulders up and tense.

"The clothes are all right?" asked the emperor.

Jon looked down at the outfit he had been given. The soft, grey silk tunic and flowing trousers were mere whispers against his skin, barely felt.

Not too forward, not too fawning, he thought to himself.

"Yes. Thank you," he murmured, glancing up shyly at the emperor for a moment before looking down at his hands. "I… have never been given silks to wear before, Your Excellency." Jon knew that the best lies were built on the foundation of the truth.

He risked another look at the man across the low table, this time without raising his head. He knew his lashes would shadow his eyes and that he looked absolutely guileless; the important thing was to make sure that the emperor saw no artifice in Jon. He launched into his prepared words.

"I want… to thank you," he said, letting his voice waver a little. "For–for freeing me." He blinked his eyes rapidly to give the impression that he was tearful before looking back down again. In reality, he was fighting the urge to leap forward and snatch the knife from the wooden board to sink it into the emperor's neck to the hilt. He allowed himself a hidden smile at the thought and then frowned. Maybe the reason he had been so hysterical over Migri's death wasn't that he had killed a man, but because it had been strangely *satisfying* to feel the knife slip into him. His heart knocked hard twice before settling into a fast rhythm, and his mouth tasted sour. Since the emperor hadn't invited him to partake in any food or beverage yet, he simply sat with his fists clenched in his lap, waiting.

"Are you all right?" purred the emperor softly. "You seem distraught."

Jon nodded quickly and brought a hand up to his eyes to rub at them.

"I'm sorry, Your Excellency," he whispered. "It has been a

terrible time for me. I can hardly believe it to be over." He heard the emperor shift on his bed of cushions with a soft sigh. "If only you knew..." He let his words trail off and wrapped his arms around himself.

"Jon, look at me," said Ah'puch. When Jon raised his eyes again, the man smiled kindly at him. "Please, have some wine. It will make you feel better."

The emperor motioned, and a fluted glass was filled with wine and held out to Jon by a petite slave woman. He reached for it, his eagerness completely sincere. He drank down the small glass quickly and placed it back on the little table where it was immediately refilled by the emperor himself.

"Do you wish to speak of it? I will not judge your words. We are but two men speaking, but I may be able to help you further. I could try to give you ways of dealing with your trauma. Can you trust me with your story, Jon?" said Ah'puch as he sat up and held out a plate of fruit. Jon chose a plum and turned it in his hands, contemplating its glossy, nearly black skin for a moment before answering.

"Yes. I guess I can speak of it," he said, and lifted his eyes to the emperor again, smiling shyly. "I... trust you." *To die by my hands*, he decided grimly. He took a bite of the plum and chewed it thoughtfully before continuing.

"He... *they*... kept me in a cage," he started. When the emperor nodded in encouragement, Jon looked away, as if in shame. "The captain tied me up," he continued, thinking of the red hempen rope. "They both made me... do things." Jon began to feel both uncomfortable and weirdly excited; he couldn't have faked the blush that infused his cheeks if he'd tried. Jon licked a little plum juice off his fingers, knowing that the emperor's eyes were on him. It was done as though innocently, but when Jon looked at Ah'puch, he saw that both his words and actions were having the desired effect.

"What *kind* of things?" asked the emperor as his dark eyes widened eagerly.

Ah, there it is, he thought to himself. *Ceara was right about him.*

He waited a moment, letting the silence drag a little, and bit the corner of his lip before responding.

"He…" Jon swallowed, his discomfort only partially an act. "He liked to make me… make me… *beg*…"

"Beg?" The emperor's voice had taken on a breathy quality, and he leaned forward slightly. "Beg for what?"

T om pulled the thin comforter over his head and let out a little pathetic groan. His mouth still tasted of the plum-flavoured rice liquor that he and Jarrod had drunk until the wee hours of the morning, and his skull felt like it was too small for his throbbing brain. The slave with the missing digits had proven to be a surprisingly adept drinking partner, given that Tom outweighed him by at least seven stone.

And a hell of a gambler.

Tom rubbed his face and scowled at the memory of losing his favourite dagger. His stomach gave a rumble of hunger; maybe there was more of the spicy goat stew from the night before.

Just as he was contemplating sitting up, he heard a soft noise. Tom pushed the covers away and reached for his knife. When his fingers closed on nothing, he swore under his breath.

"Relax," said a familiar voice. "It's just me."

Tom raised himself onto his elbows and grimaced at the spymaster. She was perched on the windowsill with an amused look on her freckled face.

"Yer a sneaky little thing. I'll give ye that much. What the fuck do ye want?" he asked groggily. As he sat up fully, his vision swam with dark shapes. He swallowed against the nausea that had reared up inside him at the motion.

"It's nearly noon, Tom. I came to see you off to your ship," said Ceara. She slid off the windowsill and threw something dark at his head. Tom grunted with surprise and caught it with one hand.

When he opened the cloth sack, he saw that it was filled with clothing.

"I don't know if any of it will fit," admitted Ceara as she stepped closer to him. "But you need to cover up those tattoos to get through town. You're a free man now; congratulations."

Tom snorted in derision and began pawing through the sack. The first shirt he found turned out to be too tight over his shoulders and biceps and the second, too tight across his chest. He scowled in annoyance and was ready to toss the sack at Ceara in frustration when he pulled out a loose black tunic with sleeves long enough to cover his arms. He yanked it over his head and it fit, but only just. Next, he found a pair of thin, dark-blue trousers that seemed to be the right size. He glanced up at Ceara as he lowered his sweat-soiled pants and grinned at the blush that infused her cheeks before she rolled her eyes and looked away.

He folded the sleeves up over his tanned forearms and tucked the hem into his pants before tying on his leather belt. Then, Tom held out his arms.

"Well?" he asked.

Ceara turned to him. From the look on her face, Tom gathered that the clothes suited him. The petite woman stared at him for a moment, and then her face closed down into the slightly haughty expression she normally wore. She clucked her tongue at him and reached for the shirt.

"The purpose was to conceal your markings, you dolt. Not to walk around with your tits hanging out," she sighed. Tom frowned and looked down at himself. The shirt was undone nearly to his navel. "Listen, you can go about like a half-naked savage on your own time but—" She tweaked his nipple mischievously as she quickly buttoned him up to the throat; the teasing touch caught him unawares, and he let out a short, startled laugh. "—in Balor, free men tend to dress a little more conservatively. *Savvy?*"

Tom grinned even wider at her use of mainlander slang. Part of him hoped that they wouldn't be forced to kill the gutsy Ceara;

he could her see getting along with the rough louts aboard the *Heart*. Maybe the captain would—

His face fell, and he snatched one of her small hands in his.

She blinked up at him, surprised.

"How's Da?" he asked quietly. Baltsaros was stronger than anyone he knew, and his mind was like a blade of folded steel, but from what Ceara had told him, the emperor was very good at breaking strong men. When the woman shook her head in response, he let out a slow exhale. He hated being so fucking powerless.

"I don't know. I wish I could give you news, but I have no way of getting to him, and the men who guard the laboratory are profoundly loyal to the emperor. I'm sorry, Tom," she said, squeezing his fingers.

He dropped her hand with a sigh. He just had to trust that the captain was able to withstand whatever was being done to him.

"And Jon?" he asked, hopeful.

Ceara reached up and draped a dark-grey silk scarf around Tom's neck to hide the slave collar until he could get it removed. Her forehead creased at his question.

"Jon... is... fine. He's actually doing better than I'd hoped," she said with a tight smile. "He's going to have Ah'puch eating out of his palm, literally, if he keeps it up. Hells, if I didn't know it was an act, I would swear to the heavens that the boy is really looking to be bedded by the emperor."

"What?" growled Tom, confused. "What the fuck do ye got him doin'?"

Startled, Ceara backed away from him quickly, and Tom reached out and grabbed her cloak, twisting the fabric in his fist.

"Shit! He's buying us some time. Ok?" she exclaimed as she pulled on her cloak. "Tom, I swear to Bal... You've got to stop thinking that I'm the bad guy."

As Ceara explained the plan to him, Tom sat down on the edge of the bed slowly. His nausea had returned, and the image of Jon and Ah'puch together was like cold seawater in his veins.

"He hasn't *touched* Jon, has he?" he asked in a bleak voice when she was done. He could feel his pulse in his clenched fists. Thoughts of that slimy, hooked-nose bilge rat putting his hands on Jon coursed through his mind. He imagined Jon trembling in a corner, his clothing ripped and his limp cock exposed while the emperor stroked his own tiny, twisted shaft and laughed. Tom tasted bile in the back of his throat.

"I don't think so," said Ceara, her expression softening at the look on his face. "Tom, honey, it's the only way. The faster you can get to your ship, the safer everyone will be. I will come up with a plan on my end. It can work."

"Then what the fuck are we waitin' for?" growled Tom as he lurched to his feet. He had to get back to the *Heart*. Polas was sure to have an idea.

"No... I see that look," she frowned, placing a hand on his arm. "You have to stay on board until *I* come up with something. You can't just barge into Balor with men and weapons and think you can rescue the captain and Jon. You don't have enough manpower."

He scowled at her for a moment and then he blinked as something occurred to him.

Tom smiled.

"Actually... I think we do."

2 6

LEARNING TO SPEAK

Lust is to the other passions what the nervous fluid
is to life; it supports them all, lends strength to
them all ambition, cruelty, avarice, revenge,
are all founded on lust.

— MARQUIS DE SADE

Jon peered at the open book on the low table. On each page
was a beautifully rendered illustration depicting the life of a
god the Balorians worshipped. One page showed a tall,
blue-skinned, three-headed man with what looked like a
giant axe over one shoulder; the next showed a hunched, leathery
demon with a lolling red tongue and fangs edged in gold.

The emperor tapped the image.

"There he is," he said. Ah'puch was so close to Jon that the
man's breath tickled his neck as he leaned over. "That's Bal. *The*
eater of hearts."

At the base of the image, Jon saw that there was a jumble of
red hearts; the paint was so shiny and thick there that it seemed

the page itself bled. He held his breath as the emperor touched his shoulder. Ah'puch smelled like flowers, a sickly sweet scent that made Jon a little nauseous. However, he forced himself to keep still as the emperor pressed his chest to Jon's back with the pretence of getting a better look at the god's image. Jon swallowed and nodded.

"I see! That is very interesting," he said in a bland, friendly tone that belied his utter loathing for the man. After a moment he frowned; he wasn't going to keep the emperor's interest with empty pleasantries. It was only a matter of time before the man tired of showing him knickknacks and retired to the dungeons to continue carrying out his "work" on Baltsaros. Jon stared at the god Bal atop his gory mound of hearts and had an idea.

"He tried to cut my heart out," he said quietly. He felt Ah'puch tense. A gentle hand closed over Jon's shoulder.

"The captain?" asked the emperor.

Jon pulled away slowly and climbed to his feet. He took a step back, nodding as he looked at the ground. When he lifted his eyes, he saw that Ah'puch was staring up at him with a strange expression. The emperor was trying to look sympathetic, his brow wrinkled and mouth turned down at the corners, but Jon's gift read only morbid curiosity and a sense of validation. A black tide of emotion rose up quickly in Jon, and he nearly stumbled when he stepped back again. In painting a picture of the captain as a depraved sadist who only kept Jon as a bed slave, he wound the truth and fiction together tightly to make his words credible; but, as he forced himself not to think of the real captain, locked away and suffering beneath the palace pyramid, he found himself getting confused. Reality was leaching away, and the truth of the past was undermined slowly by his clever lies and the constant anxiety that plagued him. Jon was adapting to the strained situation too readily, his brain finding ways to blur the edges of the worry and abandonment he felt. How long would it take before he believed his own words?

He grimaced at the emperor.

"Yes... the captain," said Jon. He lifted the hem of his tunic, at first thinking just to pull it up high enough to show the evidence, but instead, he slid the thin, grey silk shirt up over his head. Emperor Ah'puch let out a small noise and rose quickly to his feet with the help of his cane, his eyes on Jon's chest. Jon looked down at the twisted scar that Reginald had given him. Fingering the slightly raised flesh, he blinked sadly at the emperor.

"He nearly killed me," Jon said. He turned to show the matching scar that Baltsaros's knife had left a few weeks earlier. "And then he tried again."

"You poor boy," breathed the emperor. "You poor, poor boy."

When he turned back and saw that the man's eyes had focused lower on his body, Jon looked down and was suddenly made extremely aware of just how thin the silk pants were. Without the tunic covering him to mid-thigh, Jon could see the bulge of his cock through the material. He felt appallingly exposed. Heat flushed his face.

You can use this.

With a disgusted little shudder, Jon glanced back up.

"I... I need to sit," he said in a choked voice, passing a hand over his eyes. "I don't feel so well."

"Of course!" exclaimed Ah'puch and stepped forward hurriedly. He grabbed Jon's arm before he "fainted" and helped him onto the low settee. The emperor then filled a beautiful glass goblet with water for Jon.

Jon accepted the glass with a meek, thankful smile. He took a small sip and sighed.

"I'm sorry, Your Excellency," he said. "I don't know what's wrong with me." He tried not to cringe when the emperor's hand slid around his back.

"It's perfectly understandable," said Ah'puch. His fingers squeezed Jon's side, and the younger man winced. "You've been through so much." The emperor's other hand patted his knee kindly; the sweet, cloying smell of the man's perfume made Jon's head swim. "Maybe it would help to talk more about it?"

"Maybe…" said Jon uncertainly. Up until this point he had only skimmed the topic, not going into detail but giving the emperor choice tidbits to keep him hungry. Ah'puch, in turn, had taken every opportunity to ply Jon for more overt descriptions of the acts he had been "subjected" to.

He took another sip of water but pretended to choke on it this time, making sure to spill some from the goblet as he coughed. A cold splash landed squarely in his crotch, and Jon heard the emperor's quick intake of breath. He looked down and felt a blush sear his face again. For one long second, he thought he had completely overdone it. The water had rendered the pale grey silk almost translucent, and the thin material clung to him like a second skin. He might as well have just taken his pants off for all the cover the wet silk afforded him; Jon hadn't meant to be so *blatant*, but it was too late for that. The best he could do was to appear as if he hadn't noticed that his cock was on display. He coughed again belatedly and looked around the room, only too aware of the emperor's eyes on him.

"I know. You spoke about Captain Baltsaros tying you up… Tell me about that," murmured the emperor. "It will help you to talk. Trust me."

"I… guess so," Jon conceded, his jaw tense.

Ah'puch's eyes flicked down to Jon's wet crotch, and he nodded eagerly.

"The captain has a chest full of… objects," Jon started awkwardly. "Things that he likes to use on me. When I've been bad. You know, when something gets broken or I misbehave; Baltsaros has a terrible temper," he explained. The emperor nodded again in encouragement, his fingers stroking Jon's thigh lightly.

"There was one time when I was clumsy and knocked over the captain's coffee as I was reaching for something," Jon said, leaving out the part where he had done it on purpose. He'd wanted to provoke Baltsaros into some anger-fuelled play, and the captain had known it too. Jon had to keep himself from smiling at the memory, and then realized that his hands were shaking. That, at least, wasn't an act.

Baltsaros. Don't think.

He licked his lips and continued.

"He made me get on my knees on the floor, and he took a rope and tied my hands behind my head. But not just at the wrists... The rope was all the way up my arms and around my throat. Then he... He told me to spread my legs, and he tied rope around the top of my thighs and— You're sure you want to hear this?" he asked, narrowing his eyes at Ah'puch. "I thought this was unlawful. Forbidden. Isn't my talking about it just as wrong as the act?" He knew that pointing out the hypocrisy would allow the emperor to justify it somehow.

"You can speak of it to me, Jon. This is a safe environment. Your tormentor is in a cage, and you have nothing to worry about from him," said the emperor calmly. However, when he squeezed Jon's leg, Jon saw that Ah'puch's forehead was shiny with sweat. "I am but an ear to listen to you. It will cleanse you to speak of these things. Go on. He tied rope...?"

"Around my thighs. I could feel it against my... um... buttocks. I was so scared of what he would do that I was shaking. I couldn't move my arms or look around to see what he was doing because of the rope around my neck. And then... Then he put a blindfold on me," Jon said in a low voice.

He swallowed thickly at the memory. The blindfold was never easy for him to accept, but in the end, he always found a sort of peace in the dark. Ah'puch didn't need to know this.

"I heard him walk away and open the chest, but I didn't know what to think. Baltsaros likes to hit me with a bamboo switch or a bundle of leather strips tied to a handle. They both hurt in their own way, but when I heard him opening the drawers to his armoire too, I got even more scared." The emperor's fingers tightened on Jon's leg. The man's breathing sounded a little faster. Jon didn't dare look at him. Instead, he concentrated on the abstract tapestry on the opposite wall.

"What was it, Jon?" asked Ah'puch quietly.

"At first I didn't know. He... the captain... pushed me down on the rug so that I was on my chest and knees. Then, something cold touched me... it touched me right on my—" He fumbled for the right word. "—my *opening*." Jon's breath hitched in his throat, and he coloured, his heart hammering his ribs. In dismay, he felt himself stir and closed his eyes. "It was something hard and smooth that the captain had oiled. He *pushed* it, and it slid inside me. I couldn't fight it, I couldn't move. The thing was thick and it *hurt* me," whispered Jon. He was caught up in the memory. The captain had fucked him slowly with the wooden phallus to let Jon get used to the girth of it, but the stretch hadn't been the bad sort of pain. No, it had made Jon's cock rock hard and had coaxed needy little pants and moans out from between his open lips.

"He fucked me with it, pushed it deep into me, and he laughed." In truth, it had been Tom who had laughed when he had walked in and seen Jon tied up. The captain had said something in his mother tongue, and Tom had replied, his voice husky. A moment later, Jon had felt Baltsaros secure the phallus somehow using ropes stretched across his ass before doing something with the bindings around his ankles.

Jon clenched his fists against the burgundy brocade of the low divan and let out a shuddery breath.

He blinked as the blindfold was removed, and Baltsaros lifted Jon back up onto his knees with a smile. His large hand closed over Jon's stiff cock, and he leaned forward to brush his lips to Jon's in a brief kiss before gesturing to Tom.

Jon watched as the first mate quickly rid himself of his pants and positioned himself on the floor where Baltsaros pointed, broadside to Jon. The muscles in Tom's wide shoulders rippled as he supported himself on fists and knees and waited.

The captain took his place behind Tom, cock in hand, and rubbed it into the furrow of the first mate's ass. Jon watched the shiny, purplish head peep out above Tom's ass as it slid between his cheeks, and he was held rapt and aroused by the sight. The captain narrowed his eyes at Jon, and the corner of his lip curled up in an amused smirk. With one hand, Baltsaros pushed between Tom's shoulders, and the big man obediently let himself down onto his elbows. Tom looked up at Jon, the excitement and desire yawning dark in his pupils before he closed his eyes.

"Knocking things over on purpose is a crude way of getting me to do what you want. You can't just act out to force my hand. You have to learn to speak your thoughts and desires, my love," murmured the captain. "As your punishment, you get to watch me fuck Tom. Maybe it will teach you a thing or two. How do you like that?"

Jon pinched his brows together and shook his head. This isn't at all what he had expected. How was he supposed to do anything while he was tied up? However, the disappointment did nothing to slow his pulse as he watched Baltsaros oil his cock slowly and plunge it deep into the first mate with a soft grunt. Tom's lips parted with a low moan, and Jon felt his cock tense and bob up in response. Baltsaros fucked Tom with a few quick thrusts, and then he stopped.

Jon could see the first mate move eagerly up against the captain, wanting more. However, Baltsaros kept his eyes on Jon and just smiled. A moment later, Tom let out a pathetic little sound.

"Fuck, Da. Please. Please, Da. Fuck me," gasped Tom. Jon's heart leaped with the first mate's shameless words. Baltsaros slapped Tom's ass before sliding his length back into him a few times. Jon saw that Tom's cock swung heavy and hard between his legs, but he knew that the first mate wouldn't touch it unless the captain gave him leave.

"Tell me what you want, Tom," purred Baltsaros with another wicked smile. He pulled himself out to slide his length up along the furrow of the first mate's ass again. Tom's lids lifted slowly and his forehead creased. With his eyes on Jon, he began to speak as Baltsaros waited.

"I want ye to fuck me, Da. I wanna feel yer thick cock fuckin' me deep," Tom gasped. "I want ye to drive yer cock into my ass, Da. Please, Da. I want yer cock… please, Da."

The words made Jon's groin ache, and his ass throbbed over the phallus lodged inside him. However, when Jon squirmed slightly in discomfort, he noticed that while the wooden cock was held inside him by one rope, the rope around his ankle pulled it out a little. He experimented by moving his hips forward and was rewarded with a shallow plunge. He gasped at the feeling.

"More, Tom," he whispered. "Say more…"

"He wanted me to say 'I want you to fuck me hard, Daddy' while he watched me play with myself," breathed Jon, paraphrasing Tom. "And 'I want you to cum in my ass'…"

"And did you?" The emperor was almost panting.

Jon closed his eyes and leaned his head back on the couch. He realized he could do absolutely nothing about the fact that his cock was getting hard from telling the story. He gritted his teeth and took a few shallow breaths. The room was too hot and the emperor too close. He was getting shamefully aroused. He wanted to stop. To leave.

No, you don't. You want him to touch you.

However, when the emperor's fingers crawled up his thigh and tentatively traced the length of his cock a heartbeat later, lingering over the flared edge of its sensitive head, Jon hesitated only a second before pushing himself off the couch.

His mind raced.

Say something, he thought. He blinked rapidly.

"I'm sorry," he groaned. "I'm sorry!" He covered his cock with both hands and took a few steps backwards, frantic to get out.

He turned quickly and without a backwards glance raced out of the room.

S tartled, Jon looked up when he heard something strange. He saw the handle of the door slowly move in the dim light, and his breath left him. The emperor had followed him to his room.

I'm going to have to fuck him.

His pulse spun out of control, and he pushed himself off the bed, fumbling for the light globe. He prodded at it with shaking hands, and the room darkened. A few quick steps brought him to the door where he waited with the gold statuette of a fawn clutched in his hands. A dark shape slid into the room, and Jon swung at it. He didn't care about the ruse he was supposed to keep up. There was no way he was actually going to submit to the emperor. The dark figure grabbed his wrists, and he let out a frustrated sound as the gold fawn dropped to the floor. In terror, Jon struggled to get free.

"Whoa, whoa there," rumbled Tom's distinct voice. "Jon, it's Tom. It's me, lovey. Quit yer fightin'!"

Jon went limp from shock and relief, and his wrists were freed. A moment later, the light came on, and he saw Tom, dressed in long-clothes and boots, standing by the bed. With a wry grin on his roguish face, the first mate held out his arms.

"Tom!" Jon nearly tackled the first mate in his desire to bury himself in the big man's embrace. Tom smelled like tobacco and sea air.

However, Jon quickly pulled away.

"Three days," he said in a hoarse, furious whisper. "Three long fucking days, Tom. Where the hells have you been?" Not waiting for him to answer, Jon took handfuls of the first mate's shirt and began to tug it off of him. Startled, Tom laughed and lifted his arms. Jon attacked him again when his shirt was off and sank his teeth into the first mate's shoulder. Tom let out a pained gasp, but his hands tightened around Jon's waist.

"I missed you," Jon growled. "I was worried about you. I have been going fucking crazy here by myself. Where have you been?"

"*Baal's Heart* mostly. Here and there. But, this is the first time I could get myself snuck in here, lad. Swear to fuckin' gods," said Tom, submitting to Jon's bites with little grunts.

Jon scowled at him and fumbled at the fastenings at the front of Tom's pants. He had them undone in a few seconds and then pulled Tom's pants halfway down his thighs. The first mate's cock hung limp against the coarse, dark-blond curls.

"On your hands and knees," choked Jon, pushing Tom back on to the bed. "I want to fuck you. I want my cock inside you *now*." His lips were salty from Tom's skin. All the pent up arousal from earlier churned wildly inside him; he felt desperate and brittle. Out of control.

With his eyes narrowed with understanding, Tom reached up and threaded his fingers through Jon's hair, pulling his head down until their lips met. All at once the tension left Jon like a flame going out, and he sagged against Tom, melting into the kiss.

"I'm sorry," whispered Jon against Tom's jaw, the first mate's stubble sharp against his lips. "I've had a rough few days. You're right; it can wait. I'm sorry." He pulled back and stared at Tom, wide-eyed. "What are we going to do?"

"We're goin' to take everythin' one step at a bloody time, love," laughed Tom. "First, we'll work on this." Tom's hand slipped between skin and silk to take Jon in a firm grip. "I didn't mean to stop ye just now... I only wanted a kiss first cuz I bloody missed ye too." With a grin, Tom ducked his head to nuzzle Jon's cock through the thin fabric, his breath hot and moist.

Jon let out a slow sigh; it felt incredibly good. Tom tugged down the waist of Jon's pants and licked him slowly from root to tip, his callused hand holding Jon's cock upright. Over and over his rough-velvet tongue stroked him. Then, Tom's lips pushed back his foreskin gently so that he could lick the underside Jon's cockhead and up over the taut skin before sucking him down into the wet tunnel of his mouth. Jon groaned, twisting his fingers in Tom's hair. Tom's instincts were good; Jon had been too wound up before. This was better. However, now that he was calmer, Jon realized that the first mate's hands trembled slightly. It occurred to him then that Tom was being thorough and slow because he was trying to control an overwhelming sense of relief. Closing his eyes, Jon smiled though his chest felt so constricted that it was several seconds before he could take a clear breath.

Soon Jon arched his back with a groan, sweat running down between his shoulder blades, his hands locked behind Tom's head to hold him in place as he fucked his mouth slowly, savouring every languid, deep thrust. Tom made small, hungry noises, his throat open and willing as he clutched at Jon's hips to pull him in. He trembled, softly panting as his lust unfurled its tendrils inside him.

When he let go, Tom didn't need any coaxing to get up onto his hands and knees. Jon spat on Tom, thumbing the thin saliva into him before spitting again, this time into his hand to stroke his cock with. When he pushed himself into Tom's body, it was with a low moan of pleasure, and he moved slowly for a few strokes, letting Tom's passion catch up as the first mate jerked the thick cock between his legs.

Jon fell forward with one arm locked around Tom's neck, the other around his torso, and his forehead pressed to the scars and tattoos on the first mate's back as he slid his length into Tom's heat. He brought himself close twice, three times, four... stopping each time on the very brink to rest shaking and panting against Tom. Jon could feel the first mate's heart beating hard and fast, his tanned skin slick as he also held himself back. Finally, even the slightest movement became too much, and Jon pushed himself up off Tom to pound quickly into him, his hands tight around the first mate's narrow hips. With a strangled cry, Jon spilled over, his cock throbbing as the hot, liquid current crackled through him, and he shuddered, blind and deaf to anything but his fevered, breathless climax.

Tom breathed slowly, his fingertips stroking down Jon's back gently as the young man lay against his chest. It felt like forever since they had lain together like this. Tom was exhausted. Sated. But he couldn't let himself drift off like he wanted to. There was still so much to do. For the moment, however, this was what he needed, and therefore this is where he would stay... at least for another hour. He stared off into the blackness, deep in thought. The unknown state of the captain was like a raw, open wound hidden beneath the thinnest bandage. He knew it was there, but he didn't want to look at it. Tom had to trust that Baltsaros was strong enough to withstand the torture, if that's what it was.

Or still alive.

With a grimace, Tom turned his mind to another of his worries.

"Has he touched ye?" he rumbled softly.

He felt Jon tense, and it took him a long moment to reply.

"Yes," was the quiet response in the darkness.

Tom furrowed his brow and rubbed his thumb along the curve of his jaw, trying to push away the ache in his chest and the sharp sting of guilt over leaving Jon at the hands of a twisted pervert.

"It's ok, Tom," whispered Jon, lifting his head.

Tom could only see the outline of Jon against the pale sandstone walls and was thankful that he couldn't see the soft pain in Jon's eyes that he could hear plain as day in his voice. Tom's big hand cupped the back of Jon's head, and he grunted in reply. What was done was done; getting misty over it wasn't going to solve anything. He clenched his jaw.

"Aye, it'll be ok once my blade cuts that mongrel cocksucker's balls off tomorrow, lad. Not before," he growled. He felt Jon move and saw his silhouette shake its head. Confused, he opened his mouth to speak, but Jon leaned forward to press a kiss to his lips.

"No," said Jon in a strangely sanguine tone, smiling against Tom's mouth. "His balls are mine."

COMING ABOUT

The god opened Its eyes before dawn. It could smell the living creatures around It—a meaty richness that coated Its nose and tongue—and hear them scurrying in their cages. The god was hungry. Flaring Its nostrils, It raised Its head, scenting the air and searching for the one that ruled this degrading little prison.

The man who had sent bolts of lightning into the god's head.

The tiny, disgusting mortal who had strapped It down and caused It pain.

The gaoler with the golden key.

The god couldn't see, smell, or hear Its tormentor. Curling Its claws into fists in Its lap, the god sat still on Its cot and waited.

Jon stared down at his hands.

"I'm sorry, Your Excellency," he whispered. "My time with the captain... it's made me"—he glanced up and licked his bottom lip nervously—"*corrupt*. I'm sorry for yesterday." He quickly looked back down again and let out a little uncomfortable huff of breath.

As if I was the one who tried to cop a fucking feel, he thought in disgust. He twisted his fingers together as he waited to see how the emperor would take his words. When Ah'puch's hand closed on his bicep, Jon only barely kept himself from cringing; Tom's touch was still fresh in his mind, and Jon instantly felt sullied by the unwanted contact. However, he curled his lips into a soft, graceful smile and peered up at Ah'puch through his dark lashes.

"It's all right, Jon," said the emperor, charmed. His thumb stroked Jon's skin gently. "Talking will help. Even if there are, ah… steps backwards, in time you will heal."

Next, he'll be asking me to demonstrate what the captain did to me.

Jon wanted to pull away, but he couldn't think of a way to do it without making it seem like he was trying to escape. He shifted slightly; the dagger strapped to his calf felt conspicuous even though it was well concealed by the loose grey pants.

Eyeing the overlarge guards that bracketed the door to the audience chamber, Jon nipped at the inside of his lip in worry. The emperor was never truly alone, and there was no way he could take the two slaves by himself. He thought about what Tom had said before leaving that morning.

"Who watches over the slaves?" asked Tom, his voice rumbling against Jon's ear. Jon frowned.

"Guards, taskmasters… but they're all slaves, really. Yeah, I'm beginning to understand why the sacrifices have to be so frequent and gruesome. Fear is the only way that a system like this could work. Otherwise, it would be nothing for the slaves just to up and take over. They outnumber free men something like five to one." Jon felt Tom nod. He could see the outline of the chair across the room and realized it was getting lighter.

"Aye, loyalty ain't about worryin' over yer own skin,"

murmured Tom. "Ye can't whip someone into wantin' to save yer life. Trust me on that one." The big man laughed and then let out a quiet groan. "Shit, I have to go, lovey."

Jon closed his eyes and let out a small sigh before rolling off Tom. He watched quietly as the first mate sat up and stretched his shoulders with another soft groan. Scratching his stomach, Tom peered around blearily, and Jon smiled.

"Don't forget that you were wearing a shirt," he said teasingly, trying to ignore the fact that he was getting increasingly anxious about the coming day.

Tom let out a chuckle and stood. In the hazy light of breaking dawn, all Jon could see on the first mate's broad back were the twisting black curls that decorated his skin; the raised ridges of his layered scars were hidden in the penumbral gloom, and the illusion brought a lump to his throat. He pressed his lips together and sat up.

"There has to be a better way," he whispered, the earlier comment about the whip and loyalty finally sinking in.

The first mate stopped groping around the foot of the bed looking for his clothes and glanced up at Jon. Though it was too dark to see his expression, Jon knew that there would be deep lines in Tom's forehead and that his ocean eyes would be narrowed in determination ghosted by the slightest hint of sorrow. It was an expression Jon knew well.

"Aye, love," said Tom, resuming the search. When he found the black shirt, he pulled it on before reaching out to swat Jon playfully on the side of the head. "But I don't see *you* comin' up with a plan, hm? Ye'll jus' have'ta put up with ol' Tom's crazy schemes to get our asses out of here." Tom pinched Jon's cheek and then patted it with a laugh.

Jon pushed himself up onto his knees and slid his arms around the first mate.

Tom sobered.

"I just can't sit around doin' nothin' and waitin' to take the safe road, Jon," muttered Tom against his hair. "I have'ta save him."

"Jon?" The emperor's voice snapped him back to the present. Jon quickly put a smile on his face and nodded.

"Sorry," he said. "I'm just a little tired." He glanced around the room, looking for ways to get the emperor alone. It had sounded like something so easy to accomplish when Tom and he had talked. His eyes went back to the silent pair of guards at the door.

The guards are slaves.

He had an idea.

"How do you keep your slaves from rising up against you?" Jon asked shyly. He stood and took a step towards the door, peering up at the men there.

"They know that they are part of the gods' cycle and that if they are obedient, they will be granted freedom in the next life," replied Ah'puch.

"But not before you carve them up alive, right?" said Jon, the picture of innocence. Though he hadn't been sure earlier that the guards could understand him, he was now. The man on the left had curled his lip into the tiniest sneer at Jon's words.

"Ah... well... We generally only perform blessings on the disobedient. Their blood goes to feed the gods, and their souls are bound to serve them for all eternity," said the emperor.

"Oh, I see," nodded Jon. "And you give rewards to those who are loyal to you? I only ask because we had a similar slave system in my lands, and I'm trying to figure out where we went wrong."

"Wrong?"

"Yes, well, my da was the lord of a grand castle," explained Jon. "We had many, many slaves, and we too had gods to keep them in line... but one day, the slaves rebelled anyway. There were so many of them and so few of us that it was over in just a few hours! I'm wondering if we had rewarded them more whether it would have caused them to be more loyal. We only barely got out with our lives! It was a massacre." The guard's eyes flicked to

Jon's for a moment, and the man frowned at him before looking away.

Good, I have your attention.

"Can free men become slaves here?" asked Jon. He glanced at the emperor. Ah'puch's dark brows were low over his eyes.

"Yes, they can," replied the emperor slowly.

"But slaves can never, ever become free men, no matter how loyal they are?" asked Jon, his eyes wide and guileless. "Is it because of blood? No, wait, that would make no sense. I think I'm getting it wrong... Does the blood of the condemned-but-born-free and the blood of a slave feed the gods in the same way?"

"Ye-s? I don't understand this line of questioning, Jon," said the emperor, his face suspicious.

"I'm sorry," Jon said in a rush. "It just seems to me that if the gods don't care about who gives them blood, what is keeping the slaves from just sacrificing the free men to them? I think that was the logic behind the uprising in my lands. Or not. I'm not sure. But whatever it was, it certainly worked." The guard's eyes met Jon's again, his brows high. Jon knew he wasn't feeding them anything they hadn't thought of before, but the story of a successful coup was sure to spark something among the slaves. "All it really took was a few slaves to—"

The emperor said a few words loudly over Jon, and the two guards bowed before leaving the room.

Success.

"Slaves and their gossip," smiled Ah'puch apologetically when the younger man turned to look at him. "Not that I think any of mine would try the same, but..." The man chuckled and shook his head. He sobered a moment later. "Jon, I'm sorry about the massacre. How insensitive of me."

Jon needed a way of getting to the knife without alerting the emperor. He had to take him by surprise. There was no way of telling how far the guards had gone; Jon was only one man and not terribly skilled with a knife. He took a few steps towards one of the couches.

"Yes, it was terrible," Jon said, sitting down. He thought to put one ankle over his knee but decided against it in case the knife showed through the silk when he moved. "Awful." Besides, he needed the emperor closer.

"What happened to your father?" said the emperor softly.

Jon remembered the way that the blades had slid through Reginald's neck, splashing him with hot blood.

"He was beheaded," he murmured, rubbing his face with his eyes closed. After a moment, the couch sank down next to him, and Jon's nose was filled with the emperor's flowery perfume.

If I lean forward, I should be able to get the blade, he thought to himself and let out a shuddering breath as if he were on the verge of tears. When Ah'puch's gentle hand stroked across his back, Jon bent at the waist, and his fingers slid down the inside of his calf. *Perfect.*

"Who murdered him?" asked the emperor in a kind voice.

Jon lifted up the cuff of his pant leg and touched the leather sheath strapped there.

"Captain Baltsaros," said Jon distractedly, grimacing in concentration. *Only a little more...*

The emperor's hand ceased its soft caress.

"The evils this man has done to you!" growled Ah'puch. "I will make him pay for all of them."

Jon frowned, and he stopped pulling the blade free, startled by a sudden thought. He dropped his pant leg and straightened, staring wide-eyed at the emperor.

"I would like to see this," he said quietly. "I would like to... help you." He knew that the jagged emotion in his voice could be mistaken for passion born of anger. The barest hint of suspicion flickered across the emperor's face, but when Jon curled his hand around the man's thigh, Ah'puch's pupils expanded and his lips parted in a sigh.

"Please, Your Excellency?" asked Jon urgently, squeezing the man's leg gently. It was a hell of a risk—he was being way too forward—but it was worth a shot. Maybe he didn't need to force

Ah'puch to take him to Baltsaros at knifepoint. There would be less opportunity for error this way.

His heart thrummed hard a moment later when Emperor Ah'puch closed his own hand over Jon's.

"Of course, Jon," said the man in a husky voice. "It would be my pleasure."

T om grunted as the chain tugged him forward, and he stepped nimbly over the exposed root that had tripped up his fellow "slave".

"Watch yer bloody feet, Harris," he growled, and yanked on the chain that bound the line of men together from slave collar to slave collar.

"Yessir," coughed the tall, rangy pirate and resumed walking, this time lifting his feet high so that he didn't stumble over anything.

Ceara caught Tom's eye and scowled; she was afraid there might be spies not her own in the jungle. Tom ducked his head and continued to shuffle forward like the captured slave he was supposed to be.

In under an hour they found themselves at the gate to Ereme'ia Balor. Instead of waiting like the rest of the bloody fools who lined up to get into the city, they were ushered in immediately thanks to Ceara. As he trudged forward, Tom lifted a hand to his head and stroked his bare scalp slowly with his palm. The disguise was simply a precaution as no one really paid attention to slaves, but it made him a little nervous regardless to be re-entering the city without the cover of night. He scratched at his shorn head and thought how much it felt like dried sharkskin, rough even to his callused fingers.

"Stop that," murmured the woman who walked by his side. "You're going to make a mess."

Tom quickly lowered his hand and saw that his fingers had

rubbed away some of the dark oil they had smeared on his scalp to match the deep tan he had everywhere else.

"Sorry," he muttered. He was keyed up and jittery, and that wasn't going to do a lick of good for anyone. He straightened his shoulders and stared ahead, thinking only of how good it would feel to squeeze the life out of that scrawny, ridiculous little man that held the captain captive.

Jon stared in horror at the man that paced in front of the bars. The captain's hair was loose, and it hung matted and dirty over his shoulders. His beard was wild; chunks looked to have been torn out of it, and the skin on his face and chest was raw and blistered in patches. The worst thing, however, was how utterly filthy he was. Baltsaros despised being dirty, but this creature trudging back and forth was absolutely covered in dried blood and dirt. From the finger marks in the filth, it seemed like Baltsaros had smeared it on himself.

Baltsaros's head swung around like a wooden doll's, and the captain fixed him with a wide stare. Jon struggled to take a breath as the world narrowed down to a tunnel in front of him. There was no recognition in the man's bloodshot eyes.

"What have you done to him?" whispered Jon. Ah'puch's arm brushed his, and Jon almost shuddered in revulsion.

"Meet the god Bal," chuckled the emperor with a little flourish of his hand. Ah'puch was completely oblivious to Jon's distress.

The man... The *thing* in the cage growled and resumed its pacing, the wide shoulders tense and muscles twitching jerkily.

"It's a little rough yet, I know, I know," said the emperor walking away. Jon could hear him fiddling with something, but he couldn't tear his eyes away from the captain. "But this is after only what... six sessions? Imagine what he'll be like after a few more!" The man's laugh was high and nasal. "Let me just get him restrained, and then I'd like you to use your talents to see what you can tell me about him. I'm curious to know what you see when I ask him questions." There was a clinking of metal behind him. Jon kept his eyes on the thing in the cage; there was a sick, hopeless feeling in his stomach. It was like a waking nightmare.

"Do you know what the most ridiculous thing I learned was? The captain actually believed he was doing these awful, demeaning, perverted things to you out of *love*! How depraved is that?" chuckled Ah'puch.

All Jon could hear was a rush of white noise as his pulse sped up. He staggered a step backwards, his mouth dry.

"What?" he breathed. "What did you say?"

Ceara pointed to Tom and the pirates.

"These lot are to be put to the mines," she said dismissively. "The big one here is about as strong as they come. Put him in a harness, and he'll be pulling out twice the load of your usual. Don't say I never do anything nice for you, Loma. I could have given him to the stonemasons."

The big slave with the eye patch nodded with a grunt and stared hard at Tom. The first mate focused on nothing and just waited with his head low. Ceara had said that Loma was a real ball-breaker with his slaves but that he didn't dole out the whip as often as the other slave masters, and for that he was glad. Just the sidelong glance at the glossy brown whip curled at the big man's side was enough to send a trickle of ice into Tom's veins. He flared his nostrils and clenched his fists tighter.

"Harness," grumbled Loma, and he motioned with a long, hairy arm bulging with misshapen muscle.

For an instant, Ceara's crystalline blue eyes met Tom's, wide with fear or excitement, and then she was gone in a swirl of purple fabric.

Tom lifted his arms obediently as he was fitted with a half-harness, the kind that went from one shoulder to the ribs opposite. He'd worn one like it during his time as a slave in the mines. Closing his eyes as the buckles were tightened over his chest, he thought about how he'd been made to wear the same harness day in and day out. His skin had been thickly callused from where it rubbed him while he hauled iron-rich rock and from how, when Tom was down on his knees, the master's hands tugged hard on the straps. When Baltsaros had bought him, the buckles had been so rusted that he'd had to cut it off of him along with his slave collar.

Tom clenched his jaw and took a deep breath, thinking of what Ceara had told him.

In trying to find every available scrap of iron buried in the ore-scant rock beneath the city, the miners had dug tunnels that reached under the pyramid that Ah'puch used as his palace. Sometime during their excavations, the old bricked-up corpse-chute from the converted dungeons had been breached, and it was to this tunnel that Tom was to go to while the others secured the route back out again. There was no telling what condition the captain would be in, and Tom would need every bit of help he could get if he had to carry the man out of the mines.

Finally, the man adjusting the harness stepped back when he was done and pointed wordlessly to the entrance to the mine. With a surly nod, Tom walked towards the dark tunnel. After only a few steps he paused and pictured the map that Ceara had drawn for him. With a quick jerk of his head, he made his way down the right-hand fork, Harris and the others trailing behind him.

Dazed, Jon blinked and saw that the emperor was looking into the cage where Baltsaros continued to pace. Ah'puch was admiring his *work*.

"He thinks... or at least he *thought* he loved you," Ah'puch replied. "He kept saying it. Maybe he thought I was you... the dark hair and blue eyes, hm? He kept saying 'I'm sorry, Jon' and 'I do love you' over and over again. *Pathetic*. What kind of monster is so sick in his mind that he thinks that he's in love with his victims? So *sick*. And all those things he did to you! Dis*gusting*."

The captain looked again at Jon and let out a small, feral noise before he started to speak in a language Jon didn't recognize. Jon could barely think. He *hurt*.

The long, gentle fingers that liked to stroke Jon's cheek were now curled into hooked claws. The dark eyes that used to narrow in fondness at Jon were now wide and staring. The graceful lips that could stretch into a pleased smile or press fervid kisses to Jon's skin were now twisted into a bestial snarl. This was the *real* Baltsaros. This was the beast that lived inside the man Jon loved.

"See, he's not actually saying anything," said Ah'puch. "I just gave him the *suggestion* that he was the god Bal, and his damaged psyche did the rest. It's not a real language, just a series of sounds strung together, listen…"

Jon turned to the emperor, his heart thundering. He took a step towards the man.

"It's utter nonsense. Fascinating. And the only thing he's eaten in three days has been raw meat. I wonder what would happen if—"

The emperor looked down at the knife sticking out of his chest in confusion. He dropped the manacles he held and grasped at Jon's hand clenched around the wooden handle. Ah'puch scrabbled at it with a gasp, but Jon just stared him down, motionless.

"Jon?" Ah'puch said, sounding bewildered. "Guards…" The word was just a whisper that trailed off when he remembered that they were alone.

Jon pulled the blade out, and it made a sucking sound. Immediately, blood welled up with a slight froth as Ah'puch let out a pained gasp. With a grunt, Jon stabbed the emperor again.

And again.

And again.

T om closed his eyes and pictured the map in his mind again. Ceara had assured him that it was up to date. So far the woman had been right. However, a moment later, Tom turned down what was supposed to be a rarely used side tunnel and emerged into a brightly lit room. In dismay, he saw that there was a slave driver seated at a small table eating soup from a wooden bowl.

"What the hells are you doing here?" grunted the man as he stood up. His thick fingers lifted the whip from the hook on his belt. "There ain't supposed to be work done in this end until the next blessing cycle! Get back to your post!"

At the sight of the whip, Tom froze. A cold icicle of dread speared his guts and spurned his heart to gallop high and fast in this throat. All thought left him as his eyes watched the tip of the whip trail through the dust as the man held it looped in his fist.

"Did you hear me?" bellowed the fat man with the whip. "Are you deaf, boy?"

Tom was alone. The other pirates had split up to begin either incapacitating or recruiting the slaves in the tunnels. He took an unsteady step backwards, all his senses screaming at him to bolt.

Think.

He blinked and took another step back. The room was new. He could see the walls were freshly dug. If this used to be the old tunnel, then the entrance to the laboratory would be just beyond this room. He had to move forward, which meant getting past the slave driver.

Tom lifted his hands in a gesture of supplication.

"Listen. I don't want no trouble," he said quietly. "I'll get back to my post, but I need to be goin' *that* way." He pointed past the man.

"The hells you are," growled the big man with the whip. The slave driver hefted the handle and let the coil drop to the ground.

The first sting wouldn't be so bad. Nor would the second. But his world would shatter and his mind would be tossed into the black pits of hell as he begged and pleaded. He let out a low sound and took another step back.

Coward, he thought. *I'm a bloody coward.*

It's just a thing, said the captain reassuringly. *You're not a coward, but you are foolish at times, my tomcat. Why fear an object? An object has no power on its own. It's a man who wields it, and when have you ever been afraid of a man?*

Tom's brows pinched over his nose, confused. He fell to his knee with his arm up to protect his face as the first lash came down. A whimper burst from between his lips, and he quailed as the whip came down again. It cut into his forearm as it looped around, and Tom let out a cry.

He was almost blind with fear, crazy with it, and hearing voices in the dark that weren't there.

Crazy is better than afraid, no? laughed the captain. *Come, you're better than this. Be my fearless tomcat. I need you. Jon needs you.*

Tom blinked, realizing that the whip was still around his arm. He looked up at the slave driver wielding it and saw the *man*, not the object. This wasn't his Master. This was a tired-looking, over-weight, middle-aged slave that had snuck off on his own to have a bite to eat, probably worried about being caught. There was soup on his stained, brown tunic, and his body sagged with flaccid muscle.

He was faintly ridiculous.

Then, Tom noticed that the whip the man held wasn't tightly woven and well-kept at all; the leather was coming apart in places, and it had a few kinks in it where it had obviously been repaired.

It too was faintly ridiculous.

Tom began to laugh. He threw back his head and laughed loudly, not caring who heard him. The ridiculous slave driver goggled at him, his face twisted into a fearful expression at Tom's reaction.

Baltsaros was right. He wasn't afraid of any man, and this thing, this flimsy weapon held no power over him. He looped his fist around the whip and pulled as he got to his feet. Blood dripped down his forearm where the whip had sliced into him, but the cut was superficial. It would heal and life would go on. Tom grinned wide as he tugged the whip again. This time it came out of the man's hands, and the slave driver took a few shuffling steps backwards before hitting the wall behind him. He put his hands up.

"Aye... There we go," said Tom. "That's what I like to see."

"Don't kill me," stammered the slave driver.

"Now, see... I'm gonna let ye go," smiled Tom, curling the whip into a few big loops. "I got better places to be, aye? But I can't have ye hootin' and hollerin' about me, savvy? So what am I goin' to do?"

He let a few seconds go by in silence. The slave driver stared wide-eyed at him.

"C'mon. Guess," grinned Tom.

"You're... going to... knock me out?" said the man hesitantly.

"Bingo!" replied Tom, and he hit the man as hard as he could with the heavy whip handle clenched in his fist. The slave driver thudded to the ground like a sack of wet potatoes, and Tom nodded to himself.

"That's a good boy," he grinned. "Sleep, matey. I hope they won't skin ye in the mornin'... Ye didn't seem like such a bad fella after all, aye?"

He turned and made his way down the tunnel, whistling to himself as he passed his arm through the loop of the whip and settled it comfortably on his shoulder.

28

RED HANDS

The god stopped Its pacing to watch the young one kill the gaoler. Blood arced up into the air and landed in drops at the god's feet. It was glorious, this sacrifice. Watching the wolf pup pierce the man with his shining tooth made the god smile, and It wrapped Its claws around the bars to get a better look... at the boy with eyes like a storm at sea. Jon.

Jon? Where was Tom?

The god blinked Its eyes and chased the poisonous, painful thoughts away.

The god waited.

Jon's chest burned, and he dropped the gory dagger. Taking in great lungfuls of air, he struggled to get his breathing under control. The man beneath him stared sightlessly, his face frozen in a rictus of pain and terror. The pool of blood spread out, soaking into Jon's pant legs, and the wet silk stuck to him uncomfortably. With a grimace, Jon planted a hand in the middle of the dead emperor's chest to push himself to his feet.

Frowning down at the corpse, he realized that he felt no

horror over killing Ah'puch. As his heart rate slowed, Jon took stock of his feelings. His anger had drained away, and he felt... justified. Jon wiped his hands on his pants. No, he would not be crying or pissing himself over this death.

Or maybe over any death again? he wondered.

Jon shook his head. No, maybe not, but he wasn't about to become a depraved killer just because he ended some asshole's life. He blinked slowly at the dead man and then spat in his face before finally walking away.

There was complete pandemonium in the cages. In the one closest, the man inside shrieked and howled like a monkey as he hung from ropes strung across the space. In another, a tiny, frail-looking woman rammed her head against the bars repeatedly. Blood leaked down her face but she was unrelenting. Jon grimaced. Putting them out of their misery might be the kindest course of action since the emperor couldn't cure them now. For all he knew, they could be past helping anyway.

But... What about Baltsaros?

He clenched his jaw and made himself turn to the captain's cage. The first sharp pangs of regret made themselves known at the sight of the man beyond the bars. By killing Ah'puch, Jon had condemned Baltsaros to live out his life as the monster he'd always tried to hide.

The captain stood with his hands curled around the bars, his eyes wide as he stared at the blood on Jon's clothes. A smile sliced open the ratty, wild beard, and Baltsaros licked his lips. He pointed to Jon as he began to speak the guttural language he had spoken before.

Jon's eyes blurred. The emperor had awoken the beast inside Baltsaros and destroyed any good that had been there. This was the creature that had hidden behind all of the captain's easy smiles; this was the coldness in Baltsaros's eyes. This was the thing that had pushed Baltsaros to kill and kill again. It was the monster that had tried to murder him in the mists. Jon breathed quickly through his clenched teeth.

"You killed him," Jon whispered hoarsely. The captain's incomprehensible words continued to hiss and growl in the air between them without pause. "Ah'puch might have been the one to let you loose, but you were the one who killed Baltsaros in the end. I think you've been slowly killing him for a long time now, haven't you? You've been biding your time, waiting for your chance…" Jon's voice broke and he took a step forward.

"What *are* you?" he spat, his anger sparking briefly, but the thing behind the bars didn't reply. Instead, it continued speaking, one finger pointed at him. Jon sank down to the stone floor; he felt weak as the adrenaline left his system. Tom would be here soon, if he made it through the mines. What would he make of this?

It didn't make any sense. This couldn't be a god. There were no gods. That's what Baltsaros had said. Jon rubbed his face; the cacophony of the other prisoners was beginning to give him a headache. Nothing made sense.

Then the emperor's words came back to him, and he frowned.

"Wait… Why would you be speaking a made-up language?" he asked. "When you attacked me that night, you were speaking your native tongue, weren't you? Why the nonsense now?"

Jon narrowed his eyes at the captain. Something felt strangely *off* now that he thought of it. Before, when he had caught glimpses of what Baltsaros's charming mask covered, he'd felt a sort of primal fear. This creature in front of him now didn't scare him. It was like a pale version of the darkness that lived inside the captain.

"I don't think you are what you think you are," he said slowly, an idea forming in his head. "I think you have this deep-seated belief that you're truly *evil*, whatever that is. When I saw it in your eyes, I think that I felt fear because *you* felt it. I think you've always been terrified of what you believe yourself to be. Now that you're 'transformed' into a monster, you're not afraid anymore, are you? In fact, you *should* be relieved. Happy, even, because you can finally just give in to it. But... Why do I still sense conflict when I look at you?

"This compulsion, this murdering spree you've been on for gods know how many years. Where does it stem from? What triggered it? Ah'puch said something that I almost missed. He said you had a damaged psyche. I don't know what *psyche* means, but I'm guessing it has to do with your mind. I've called you damaged in the past, and you really are, aren't you?" As Jon spoke, the captain's voice got quieter until he finally fell silent. The man stared at him, expressionless.

"What could have happened to you to make you honestly believe that you're a monster? And it wasn't the time you were dumped overboard in a barrel by your uncle. I think it happened when you were younger. Much younger," murmured Jon. He had a sudden thought. "Baltsaros... *how did your parents die?*"

Jon climbed to his feet as the silence stretched on. The man behind bars watched him, his dark eyes wary.

"You never told me," explained Jon. He took a step towards the bars and saw a flicker of apprehension cross the captain's face. "Tell me. I know you can understand me. How did they die?"

He was rewarded by another long stretch of silence. Then the captain spoke two words in his native tongue that Jon recognized.

Red hands?

"What does that mean? Red hands... Your red hands? My red hands? I don't understand," said Jon softly. Slowly, tentatively, he reached his own hand out. The captain's eyes widened as Jon's fingers touched the older man's hand gently. Instantly, Baltsaros recoiled with an angry growl. Jon watched in dismay as the captain began to pace anew, muttering to himself quietly.

A grinding noise startled Jon, and he spun on his heel. From a small metal door at the end of the row of cages emerged a familiar figure. Jon felt relief crash over him.

"Tom!"

The first mate straightened and looked around, his eyes wide at the sight of the cages and their crazed occupants. He stepped forward, barefoot and filthy from his time in the mines. When he reached Jon, he cupped the back of his head and pressed their foreheads together quickly.

"Thank the gods," breathed Jon.

"Thank the gods my arse, lad," smirked Tom. "It was a piece o' cake."

Jon's eyes slid from Tom's narrow, tufted strip of hair to his black-ringed eyes and down past the harness, the tattered whip, and blood on his arm; he raised his eyebrows, curious.

"Where's Da?" asked Tom, looking past Jon. When Jon pointed to the raving madman in the cell, the first mate paled visibly.

"Bloody hells, what the fuck is wrong with him?" choked Tom. He curled his fists over the bars. "Da?"

The man inside the cage stopped his pacing and turned to look at the first mate. Jon let out a slow breath. There was recognition there. Brief, but he had seen it.

"We have'ta get him out of there. What the fuck is wrong with him?" growled Tom. "Where's the bloody key?" Tom's knuckles whitened.

"It's probably on Ah'puch," replied Jon.

Tom's head swung around.

"Where is that fuckin' cunt?" snarled Tom. When Jon pointed to the open space beyond the row of cages, the first mate's face went momentarily slack with surprise. With eyes narrowed, he looked at Jon.

"Yes, it was me," replied Jon to Tom's unvoiced question.

The big man squeezed Jon's shoulder before walking towards the body.

"I'm not sure it's a good idea to let him out just yet," said Jon, watching the captain. The man had resumed his pacing, but now he threw glances at both Jon and Tom. Jon could see confusion like cracks in his eyes. "He's not himself."

"That's for fuckin' sure," said Tom, returning to Jon's side. There was a golden key in the first mate's bloody hand. Jon stared at it a moment.

"Tom, do the words *red hands* mean anything to you?" he asked. Tom turned to him, and shook his head.

"Nay, love. He spoke 'em?" Tom frowned at the captain.

"Yes. I asked him how his parents died, and that was his answer. Do you know the story?"

Tom shook his head again. His shoulder was warm against Jon's.

"No. He never said. I never asked," admitted Tom. "Why?"

Jon quickly told Tom about what Ah'puch had said.

"If he's a bloody god, then I'm the king o' the world, love," scoffed Tom.

"No, he's not an *actual* god. Ah'puch just made him believe he was one, or at least what Ah'puch thought a god was like... all mixed up with the guilt that Baltsaros has over something."

"Da? Guilt?" The first mate peered at the captain.

Baltsaros had stopped pacing and simply stood motionless in the centre of the cage. Jon tilted his head at the captain and thought hard.

"What if something terrible happened to him when he was really young. Something that he thought was his fault and left a scar so deep and so horrible that, somewhere inside, he began to think of himself as a truly evil person. Not consciously, I mean... Hells, maybe he doesn't really remember it."

Jon watched Tom mull over his words.

"Ye think Da's been killin' because he thinks he's *evil*?" asked Tom. The first mate slowly rubbed the stubble on the side of his head with his palm, a deep comma of confusion between his brows.

"Yeah. Because he thinks he has to for some reason. I've seen it in the dungeons—men who thought it was ultimately in their nature to kill. But the people the captain's been killing... They've all shown some kind of prejudice or hate, right?"

Tom thought a moment and nodded.

"It's like he was having some sort of fucked-up, good-versus-evil war in his head and the emperor tipped him over into... this.

This has to be just some kind of reaction to being told that he's an evil, heart-eating god. There's just enough behind the legend that it fits with Baltsaros's past somehow. Ah'puch worked with that." Jon decided not to give voice to his conflicted feelings about the peculiar string of coincidences that seemed to follow them... if that's what they were. The alternative was just too strange to think about. He watched the captain for a moment, letting his clever brain sort through theories.

"See, now he's off the hook for his past behaviour," Jon finally continued. "Ah'puch granted him permission to be the evil thing he always feared he would be. So he's retreated into this... *performance*. I think, at least partially, to free himself of the guilt he feels over almost killing me."

Baltsaros let out a small, strangled noise and sank down to his knees.

Jon nodded, his heart beating quickly. He was definitely getting somewhere.

"He'd stopped murdering, and he'd truly begun to pull away from this notion that he was a monster... and then he nearly killed me. It must have been quite a blow."

Tom slipped the golden key into the lock and turned it. With an anxious look at Jon, the first mate pulled the door open. The captain didn't move; his eyes were red.

"He thinks," Jon said, stepping into the cage, "that if he admits to having feelings, having weaknesses, the monster inside him will get out and destroy everything he holds dear."

Baltsaros moaned softly. He flinched when Tom placed his hands on his shoulders, but his eyes closed, and he leaned into the first mate's touch.

"But that makes absolutely no sense, Baltsaros," said Jon. "You *know* that. How can you protect something you care about without acknowledging that you care about it to begin with? Think about it."

"Why would I try to kill something I love?" came the whispered reply. Baltsaros opened his eyes and stared at Jon. One tear spilled from the corner of his eye, tracking a path over his cheek-bone and into his beard. A tremor shook him, and Tom sank down to his knees, folding his arms around the captain. Baltsaros took a hoarse breath, clenching and unclenching his fists in his lap. "What kind of monster would do that?"

"No monster at all," replied Jon. His throat felt tight as he crouched in front of the captain. "What about all the others? You're not the only person who attacked someone that night. People killed, Baltsaros, and it wasn't because they were monsters."

"What about... the others? Before..." rasped the captain.

"Yes, you are guilty of murdering people," said Jon with a nod. "There's no way around that, but you'd no more kill Tom or me than you would take your own life. So, instead of trying to find secret, crazy ways of 'purging' this so-called monster inside you, you're going to help me find out what started it to begin with."

"But I... don't..." Baltsaros sounded lost, afraid, helpless. Jon caught a flash of the boy he had seen before.

Help me.

It gave him hope.

T here was a thundering at the door. Tom was up on his feet in an instant. Jon stood and glanced at the entrance. The emperor's absence had probably been noticed; he also hoped the ruckus at the door wasn't because the pirates had been captured in the mines.

"Shit," Tom muttered. "Looks like we're outta bloody time. Can ye walk, Da? Or are ye gonna make me carry ye?"

"I can walk," said Baltsaros, his voice stronger. However, when he stood, he stumbled forward, and Tom had to catch him before he fell.

"The fuck you can," grunted Tom. He grabbed the captain's wrist and bent his knee, preparing to lift him over his shoulder, when the captain stopped him.

"Wait, no, I'll be ok," said Baltsaros with a short huff of breath, nearly a laugh. "The day I let you carry me out of somewhere…" He shook his head. "We need to find the antidote to the spores first. It's there." Baltsaros pointed to the long row of shelves above the burnished worktable. "Somewhere."

Tom stepped up to the shelves and peered at the gleaming bottles. The pounding on the door doubled, and Jon thought he could hear shouting. He wondered whether someone else in the emperor's employ had the key.

"Da, which one?" asked the first mate, his ocean eyes wide. "I can't fuckin' read half o' these."

"Ah'puch showed it to me. When he was… *working*. He liked to talk. Brag," Baltsaros said. He coughed into his fist, and Jon saw another tremor go through him. "It's a bluish-white powder." The captain shuffled to the wall full of bottles and began to search with the first mate.

Jon walked over to the emperor's corpse and grabbed the dagger. The patients in the cages had begun screaming and crowing all over again in agitation, and he could barely think. He heard Tom let out a long string of curses as bottle after bottle crashed to the floor.

"Come on, we have to go," Jon said urgently. The corner of the door was denting out. There was no way that the hinges would hold much longer.

"Is this it?" yelled Tom over the ear-splitting noise. Jon watched the door shake in its frame and held the dagger out in front of him. They were out of time. Then something caught his sleeve, and he spun. Tom pulled at his arm again with a glance at Baltsaros, and Jon helped the first mate support the captain as they ran to the corpse-chute. The woman who'd been bashing her head against the bars was unconscious or dead in a pool of blood, having finally succumbed to her self-inflicted injuries. He caught a glimpse of a figure at the back of the cage and stopped in surprise.

"Oren?" he yelled.

The boy lifted his head, a dazed look on his face.

"Jon! We ain't got time, lad," shouted Tom. He grabbed the metal door and lifted it. Baltsaros ducked through the low opening.

Jon nearly tripped in his hurry to get the key, and when he turned it in the lock to Oren's cage, the willowy youth staggered to his feet.

"Jon..." growled Tom. His muscles bulged from holding the heavy door up. Jon grabbed Oren's arm and half dragged the younger man out of the cage before pushing him to follow Tom. He slipped into the narrow space behind Oren and slid down the chute, half landing on the young fisherman at the bottom. He quickly got out of the way as the door above clanged shut. Tom slid down the incline and landed with a grunt.

Jon and Oren helped Baltsaros to his feet, and the three of them made their way down the rock-hewn tunnel with Tom following close behind. When they reached a juncture, Tom stopped and put his back to the wooden beam that reinforced the tunnel ceiling.

Tom let out a roar, and the tendons in his neck stood out in stark relief as he pushed as hard as he could. There was a crackle and then a high squealing noise. Finally, with a spray of rock dust, the beam shifted. After a few more heaves, Tom managed to push it over. He leapt forward as it collapsed across the tunnel entrance followed by a shower of loose rocks and a few large boulders.

"That should slow 'em down at least," said Tom. He took off at a slow lope and squinted down the tunnel, motioning for the others to follow a moment later. Behind them came the noise of the metal door slamming, and Jon hurried Baltsaros forward. Tom led them down one tunnel and then another, the passages twisting and sometimes doubling back on themselves until Jon was convinced they were lost. Tom stopped again at the entrance to yet another side tunnel and pressed his back to the wall before glancing into the space beyond. It was pitch dark.

"All right, quick as ye can, after me," he rumbled. "The exit's not far, but since we ain't seen Harris or the boys yet, we can't be sure it's clear. Someone's broken the lantern so watch yer feet, lads."

Jon nodded quickly and looked at the captain. Baltsaros's skin had taken on a greyish tinge, and his eyes were half-closed.

"Baltsaros?" he said, adjusting the man's arm on his shoulder. "Stay with me."

"I'll always stay with you, Jon," whispered the captain. "Always. I promise. Always."

Jon was suddenly short of breath from Baltsaros's words even though it was obvious that the man was starting to lose his senses again.

"Shit, don't do this to me now," gasped Jon with a half-laugh over the helpless tears that rose in his eyes. "I love you. We'll get you out of here, and then we'll have all the time in the world for promises. Just put your weight on me. One foot in front of the other. Come on now."

Tom shoved Oren roughly out of the way and took Baltsaros's other arm. The skinny, bruised young man stood uncertainly, blinking his large blue eyes slowly for a moment before he turned and ran quickly up the tunnel. Jon thought he had simply fled until he heard a quiet, "Come, come, it's safe," from the dark. With the help of Tom, he manoeuvred Baltsaros into the tunnel, the two of them supporting the captain almost entirely. Jon felt Baltsaros's head loll on his shoulder, and he ground his teeth in frustration.

Up ahead, they could hear the sound of fighting. Jon and Tom slowed down, nearly crashing into Oren in the dark.

"What's happening?" whispered Jon. He couldn't see Oren's face, but he saw the faint silhouette shake its head.

"I can't be knowing," replied Oren quietly. "I go look. You stay." The youth took off at a quick step, barely visible in the dark.

A few seconds later, they heard Oren cry out, and Jon assumed the worst. However, when the boy let out a relieved laugh, he frowned. Jon tensed as a tall shape came up the passageway towards them. A match flared in the dark. Polas smiled at them, and the tears in his eyes glittered in the light of the flame.

Tom gave a whoop of laughter.

"Bloody fuckin' cocksuckin' bloody hells am I fuckin' glad to see yer fuckin' face!" he exclaimed.

Polas's smile widened, and he reached out to pat Tom's shoulder.

"Come, come. We will get you through here. Come. I see the captain? He is injured? We will carry him. I have so much thanks for my grandson. So much. So many?" said Polas with a laugh as he led them down the tunnel towards the light. "I lose my speaking, I am so glad!"

When they emerged into a wide main tunnel, Jon saw a group of fisherfolk assembled. Each held a double-pronged spear in one hand and a net in the other.

"What's happening? How are you here?" asked Jon. He let the captain down onto the tunnel floor gently, and Baltsaros slumped over. Tom knelt at his side and lifted a waterskin to his lips. Jon watched the captain take a few sips and sighed in relief.

"A revolution, Jon," said Polas, his face creasing in another wide grin. "A beautiful revolution. And it is to you and Tom that it is thanks."

29

BROKEN GOD, WOUNDED BEAST

Jon sat cross-legged on the captain's wide bed watching Baltsaros sleep. Gone was the straggly, dirty beard; Tom had very carefully shaved the captain before he left to help Polas and the marked slaves take out the last of the resistance. Without his beard, Baltsaros suddenly looked like a stranger... older for the deep lines to each side of his mouth; frail, even. Jon frowned and reached out to move a loose strand of hair away from Baltsaros's face. The captain was covered in sweat, and the hair stuck to his forehead; at Jon's touch, Baltsaros let out a small moan and a shiver as his body fought the damage done to it.

The boom of the cannon startled Jon, and Baltsaros's eyes flew open, sightless, before closing again. They were anchored in the mouth of the harbour outside of Ereme'ia Balor, and the *Heart's* guns were being used in aid of the rebellion. Jon wondered how long it would be before the last of the lords and slavers of the city finally gave up or were defeated.

Without opening his eyes, Baltsaros murmured a word.

"Water."

It was the first thing he'd said since he was carried aboard the previous evening.

Jon slid off the bed quickly and went to the icebox to get cold water for the captain. When he turned back to the bed, Baltsaros was up on one elbow, his red-rimmed eyes on Jon. Jon sat on the edge of the bed and handed over the metal cup, unsettled by the way the captain's hand shook.

"What's happening?" rasped Baltsaros after he had taken a slow swallow.

Jon quickly brought the captain up to speed as he sat taking tiny sips of water.

Shortly after the guards had been dismissed from Ah'puch's chambers, they began to spread Jon's story of the successful slave rebellion. It didn't take long before the news made its way out of the palace, at which point Tom and the pirates had already set off towards the mines. After leaving Tom with the slave drivers, Ceara learned about the rumour from her spies. Seeing her chance to create a distraction to help with the captain's rescue, she had sent word to Jarrod and the bevy of escaped slaves in the sprawling *madina* to spread the story ever farther. On hearing the rumour, Ertos the fishmonger had sent a runner to *Baal's Heart* to tell Polas that the slaves were being whipped into a frenzy by stories of a rebellion; one that grew more and more outlandish with every retelling. Polas had taken a few of Baltsaros's men with him to Balor by jolly boat to lend support. He had arrived at the mines only moments before Oren had come running out of the dark into his arms, leading the three men to safety.

Baltsaros listened quietly as Jon talked, his dark eyes slightly unfocused. When Jon had finished, the captain narrowed his gaze at him.

"Why?" he asked softly.

"Why what?" replied Jon, confused. "Why were the fisherfolk

so quick to help the rebellion? Why had the slaves rebelled so easily?"

"Why do you love me?" asked Baltsaros.

Jon frowned and wondered if the captain had heard anything he had said. When he didn't reply right away, Baltsaros's fingers closed around his forearm and squeezed hard. Jon winced but didn't move.

"Why? Jon... why?" repeated the captain, searching his face.

Jon's first impulse was to blurt "I don't know", but the crazed, desperate look in Baltsaros's eyes demanded more. He took a deep breath.

"Because, despite everything, despite all the shit you've put me through, despite the fact that I've wanted to kill you myself more than once... I still find solace in you. A place where I belong. You gave me the gift of freedom, and I took it willingly, and I just as willingly bound myself to you," Jon said and let out a small, pained sound as Baltsaros's fingers tightened on him. "But... I love the man you are and hate the monster. Or do I? See... This is the problem. My feelings, my thoughts get all fucking tangled when I'm with you. Part of me just wants to follow you blindly to the ends of the world. The other would see me far, far away where you couldn't hurt me anymore. Because that's what you do, Baltsaros. You *hurt* me. Over and over again. And you do the same to Tom." Jon was getting angry. He wrenched his arm out of Baltsaros's grasp and stood, staring down at the older man.

Baltsaros's expression had shifted to sadness. There was a tic in his cheek as he looked up at Jon, but his eyes were clear.

"Find the man," murmured Baltsaros, "and you'll help me defeat the monster. But... Jon, do you truly love the man?"

Jon looked hard at Baltsaros. His handsome, chiselled features framed brown eyes wide with rare emotion. His broad, muscular shoulders, sun-dark despite his sickly pallor, were stooped as he waited for Jon's answer. His long-fingered hands that could be gentle or cruel lay limp in his lap. He was a man defeated, but as

Jon watched, Baltsaros's face creased into a wan smile though he seemed a shadow of his usual self.

"You're being cruel in your silence, Jon," he said. "You've already followed me to the ends of the world, but you didn't do it blindly. You succeeded in stripping me of lies I didn't even know I had... Did you also want my blood?" Baltsaros lifted his arm, showing Jon the scabbed wounds left behind by the emperor. "You can have it. You can have everything I am. I give it all to you."

Jon let out a small sigh.

"Of course I love the man. Didn't I just say that?" he smiled sadly. He sat back down on the bed and took the cup from Baltsaros; Jon set it on the floor. "I don't want your blood. I've had quite enough of that this past week. All I want, Baltsaros, is to leave this place. I want long days of sunshine and hard, satisfying work aboard the ship, *our* ship, without feeling the need to look over my shoulder all the time. I want, at the end of those days, when my muscles are sore and I'm filled with simple happiness, to fall into your arms and have you show me how to be yours all over again." The words poured out of Jon as if a dam in him had broken. He felt a desperate hope. "I want you to be sane and whole. I want to spend my nights with you and Tom, playing and fucking and loving until I'm sore all over again. And then I want to fall asleep, and dream stupidly happy dreams, bothered by nothing more frightening than Tom's snoring."

Baltsaros laughed and reached for Jon. He let himself be pulled down and stretched himself out carefully beside the captain, mindful of his wounds. He lay there quietly while Baltsaros trailed his fingers over his cheek and down to his shoulder and back again, the touch as soft as a whisper.

"We can do that, Jon," said the captain after a time. "I promise."

Jon nodded and closed his eyes.

A metallic clinking pulled Baltsaros from sleep. He opened his eyes and saw that the room had darkened. He had slept the entire day away. Or... had he? His memory felt full of holes, and time was unfolding strangely. He hoped that the damage to his brain wasn't permanent. There was another clink and then a crash followed by a muttered string of curses. Tom bent over to pick up the fallen plate and saw the captain's eyes on him.

"Oh. Sorry, Da. Didn't mean to wake ye," said the first mate, placing the golden plate on top of a precarious stack of dishes. The long mahogany table was piled with riches: golden cups, statuettes, and platters sat amongst chests filled with jewellery that glittered even in the muted light of the captain's quarters. "I was just pickin' out the things I thought ye'd like. Ye know... for yer fancy meals and, ah... things." The first mate held a heavily ornamented spoon aloft, the smile on his rugged face enthusiastic.

"I take it that the rebellion went well?" asked Baltsaros with a wry grin. He tried to sit up, but halfway there he gasped with the pain that erupted in his groin. Tom was at his side in an instant, pushing him back down. Jon was nowhere to be seen.

"Hang on, Da. Lemme get ye some painkillers," said the big man, his eyes worried. Baltsaros shook his head.

"Not yet," he said. "My head is clear right now. I want it to stay that way, at least for a little while." He gingerly touched the thick bandages that swathed him from hip to mid-thigh and hid the worst of the damage done to him. Hopefully, he'd retain the use of his cock once the burns healed. He grimaced. To hells with his cock; he was lucky to be alive.

"You sure took your bloody time rescuing me," he said goodnaturedly and smiled wide at the look of chagrin on Tom's face.

"I'm sorry, Da," mumbled Tom, stooping to crawl onto the bed.

Baltsaros sobered as he watched Tom sit at his side, his blue-green eyes narrowed with misery.

"Thank you, Tom. Truly. I owe you my life," said the captain.

He reached for the first mate's hand and realized, as he did so, that though he often held or touched Jon's hands out of simple affection, he had never really done so with Tom. The brawny young man looked away, and Baltsaros thought he detected a flush in his face.

Curious, Baltsaros turned Tom's hand over in his. The back of the first mate's hand was covered in a smattering of small scars—old burns and wounds acquired from his life of servitude and from working aboard the old pirate ship. His knuckles were criss-crossed with raised, white lines where the skin had split and healed over and over from his penchant of using his fists to get his point across. Even now they were red, and on the first two there were fresh scabs. The third knuckle had a squashed look to it, and Baltsaros remembered when the first mate had broken it in a fight the first year he was aboard. They were hands that he knew almost as well as his own. He rubbed his thumb softly over the scarred skin before lifting Tom's hand to his mouth. He kissed Tom's battered knuckles gently, one by one, before turning the man's hand over in his to press his lips to the deeply lined palm. When he looked up, Tom was staring at him, a glimmer of wetness in his eyes.

The sight made Baltsaros hurt.

"I'm sorry, Tom," he whispered. "You've put up with too much."

Tom made a small noise deep in his chest and lifted his shoulder up in a shrug.

"No. Listen to me," growled Baltsaros. "I am sorry. I've never told you enough how thankful I am that you came into my life—"

"Or ever," interrupted Tom with a twisted grin. He closed his callused fingers over Baltsaros's and squeezed softly. "Save yer godsdamned words, old man. I ain't a soft thing that needs to be coddled, aye?" However, the tears that threatened to spill from Tom's eyes belied his words. The first mate dashed them away with his wrist and clenched his jaw.

Baltsaros lay there holding Tom's hand and closed his eyes.

"When Jon wanted to leave, just you and him together, how

long were you tempted?" he said. He felt Tom tense and he smiled.

"Not a godsdamned bloody second, Da," said the first mate. It was a lie, Baltsaros was sure of it, but he liked the answer regardless.

Tom found the ingredients that Baltsaros had jotted down the last time he was conscious. *Aloe, turmeric, yellow dock, powdered ephemroot mould, calendula, qaphberries...* Tom took out the small jars one by one and placed them on the table along with the mortar and pestle. Some of the ingredients were powders; others were just leaves kept in clear alcohol or oil. Mashed together in the right proportions and cured quickly over fire in the metal tablet mould, they would make a powerful medicine to fight the infection that had taken root in Baltsaros.

Jon's face was drawn as he looked down at all the ingredients.

"You sure this is everything?" he asked, his brow furrowed.

Tom read over the list again and nodded.

"How are we supposed to know if these are the right ones? He hasn't been the most lucid. I barely understood half of what he said earlier," said Jon, glancing up at him.

Tom grimaced. It was true. Baltsaros's waking periods had become shorter and shorter over the past few days and were often punctuated by strange turns in the conversation and periods of delirium.

"What else can we do?" Tom said quietly. He stroked the side of his jaw, the stubble sharp against his palm.

Jon stared at him; his blue-grey eyes were bleak.

"What if I mix it wrong?" he said.

Tom looked away as he put the thin black cigar between his lips and started rooting around in a drawer for a match. He was sick with worry over Baltsaros, but Jon didn't need to know that.

"Ye'll mix it the way ye mix it, and it'll all work out in the end, lovey," he said, keeping his tone cheerful. "Da's got the luck of the black devil himself. Don'tcha worry one bit." He struck the match against the corner of the armoire and put the flame to the end of the slim cheroot. Thick smoke filled his lungs as he puffed on it, and he felt the welcoming tingle of the mild narcotic make his head feel momentarily light.

Tom turned back to Jon and saw with relief that he had squared his shoulders and set his jaw with a nod.

"Okay," said Jon, "tell me again what to do."

Tom pulled out a chair and turned it around so he could straddle it and rest his arms across the backrest. He read out Baltsaros's instructions, one step at a time, and watched Jon grind the ingredients together. Tom felt like a coward making Jon do the work, but he just couldn't do it himself. What if he killed the captain? He would never be able to live with himself.

When Jon finished mixing everything together and pressed the resulting greenish paste into the mould, Tom struck another match and held it beneath the piece of tin; he kept the flame close until it burned the tip of his fingers, and he dropped the match to the tabletop with a curse.

The two of them stared at each other in silence for a moment, and then Jon's lips quirked up into a slight smile.

"All right," he said. "Let's see if we can't get Baltsaros back to the healthy, black-hearted scourge of the seven seas we all know and love, shall we?"

Tom was surprised by his involuntary bark of laughter; trust Jon to suddenly turn a tense situation on its head. With a smile on his face, he lurched to his feet to grab some water as Jon popped the cooling tablets onto a plate.

The god awoke in the dark, Its prey mere feet away. It could smell them. The two entwined on the bed. It made him sick.

Wait. Sick?

The god... The beast? The beast sat up despite the pain. Pain is mortal. Pain is nothing. Gods don't feel pain.

Wait. Beast or god?

The world tilted on an angle as he tried to stand. He fell on one knee.

Pain.

Pain.

PAIN.

Baltsaros dry-heaved on hands and knees. His mouth was sour. His head pounded. He blinked in the dark, trying to make out his surroundings. With a trembling hand he reached up and touched the black shapes in front of him. Bars. Cold, flattened iron.

It took him a few seconds to realize that he was in the cage in his quarters.

The captain groped for the narrow cot and pulled himself back onto it.

Not a god. Not a beast. Just a man. A very weak, sick man.

His brain burned.

He tried to remember what he had done to get himself locked in the cage, but he came up empty. How much time had passed since he had been rescued from the menagerie of the mentally abused? He touched his chest and his fingers came away sticky with salve. The electrodes had burned into him, again and again. The lights. Bright.

Pain.

Pain.

Pain.

When the warm hand reached through the bars and stroked his hair back from his face softly, Baltsaros realized he was weeping brokenly.

"Hush, Da. Hush," rumbled Tom.

A second hand reached through and clasped his shoulder.

"It'll be all right," whispered Jon.

Baltsaros closed his eyes and drifted off, the pain chased away by the touch of two souls that would watch after his own.

THE LAST SACRIFICE

Baltsaros ran across the ice. His tears froze on his cheeks. He was furi-ous. They would pay. All of them. His skinny legs were a blur. He was fast! Fast like the lion on his family crest. His breath heaved in his bony chest. They would pay. Pay for being so... being so mean! Baltsaros tripped over a chunk of ice and went sprawling. He let out a cry and pulled himself up, wrapping his thin arms around his knee and rocking as he sobbed. There was blood on the ice. He had torn open his knee. He had ripped his pants. Mother would be furious about the pants. He sat and wept like a baby. It wasn't fair! Then he saw the men on the ice. Strangers. Red hands. Red feet.

The captain jerked awake, his strangled yell like a distant memory to his ears, and he blinked rapidly a few times to clear the strange vision. The portal above his head was a circle of cloudless blue, and he could hear men shouting outside. He waited until his heartbeat slowed a little before sitting up. After a moment, he smiled. That was no fighting; it was just the simple sounds of the rough men working aboard *Baal's Heart.*

From the way that the boat gently rocked beneath him and the water softly slapped the hull, he knew they were still anchored.

Baltsaros grimaced, hauling himself to his feet with one hand hooked into the flat iron bars to hold his weight as he shuffled forward like an old man. Standing over the piss pot, he gingerly eased down the thick, clean, white bandages at his groin. He peered at himself with a sigh; his skin was a mess of burns and contusions. Wincing, Baltsaros pulled his cock out, handling it as lightly as possible as he pointed it over the earthenware pot. When his stream came, the captain gritted his teeth against the searing pain. Ah'puch had really done his best to "cure" him of his sexual deviancy. With a muttered curse, he shook himself and pulled the bandages back over his damaged skin. Ah'puch would pay.

Ah'puch is dead, he reminded himself.

Yes, your wolf cub is turning out to be quite the little killer, said the beast, looking at him with burning eyes. *Just like you wanted him to be. Like I wanted him to be. What fun we will have together when I take his mind like I've taken yours.*

"Shut up!" snarled Baltsaros, lashing out at the air.

"Da?"

Baltsaros started and turned around. Tom stood in the doorway to their quarters with a worried expression. All that remained of the damage done to his face was the healing cut on his lip and a little yellow-greenish hue in the corner of one eye.

How long had he been sleeping?

"Sorry," muttered Baltsaros, easing himself slowly back down on the cot. "I'm all right. I'll be all right."

"Who were you talking to?" asked Tom as he stepped towards the cage on silent feet. In his hand, he held a plate of food; Baltsaros could see that there were two pieces of battered fish and a scoop of Cook's spicy vegetable stew. His stomach rumbled.

"No one. Is that for me?" asked Baltsaros with a smile.

The big man nodded slowly, his eyes narrowed in skepticism. However, he unlocked the cage door and handed the plate to the captain, pulling up a chair a moment later to keep Baltsaros company while he ate.

"So yer feelin' better?" asked Tom. Gone was the black kohl around his eyes that he had worn at the captain's rescue, but the strip of short hair that stuck up from his shorn scalp remained... as did one other thing. Baltsaros ignored Tom's question and pointed.

"Why are you still wearing *that*?" he asked.

Tom's fingers touched the slave collar, and Baltsaros could swear that the first mate's face reddened a little. Tom looked away and then up to the ceiling where there was the creak of someone walking above them on the quarterdeck. He shrugged, and his lips parted in a coy, almost sheepish grin.

"Ah. I see," laughed Baltsaros, shaking his head. Pangs of jealousy should have had no place in the deep well of gratitude he felt towards his boys for rescuing him, but there they were. Something of his thoughts must have shown on his face because Tom's eyes went wide, and he pushed himself off the chair and down on his knees in front of the captain.

"Yer gettin' better, Da. There's no more infection. Jon did ye up good. Ye'll be back to slappin' me around in no time," said the first mate, his voice gruff and full of forced cheer.

Baltsaros nodded with a sigh and, after an idle thought, pulled a piece of the tender fish apart with his fingers, holding it in front of Tom's lips. He smiled at the surprised grin on the young brute's face; Tom opened his mouth and took the fish obediently. After he had swallowed, and without prompting, he licked Baltsaros's fingers clean. So many possibilities that they hadn't yet explored in this capacity.

The captain let out a sharp cry and nearly dropped the plate.

"Da? Bloody hells, Da? What's the matter?" asked Tom. His hands steadied Baltsaros, fear making deep pools of his pupils as he stared at him helplessly.

Baltsaros began to laugh. He curled one hand around the tender mound in his groin, the one that had begun to harden at the touch of Tom's warm tongue against the whorls of his finger-tips. The pain had startled him more than anything, and the sheer relief made him laugh even harder. Tom watched him in total confusion as the captain laughed himself to tears in front of him.

"Da, yer scarin' me," said Tom. True enough, there was a hint of fear in his voice.

Baltsaros waved his hand, tears streaming down his face as he tried to get himself under control. He couldn't remember the last time he'd laughed so hard.

Tom lurched to his feet and bellowed in the direction of the stateroom door.

"Jon! Get yer ass in here. Da's having some kind o' turn. Jon!"

Baltsaros grabbed Tom's hand and shook his head, the laughter crushing his insides and making him gasp for air.

There was the thunder of boots on the stairs outside, and Jon appeared at the door, his blue-grey eyes wide with fear.

Finally, Baltsaros could breathe again. He rubbed at his face, still chuckling.

"It's ok. It's fine. I'm fine. It's just that it seems that my recovery is going... better than expected," he smiled, looking up at Jon and Tom. "I'm sorry. I didn't mean to worry you. It's just that part of me is rather eager to get behind the wheel, so to speak."

Tom looked unconvinced, but Jon nodded slowly.

"Da's never laughed like that before," said the first mate quietly, his voice like velvet-covered gravel.

"No. I wouldn't think so," replied Jon, his eyes on the captain.

Baltsaros sobered at the expression on his young face. It was a knowing look; Jon understood something that he himself had yet to grasp. It made him angry all of a sudden. And then very sad. His chest hurt. Emotions punched through walls as thin as paper. He groped around looking for his sense of self and found that the well of peace that he depended on was empty. So much confusion mixed up with pain and... relief?

"I think you're going to find that the captain's going to

surprise the ever-loving hells out of us in days to come, Tom. And not necessarily in a bad way."

J on smiled reassuringly at the captain. Baltsaros's eyes went flinty as he appraised him like he was a morsel of food or a small rodent trapped in his claws. Then the warmth returned to the captain's face, and the older man smiled back with a small nod. Watching the naked emotions flit across Baltsaros's face like ripples in a clear lake was startling and worrisome. He wondered if the captain could recover on his own or if he needed something that neither Jon nor Tom could provide. Baltsaros glanced down at his plate and resumed eating with a slightly lost look in his eyes.

Abetha, said a small voice inside him.

It made sense. She had helped Baltsaros find answers about himself before; maybe she could do it again.

"We should get him to your mother," he said quietly to Tom. "She might be able to offer some insight."

A deep furrow appeared in the first mate's brow, and he scratched at the short stubble of his jaw.

Jon almost laughed at the fear he saw there.

"She's your mother. Not the black devil," he scolded Tom, bumping his shoulder.

"Indeed, Tom. Your mother has been a boon to me in the past. Jon's suggestion is sound," agreed the captain, setting down his spoon. He passed his plate to Jon, his eyes clear again. Baltsaros's mercurial moods were disconcerting, but at least he seemed happy enough to defer to Jon's judgment until he had recovered.

Jon frowned. There was something else that needed to be resolved.

"We need an interim captain until you're well again," he said to Baltsaros. He watched anger and resignation battle for dominance in the captain's eyes. "You know that's a fact."

"What? You don't want a madman at the helm?" grinned Baltsaros, instantly full of good humour again. "Yes. You're right, Jon. Tom, you will replace me—"

"Nay, Da," grunted Tom, crossing his arms over his bare chest. "No fuckin' way. Ye know I like to make the crew hop, but I ain't the one who makes the bloody orders. No."

"Then, who?" grimaced Jon. "Calum's dead. Polas is staying here to help rebuild the city. Shit, I wish Katherine were here; she could have..." he trailed off when he saw Tom's lips stretch into a wide, playful smile. Baltsaros was staring at him with a shrewd look. Jon blanched when he realized what they were thinking, and he shook his head. "What, *me*? You've got to be kidding. Who the hell is going to listen to *me*?"

"Jon. Tom listens to you. If Tom listens to you, the crew will listen to you. Besides, what have you been doing for the last two weeks?"

Jon sat down slowly on the chair Tom had pulled out, his heart in his throat.

Polas walked with long strides, surveying the damage. At his side, Jon stepped over the cobblestones torn up by the ship's guns. Everywhere they went, there were men and women wandering around in a daze with white bands of sun-virgin skin around their necks where metal collars used to sit. Many of them held the cut collars in their hands, the steel in them the only valuable things they owned. The blacksmiths in town were offering to melt down the collars to mint new *dokschas* in return for a small fee; Jon wondered if their current economy would survive the upheaval.

Reading the worry on his face, Polas laughed softly.

"With big changes come bad things. But I think the good will come soon," said the white-haired man sagely. He had reclaimed the role of headman shortly after helping to free the captain. The part he played in the slave emancipation had raised him in the esteem of his people, and he now held his head high as he walked. "This is not the first big change. It's not the last. The world is very old, and she has the seeing of many things before."

Jon nodded, looking up at the damaged pyramid they had arrived at. The interior had been gutted, and all valuables had been stripped away. The other four pyramids were in a similar state, but this one had held the motherload, the majority of it now safely secured in the *Heart's* holds.

"What are you going to do now?" he asked the old fisherman.

Polas smiled wide, his face creasing in easy amusement.

"I am not of the knowing. That is up to the gods. The older gods. The gods before the filthy blessings. We fishermen will fish free. The barbarian tribes will come back. A city stays or falls, and we hope new things will taste of good instead of tears," said Polas. He turned at the sound of a woman's voice raised in distress, and Jon followed his gaze. The woman cried out again. A man had snatched the collar from her hands, her only wealth. Seconds later an ex–palace guard tackled the fleeing thief to the ground, and the collar was returned. Polas chuckled and pointed. "See? Good. Maybe for more than an eye blink, eh?"

Jon smiled tightly. Ereme'ia Balor had existed on the backs of slavery and bloodshed for so long; how could it be kept from returning to its former state? His eyes slid to the top of the pyramid, an idea forming in his head.

"How many so far know that the emperor is dead?" he asked. They had kept the information secret for fear of adding to the chaos that had followed the slaves' rebellion.

The old man turned to him, his bright-blue eyes curious. He thought for a moment before answering.

"Ten. No more."

Jon nodded.

"Polas, send a runner to fetch Tom. I'm going to need him for this. Have him meet me at the top of this pyramid in, uh… half an hour," he said, setting off at a brisk pace.

"Where will you go?" called Polas after him.

"Me? I have a date with the dungeons," replied Jon with a tight smile.

An hour later, Jon stood atop the pyramid, clothed in robes of deepest purple and wearing the emperor's massive, gilded crown. His ears keened in protest following the ringing of the great bell, and he felt a little ill looking down at the hundreds assembled below; steeling himself, he held his back straight and stared down at the crowd through his mask. In the midst of all the fallout, the only ones who had turned up at the square were the curious or those who desperately wanted some kind of order to return. Hopefully, it was enough. He thumped his walking stick a few times, mimicking the emperor's behaviour.

He searched the almost-silent crowd and quickly found Ceara. The woman nodded once when she met his eye; the players for this performance were in place. He glanced at Tom who crouched beside him. The big man grinned and winked. *Now or never.*

"You traitors!" bellowed Jon, pointing his staff at the assembly. He could do the emperor's accent; he just hoped no one would find it so unusual that the man would give his "sermon" in Common. However, he was gratified when the crowd recoiled in reaction to his words. Some started weeping. More than a few fell to their knees. "You have defied the gods! You, who were born into slavery, who were pressed into service of the gods... Your blood is their payment for our lives, for our health, for our crops! Do you think that the gods will stand for this? Do you think they will allow you to shirk your *gods-given duties?*" He let his voice take on the edge of hysteria, spittle flecking his lips. The eight warlocks stood in a line to his side. They lifted their hands and began to chant at Jon's glanced signal. "You will pay with your blood! All of you! The gods will take you!" he shrieked at the citizens of Balor. He stalked back and forth, warming to his subject. He railed at the crowd, gesticulating wildly, stalling until the sun dipped below the tree line to shroud the city in the gloom of dusk. By the time he gave the nod to Tom, half of those below were sobbing and screaming for forgiveness.

Tom ran below, heading for the great spoked wheel of the electricity generator at the rear of the palace. Jon eyed the men in red cloaks, chanting in unison. The front of their robes bulged awkwardly but that couldn't be helped. Jon had been firm about this part of the plan: no more death.

Suddenly, all the lights of the pyramid went on at once, an eye-watering, sensory explosion. The crowd wailed in surprise, but Ceara's network of spies at the edge of it had silently put up barriers to keep anyone from escaping. Jon worried that if he didn't end this performance soon, those assembled below would start to trample each other in panic, and the square would turn into a complete bloodbath.

Jon lifted his arms into the air and let out a terrifying roar that would leave his throat sore for days. The warlocks let their chanting reach a crescendo of ululations before falling utterly silent; the Lords of the Knife were well schooled in theatrics. The crowd hushed into silence as everyone atop the pyramid ceased moving. The light globes began to flicker as the first mate had Harris and the boys slow their turning of the generator. Jon lowered his arms, letting them fall limply to his sides. Using his own accent for once, he began to speak as if in a trance.

"My sons and daughters," he said, "you have freed me. The age of tyranny is over! I am free as you are! Gone are the false gods of the false emperor." He stood quietly and waited. The crowd started to murmur, confused.

"Who are you?" yelled someone. Jon thought he recognized Jarrod's booming baritone.

He pulled the crown off of his head and set it on the ground.

"Have you forgotten me? My sons and daughters?" he said sadly. "I am Lakkim. Your father. The father of this land." Polas and Jon had narrowed it down to the god of agriculture since Lakkim presented a nice counter to the claims that only blood could grow crops. Despite understanding the need for the act, the old headman had seemed slightly scandalized by the idea of using what he considered a true god, an old god, in this ruse. However, he agreed that Lakkim probably wouldn't mind, if it meant the end of the false gods.

"Lakkim?"

Jon could hear the people murmuring to each other, memories refreshed by Ceara's men scattered among the crowd. Though he now knew that she had helped slaves all these years, counter-manding the emperor rather than working for him, he still didn't quite trust her; however, she was playing her part well this evening. Soon the crowd started shouting things on their own, no longer in need of prompting. The warlock closest translated quietly for him when needed.

"Lakkim! Who trapped you?"

"Lakkim! I remember you!"

"Will you punish these evil men?"

Jon held out his arms, and silence fell over the crowd again.

"The man you see before you, the flesh in which I stand, trapped me in servitude while he forced his false gods upon you. For this he will die, and I will depart to the sky to watch over you. Together we can rid the land of the evil this man has done! These agents of evil... These *warlocks* as they call themselves, they have no power over you! They took your blood to feed false gods. I will take theirs and give you something better!" Jon shouted the last and the globes returned to full brightness.

Each of the warlocks raised their sharp daggers one by one, and one by one they plunged them into the bladders filled with cow's blood attached to their abdomens. Blood poured out from their "wounds" and into the tracks made for that gory purpose down the front of the pyramid.

The crowd shuffled quietly below, uncertain how this differed from the usual ceremonies they'd been forced to attend. There was a gurgling noise in the square and when the last of the warlocks fell "dead" at Jon's feet, a great, warm gush exploded out of the holes set in the paving stones. However, instead of blood, it was clean water pumped in from the river and through the heated pipes that ran through the palace floors. Polas and his men had made the switch earlier, using swim bladders from the gigantic bowfin that they routinely caught to bridge the two systems. The cow's blood drained below the palace and into the soil; hopefully the last blood sacrifice this land would see for a long time.

The people below stared up at Jon in a daze, soaked to the skin. He could see a few smiles here and there and more than a few skeptical looks. He needed to drive his point home. He heard a grunt and saw that Tom had hauled the emperor's corpse to the top of the stairs, hidden behind the tall screen. They had laid the body atop some heating vents to make it warm again. However, the emperor's skin was grey from lack of blood and his face had a sunken look. Ah'puch was starting to go gassy and bloat; Jon hoped no one would notice. He grimaced at the first mate before turning back to the crowd.

"Listen to me, my sons and daughters! My time here is nearly done. Take my laws to heart and your lives will be filled with joy: Never again shall blood rain down on you! Never again shall man bow his head in slavery to another man! Never again shall false gods rule over you!" he shouted, his voice growing hoarse. Then for good measure, even though he saw Tom shake his head from the corner of his eye, "Never again will man be persecuted for lying with man... nor woman with woman." He heard Tom snort in amusement. Even as he said it, it sounded foolish, but Jon felt it was right to add that "law". It was only fair. Besides, if they were ever to return to these lands, he sure as hells didn't want to wind up on the wrong side of the law again. The murmuring from below grew louder. He could hear that a few arguments had broken out, but as Polas had said, everything would work itself out for better or for worse; Jon was just helping it along.

He looked at the warlocks lying at his feet, their eyes on him. Each man had been promised a reduced sentence in the dungeons if they worked to uphold "Lakkim's" laws. Polas's men would make sure they kept to their end of the bargain; it was lucky for them that their identities as warlocks were known only by a select few; otherwise, Jon might have been forced to have them killed. Tom hadn't agreed with him on letting them loose, but Jon saw no reason for more bloodshed. It was the end of an era.

It was also the end of his performance.

He let out another throat-searing roar that rendered the crowd silent. Then he pretended to convulse and shake, tearing at his clothing as though possessed by a demon.

"No! No!" he yelled in the emperor's accent. "You cannot take my slaves away! You cannot take my city! I have fooled them for so long! They believe in my false gods! I will lock you away, you —" He let out a burbling scream, laying it on thick so there was no doubt in anyone's minds that he was fighting with a higher power. Then, he yelled out in his own voice:

"You have led your people astray for too long! You will die, and I will be free!" Jon tossed up his cloak and fell back just as Tom heaved the emperor's body over the edge. The dead man rolled like a ragdoll down the stepped slope of the pyramid, bouncing into the air, his dark purple robes flapping. Jon heard the commotion below, but he didn't look over the edge. Instead, he gestured for the former warlocks to follow Tom down the stairs and into the ravaged palace.

Jon was exhausted, both mentally and physically. Ceara would make sure that the crowd was incensed enough that they would tear the emperor's body to pieces. Jon had no wish to see it happen. At the foot of the stairs, they were met by Polas and his men. Oren stood with them, his expression unreadable as he stared off to the side. Jon knew that the young fisherman would never forgive him for killing his father, and Oren was uncomfortable with the fact that Jon had saved his life. He just ignored the young man. Some things were better left alone. Polas clasped Jon's arm, his smile like a proud father's.

"Did good, you did. Loads. I'll be seeing more happiness, I think," said the old man. "You're a good man, Jon."

Jon let out a tired chuckle and nodded, clasping the man's arm in return before he turned away and walked to Tom.

The big man wrapped his brawny arms around him and hugged him close, the heat of his skin soothing to Jon's tired body.

"C'mon, lad," said the first mate softly against the side of his neck. Jon felt the little hairs at the back of his neck stir with Tom's warm breath and he sighed into the embrace. "Let's go home."

J on looked between Tom and Baltsaros. Captain? Him?

"Listen, love: if ye can pretend to be an emperor and a god, ye sure as hells can pretend to be a lowly boat captain," said Tom with a chuckle.

"Lowly?" smirked the captain, a spark of his old self in the curl of his lips.

Jon shook his head.

"I don't know. *Captain Jon* doesn't sound very impressive," he laughed. The idea had merit though. He could see himself shouldering part of the responsibility with Baltsaros's counselling and Tom's fists. Not quite a figurehead... and it would be temporary.

"Aye, but *Captain Jon, The Black Brigand* is a great fuckin' pirate name," grinned Tom, squeezing his shoulder.

Jon blinked.

"All right, but let's make it simple. I had a great-great-uncle or something who was a pirate; did I ever tell you that? *Captain Black*. If I'm going to follow in his footsteps, I might as well take his name, aye, matey?" he said with a jaunty tilt of an imaginary hat.

There was a girlish laugh from the open door, and he turned, startled. Ceara, in a pair of tight leather pants and a high-necked, sleeveless black shirt, stood leaning against the wooden frame with a bag at her feet.

"Captain Black? It does have a nice ring," she smiled.

"Well, lookee here," drawled Tom, a mischievous sparkle in his green-blue eyes. "It's the new chambermaid! Go get in t'yer skirts, wench. That ain't no sort of uniform."

Ceara looked uncertain for the span of a heartbeat before she realized that Tom was joking. She smiled at him, but there was a brittle edge to it. Jon knew that beneath her sass and easy confidence, there was a damaged girl who knew only too well how to put her back to the wall to defend herself. He wondered how long it would take before Tom would realize that too. Jon thought about the twisted red scars that covered her from neck to waist and what Tom's reaction might be when he saw them. A little jealous flame licked at his heart, but he nearly laughed out loud as he shoved the worry away. Tom was his. His and Baltsaros's and no one else's. Jon smiled at the collar around the first mate's neck; Tom knew it.

"All right, then... *Captain Black*," she said with a tiny bow. "I'll do what I can to spread words of your newfound bravery and appetite for cruelty around the crew. It's the least I can do."

Jon dropped his smile and walked quickly up to her, his face set in deadly seriousness as he stood almost touching her. He looked down into her crystal-blue gaze and could see the tiny tremor in her eyelids.

"I don't trust you," he said, soft like silk against steel. "Not yet. So I will be watching you, Ceara, and gods help you if I so much as hear a single whispered word to make me doubt your loyalty, you'll find the truth in those *rumours* you just offered to spread. *Do I make myself clear?*"

Ceara's eyes widened even more, and he saw real fear in them. She quickly nodded her head, and he stepped back, letting his expression settle into a grim smile. One look at Tom and his slack jaw nearly broke Jon's act.

C'mon, Jon... an act? Do you still think you're acting? whispered the little voice inside him with an evil chuckle. Jon blinked and turned his eyes to the captain. The steely, cold creature stared at him from behind the captain's dark-brown eyes. Jon scratched the back of his head and turned away to hide the shiver of unease that took him.

He straightened his shoulders, his eyes settling on the map on the far wall. Nathaniel had been adding to it as the *Heart* made its way along the coast during the two days Polas had kept the ship out of harm's way, waiting for their return. He squinted at it.

"I guess as captain, my first act is to decide what in hells we're going to do until the passage opens up again at the Devil's Isles, right? We've got months to wait before we can start making our way back again," he said with a sigh. "Any suggestions?"

"What do you mean months?" asked Ceara with a twist of her cupid's-bow lips. She approached the map with her head tilted, her confidence having recovered from Jon's threat.

"We can only get through the spires once the weather has grown warm enough that the ice has melted. Otherwise, we will be trapped there," said Jon.

Ceara let out a small laugh and shook her head.

"Think, gentlemen: what kind of trade could we *possibly* maintain with such a limited window of opportunity? And trade, as you have surely seen, has been quite good," she said, sliding her fingers up the drawing of the impassable mountains. She stopped and tapped a point northeast of where they were located. "No, trade with your lands to the east would have surely been tedious and unprofitable were it not for a very, very well-kept secret."

"Spit it out, woman," frowned Jon, made impatient by her gilded showmanship.

"A deep fissure in the mountain, twisted and fraught with dead ends called simply *The Rift*," Ceara said with a smile. "And you just so happen to have taken aboard the one person who knows exactly how to get through it."

"Who's that?" grunted Tom, a comma of skepticism etched in his brow.

At this, Jon burst out laughing. He clapped the first mate on the shoulder hard, and gave Ceara and genuine smile.

"She means her, you lunkhead," he said affectionately, his

mood much improved by the sudden possibility of a swift journey home.

Ceara looked relieved by his reaction, and he felt a little easier about her. What would she gain to win if she led them astray? No, she had to be telling the truth.

Jon ran a hand through his curls and walked to the door.

"Tom, make sure everyone's ready to leave. I want the last of the men on board and the supplies stowed by the time the sun comes up tomorrow morning. Any who dawdles gets left behind. Go. Now," he said. Tom was out the door and shouting orders in moments. Jon turned. "Ceara, you'll be staying in the smaller of the two bunkrooms. Go put your sack on your bunk and report to Cook. Don't think this is going to be a pleasure ride just because you can get us through some crack in the mountains."

"Yes, Captain," she said in all seriousness and picked up her sack before following Tom out.

When they'd gone, Jon walked to the cage where Baltsaros sat quietly on his cot, staring at him with amusement. Jon sat down next to him with a wry grin.

"How's that?" Jon asked him. Baltsaros nodded, his fingers coming up to curl comfortingly around the back of his neck. Jon leaned into Baltsaros and pressed his forehead against the older man's cheek, letting out a sigh when Baltsaros wrapped his other arm around his shoulders.

"You'll do fine, Jon," murmured Baltsaros. "I'm proud of you." A tremor shook the captain, and he tightened his hold on Jon with a laugh. "Seems we've changed places, you and I."

Jon pulled away with a soft smile before leaning in to brush his lips softly against the captain's.

"It's only temporary," he chided Baltsaros. "We'll be back under the swinging lanterns of the *Blossom* in no time, a glass of Maya's good brown beer in front of us, and the night air fragrant and warm. This will all seem like a dream, a bad dream. Just think of your carved bed and crisp sheets and the three of us falling asleep to the sound of waves breaking on the white sandy beaches below."

Jon frowned. Baltsaros's eyes had gone glassy and he'd turned away; Jon knew that he was no longer listening to him. He reached for Baltsaros's cheek to turn his head, but when Jon touched him, the captain cringed. There was no recognition in the dark eyes that widened at him, but Jon pulled Baltsaros against him regardless with a desperate whimper fighting for release deep in his chest.

"I'll get us there," he whispered into the trembling man's hair. "I will."

After a moment, Jon released Baltsaros and stood. Baltsaros looked lost and confused as Jon left the cage and locked the door behind him. After taking up Baltsaros's long coat to shield him against the slight chill in the night air, Captain Black left the stateroom. As his step crossed the threshold, he left behind his weaknesses and doubts, finally setting aside the boy to become the man he had to be.

END OF BOOK II

EPILOGUE

Jon smiled as Tom let out a soft groan, muffled by the red silk of his gag. The first mate was kneeling on the bed, thighs wide and pelvis forward, with his wrists secured tightly to his ankles behind him. This had the effect of bowing his back in such a way that his ribs were starkly outlined, and the thick tendons in his neck stuck out as he held up his head, blue-green eyes fixed on Jon. He trembled from the strain of keeping the uncomfortable pose, but Jon had told him if he let himself sink down onto his calves, he would be denied release again.

With a pleased sigh, Jon leaned forward to lick another slow line down Tom's chest before closing his lips over a nipple to worry the bud with his teeth. Despite how the first mate's muscles bulged and strained against his bindings, he didn't struggle. Jutting from the thatch of dark-blond hair at his groin was the reason why; Tom's cock was a thick, hard, upward curve that jumped up every time Jon bit down harder.

This was the first mate's idea of a good time.

Jon chuckled against Tom's skin, almost lazily stroking his hands down the big man's sides to grasp his muscular buttocks before biting him again. This time he took the metal ring between his teeth and tugged on it. In response, Tom's cock grazed Jon's bare stomach and left behind a slick streak. Jon grinned and sat back on his own heels, grasping his cock in one hand to rub it against the head of Tom's. The first mate let out another low sound, closing his eyes as he thrust his hips further forward. Jon obliged him for a moment; taking the wide head in one hand, he thumbed along the underside, teasing Tom as he stroked his own cock. They'd been at this for the better part of an hour.

"Do you want it?" asked Jon with a wolfish grin.

Tom nodded quickly, a plea in his eyes. Jon reached for his jaw and tugged down the gag.

"Let me hear you say it," said Jon softly. His fingers stroked along the edge of the slave collar Tom wore. The first mate's skin was hot and wet to the touch, and his pulse thumped against the tips of Jon's fingers.

"I want yer cock," rasped Tom. Another drop of arousal slipped from the slit of his cockhead and perched there for a moment, shiny and clear, before sliding down along the thick vein and over the smaller metal circlet that he wore tight around the root of his cock. "Please, Jon. I want ye to fuck me. Hard. Please. I'll do anythin' ye want. Just… please."

Jon patted Tom's cheek lightly with a smile and looked up. The captain's tanned face was creased in amusement as he lounged behind Tom on the bed stroking his own cock and watching Jon taunt the big man. At Jon's nod, Baltsaros sat up and moved forward to quickly free Tom's wrists. Jon watched the captain narrow his eyes in concentration as he undid the knots.

Jon smiled softly. The captain's body had healed, but his mind had taken longer. For the past week, however, Baltsaros's eyes had been clear and his strange turns had all but vanished. That the captain felt "sane" enough to participate in some slightly rougher play with him and Tom gave Jon hope that things would soon return to normal.

Whatever that is, he thought.

He turned back to Tom and saw that the first mate was looking at him with pupils blown out from lust and *char*, completely oblivious and lost in the moment. He was absolutely gorgeous like this, willing to do almost anything for the sake of pleasing him... a living plaything, but so much more.

Someone to cherish.

Jon widened his grin and ducked his head to cover Tom's lips with his own, nudging them open to begin kissing him slow and deep. When Tom's arms finally came free of the rope, he curled them around Jon's waist and surrendered to the embrace, his chest rumbling with small growls of pleasure. Then Tom tensed suddenly against Jon, breathing a gasp into the kiss. Curious, Jon slid his hand down Tom's hard stomach, past his cock and sensitive sack, to discover that the captain had slid two fingers into the first mate. Baltsaros let out a slow breath when he felt Jon's tentative touch, and leaned over Tom's shoulder to press his lips to Jon's cheek.

Jon broke the kiss to share breath with Baltsaros for a moment. Smiling against his lips, he slid his own finger next to the captain's and into Tom. The first mate trembled between them as they fucked him using their fingers, opening him up, their hands slick with oil. Soon Tom's normally gruff voice broke on a whimper as he begged.

"Please, Jon... Da. For love's sake," said the first mate. "I've been good, aye?"

Jon laughed, breathless and wild with desire, and he shared a look with Baltsaros. It was tempting to make the first mate wait longer, just to hear how desperate he could sound, but instead he grabbed the back of Tom's head and kissed him again.

"Yes, you've been a good lad, Tom," murmured the captain. His long-fingered hand stroked up Jon's arm, the touch gentle. "How would you like to take the both of us? Hm? Would that make you happy?"

Tom pulled away from Jon, his eyes glazed and fervid, lips parted on a slow pant.

BEY DECKARD

"Oh… fuck yes, Da."

Jon's heart pounded, and his cock throbbed in his hand as he watched Tom straddle Baltsaros and then lay back against the man's chest, bracing himself on his heels. The captain cushioned the big man's weight with one hand, moving to push his thick cockhead against Tom's puckered opening with the other. Jon licked his lips, an involuntary moan expelled with a hitched breath at the sight of Baltsaros's cock stretching Tom open and sliding deep into him. Tom let out a shallow grunt and closed his big fist over his own length. Jon watched hungrily as the captain fucked the first mate slowly for a few thrusts.

He felt suddenly uncertain, wondering if Baltsaros had been serious about what he had offered. It didn't seem possible. He might hurt Tom. With a crease between his brows, he climbed back up on the bed and stroked himself, unsure about how to approach. Tom's eyes were closed, but when Jon made no further move, the first mate lifted his head and frowned at him. Tom held out his hand.

"Come," he said with a smile that faltered into a grimace of pleasure as Baltsaros's cock thrust deep again. "You can't hurt me, lovey."

Jon nodded weakly. Dizzy and excited, and a touch nervous, he found a place for his legs, straddling the captain, and leaned forwards over Tom. The first mate's legs hooked over Jon's hips as he stroked the head of his cock over the captain's thrusting length and then eased in slowly when the man paused. He pushed hard, and Tom's eyes closed once more. It was tight, almost too much. When Tom let out a pained breath, Jon stopped, but the first mate just chuckled a shaky laugh.

"Don't ye dare stop, Jon. Don't ye stop…" Tom groaned and let his head fall back over Baltsaros's shoulder. Jon's fervour took over. He plunged his cock into Tom's heat, sliding tight against the captain's length. It was glorious, and he found himself teetering on the edge of climax quickly. He paused, eyes closed and so sensitive that he was almost in pain. For a moment Jon just

426

held back, waited, and relished the feeling of the captain's cock sliding against his before resuming. However, it wasn't long before he couldn't stop himself from spilling over, the swell of pleasure breaking out into molten waves of intensity that tore the voice from his throat and left him breathless and weak. When the liquid pulses that rocked him slowed, then stopped, he leaned his head against Tom's furry chest and eased out slowly, wincing as he did so.

Tom let out a grunt of surprise a moment later when Jon moved over to begin working his mouth over Tom's cock. The first mate buried his shaking hands in Jon's dark curls as Jon gagged trying to take all of Tom in. Jon swallowed and tried again, keenly wanting to reward Tom. He relaxed his throat, shifted his position, and lapped at the head of Tom's cock before sliding it back into his throat.

With Baltsaros thrusting into him from below and Jon gorging himself on his cock, Tom soon started breathing through clenched teeth with a low, rumbling moan that Jon knew meant he was close. Jon curled his fingers around the base of Tom's cock and tightened his lips, spit running down the sides of the big man's shaft and over Jon's fingers.

Suddenly Baltsaros let out a low growl, fucking Tom faster with his arms tight around the first mate's chest, the muscles taut and twitching as his body rocked beneath him, caught in the feverish, frantic surge of orgasm. Then, with a strangled cry, Tom finally let himself cum, his bitter seed gushing over Jon's tongue as his body shuddered and hands clutched at him before falling limp to his sides.

Jon almost laughed with giddiness. With a grin he came forward to press kisses to Tom's sweat-slick skin when the captain rolled the first mate gently to his side and began murmuring soft praises.

"Good boy."

Jon woke a few hours later, curled against Tom's side. Tom slept soundly, his broad chest rising and falling with every deep breath. On his other side, the bed was empty. Jon frowned and sat up. The early morning light streamed in through the curtains and painted the room in a hazy, golden hue. After climbing out of the huge four-poster bed, Jon padded quietly to the front room to see where Baltsaros was. He still didn't trust the man out of his sight. Not after everything that had happened. When he saw that this room too was empty, a finger of worry stole into his heart. Then he saw the note. He picked it up from the big desk and peered at it.

J & T,

All hands needed to stock up and ready the ship. We leave tomorrow at noon. Meet me below when you wake.

— B.

Jon pulled the thick velvet curtain aside and squinted at the beach. Sure enough, there was a bustle of activity. He could see a jolly boat making its way to the ship with a load of supplies. Confused, he turned back to the desk. There he spotted a letter written in the spiky alphabet of the northerners. He snatched it up and ran back to the bed, shaking Tom from his slumber.

Tom rubbed his face blearily, blinking around him in confusion with eyes tinged in red before he scowled in annoyance.

"What?" he rumbled.

Jon shoved the letter into his hand.

"The captain is down at the ship, getting her ready to leave tomorrow," he said, his heart skipping in his chest. "Does this have anything to do with it?"

After swiping at his face again, Tom focused on the letter. A deep crease formed in his forehead, and when he looked back up at him, Jon saw deep concern.

"Aye, lad," said Tom quietly. "Seems we're headed north. Far north."

WANT TO KNOW MORE?

See maps, a pirate glossary, diagrams, soundtracks, and details of
Baal's Heart at <u>baals-heart.com</u>.

—Bey

SACRIFICED - NARRATED BY MICHAEL FERRAIUOLO

Sacrificed is available in audiobook format (*whispersync* ready). Relive the adventures of Jon, Tom, and Baltsaros, now exquisitely narrated by the very talented Michael Ferraiuolo.

Find it here: http://geni.us/pageSacrificed

BOOKS BY BEY DECKARD

FOR AN UP-TO-DATE LIST OF TITLES, VISIT:

https://beydeckard.com/blog/buy-my-books/

MAX, THE SERIES

Max

Max, the Sequel

BAAL'S HEART SERIES

Caged: Love and Treachery on the High Seas

Sacrificed: Heart Beyond the Spires

Fated: Blood and Redemption

Careened: Winter Solstice in Madierus

F.I.S.T.S

Sarge

Murphy

F.I.S.T.S. Handbook For Individual Survival in Hostile Environments

THE ACTOR'S CIRCLE

The Complications of T

The Last Nights of The Frangipani Hotel

THE STONEWATCHERS

Kestrel's Talon

STANDALONE BOOKS

Better the Devil You Know

Exposed

Beauty and His Beast

The Blacksmith's Apprentice

SHORT STORIES

Don't Touch Me (UnCommon Bodies Anthology)

Rakka Surprise (UnCommon Lands Anthology)

ABOUT THE AUTHOR

Artist, Writer, Dog Lover

Bey Deckard is the author of a number of novels including the *Baal's Heart books, Max, Beauty and His Beast,* and *Better the Devil You Know.*

Bey lives in Montréal, Canada where he spends most of his time writing, doing graphic work, painting portraits, speaking French, cooking tasty vegetarian eats, or watching more movies than is good for him. If you're the curious type, www.beydeckard.com is where you'll find art and free stories by Bey as well as information on his published works.

bey.deckard@gmail.com
Look for Deckard's Diablerie on Facebook

f facebook.com/authorbeydeckard
twitter.com/BeyDeckard
instagram.com/beydeckard
g goodreads.com/beydeckard
BB bookbub.com/authors/bey-deckard
m pettingzoo.co/@Beybey